RELOCATING MIA

REBECCA LERWILL

Relocating Mia
Published by Bridgeway Books
PO Box 80107
Austin, Texas 78758

For more information about our books, please write to us, call 512.478.2028, or visit our website at www.bridgewaybooks.net.

Printed and bound in the United States of America. All rights reserved. No part of this book may be reproduced in any form or by any electronic or mechanical means including information storage and retrieval systems without permission in writing from the copyright holder, except by a reviewer, who may quote brief passages in review.

Library of Congress Control Number: 2007921664

ISBN-13: 978-1-933538-87-7
ISBN-10: 1-933538-87-2

Copyright© 2007 by Rebecca Lerwill

This is a work of fiction. All of the characters and events portrayed in this book are fictional, and any resemblance to real people or incidents is purely coincidental.

10 9 8 7 6 5 4 3 2 1

Acknowledgments

Someone very smart said once "Friends are family we get to choose." I couldn't agree more. Writing a book is a journey. It's wonderful, exciting, and sometimes very lonely. When things were flowing and my characters took over, I felt like their servant telling their story.

But in the beginning I could not have done it without the endless encouragement I received from the people I'm proud to call my friends, and who believed in me. Thanks guys, I love you all!

Foremost: this is for my husband Troy—my rock, who has been incredible through this adventure. Also many thanks to Wayne for the nudge in Florida, Gabi and Mingo for giving me their genes, Bob for his wisdom, Boyd for the heart, Kelly for the laughter, Heike for her inspiration, Ann and Linda for their advice, and Kim for her honesty.

There are many more to thank, especially all of my family and the people responsible on the business side of things at Bridgeway Books. But I also like to include the troops who keep this wonderful country out of harm so it has allowed to me to live in safety and pursue my dreams.

Prologue

St. Petersburg, Russia

THE SMALL MAN SHOOK his hand.

"You will see the plan is perfect. There is no need to worry." The small man's intense blue eyes mesmerized him, and he wanted to believe what he said. He finally let go of his hand and continued his persuasive speech. "All you need to do is focus on your family now. They need you. Let *our* family take care of the rest."

He nodded. It all sounded fairly simple and risk-free. And the small man was right, he needed to focus on his family, put all his strength into making her better.

The small man studied him for a while and said, "As you know, the equipment has already been shipped, and they are preparing the lab as we speak. I will send you a final report in the next few days, but if everything continues to go as planned, the production will start very soon."

He felt more and more confident that this arrangement would be for the best. He checked his watch; it was almost time to catch his flight back east to Irkutsk.

"Is there anything I can do for you in the meantime?" The small man intensified his captivating gaze.

"No." He shook his head. He really felt good about this now. "I will wait for you to contact me with any proceedings, correct?"

A quick nod. "Yes, that would be correct. Now, please." The small man showed him toward the door. "My driver will drop you off at the airport. Please enjoy your flight home." With this, the small man excused himself.

He looked after the small man as he walked down the carpeted corridor; he had never met anybody more charismatic. Yes, there was no doubt in his mind that he was doing the right thing. Satisfied with his actions, he straightened his shoulders. As he turned to walk out the door, he caught a glimpse of himself in the tall wall mirror.

He adjusted his tie and looked himself in the eye. Lagunov nodded at his image and disappeared into the darkness.

Chapter 1

When Mia got the call at lunchtime, she was thrilled.

She hadn't worked in a few months and was growing bored of just hanging out with the locals.

"When can you depart?" Simon asked. "We need you there by latest Sunday."

Mia could hardly hide her excitement. "Shouldn't be a problem, Simon. Let me get back with you by tomorrow."

As she put down the receiver, she checked herself in the little, antique, oriental mirror she had brought back from a previous job.

She would have to get her hair done before she took off. "What do you think, Blue?" she asked her bright-eyed Akita–Australian Shepherd mix. "Do we deserve a little pampering at Rosa's Salon?"

Mia wouldn't have to worry about making an appointment. Waiting in line was one of the few entertainments in Stoney Creek, a rural town of some seven hundred people. Most of them were Native Americans, but some of them were the leftovers of a generation of the gold diggers. Mia had fallen in love with Stoney Creek and its people during a ski vacation at Moose Mountain, a resort just thirty miles east of Flathead Lake in Montana and a stone's throw away from the Canadian border.

She worked for a small, but very successful, relocating company based in Seattle.

It had been almost two months since her last contract with Worldmove Incorporated had ended. Her status with the company was unique. She didn't work with a team and was therefore responsible for her own assignments once she had accepted them. As a relocation specialist, she never quite knew when the next job would come along, or where it would take her. But Mia loved to travel and adapted as easily to new surroundings as a chameleon changes color.

Being fluent in four languages, she was a professional in demand. Her responsibility was to scout out the cities where individuals would be relocated to by their employer. Sometimes her clients moved within the United States, but mostly her assignments took her overseas to Europe and beyond.

When Daimler and Chrysler had merged, she'd had to relocate several European executives to Pontiac, Michigan. Eventually it was as easy as finding the right top-floor, high-end condominium located within walking distance of—but still discreetly neighbored to—a pricey nightclub. The arrangement had been perfect for the recently divorced, golf-playing, middle-aged German engineer.

Other times Mia had to tolerate all the "what we don't wants" before she could even start finding just the right flat for people like the Dunham family from Los Angeles. After a joint venture with an Asian computer company, Dunham Enterprises needed to relocate to Singapore.

Dunham Enterprises had consisted of a team of four young and dynamic software designers, the owner (Dunham himself), and his family. Mia had eventually found the perfect apartment unit in busy, downtown Singapore for Dunham's aspiring team.

The Dunham's themselves had been a bit more of a challenge.

After extensive research she had found an American-owned private school for the three little ones. Just as important as finding the right school, she'd also found a ballet instructor for the girls and little league practice for the boy. Of course the Singapore Island Country Club for Dad Dunham and the utmost modern wellness center with English-speaking staff for Mom also had to be within reasonable driving distance from their new home.

A smile tweaked Mia's lips as she remembered Mr. Dunham's inquiry about any "special services" she might provide. He'd had an itch since his wife had gotten a little too comfortable a little too quickly in their new home—thanks to her chiseled, Polynesian yoga instructor.

Sometimes she had to deal with the occasional flirty CEO who confused her job with that of a hostess. Usually her clients really appreciated her professionalism. She thoroughly researched the options a new city had to offer and made sure the right environment was found for each individual and their family. "The easier they are relocated, the happier the client and the faster they get back to work. That's what the employer is looking for," Scott Hensley, the owner of Worldmove, had told Mia during their accidental encounter two years ago at a TGI Friday's when she had still lived in Seattle.

A cold, wet nose brought her back to reality. Mia was still standing in the small front room she used as her office, wearing running shorts and a T-shirt, trying to decide about that haircut. Blue nudged her bare leg, reminding her about his promised run.

Blue enjoyed running just as much as she did. In the past weeks, Mia had concentrated on lengthening her distance and had added a weekly hill climb to develop her muscle strength. By spring she hoped to be ready for her first marathon. Today she had planned on another workout on Blue's favorite hill. He would have chased the groundhogs while Mia enjoyed the yellow blossoms of the sage brushes on this pretty, early autumn day.

"Oh, I'm sorry, Blue Eyes." Mia bent down to cuddle her dog. "I guess we need to postpone our workout for today. Looks like you're in for another vacation with Uncle Phil."

She felt a little guilty, but she knew Blue didn't mind. There were just too many squirrels to chase on Uncle Phil's huge ranch just outside of Stoney Creek. Since Mia had moved here eighteen months ago, she had known Uncle Phil as just that. Everybody called him Uncle even though he didn't seem to have any real family anymore. His rusty, 1968 Ford pickup had "Uncle Phil's Farm Fresh Eggs" painted in orange script letters on the driver's side door. He was a leather-faced old farmer who took in everyone's pets during the occasional vacation time away.

Mia got herself a Perrier out of the tiny refrigerator in the even tinier kitchen she shared with Zulanda. Mia rented a room from the older native woman—Zulu to her friends—who taught two different grades in one classroom in Stoney Creek's only elementary school.

During her ski vacation, Mia had met Zulu browsing the local library. After a long conversation between the two strangers, Mia had fallen in love with the uncomplicated ease in which these people seemed to live their lives. Mia had needed to simplify her own life and wanted to move away from Seattle. The arrangement in Stoney Creek had sounded too good to be true. Zulu had offered to rent Mia her second bedroom with an adjoining bathroom. Zulu didn't own a car, so Mia's personal belongings could be stored in the garage.

Zulu's husband had died several years earlier and she had needed someone around the house who could take care of smaller maintenance projects, like painting and the garden work. The two women had quickly worked out the details, and despite the thirty year age difference, Mia and Zulu had soon developed a deep friendship.

The sun was setting earlier now in mid September, and cool air streamed through the open front door. The sound of Zulu's many wind chimes hanging from the white porch reminded Mia of fall. She decided to change into some warmer clothes before making her call.

Stoney Creek sat in a beautiful valley between majestic mountains. The setting was magnificent, but it also meant there was no such thing as cell phone service. When Mia had first moved here, time had seemed to stand still, and she'd liked that.

I need to get a hold of Oliver McGee before the day is over, Mia thought. She'd schedule a flight out to Kalispell with him. McGee owned and operated the local crop-dusting business. When he didn't go after bugs or assist the smoke-jumpers during the wildfire season in the nearby forests of Glacier National Park, he happily provided flights out to the city. Getting to Kalispell on short notice was almost impossible since the drive around Flathead Lake took several hours. But the international airport in Kalispell was small, so they allowed personal aircraft traffic, and Mia liked to take advantage of the local service.

McGee was a veteran. His Korean War stories kept changing, and he recounted his past hockey days every chance he got. He was interested in talking to Mia partly because she'd grown up in the Midwest.

She went upstairs to her bedroom, took off her exercise gear, and slipped into a pair of blue, fleece-lined pants and a zip-up Michigan Spartans sweater. If she still planned on a quick visit to Rosa's Salon, she'd better be prepared for the early evening's chill. The weather could change drastically in a matter of minutes this time of the year.

Chapter 2

"Honey, you're out of your mind!" Rosa exclaimed dramatically. Mia had just told her about her newest assignment. "Siberia? Like in Siberia, Russia?" Rosa could have easily passed for one of the dusky maidens from the early 1930s movie era. Gracefully she walked around Mia as she trimmed the ends of her shoulder-length, chestnut hair.

Just an hour earlier, Mia had run into Oliver McGee out at Uncle Phil's Farm when she had dropped off Blue. Both men had been sitting on Uncle Phil's front porch sharing a few good ol' boy stories and drinking black coffee. They had offered Mia a cup, but she had declined, knowing from past experience that Uncle Phil's bitter brew would tear up the lining of her esophagus. Mia had made arrangements for McGee to fly her out to Kalispell the following morning. From there she'd driven back into town to visit Rosa's salon.

"It must be winter there by now. You better make sure you don't freeze right to the doorknob." Rosa placed her hands onto her wide hips and looked exasperatedly at Mia through the mirror.

"I'll wear mittens," Mia promised.

"Who in their right mind would move there anyway?" One of the older ladies asked, poking her head halfway out from under the dryer.

"Well nobody yet, actually," Mia explained. "I'm not relocating a person. This job is a little different; they want me as an advisor to find a new location for their expanding company."

"What is it they do?" Rosa sensed new gossip, eyeing Mia in the mirror.

"I'm not sure," Mia lied. "Something petroleum."

"Good grief! You're not gonna help digging some pipeline are you, Mia Maria?" Rosa's husband, Theo, joked from his seat in his barber chair, hiding behind his paper.

"Theodore, you wouldn't know nothin' 'bout no pipelines, now would you?" Rosa shot at him.

"No, Ma'am sure don't." Theo winked at Mia.

Married and in business together for over forty years, Theo had said before that the only dull moments they'd had was when his scissors had lost their sharp edges. It seemed that nobody actually knew how this black couple had found their way to the Northwest. The southern drawl never vanished from either one of them, even after such a long time away from their Georgian home.

After finishing Mia's coif, Rosa turned her chair so Mia would face her. She cupped Mia's delicate face in both hands and said, "Just take care of that beautiful skin of yours. We don't want to be treatin' no frostbites when you come home."

Mia took a minute to look at herself in Rosa's huge salon mirror. She did have her mother's beautiful, fair skin and high cheekbones, typical for her Prussian roots. Her father's side was Italian. Mia had inherited his big, brown eyes and thick hair.

"I guess I better get packing." Mia got out of the chair.

"Send us a postcard 'from Russia with love,' or something," Rosa said and gave Mia a hug. Rosa was a big lady and almost crushed Mia and her slender, five-foot-six frame.

"See you soon," came from behind the paper as Mia left the salon.

It was still dark when Mia woke up the next day. She had always been an early riser and enjoyed the quiet time before nature came alive. With a fresh brew of a Columbian blend, she turned on her computer to print out her itinerary. She had made the reservation with Delta the night before. Seattle's time zone was an hour behind hers; there was nobody in the office yet. To pass some time, Mia took care of her personal correspondence. An e-mail from her sister Corinne in New Hampshire was waiting for her.

"Geez, Cora," Mia muttered out loud. "Ed needs to take that camera away from you." Corinne and her husband, Ed, had a new baby boy. Mia got showered with picture attachments of her new nephew on a weekly basis. With only dial-up it took Mia some time to download all the photos. Her sister took the modern city amenities, including high speed internet, for granted and seemed to forget about Mia's limitations out here in rural Montana.

A little agitated, Mia thought about how many times she had asked Corinne to keep the e-mail files smaller. But as Mia watched her new nephew appear on her screen, she laughed out loud. The eight-month-old sat in a high chair, his mouth grinning toothlessly into the camera with enough chocolate pudding around it to feed the whole family.

Mia forgave her sister. Obviously it was just too tempting to keep shooting away.

She decided to give her mother in Michigan a quick call to let her know she would be out of the country for a few weeks.

"Yes, Mom, don't worry. Of course I will call you as soon as I return. I love you too. Hugs to Dad." I should just call them when I return, she thought. Her mother always worried. Mia was younger than her sister and would always be the baby to her Mom

She went back into the kitchen to pour herself a refill of hot, steaming coffee as her roommate Zulu came down the stairs. In her pink, flowered nightgown and with her black, unruly hair a total disaster, she made Mia laugh.

"I'm sorry, Zulu, but you have a serious case of bed head," Mia teased.

"If you had to deal with a bunch of third graders like the ones I've got this year, your hair would be the least of your problems, Darling!" Zulu sat next to Mia after helping herself to a cup of coffee. "Hmm, I don't know where you got this stuff, but it sure is the best coffee I've ever had."

"Leftover from what I bought in Rio. I found it way in the back of the freezer the other day."

The two women's casual morning conversation went on for a little while until Zulu had to get ready for school.

"Do you know when you'll be back, Mia?" Zulu gave her a hug good-bye.

Mia shrugged. "They suggested two weeks, but you know how it goes sometimes. Would you check on Blue for me?"

"Of course, don't worry about him. I'll ride out to see Uncle Phil in a couple of days. You just make sure to take care of yourself."

It was eight thirty by now in Seattle. Time to check in with Worldmove headquarters.

"Change of plans, Mia," Simon, Team Coordinator and her boss' right hand, informed her. "Scott wants you to come out to Seattle before you head back east."

"West, Simon, I'm heading west, even if Russia is considered an eastern country." Mia rolled her eyes, not knowing if she was more annoyed by Simon's ignorance or her boss's request. "Why do I have to re-schedule?"

"I don't know, Mia. But I've got you booked on Alaska Airline at 11:35 this morning."

"Geez, Simon, a bit more notice would have been nice." Mia hated complaining, but was struggling with the aggravation of having to go to Seattle. Not her favorite place in the world. In fact, if she never saw the Space Needle again, it would be just fine with her.

"He just notified me about it. Scott would like you to be here for a two o'clock meeting," Simon said and quickly hung up, not wanting to deal with Mia's mood.

Mia called McGee to confirm her flight out to Kalispell. She would have to hustle now, and as she finished up her packing, she wondered what in the world could be so important that it couldn't be discussed over the phone. Mia would have to cancel her mid-afternoon flight to Los Angeles. Her plan had been to fly from there to Beijing and continue on to Irkutsk, Siberia the following day.

Scott Hensley usually didn't throw her a curve ball like that right before meeting a new client. And from the bits and pieces

Simon had told her, this was a big client who seemed to be in it for the long haul. If this company expanded and built new facilities, housing would have to be found and people would have to be re-located.

Mia went back upstairs. She would have to change her travel attire from a comfy pair of beige, linen slacks and a matching blouse, to a smart, dark blue Ann Taylor suit and black Roberto Cavalli pumps to be presentable for her meeting. After applying a touch of makeup, she gathered her things and fixed a last cup of coffee to-go.

At Stoney Creek's municipal airport, Mia boarded McGee's PAC Cresco, secured herself in her seat, and closed her eyes. She was a little nervous, as usual, starting a new assignment. She loved meeting new people but never knew what to expect.

McGee was saying something about the NHL and his blown-out knee in college, but Mia signaled him that she could not understand. It was too noisy for civilized talk in the small airplane.

Mia leaned her head on the glass and enjoyed the view of their thirty minute flight. McGee had flown her several times from Stoney Creek due northwest to Kalispell. They would cross the deep blue waters of Flathead Lake, and Mia loved the relaxing effect the huge Lake had on her.

It was surrounded by deep, green forest and the roads snaked their way through the rolling hills. Sometimes Mia would catch the mirrored image of McGee's plane on the lake's smooth surface. A few boats looked like tiny white dots followed by white, wavy streaks.

Mia was on the lookout for her favorite place. Down below, a small group of islands came into her view. The biggest of them was at least several hundred acres in size. It had a hill right in the center, and nestled on top, surrounded by trees, sat a huge villa.

Breathtaking. It's gotta be the size of a freakin' football field, Mia thought as she looked at the light-colored, Mediterranean-style mansion. Mia imagined the peace and quiet it must provide. Someone had told her once who it belonged to. Some fashion designer? She couldn't remember.

Unfortunately, the fun part of the trip was over too soon, and Mia had to focus on reality. She thanked McGee, who helped her unload her luggage before he took off again.

"How are you today?" a friendly member of the ground crew greeted Mia as he arranged for someone to pick her up at the runway and drop her off at the terminal. Mia knew he was checking out her rear end as she walked away from him. She hated chauvinists, and this one was not even trying to hide it.

The terminal was not too busy, and after Mia had checked her bags, she went through security surprisingly fast. All seventy seats on the small turbo prop to Seattle were taken, and Mia wrinkled her nose after she had taken her seat. The guy next to her obviously didn't believe in personal hygiene. She sighed and thumbed through a magazine from the pouch in front of her. Her carry-on was unreachable above her. She would have liked to retrieve it and nonchalantly spray a little of her lavender-scented Panhaligon's on him.

Chapter 3

DOUGLAS FARLAND WAS EARLY for his one-thirty meeting. He sat in a bistro on the ground level of the old Sears Building. Worldmove Inc. had their office on the sixth floor, above a trolley stop on Elliott Avenue, just north of the port of Seattle.

He had been offered this job a couple of weeks back and now the time had come to meet up with his new employer and the associate he'd be working with.

"Can I get you a refill, sir?" This pretty, blond waitress had started flirting with him the minute he'd stepped into this place. She was young—too young. He declined and left a rather generous tip. Douglas took the black, Armani suit jacket he had casually draped over the back of his chair, gathered his leather Louis Vuitton briefcase, and avoided the elevator; he liked the stairs.

The wall clock in the bright, roomy reception area showed 1:25 p.m. Perfect timing. He walked down the white, marble-tiled hallway. The receptionist gave him a genuine smile. "Of course, Mr. Farland. Mr. Hensley is expecting you. Please, it's all the way down the hall."

Douglas nodded thankfully, smoothed his pale orange, silk tie, and proceeded toward the heavy, oak door with "Mr. Scott Hensley, CEO" engraved in gold letters on it.

He entered after a short knock and found his new boss with his back to him on the phone. Douglas eyes went to the eight-foot-tall windows, which offered a breath-taking view of the sea.

Scott Hensley swiveled his black, overstuffed leather chair around, and used his free hand to signal Douglas to take a seat. Douglas sat opposite of the man and let his eyes wander over the beautiful, hand-carved antique desk. He was surprised to see a guy not older than himself in a casual, white cotton shirt and designer jeans. With neck-long, reddish hair and a five o'clock shadow, Scott Hensley looked more like a musician than the owner of one of the most successful relocating firms in the U.S.

He finished his phone conversation with a few words, put the receiver down, and looked at Douglas.

"Well, Mr. Farland, welcome to Worldmove. We're glad you are here." He paused and then added, "I think."

"Thank you, sir, for the opportunity. I'm glad to be here." The two men shook hands.

"Mr. Farland," Hensley continued, "I have only a few minutes to explain something very important to you." He leaned back with his elbows on the armrest. He folded his hands in front of him and pointed both index fingers onto his lower lip with a thoughtful look.

"Since we have discussed your job description thoroughly over the phone, I'm gonna cut right to the chase."

Douglas listened. He liked it when people didn't waste time. "As I explained, you will be working with an individual who is a huge asset to this company. Frankly, outside this office this person is the company. I need to make it very clear that you both will be working together as a team. I can not allow any competition between the two of you that would hurt our relationship with our clients."

"Understood." Douglas looked straight at Hensley.

Hensley paused, looked at Douglas, and grimaced a painful smile. "I have no doubt that you understand. It's not you I'm worried about."

Douglas was a bit confused. "What are you saying?"

"For the last two years your future team partner has been, shall we say, alone in the field—very comfortable traveling all over the world to relocate our clients' employees and their families. Now that our little company is growing, I've found it necessary to add someone like you to make the job more efficient. I believe this assignment in Russia would be a perfect start."

Hadn't he said he was going to cut right to the chase? "Mr. Hensley, you could just tell me what my hurdles are," he said and sensed trouble. Douglas wasn't sure from which direction it might be coming.

Hensley studied him for a long moment and then he explained. "The hurdle, as you put it, is to introduce this idea to the lady I just described." Douglas raised his eyebrows. What was this guy? Nuts? Douglas thought and asked, "Am I understanding this correct, sir? The person I'm going to work with doesn't know of my existence?"

"I'm afraid not," Scott exhaled, "but she's going to be here in about twelve minutes and I've gotta come up with a plan." He looked more serious as he added, "You have to understand, under no circumstances do I want to lose her."

"May I offer a suggestion, sir?" Douglas analyzed the situation in his head.

"Shoot." Hensley seemed hopeful.

"Why don't I step out of your office for you to have a private meeting with the lady?"

Now Scott Hensley showed some wrinkles around his youthful blue eyes as he laughed. "You don't understand, man. She's half Italian—I might need protection."

They laughed and Scott went on, "Seriously, I hope you don't find this unprofessional, but you'll see, it's the best way to handle things."

Unprofessional? "It's your company, Mr. Hensley, I certainly think you know best."

"I like to believe so, Douglas. And please, call me Scott."

Chapter 4

MIA'S MOOD SANK AS fast as her plane descended once she saw the city of Seattle from above. Everything looked gray, even the Pacific, and she hated the color gray. Maybe her demeanor had something to do with her past in Seattle? She bit her lip. Hardly, she thought sarcastically.

Mia had first come here four years ago with the ink on her master's degree in business administration still wet. Fresh out of Michigan State University, she scored a job as a business developing manager with Boeing, starting a promising career. During the initial job interview they had told her they were looking for someone more experienced but couldn't pass up her linguistic skills. She was fluent in German, Italian, and Russian.

As a teenager Mia's focus was on sports. She'd still had one grandparent from either side who had been speaking with her in their native languages all her life. She had proven herself on the track and swim team in high school and it had not been a surprise when she got a scholarship at MSU.

Mia had been very close to her family, and it was hard for her to move as far away as Washington State. Despite feeling a bit lonely on her own, she had fallen right in love with the city's cosmopolitan flair, the pulsing downtown, and its world-famous Pike Place market. She had spent hours at the harbor watching the sailboats heading toward the horizon, letting her imagination run free.

The job with Boeing had worked out to be just what she wanted. She had moved into a beautiful, downtown apartment and introduced herself to the social circle of Seattle. The city had so much to offer to a young woman. Mia had often visited the Burke museum, she loved cultural heritage. Once in a while she had gone with a group of people to watch a Seahawk game and had the occasional beer afterward at the Blue Moon. Sometimes she had roamed the jazz clubs downtown; her favorite had been the one on Pioneer Square.

Eventually she started dating, and after a few disappointments, she fell in love with a fellow coworker at Boeing, an aviation engineer. After just six month of dating, Mia moved into his house and they got married. She would have liked a low-key ceremony, but Thomas' extravagant mother insisted on a lavish wedding.

Now Mia wished she had been more sensitive to the early warning signs of Thomas' conning and manipulative behavior, but by the time she had finally realized that her very intelligent and handsome husband was turning out to be a control freak, it had been too late.

Mia had kept herself busy with her work schedule and had tried to work on her marriage, but when she had caught Thomas lying about some messages her friends had left for her, she began to investigate further. It had not taken her long until she discovered that he had been reading her personal e-mails on their shared computer in their home. Thomas had also gone through her paper mail regularly, throwing away letters from her mother and grandmother in Michigan.

When Mia had confronted Thomas he had shown a new and very frightening side. After his yelling finally died down, he had pinned her against the refrigerator, and with a cold demeanor, he had made it very clear who was to be obeyed in his family. It was only a couple of hours later that Mia had packed some of her belongings and moved into a local motel.

She had been toying with the idea of returning back to Michigan, but she had not been quite ready to give up her life in the Northwest. Just a week later she had bumped into Scott Hensley at a restaurant during lunch. After an interesting offer, a little negotiation, and not much to lose, Mia took the job.

She quit Boeing and dove headfirst into a career filled with adventure. Her first assignment took her to Sydney, Australia. She had spent several weeks far away from abusive husbands, nasty mother-in-laws, and Seattle with its sad memories. When Mia returned from her first successful assignment, she had divorced Thomas and treated herself to the ski trip to Montana where she'd found Stoney Creek.

All this had happened about two years ago. In the beginning Mia had worried about Worldmove's headquarters being located in Seattle, but she very rarely had to come out for a meeting like today.

Hello, old demons, Mia thought as she stepped through the glass door at SEA TAC International Airport after collecting her bags. The cool autumn air caressed her skin and a shiver overcame her. Was it the wind or was it the city? Mia couldn't tell. But one thing was for sure, the funny feeling she'd gotten in her stomach after the call for the meeting this morning had started to intensify.

She checked her platinum, Dior wristwatch. If she wanted to be on time for her two o'clock meeting, she'd have to skip lunch.

Damn, it was breezy. Mia wished she hadn't packed her Eltro wool coat in her suitcase. She would have much rather had it now instead of being uncomfortable in her very chic, but very thin, business suit. She took a deep breath, squared her narrow shoulders, and waved down a cab. Of course the driver talked the whole way on a cell phone, to her surprise in English. He didn't help her with her luggage and barely paid attention when she gave him her destination.

Mia leaned back in the cab seat. No voice or text messages on her cell phone. She thought about checking in with Simon at headquarters but quickly changed her mind.

What's wrong with me? Mia wondered. Usually she was a very easygoing person. Today, she felt frazzled. Was the last-minute meeting really throwing her off this bad? Or did Seattle still have this strong an influence on her? It was time to get her act together. This was an important day, and she was not going to mess up a meeting with her boss. Scott Hensley could always count on her, and she had never disappointed him. She certainly was not planning on starting now.

Mia relaxed a little. She actually felt good after eight weeks without an assignment. She had used the downtime to study a certain Russian dialect. And she had been running—her passion. She had expanded her distance to fifteen miles and she got stronger by the workout.

Relax and expect anything, she told herself. Mia made the decision that whatever it was that had brought her here today was not going to compromise her composure, nor her job, in any way.

Chapter 5

AT WORLDMOVE INC. THE fax line rang and Simon retrieved the documents off the tray. He mustn't forget to make copies, he reminded himself and startled when Mia stepped into the room.

"Oh, hi, Mia. Good to see you. I'm just finishing up your paperwork for Russia."

"Thank you, can I have it now? I'd like to review things before my meeting," Mia asked patiently.

"Well, I'm not quite done. Can you give me another minute?" Simon seemed a little nervous. Mia knew him to be a geeky but very organized person. She had only met him in person once before, since he handled all her company business over the phone.

Today he almost seemed comical behind his messy desk, with his round glasses and his beige slacks a few sizes to big. Simon was only her height and seemed skinnier than she remembered.

"I'll wait." Mia watched him curiously, wondering if his behavior had anything to do with this short-notice meeting.

After shuffling papers around and doing some clicks on the computer, Simon handed Mia a yellow file folder about half an inch thick. "Good luck, Mia. Have a safe trip." He didn't even look at her.

Weirdo, Mia thought as she left his office. She leafed through the file. Everything she needed was right here, including her airplane tickets.

She decided to use the ladies' room to freshen up before she met with her boss. She wanted to powder her nose, but had left all her luggage with the receptionist, including her purse. A thin strand of hair came loose, and Mia tucked it behind her pearl-studded ear. There was no time to undo the knot she wore her hair in, and her comb was with the rest of her makeup kit in her purse.

Her tailored suit jacket had a few wrinkles from the trip, but Mia was glad she had chosen the light purple, silk blouse with her dark attire. It gave her a classical, feminine look. And her makeup was still meticulous—even her natural-colored lipstick had lasted through two cups of coffee.

"Not perfect, but it'll do," Mia thought and stepped out in the hallway.

"Ah, there she is. We thought you must be hiding."

Mia froze. Startled, she looked up at Scott Hensley, who was leaning casually against the hallway wall, both arms behind his back. He was accompanied by a tall, dark-haired man dressed in an expensive looking business suit and an orange tie.

Mia stood in the ladies' room doorway, feeling caught off guard. For a bizarre moment she wondered if they were considering whether or not she had washed her hands. She smiled at her strange thought and briskly stepped forward. With her chin up, she stuck her right arm out to greet her boss with a firm handshake.

"Scott, how are you!" Mia said, sincere. She couldn't help herself from eying the orange tie standing next to Hensley as she exchanged some short pleasantries with her boss.

"Mia, I would like you to meet Mr. Douglas Farland, a new associate with Worldmove. He will accompany you to Siberia." He studied Mia for an instant and added, "But here, why don't we step into my office?"

Mia was baffled. To accompany her? Did she just hear correctly? So that was what this meeting was all about. She felt a quick heat flush her cheeks but immediately suppressed the feeling that her territory was being endangered. Be nice, she warned herself and turned to greet the orange tie. He seemed taller now as he shook her hand, and Mia noticed that his eyes were the same color as his bright blue shirt. Whoever had talked him into buying that suit should be arrested.

"It's my pleasure, Ms. Trentino." His deep voice matched his physical size and she detected a bit of a drawl. Mia ignored the tingle on the back of her neck and stepped ahead of the men into Hensley's office. Scott wouldn't have to explain it to her. She had wondered in the past if there wouldn't be some sort of addition to her in the field.

Her boss's move to just casually bump into her in the hallway was pretty smooth. Mia was surprised he thought she had to be introduced this way. Strangely, it pleased her, too. Scott seemed to fear her—at least a little.

"Mia, you look fantastic," Scott complimented on their way into his office. "Have you been running a lot? What's your distance now?" Mia could appreciate his interest. As far as she knew, Hensley ran the annual Seattle half marathon himself. But she didn't like her private matters being brought up in front of a stranger. She could feel the men's eyes on her, but she was too confident to let them intimidate her.

"Oh, a few miles a week, to exercise the dog," she answered vaguely and then steered the conversation toward the assignment.

Four, comfortably deep-seated chairs surrounded a large, hardwood coffee table in one corner of Scott's huge office. Hardly the right environment for a serious business discussion, but Scott was a laidback character who loved having his meetings held in such a manner.

Mia was glad she had chosen a pantsuit. She would have shown way too much leg and never been able to get up elegantly out of this chair in a skirt. Scott took the seat next to Mia to discuss the assignment. There was sexual tension in the air and she wasn't sure which side it was coming from. Scott was in an awfully good mood. He must be excited about the new contract.

While Mia went over the details with Scott, the orange tie mainly observed. He asked a few intelligent questions, and by the time the conference call came from Russia, she felt in her element. Mia handled the dialogue between the Chairman of Yukoil, the Siberian Oil Company they would be working with, and Hensley very well. She went back and forth with the translation like she had never done anything else.

The Russians seemed a little vague about the exact dimensions of their situation. Mia thought that they seemed a bit unorganized and they didn't have answers to a few of Hensley's questions. By the time the call was over, Scott was very pleased with their meeting. Mia seemed to be taking it quite professionally that, from now on, she had to be a team player. Simon had been extremely efficient with research and flight schedules, so they could head out to their destination in Russia the following day. Mia respectfully declined her boss' invitation to a casual business dinner, wanting to get some rest and study her workload before heading out to Los Angeles on an early morning flight.

After Hensley dismissed them, it was clear to Mia that she had done well in keeping her composure. She had managed to handle the last two hours gracefully.

Of course, she was infuriated!

Her boss didn't seem to have noticed. He was too busy talking about Worldmove's great future, now doing business with the Russians. Mia was not so sure about the orange tie. He had been watching her during the entire meeting, his penetrating, blue eyes rarely leaving hers. He had not had much to say.

Mia couldn't wait to get the hell out of there. She felt betrayed and yearned for a long, hot shower. She would regain her composure in her hotel room with a nice glass of Chiles Canyon Red Zinfandel.

"Ms. Trentino, may I help you with your luggage?" Orange tie stood close behind her, invading her comfort zone, as Mia spoke with the receptionist.

"Why, no." Mia unconsciously stepped aside and straightened her shoulders. "I mean, no, thank you. A cab has been called and they will take care of it." She had to be careful not to lose her tact.

Her attention focused back on the receptionist. Douglas hesitated for a moment, letting his eyes linger on her. As he turned away from her, he lightly touched the sleeve of her left arm. "I am looking forward to working with you." Then, as he was walking away he added, "Please call me any time I can be of service."

Chapter 6

SEATED NEXT TO EACH other in coach, Mia and Douglas left the U.S. and headed to Beijing, China the following morning. Simon had not had much time for their travel arrangements, and on such a short notice there had not been any business class tickets available. Hensley always made sure Mia had the best treatment during her travels. "The job in the field is tough enough, so getting there should be a breeze," was Scott's motto.

There wasn't a time when Mia would have appreciated it more than now.

It wasn't just the duration of the flights—from Los Angeles, over Beijing, China, to Irkutsk, Siberia was going to be ungodly long—but having extra room between Farland and herself would have given her some comfort.

Mia had managed to stay off of his radar at SEA TAC International Airport and during the flight to Los Angeles. But once he had spotted her at LAX, he hadn't left her side.

Farland wasn't a man of many words. He stepped in when necessary to lend a hand with Mia's luggage. She had watched him as he quietly observed his surroundings. To Mia he radiated a strange authority. He seemed overly confident, and frankly just his presence was overwhelming.

During the first hours, thirty thousand feet above the pacific, they kept the conversation purely business. Mia tried hard not to show her annoyance and patiently explained the most important aspects of her job. Douglas seemed to catch on rather quick. "In the End, Mr. Farland, this isn't rocket science. It's all about moving people from A to B with the smallest amount of disturbance to their careers as possible."

As the conversation changed from business to a bit more personal, Mia was pleasantly surprised when Douglas revealed that he had been a faculty member at a private college for almost a decade, teaching geology and biochemistry. He also spoke French, which was another asset to the Company.

"May I ask what made you decide to leave?" Mia's curiosity finally got the best of her.

"Just like every other job, I guess I grew tired of it." He avoided a more thorough explanation. Then, he leaned his seat back and closed his eyes.

In the middle of a conversation he was going to take a nap? God, he was rude! Mia wondered darkly if the real reason he'd left was because he had gotten in trouble with one of his female students.

Glancing over and studying his features, Mia thought there was no doubt; he was handsome. He must be at least six foot two. His dark hair was neatly trimmed and showed some gray around the temples. He had a good nose and a strong jaw. His neck was muscular and through his taupe, Prague suit he wore for the day's travel, Mia thought he looked athletic. The only jewelry she could detect was a stainless steel Breitling on his left wrist, and his big hands did not look like the ones of an academic.

His age was difficult to guess. He seemed like to take good care of himself, but there were some deep lines in his face revealing a rougher past. She had to admit he was a pleasure to talk to. He knew when to speak and when to let her talk. And he spoke with a little bit of a southern twang. Very soothing, Mia thought.

He was very confident and seemed to have a solid character. However, Mia knew he was a threat to her career. She wouldn't lose her job to him, but she would have to fight for her status at Worldmove. During the meeting the day before, Mia had been aware of the mutual approval between her boss and Farland. The two men addressing each other on a first name basis had clearly shown that.

Of course Mia was not Worldmove's only employee. There were several other Relocation Specialists who took care of business within the United States and Canada, but Mia, because of her linguistic skills, had the status of being the only one on an international level. For two years she had been working on her own, and now Mia had to be a team player. She thought about that for a long time and then decided she also needed to be careful not to let Farland in on all of her secrets about the business. It was going to be a challenge, and she was not sure if she liked that.

And there was one more thing bothering her besides that orange tie he had worn yesterday. Sometimes, when Mia had shown some attitude, his jaw muscles had flexed in irritation.

Douglas needed to close his eyes. He wasn't tired. Actually he hadn't felt this awake in weeks. But to keep his head clear he needed to review his thoughts so he could make sensible decisions on how to proceed.

Yesterday afternoon he had started a new job as a relocation specialist, a title he had no idea existed until just a few weeks ago. Douglas had done his research about the company. He was impressed at how much Worldmove had accomplished with this little man power. Now he was looking forward to being a part of it after finally meeting Scott Hensley, an easygoing guy. And then there was Mia Trentino;

Scott had described Mia in a way that showed a little more than just respect. He had seemed to be intimidated by her. Calling her a business-savvy woman with a feel for the needs of individuals, he had explained that she would focus on the spouses and families of the mostly male clients. Mia had explained to Hensley that it would be much easier for executives or CEOs to focus on the job when their wives were comfortable with their new homes and surroundings. He had also mentioned that Mia was very strong-willed, and that he had learned to trust her by herself in the field.

Scott and Douglas had stepped out into the hallway at Worldmove Incorporated after ending their initial meeting. After all that talk about Mia, Douglas had been a little anxious about meeting her. He had wondered what kind of feminist he would have to deal with. But when Mia had stepped out of the Ladies' room, Douglas had felt anything but intimidation. He had taken one good look at her and realized that this new job had come with a very pleasant surprise. Understandably, she had been reserved toward him. This Scott guy sure knew how to run his business, but Douglas didn't agree with how he had handled the situation with Mia. It would make it harder for Douglas to gain her trust. But he had no doubt that it wouldn't take him long.

This morning he had given her time. He had kept an eye on her, studying her first at Seattle International airport, then during the flight to Los Angeles, seated several rows behind her. At LAX Douglas had made some last necessary phone calls before checking in. He arranged meeting up with Mia before boarding the plane to China, hoping she would be easier to handle.

Manipulating the conversation from business to personal matters, he had woken her interest about himself, but Mia had carefully avoided sharing too much information about her own life. She had shown confidence, and those pretty, dark eyes had sparkled when he cornered her during their dialogue. She was intelligent, almost street-smart, but she was no match for him.

Douglas opened his eyes. He looked straight ahead to the screen at the front of the aircraft where the little airplane on top of the world map showed passengers their travel location. Out of the corner of his eye he could see from Mia's deep and steady breathing that she had fallen asleep. He turned his head to study her. Her head leaned slightly toward him, and the dim light above her played with coppery highlights in her shiny, auburn hair. The soft, lace trim of her pale violet-colored blouse only allowed a glimpse of the outline of her chest. The sleeves reached just below her elbows and exposed the flawless skin of her slender forearms. Her delicate hands were resting in her lap. She was not very tall, but her legs were long for her height.

She had one leg crossed over the other. Her ankle-length, light brown, suede skirt had parted where the side slit came up to just below her knee and gave a glimpse of a beautifully shaped calf. When he had walked behind her he had noticed that her strides where long and powerful, and that the shape of her body was slim but nicely curved. A runner, Scott had mentioned. That's exactly what she looked like.

The overnight flight into Beijing would have thrown any world traveler off. Mia was used to dealing with jet lag, but she had never gone against the time zones for such a long distance. They had served some sort of breakfast, but Mia had declined. She was sipping a cup of excellent Chinese tea as the captain greeted the sleepy passengers first in Chinese, then in very heavy accented English. The airplane started the decent and it would only be a matter of thirty minutes until arrival.

Douglas was not in his seat. Mia gladly stretched her legs over into his legroom and tried to wake up her aching muscles. She would have liked to get up but the fasten seat belt sign had already come on. She wondered where he was, but didn't dare turn around. She wouldn't want to be caught looking for him.

As Mia finished her tea, Douglas reappeared and looked clean shaven and rested. He glided back into his seat and looked at her. With his deep voice he asked "Did you get some rest?"

Mia just nodded. She still felt dazed and did not want a conversation. Turning her head toward the window, she could make out Beijing's early morning lights in the darkness far below.

Chapter 7

IN THE PAST SCOTT had asked Mia if he should have Simon arrange for a layover for travel distances over fifteen hours. Just wanting to get there, she had always declined. Once on the road, or in the air for that matter, she had never cared about how long the trip would be. Usually she passed the time by studying her new assignment. Mia would learn about the industry and status of the client who had to be relocated. She studied the area's demographics, religious and cultural diversities, and the school system.

This time as well, she had chosen not to stay for an extra day in Beijing. Once she and Farland arrived in China, she regretted that decision. Mia's state of mind had been awful since yesterday's upsetting meeting at Worldmove. She felt distracted. The fact that she was, from now on, teamed up with someone had yet to sink in, and she was working hard to try and accept the decision Scott had made. On the other hand, she had enjoyed Farland's company.

She had had trouble focusing on her material once they had left Los Angeles. She would have to do her reading on her flight from Beijing to Irkutsk.

After finally making it through customs in Beijing, they'd had just enough time for a quick meal before they had to board yet another plane. The flight duration to Irkutsk lasted only two and a half hours and she had barely made it through the list of Yukoil associates and the administrative divisions of Irkutsk and surrounding cities when they approached their final destination.

Douglas had not offered any help with the workload. He had thought about it but figured that she would reach out to him when she was ready for his help. He had managed to sleep during this flight and felt rather refreshed as he gathered his carry-on before he left the plane.

Mia's body ached.

As she waited in the baggage claim area for her luggage, she felt like falling asleep standing upright. It has been twenty-six hours since they had left Seattle, and they still had to take a drive to the hotel.

There was just a short line at customs and she was glad to be in a country whose language she mastered. She felt a little sorry for Douglas. If people didn't speak English at Yukoil, he would be totally dependent on her.

Her face felt saggy from the lack of sleep, but this thought made her smile.

"Did I miss something funny?" Douglas handed Mia a Styrofoam cup filled with something steaming hot. He studied her intently.

"Smells fantastic, thank you." Mia ignored his question without looking at him. Watching the baggage claim belt go into motion, she carefully sipped. Lavender-scented white tea—how could he know? Mia decided it must have been a very lucky point of the finger at the kiosk. She did not decline when he offered to help her with her carry-on.

The mid-afternoon sun pierced Mia's eyes as she stepped out side of Irkutsk International Airport. The temperature was pleasantly in the sixties and there was no wind. The airport was small in comparison with most U.S. terminals. It was not very light inside and the gray exterior reflected the mood this country must have experienced in the past. Mia was glad the airport was not very busy this time of day. The few travelers seemed preoccupied with their activities and the airport staff was friendly and helpful.

A driver, holding a sign with the Worldmove Business logo, waited for them near the exit. The driver was very kind and assisted with the number of bags. Mia stood aside, draped her black wool coat around her shoulders, and let the two men organize the luggage.

As the superior, Mia should be seated in the front passenger seat, but at this point she needed the comfort of a backseat more than the reassurance of being the top of the heap. She waited for the driver to get the door and took a seat in the back of the old, pale beige Mercedes sedan. She hadn't seen a taxi cab like this one since she had visited Germany as an exchange student.

Leaning back in the black leather seat, Mia tried to remember what day it was. After a moment it occurred to her it was only Saturday. The first meeting with Yukoil executives had been set up for Monday morning. She made a mental note to bring back a gift for Simon. Thanks to his efficient scheduling, Mia would have an extra day to get acclimatized.

The ride to the Baikal Hotel was surprisingly short. The four-story-high, white stucco building looked friendly, and the tall, dark blue-tinted windows gave the hotel a modern look. Mia was beat, but she still had appreciation for the pine trees and the neatly trimmed hedges surrounding the premises. Red roses and evergreen brushes thrived by the entrance, and Mia noticed the Russian flag waving calmly high above them in the breeze. She hoped for a chance to visit the famous Lake Baikal; she didn't think it was too far from the hotel.

Douglas unloaded the luggage. Mia asked the driver how far it would be to the expansion side.

"Only one hundred and eighty kilometers, but the road conditions are poor," he answered in Russian.

Roughly a hundred miles, Mia thought. Thank God she would not have to deal with that drive today. Being more than glad about that, Mia smiled and thanked the driver warmly. He bashfully adjusted his checkered wool cap and said in very broken English, "I believe I will be your driver while you are here."

Mia glanced at Douglas. His eyes showed a glimmer of hope. I've got it made. Someone speaks English, they seemed to say.

The Baikal hotel entry hall was bright and friendly. There was a conference room on the north side. A comfortable lounge with all the amenities of a world-class hotel extended from the foyer. The ground level also offered a restaurant with several big screen TVs and a full bar. I'm impressed, she thought. At this moment she would have slept just about any where, but the appearance of this place suited her very much.

The receptionist took care of their check-in with quiet efficiency, and two bell boys arranged the handling of their luggage. Their rooms were located on the second floor across the hall from each other. Mia liked the idea of a little extra privacy due to the hallway.

Her room was beautifully furnished. Light colors everywhere. A vibrant print of a Wassily Kandinsky oil painting hung above the huge, king-sized bed. The beige tiled bathroom had a deep bath tub that Mia couldn't wait to stretch out into. A lavender-infused bath would help her get the relaxation she needed. There was a business center set up, including an all-in-one printer and fax on a cherry wood office desk. A sign noted the availability of wireless, high-speed Internet. This hotel room could have been found in any western country, and Mia's uncertainty over spending several weeks in the former Soviet Union vanished.

Chapter 8

"THE AMERICANS HAVE ARRIVED," Oleg leaned back in a chair and crossed his work boot-covered feet on top of a dented, old metal table. He took drag of his filterless Palekh cigarette.

Shurnik, Oleg's superior, stood and smirked at him. "Do we anticipate any problems? How many are there?"

Oleg inhaled deeply, "Just two of them. I don't see any trouble. The woman checked out clean. She is here for the expansion. The man with her couldn't be traced, which doesn't have to mean anything."

Shurnik kicked the chair away from under Oleg. He hit the floor hard. "Dumbass! I told you before, do not take the Americans lightly! We have informants and the access to research them thoroughly. Use those recourses. Now go back to work!"

Oleg got up and rubbed his lower back. He looked down as if the dirt at his feet was intriguing. Oleg did not dare to look at Shurnik, who continued with his commands. "I don't want to see your sorry face again until you dig up some useful information on him."

Oleg obeyed and left Shurnik's dingy office. Shurnik picked up the chair and sat down. He wondered if Oleg was the right man for the job. He was worried about what Oleg had just told him. He had to be—too much was at stake. If Lagunov found out there was no existing file on the American, someone's head would roll, and it probably would be his.

He opened a metal drawer and looked for his blue-labeled bottle of Gzhelka Vodka. Shurnik took a good swig, let the alcohol slowly burn down his throat, and waited for the pleasantly numbing buzz to kick in.

God, he didn't have the nerve he used to have. As a former Polovnik, the equivalent to a colonel, in the red army he had been trained to listen to his intuition. This sense told him now that the American needed to be watched very closely.

Monday morning came and went. Mia had received a message sometime Sunday confirming their meeting with the executives of Yukoil. Douglas had joined her for a brainstorm supper Sunday afternoon at the Armenian restaurant at the Baikal hotel. Mia had heard many good things about Russian cuisine and wasn't in the least disappointed when she had tasted the Ishkhan, a trout fried in wine and filled with cherry plums. Douglas had been a perfect gentleman, not in the least flirtatious. The obvious respect he showed her pleased Mia, and she relaxed about him a bit.

Yukoil's main office was located in a beautiful, nineteenth-century Gothic building in downtown Irkutsk, just a few blocks from the Baikal hotel. The entire building had been laid out with red carpet runners covering white marble floors. A wide, wooden staircase majestically led to the first floor offices and a big meeting hall. Tall, narrow windows were framed with heavy drapes and reminded Mia of a TV program featuring a story about Russian Czars she had once watched.

It had been decided that there was no need at this point to take the drive out to the location where the company would extend to.

Mia had been very comfortable with the Russians right from the start. With the exception of a secretary, she was the only female attending the meeting and everyone had treated her with the utmost respect.

The first meeting at Yukoil had taken several hours but was well organized. In the beginning, Mia had wondered why exactly she was needed without even the construction of the expansion being completed. Back in Seattle Scott had explained some of the ideas the Russians had for this area, but they had not shared any details with him. Now the picture was starting to become clearer to Mia.

Housing in Irkutsk was limited. Besides the long commute, the only road from Irkutsk was in very bad shape. The idea seemed brilliant. Yukoil planned on not just expanding to yet another oil-drilling field—they would build a complete city to go with it. Besides housing and schools, stores and administrative offices, they would also have a small power plant, as well as everything else a small city would need to survive on its own.

The financial plan showed that it would be more lucrative to build apartment complexes on land already owned by Yukoil instead of trying to purchase property owned by the Irkutsk Oblast. Yukoil owned most of the drilling fields in Siberia. This would be the first one with its own refinery attached to it, which would eliminate the need for hundreds of miles of pipeline. The demographics showed a population density in Siberia of three people per one square kilometer. The economic boost in eastern Siberia would be tremendous.

Mia had been asked what the logistics would be to move several hundred future employees and their families into the area. She impressed the seven Yukoil board members with a quick calculation and a detailed explanation of the necessities.

A second meeting had been scheduled for Tuesday morning. A Russian Environmentalist from the University in Moscow had been invited to discuss the geology and the environmental impact of the area. This subject being Douglas' expertise, Mia had spent the evening before studying the technical terms she would have to translate back and forth.

Douglas had done extensive research that night. He was able to prepare a presentation for the board. He took the spot on the overhead projector and displayed some complex diagrams. Choosing his lingo wisely, Mia had little trouble with the translation. Douglas observed her closely and rephrased his sentences when necessary.

They had handled yet another meeting to the Russians' satisfaction. Mia was pleased. If things kept going like this, they would be able to shorten this assignment and fly home several days early.

Chapter 9

"We need to get out there." Douglas seemed determined after the meeting. "Don't you agree, Ms. Trentino?"

Mia gnawed on her lip in thought. In her mind, she went through today's tasks. There was not really anything to be done that they couldn't work on during the drive.

"Let's do it," Mia agreed. Her curiosity had grown as well, and she felt they needed to investigate the location.

After a quick lunch their driver picked them up at the hotel. Douglas had changed out of his well-tailored business suit into jeans, work boots, and a thin, black sweater.

The early afternoon sun had warmed the air a bit. Douglas pushed his sleeves up, which exposed his tanned and masculine forearms. He was aware of Mia's gaze. He casually threw his sheep's wool-lined, leather jacket over one shoulder and grinned at her,

"Feels good to get rid of that suit, doesn't it?"

"Yes, it does," Mia nodded. She herself was dressed in jeans and a violet and white checkered shirt. She always packed some casual clothes just to be prepared. But when she felt Douglas eyes she just wished she had brought her old, comfy corduroy pants instead of just her fitted Calvin Kleins.

"I have to tell you how impressed I am with your skills," Douglas complimented her. "Where did you learn to speak Russian?"

"My mother's parents came from Prussia, and my Grandma still talks to me in Russian." Mia was glad to have a casual conversation. She felt crowded by Douglas in the Mercedes' small backseat.

Heading south, they made their way out of Irkutsk around the beautifully wooded, southwestern shores of Lake Baikal. The driver explained that the lake would not be visible from the road and asked if they would like to make an excursion to it.

"Maybe some other time," Mia answered. "Today it's all business."

After a while the scenery changed and lead through the thickness of the Siberian taiga. The road snaked through deep forest and around grassy hills. There was a mountain range due south. Mia hoped the ridged dirt road would become smoother, but it didn't seem likely.

"This area looks a lot like the cow pastures in Colorado," Douglas commented.

"Oh yes? I wouldn't know."

"Tell me, you've never been in cowboy country?" He seemed genuinely surprised.

Mia turned her head, looked at Douglas, and raised an eyebrow. "Cowboy country? Mr. Farland, this may sound rude, but I'm not fond of rednecks."

Douglas busted out laughing. "Remind me when we are done with this job, and I will take you out to a friend's ranch. The air would do you good, Ms. Trentino, and I bet you'd look fine on horseback in those jeans." He tipped his invisible hat and drawled, "This coming from a true redneck, ma'am"

She looked at him incredulously, not quite sure how to respond.

When they finally arrived at their destination, Mia remembered the road conditions had been described as poor—what an understatement!

Two and a half hours and a bit over a hundred miles later, Mia felt she had lost the fillings in her teeth. They had tried to go over papers during the drive, but the rough ride had made it impossible.

The commute was an unreasonable demand. They were supposed to work out here in the following days. What would they do? How would they get here?

Holding one hand over her eyes, Mia squinted into the sun as she looked around. She was taken aback by the endless distance between her and the horizon. The tremendous depth of the south-central Siberian forests around her displayed countless hues of greens. Just a few white clouds disturbed the most perfect blue of an unbelievable, mile-high autumn sky.

It took her a while to realize that this was the place where hundreds of people would live after the completion of the project.

Douglas stretched his back. He so much preferred to work out in the open instead of in the confinement of an office building, having to deal with bureaucracy. They would be so much more efficient out here.

Mia had been watching him. He seemed energized and his amazing blue eyes showed a flicker. When he looked at her, she flushed just a little.

"Isn't this outstanding?" he asked. She smiled, distraught, and wasn't so sure. Back in Montana she would find some lonely parts during her running exercises, but this was borderline godforsaken.

Mia found herself in a camp-like base. Heavy earthmoving equipment and ATV's, water trucks, and tractors with loaders were parked everywhere. Something that looked like an old-fashioned travel trailer sat on the other side of the premises. She noticed even a helicopter pad in the distance.

A medium sized man in camouflaged pants and a dirty, green jacket approached them. He introduced himself as Oleg. "I don't expect you to pronounce my last name, so please, just Oleg is fine." He took his work gloves off and shook Mia's hand.

After Mia translated the introduction between Oleg and Douglas she asked if they could take a tour.

"Certainly, Ms. Trentino. We were expecting you and Mr. Farland. Please step this way for a refreshment."

The camp's center consisted of four olive drab, heavy duty canvas enclosures. Every tent had its own diesel generator as power supply. Several water tanks indicated some sort of fresh water system. Mia wondered if people actually lived here at this point. The whole set up seemed to have military written all over it.

They stepped into the largest of the tents and Mia was surprised to see a mess hall with pop-up bench tables. Adjoining was a primitive but functional kitchen including fridge, freezer, a big, eight-burner gas stove with two ovens, and several stainless steel cabinets with a sink. The dirt floor was covered with a tarp-like material. The whole scene had a lived-in feeling to it.

On a table were clean glasses and different kind of beverages arranged.

"Can we offer something to drink? Or maybe a bite to eat?" Oleg offered kindly. The label of each drink was in Cyrillic, but the color and layout was the same as in the U.S.

Douglas reached for a red and white labeled bottle with a brown liquid. Mia thought he must know that was a coke. He had picked up a few words in Russian and thanked Oleg for the hospitality.

Mia took a bottle of water and asked for a washroom. Oleg showed her the way. Douglas stayed behind and Mia had a suspicion that he was glad to get rid of her for a little while.

When she returned, she joined the two men on a tour of the whole complex. The other three barracks contained sleeping quarters for about twenty-five men, a shower room, and an office facility with several workstations, including an SCR300 radio. She noticed Electrical radiators in all the barracks and suspected the temperature dropped quite drastically at night.

"The Director will be joining us in a little while," Oleg explained. "He drove out to the field. They had some problems with one of the pumps this morning." Mia noticed Oleg eying Douglas with an expression she couldn't interpret. "I will notify him that you have arrived," Oleg said. "Please make yourselves at home. It should only be a short wait."

Shurnik cursed. "Why has this not been repaired at once?" He yelled at his men. Up to his elbows in grease, he investigated the pump and why the pressure was down. It seemed to just be a seal, but it could have done some severe damage to the engine.

"Useless, that's what you all are! Fix it—immediately!" Shurnik commanded in a harsh tone. The three men ducked their heads and went to work.

In the past…well, things like this just didn't happen. In the good old days, there was no room for failure.

Shurnik wiped his hands on an already oil-stained towel and headed back to his Kamaz 6x6 truck. He got on his CB and confirmed the arrival of the two guests.

Chapter 10

NICE PIECE, SHURNIK THOUGHT. As he rolled into the camp, he had spotted Mia.

He watched her walking between Oleg and another man. Both men were only inches away from her, and what must be the American was towering over her, but she walked with confidence and seemed to be arguing with the two men.

He parked the truck and killed the diesel engine. Shurnik continued to watch them and took his time collecting his worksheets. As he stepped out, he wondered what the reason for the woman's bickering could be. As he walked toward the three, his facial expression changed from plain and hard to pleasant.

"Ms. Trentino, Mr. Farland," Shurnik called out.

Mia paused in the middle of a sentence and looked, rather flabbergasted, at the approaching man calling her name. Shurnik planted himself in front of Mia, looked down to her with a genuine smile, and took her hand.

"Welcome to our little paradise. We are so pleased to have you here." Shurnik held on to Mia's hand with both of his.

At first the man startled Mia, but strangely, after a moment, Mia didn't even mind his touch.

"I'm Alexandr Shurnik, the Director of this operation," Shurnik introduced himself. His English was heavily accented.

His hand finally let go of Mia's just to offer it to Douglas. "I hope you have had a pleasant trip to Siberia? Your hotel is satisfactory? Yes?"

"Thank you." Douglas was sparse with his words. From her observations Mia knew by now that he got quiet when he tensed up.

Shurnik was as tall and athletic as Douglas, but twenty-five pounds lighter. His skin was sun-beaten, and his gray eyes stood in contrast to his tanned face. He looked fit but must have been at least in his mid-fifties. He wore camo pants similar to what Oleg was wearing and clearly had just arrived from someplace dusty.

"Please forgive my appearance, Ms. Trentino." He rolled the 'r' in her name sharply. "Let me clean up. I will return in a minute." Shurnik hesitated and then walked off. Walking back to the mess hall, Douglas took Mia slightly by the elbow. "Are you going to share your concerns with Shurnik, or would you like me to handle it?"

Mia looked up at him. "I appreciate your thought, but I have to stand my ground out here, if you know what I mean."

Douglas understood. If Mia wanted to be accepted, she'd have to fight her own battles.

After a few minutes Shurnik rejoined the group. He looked cleaned up and invited Mia and Douglas to a supper consistent of Borscht. "You still have to take the drive back to the City. I had Elena prepare an early dinner. I hope you will enjoy it."

A heavyset woman in a worn apron rummaged in the kitchen. She must have been at least in her sixties. Some gray strands peeked out from under the soft cloth she wore as a Kichka. At first she didn't pay the visitors any attention, but after Shurnik said something to her that even Mia couldn't understand, she surprised Mia with a very warm smile.

Oleg had disappeared. Shurnik waited until his guests had been served then took his bowl of stew from Elena. He snapped open his knife and cut the freshly baked bread in generous slices. Sitting down opposite Mia and Douglas, he looked straight at Mia and asked, "Ms. Trentino, please forgive me for asking so bluntly, but Oleg mentioned some, how do you say, apprehension?"

Mia used her napkin, put her spoon down, and held Shurnik's

gaze. "Mr. Shurnik, your company has hired us to advise in your operation. We feel that the most efficient way of doing so would be working on-site rather than trying to coordinate things from Irkutsk."

"Meaning?" Shurnik asked. Mia just had to get straight to the point. "The commute to and from Irkutsk would be too long on a daily basis and also—"

"The ride is terrible, isn't it?" Shurnik interrupted her.

"Yes, indeed," Mia agreed, somewhat relieved.

"You understand now why we decided to build here and move our employees?" Shurnik leaned back and folded his hands above his head. "Why don't you do the same?" he suggested and spread his arms. "There is plenty of room, as you can see."

"Excuse me?" That was not what Mia had in mind. She had thought about the Eurocopter sitting in the distance.

And just as though he had read her mind Shurnik said, "Well, I hope you did not refer to the usage of Charlie?"

"Who's Charlie?" Douglas wanted to know.

"The German EC 135, I am certain you have noticed," Shurnik studied Douglas for an instant. When he detected recognition in Douglas' expression Shurnik continued. "Our budget would not allow the daily use. Charlie is available for emergency only."

Mia wished she hadn't brought it up. Now they would have no choice but to move out here, would they?

"Of course I would not suggest to you how to do your work," Shurnik said. "But I can only encourage you to stay here with us."

Shurnik was right, Mia had to agree. It only made sense—well, as far as the project went anyway.

Helena had served a delicious, homemade pirozhkyas as dessert and left silently the kitchen after she had cleaned up.

"The choice is yours." Shurnik got up. "You are welcome here, and we would do our best to make it comfortable for you." Mia and Douglas had also gotten up and Shurnik continued. "Ms. Trentino, Elena here is our cook and nurse who takes care of us. She has her own private sleeping quarters, and I believe you have seen her washroom. There would be similar arrangements made for you. Now, please excuse me. I am needed out on the oil field."

Once again, he shook their hands. "Please notify headquarters about your decision." With that said, Shurnik nodded briskly and walked off.

Mia noticed the fine hair on the back of her neck standing up. This guy was creepy—very nice, but creepy.

Deep in thought, Mia studied the ground in front of her leaving the tent. She could feel Douglas looking at her. When she turned around to him she noticed him watching her with his eyes narrowed in concern.

"Are you going to be okay with this?" he asked with honest distress.

"Is there any other way?" she countered, knowing the answer.

After they returned to the car, Mia sat next to Douglas in the backseat and crossed one leg over the other, fidgeting. For a while she stared out of the window and then studied Douglas, who made some notes. Without looking up he asked, "What is it?"

Mia took a deep breath, "As part of the team, I have to ask you…do you have any opposition to moving out here?"

Surprised, Douglas looked up. "Me? Are you kidding? Whatever it takes to keep me out of a suit."

Mia pulled a face. "Even if it means living in this boot camp?"

Douglas laughed. "No offense, Ms. Trentino, but I doubt you know anything about boot camp," he said and studied her with probing, blue eyes.

"None taken," Mia mocked, "but I'm sure you have plenty of experience to share?"

"Yes, ma'am." Douglas proudly drawled. "I spent four years with the Marines."

Mia nodded and leaned back in the seat. God, she thought, why am I not surprised?

Chapter 11

SHURNIK ACCELERATED.

Leaving in a dust cloud, Shurnik analyzed the two Americans. The woman certainly was just a typical socialite—naive and too consumed with herself to pay much attention to her surroundings. He would have to keep his crew away from her, though. A woman like that could get herself into trouble out here. And he didn't need that kind of attention.

He sensed martial arts training on the man. The way he was built and moved had told him. Shurnik thought about the man's reaction when he had snapped open his switchblade underneath the table. He had quickly lifted his head and looked at Shurnik. And Shurnik had noticed that, just for an instant, the man's shoulders tensed up. The fact that Oleg's investigation had not brought up anything made him suspicious of the man. Of course he'd keep his eye on the American. Shurnik would have to do more research on his own about him. He would use one of his old informants for that. Markovich would do a good job. He had known him for a long time and trusted him.

Shurnik had met Markovich after the Soviet Army had recruited both of them. At that time Shurnik underwent rigorous training to be with the Spetsnaz, the Soviet's Special Forces unit. Shurnik and Markovich had fought side by side a very bloody war in Afghanistan.

Out there in the desert they had become brothers, sworn to each other until death. Still today Shurnik would do anything for Markovich, no questions asked, and he knew it worked vice versa.

Back then, Shurnik had been one of the best, an excellent sniper and a master of brutal guerilla techniques. Speaking Farsi and Pashto, he had functioned as a mole in the inner circles of the Mujahideen. With his manipulating techniques, he had been able to do some severe damage. But they also had damaged him. Shurnik had witnessed some of his comrades being tortured and suffer barbaric deaths. Shurnik had been a war animal and loved the thrill of the hunt, but still today he would wake up at times soaked in cold sweat from those nightmarish, recurring memories.

Shortly after the Soviet Union had dissolved, military forces had been reduced and hundreds of soldiers and KGB Officers had lost their posts. Shurnik and Markovich had been two of many.

The early attempts of the country to nurse along a democratic government condemned the already weak economy to a total disaster. The virtual non-existence of trade and the political uncertainty contributed to the rapid growth of the Russian Mafia.

The Bratva, the Russian Mob, began to recruit heavily amongst ex-military and former government workers. After eliminating internal feuds and perfecting corruption and crime, the Russian Mafia grew into a well-organized cartel. In a short amount of time it had established a similar organization to its European counterpart in Italy.

In the beginning, Shurnik had been a member of a group specializing in seizing control of the new, legitimate banking system. Within two years, just in Moscow alone, Shurnik had carried out as many as eight hits on new, reform-minded bank executives and leading business men. A few foreign businesses actually did get their feet on the ground. By paying Krysha up to 30 percent of their profit, they bought a guarantee to stay alive while doing business on Russian soil.

Shurnik had worked closely with the leader of the Nordex affiliation of the Russian Mob and was responsible for the collection of those fees. Sometimes he had to use the same techniques on his "customers" as his co-conspirators had suffered before they had been killed.

After the end of the cold war, Shurnik's computer-savvy friend, Markovich, had gone in the private sector of security, finding new roaming grounds in the U.K. Today he called himself a

"Contributor to the free market," spying on American and European Intelligence and being heavily involved in money laundry in France.

Shurnik had been working for Yukoil for quite some time. First in the oil fields in northern Siberia, and later he worked his way up to supervisor and was responsible for training new workers. Now his experience showed, and in a very short time the new field had yielded success.

The work out here was dirty, dangerous, and could be potential deadly. So many things could go wrong, and he had to be after his crew constantly to be on top of the dangers. Those dangers applied to the relations with the Americans as well.

Chapter 12

When Mia had explained the importance of her and Farland moving out to the field, the boardroom had fallen silent. She knew they needed her here at headquarters to help make crucial decisions, but right now Shurnik and his crew were a bigger priority.

"Ms. Trentino, you understand that, at this time, it is dangerous terrain out there?" one eventually asked. She could feel their skepticism.

"And you must know that communication between us is going to be difficult," another added. "At least until the communication unit is installed."

"Yes, I certainly do understand, but I hope you can see our reasoning," Mia replied, turning her head to Farland. Douglas was reading the men's faces. Despite their reluctance, he could tell they were going to give in.

Finally one nodded, and the rest quickly followed his lead. They were going to the field.

The meeting adjourned and Mia was quiet during the short drive back to the hotel.

She stared out the window with a worried look on her face. Douglas pretended to read his notes, but he'd been watching her since the meeting had finished. She was really fretting over leaving Irkutsk.

Douglas thought about the drastic change this assignment was about to undergo and how scary it must be for a woman to leave the comfort of a city and exchange it for the dangers of the Siberian taiga. She obviously knew it was the best for the job, and that was clearly her priority. Douglas admired that courage. He was aware of her independence and inner strength, but even Mia Trentino's bravery could only go so far.

He considered how best to be supportive without embarrassing her. Finally he said, "I need to tell you something important." In the cab's small backseat, she suddenly seemed very vulnerable.

"What is that?" she asked softly.

"I want you to know," he paused, trying to find the right words, "out there I'm not just your associate. I'll watch out for your safety, if necessary." He wanted to explain further but decided to leave it at that.

After an initial flush of embarrassment, Mia smiled at him. "I don't think it will be, but I'll keep it in mind."

Mia had arranged to leave most of their belongings at the hotel. There was no need for much business attire out on the oil field. They packed light, just the necessities for a few days' stay. Eventually, Douglas' careless attitude had leeched some of the tension out of Mia.

"This is going to be rough. Did you bring any survival gear from a previous job in one of those suitcases?" Douglas joked from across the hall. His hotel room door stood open, and Mia glanced inside.

"No, I thought that's what the boss sent you along for," Mia responded, smiling.

"Ouch. Well, maybe I will remember some of my Boy Scout days in case we have to start a bonfire." Douglas rubbed a pair of imaginary wooden sticks between his hands.

Mia sighed. To leave the comfort of the hotel seemed like a breeze for him. Apparently it would be much easier for a man to adapt out there. She was a little apprehensive of the idea. *I'm just gonna have to trust him*, she reminded herself, thinking about the two of them working together in such an unusual situation.

A faint peep came from her pocket. There was a message from home on her Palm TX. Leaning against Douglas' doorframe, she read the message and a bad feeling went through her like a lightening bolt. Her face ashened.

"Call me ASAP, Zulu," it said. "Is something wrong?" Douglas asked, concerned. He stood on the far side of his room, organizing his belongings. But she had already stormed out. Must be bad news from home or something, he thought, and threw the shirt he was folding onto a chair to go after her.

Despite the time difference, it was just after midnight in Montana, Mia had called back right away. By the time Douglas made it across the hall, Mia was sitting on the edge of her bed, and tears were filling her eyes. Taken aback, he paused just at the door. With concern he watched as she clasped the receiver with both hands.

Mia felt like someone had just ripped the floor away from underneath her.

"They don't know if he's going to be okay, Mia," Zulu explained, the worry in her voice clear even across the ocean. "Uncle Phil is so sorry. He doesn't know how he could have missed it. He was certain he had gotten to it all when he cleaned out the barn."

Mia could feel that her friend was just as scared as she was. She sounded like she'd been crying. She cleared her throat and continued. "They flushed Blue's system and put him on a drip. The Vitamin K should kick in within twelve hours, and then they can tell us more."

Mia swallowed hard. "I won't be reachable in twelve hours, Zulu. But I will call you as soon as I can."

"I'm sorry to put you through this." Zulu's voice skipped. "But I wanted you to know, in case you end up having to make the decision—"

"Of course," Mia interrupted quickly and closed her eyes. She couldn't bear to hear the words. "I'll be fine, and please tell Uncle Phil not to beat himself up," Mia reassured her friend.

She put the receiver down, still sitting on the edge of her bed, gnawing on her lower lip and deep in thought.

Blue's face flashed in her mind's eye. He had been with her for over six years, since he was a puppy. He'd moved with her from

Michigan to Seattle and had stood loyally by her side through the ugly divorce. Mia couldn't stand the thought of him being in pain, or worse. She wiped at the tears starting to run down her cheek with the back of her hand.

She just sat there, staring at the floor, still unaware of Douglas. She was trying to figure out how she would be able to contact Zulu the next day and startled when Douglas took a step toward her.

"Are you okay?" he asked carefully.

Great, she thought, getting more upset. Now he'd start nosing around in her private business. What was he doing in her room, anyway?

She knew she was being unfair—he was reacting just as she would have if he'd been upset—but she couldn't deal with him right now.

"It's nothing, not to worry. Thanks anyway. Would you excuse me, please?" Mia babbled. She felt panic swell up inside. She needed to be alone.

She stood up and turned her back to him, trying to look like she was still busy packing. But as she began to refold a shirt, she started to feel she had made a mistake. He hadn't done anything wrong. He was just trying to be supportive.

Suddenly, she felt stupid. It would be hard, but she couldn't let a sick pet ruin the good work atmosphere they'd been slowly building. If they were to continue this assignment together successfully, she couldn't be this reclusive, even with a private matter. Decided, Mia took a deep breath, ready to tell him about Blue, and turned around.

But he'd already left the room.

Rats, Mia thought, now he's mad. Standing in the middle of her room, she closed her eyes and took a deep breath. Should she care? Yes, you should, her conscious told her. Also, you need him for this job, whether you like it or not!

"Damn," she muttered under her breath. "I have to make it right with him." Angry with herself she walked across the hallway.

"Mr. Farland?" She knocked quietly on his door.

After a moment he opened it, his face expressionless. He stepped aside to let her in, but Mia stood with her hands buried in the pockets of her slacks. She looked up at him and explained. "It's my dog. He got into rat poison and..." Mia paused and then added, "I'm sorry I reacted so badly."

His face softened as soon as he saw the anguish in her dark, red-rimmed eyes. "No problem, Mia, I understand." Douglas had to beat down the impulse to take her in his arms. She had seemed like such a tough cookie in just the few days he'd known her, and that had impressed him. But this new side she was showing him touched his heart—and it hadn't been touched in a long time.

Feeling self-conscious, Mia straightened her back and decided he didn't need any further explanation. "Thank you. I will see you downstairs." And before he could say anything else, she turned on her heel and hurried back to her room.

After she had finished her packing and had rung for the bell boy, it occurred to her that Farland had called her by her first name.

Chapter 13

MIA IGNORED IT. SHE had to—there was no way she could keep her professional front if they were on a first name basis. She was old-fashioned that way. It didn't help that she was certainly aware of the attraction starting to build between Farland and herself. The isolated environment they'd be working in would only complicate things further.

I need to keep my distance, she thought. Ignore his looks and focus on the damn job!

Mia had immediately called him by his surname when they had met in the foyer, and he had done the same. Picking up on her rigid formality, Douglas kept the conversation limited on their way out to the camp. He kindly asked if her dog was going to be all right, and then focused his thoughts on what the days ahead might bring.

Helena had expected Mia's arrival and had prepared a yurt for her stay. The small living space contained a simple, wooden chest of drawers and a lockable nightstand for her personal belongings. A thin mattress sat on top of a narrow, metal bed frame, and Mia yearned for the comfortable, double pillow top mattress in her hotel room, but the linens were freshly washed and crisp. There was no room for a desk. Mia would have to do her work either sitting on her bed or out in the mess hall.

The entry was a heavy-duty, zip-up closure—impossible to lock. Mia did not worry about security; Helena's room was located just on the other side of the adjoining washroom. When she poked her head inside the shared space, she realized it had just been cleaned. She smiled, knowing that Helena had gone out of her way to make her feel comfortable.

She finished unpacking and sat on her bed. *It's gonna be okay. You won't be here too long,* Mia was telling herself.

Douglas was sitting in the mess hall. He had finished arranging his room and was waiting for Mia. *I bet she can't handle it,* he thought. She seemed too much like a city girl with her perfect hairdo and pretty clothes.

When she walked in, he couldn't help himself. "So? You think you can manage?" He asked her curiously. Mia sat down across from him and smiled. She had a small pack of peanuts in her hand and offered him some.

"Sure," she said. "Just like another camping trip."

He narrowed his eyes. "Camping?" he asked, not believing her. "Really! Tell me about it."

She nodded. "Growing up we went every summer to the Upper Peninsula in Michigan. And just last year I spent a week in Glacier National Park." She had another peanut and looked at him challengingly. *Take that, you arrogant prick,* she thought. She knew he had put her in a category she didn't belong, and she wanted to set the record straight.

Douglas accepted the subtle rebuke and changed the subject. Mia learned that his accommodations were not as private as hers. His sleeping quarter had been separated with a thin canvas from the rest of the men, and he shared the main washroom with them. She wasn't surprised when he shrugged and expressed that it didn't concern him at all.

The next two days were dominated by long hours in the open. So far the weather was being cooperative, with temperatures in the low fifties and calm winds.

Planning the layout of a small city was a little beyond the kind of work Mia had done before. Living so isolated out here would be hard on families, and Mia tried her very best to make it as comfortable and convenient as possible.

She went over the zoning of each sector several times, changing locations around until they would make the most sense. Mia paid special attention to anything involving the construction of the schools. In addition to the job security, a good education for the children would help draw in families.

Farland was a huge help. He had incredible perception for the job. It turned out they worked very well together, and Mia was quickly falling in love with the assignment. She also realized that it would not have been a success had they not come out to the field to get a feel for the environment.

The mornings started with a meeting with Shurnik. He seemed to be very pleased with their progress, and today they had decided to review the construction site for the communication unit that would be installed soon.

"I can't believe it's already been three days," Mia commented as they arrived at the site. "I can't wait for this comm unit to be up and running."

Douglas nodded. "I know. It'll be much more productive when we're able to communicate with Yukoil directly."

He held the passenger door open, and Mia stepped out of the truck. Two workers walking by nodded a greeting. Mia smiled back when they heard an earth-shaking, metallic sound followed by a deafening scream.

Mia, Douglas, and the two workers sprinted toward the noise, over where the crew was working with heavy equipment. A palette of heavy drill steel sat on the ground. Men had been standing next to it when one of the steel ties had snapped. Several pipes had rolled off the palette and one of the workers was crushed beneath them.

The man's upper body was visible and twisting in agony. Mia's blood froze and she couldn't move. In terror she watched as five men tried to free their comrade from under the heavy pipes, but it was clear they wouldn't succeed. The pipes were too heavy to lift with just brute strength, and the man pinned underneath was running out of time.

Mia panicked. She looked around frantically, trying to figure out a way to help with the rescue. Her eyes flew to the surrounding equipment and caught on one of the heavy machines. At first her mind balked at the idea taking form, but she quickly knew she had no other choice.

Yes, you remember! Her brain screamed. Do it and do it now!

Mia ran to where the heavy equipment was parked and jumped on a track hoe. She found the ignition and started up the big diesel engine. She scanned the controls and levers in the cockpit. Different from what she had seen before, but didn't they all work about the same? Her right foot pushed down a pedal, and the heavy machine answered with a billow of black smoke out of the exhaust pipe. Slowly, she maneuvered the machine toward the men.

As she approached, Mia realized the crushed man was not moving anymore. Someone was frantically talking on a handheld radio.

Douglas yelled at the men to try the other end of the pipe and then realized they could not understand him. He watched as blood spurted out of the compound fracture on the man's upper leg. Goddammit! If the main artery was severed, he would bleed to death in the matter of minutes.

Suddenly Douglas heard the loud rumble of approaching metal tracks to his left. He looked over, and it took him a second to understand what was happening. What the hell was she doing?

Douglas looked at Mia with wide eyes. She stared down at him from the cab of the track hoe. "Trust me," her eyes seemed to say, and she signaled him to communicate to her via sign language.

Mia stopped the heavy machine within a few feet in front of the men. With a shaky right hand she used the control to carefully extend the excavator's toothed bucket.

Mia held her breath and sweat rolled down her neck. She paused and in her mind she visualized how the control knobs worked. A mistake on her part could have fatal consequences. Relax! You can do this, she told herself. She exhaled, trying to force herself into calmness. It worked, and her right hand stopped shaking.

She eased the outside right tooth of the bucket underneath the end of the heavy pipe and inched it up, aware that if it slipped it would harm everyone on the ground. Her position would not allow her to see the injured man. Her focus was on Douglas, who was using one hand to tell her how far she had to raise the bucket.

The tip of her index finger touched the control, and by moving it ever so slightly to the left, the hydraulic arm lifted the steel just enough off the injured man that the others could pull him to safety. Mia could see severe damage to his lower extremities. His left leg was lying at a weird angle to his body, and the bloodied bone had ripped its way through his work pants.

Mia lowered the excavator and turned off the rumbling engine. For a few seconds all she could hear was her own blood rushing through her ears, but then she could make out the steady chopping sound of the helicopter in the distance. Still trying to understand what had happened, she just sat there, nauseated, watching the approaching aircraft. She could make out Shurnik in the pilot seat. After he gently sat the chopper down, his head turned toward the track hoe. Even with his head gear, Mia could see disbelief written on his face.

Helena climbed out of the helicopter, hurried to the badly injured man, and began to do what she could for him.

Mia jumped when Douglas opened the cabin door. "Holy shit," he shouted over the helicopter's roaring turbine. "What in the hell was that?"

Mia didn't answer. She looked at Douglas and realized tears were streaming down her face. She turned back to the scene and saw Helena securing an IV as the other workers strapped the victim to a stretcher. In moments they were carrying him to the aircraft. Once Shurnik was safely in the air, she climbed shakily out of the cab. Douglas grabbed her by the arm and helped her sit down on the wide metal track.

"I'm gonna be sick," she muttered.

Douglas pushed gently on her back. "Lean forward and put your head between your knees. That's it. Now, take a couple of deep breaths. You'll be all right." He rested one hand between her shoulder blades. Soothing warmth radiated from his palm, and when she began to relax a bit he started rubbing comforting circles on her back.

After a minute he said, "I need an explanation. That wasn't your first ride in one of those."

It took her a moment to think clearly enough to answer. "No." She lifted her head up. "Back in Michigan I worked on a similar one." Douglas' eyes narrowed, but he didn't say anything.

She let her legs hang down over the track and leaned against the heavy equipment. She thought about how long it had been and was amazed and very glad that she had remembered. She wiped her face on her shirt as the adrenaline and emotions eased out of her body and explained.

"In college I was looking for a job and read an ad about this excavation company hiring females. They told me to get a heavy equipment operator license, so I did."

He couldn't believe it. "What for?"

Mia shrugged. "You know how it is as a starving college student. You do whatever it takes to get by. I worked weekend shifts helping to build the Twelve Oaks Mall." She pulled a face and gave the huge vehicle a pat. "I guess I still remembered how to run one of these."

Douglas was astonished. He raised his eyebrows as he realized how wrong he'd been about her. "I guess you did. And I believe you just saved that man's life."

Chapter 14

THE WEATHER HAD CHANGED.

Shurnik pulled the hood of his parka over his head. The temperature had dropped drastically since yesterday and the wind had picked up. It had come early. Usually the first cold fronts didn't arrive until the end of September.

He sat in his Kamaz truck reading the notes he'd made for himself. Chewing on a toothpick, he reviewed the conversation in his head. Shurnik had used a secure channel on the radio to receive Markovich's findings about Farland. Operating out of the UK, Markovich had used Informants at SIS. From there he had been able to hack into a program at the Pentagon to retrieve Farland's file.

"No immediate threats identified; maintain risk management," Shurnik had scribbled down as he considered Markovich's suspicion about the man's history.

Farland grew up in Biloxi, Mississippi. His mother had raised him and his older brother by herself after his father had been killed in Vietnam. Shurnik couldn't find anything out of the ordinary in his early school years. During high school Farland had apparently moved to live with an Uncle in Florida.

"Several misdemeanor as a young adult. Arrests and community service," the file said. Shurnik smiled. If that was the worst of Farland's indiscretions, he was an altar boy compared to himself.

Farland's biography listed a few years of college and some job history. He had joined the military, and had been deployed to the Middle East to be part of Operation Desert Storm during the Gulf War.

Of course, Shurnik thought. His instincts were right.

The rest of the notes seemed to be insignificant. Either Farland was really insipid, or he knew how to hide things. Shurnik rubbed his unshaven jaw, thinking about what could be missing. There was just something about the American that didn't feel right. The unsatisfying content in Farland's biography was setting off alarm bells, but he couldn't pinpoint why. Not yet, anyway.

The thrill of the hunt woke in him. It affected him like a drug, and he could feel the adrenaline rush through his blood. Shurnik's anticipation grew by the minute. He knew he had to do something about it; he always followed his instincts.

Mia and Helena stepped out of the Mercedes. The two women had been to Irkutsk for a day. Helena had needed supplies and wanted to check the status of the injured worker. They had performed surgery on him yesterday at the hospital and had been able to save his leg. A long recovery stood before him, but it was clear that without Mia's quick thinking, he would have most certainly died.

Yukoil's board members had requested to see Mia. Chief executive Piotr Lagunov especially had treated her like a heroine, expressing his gratitude for saving the man.

Mia had stopped at the hotel to get more clothes, and she had bought a compatible printer for her laptop, small enough to carry places. Mia had been able to reach Zulanda and found out that Blue would be okay.

It was late when she returned to camp and she went to look for Douglas. Searching through the individual tents, she couldn't find him. She needed to meet with him—the board had raised some questions she wanted to discuss. Where are you, Farland? she wondered. The temperature was dropping quickly as the sun was setting. Hoping this weather depression wouldn't last, she draped herself in her coat.

There were men sitting in the mess hall, and she asked if they had seen Douglas. Apparently he had met with one of the communication engineers earlier in the day, but no one had seen him for several hours. Her feelings wavered between worry and puzzlement. She had combed the camp looking for him. It wasn't like there were many places to hide.

Frustrated, she gave up and met Helena for a game of chess.

The two women had become friends during the day's travel together. At first Helena hadn't been very talkative, but after a while she had opened up. Helena had given her a more broad idea of the southeastern Siberian people. It was interesting to hear how certain ethnic groups interacted. Helena had explained that 70 percent of the Siberian people lived in the few big cities, how the Trans-Siberian Railroad was constructed, and that the railroad was still one of the most important employers in Siberia. It had provided work for the same families over generations.

Helena had also told Mia a bit about her own history. Helena was a widow. Her husband had been killed working on Yukoil's largest oil-producing field in western Russia. From what Mia had understood, it had been negligence on Yukoil's part. Helena's husband had worked on tightening bolts on the connection pieces between pipelines. A fellow worker had been digging a trench next to him when the brakes on the heavy equipment had failed and wedged Helena's husband against the trench wall.

Her husband had been telling Helena for a long time about the unsafe work environment and how Yukoil was cutting corners with the safety procedures and maintenance work on the heavy equipment. There had been an investigation, but the investigators had been Yukoil's people.

They had offered Helena a small compensation and a job as an on-staff nurse. Helena had been a nurse in a Moscow hospital, but her salary had not been large enough to provide for herself and keep the small apartment her husband and she had been living in. So she'd been forced to take Yukoil's offer. When Yukoil had expanded, she'd gone along to do what she was doing now.

In tears, Helena explained that her four adult children hadn't been able to help support her, either, so she'd had to take the job. All this had left Mia with a bitter taste in her mouth. She had to remind herself that this was not the United States. There was no Union, at least not for people like Helena. And a lawsuit between an elderly women and a huge oil firm like Yukoil was unheard of.

The sky was clear the following morning. The temperature was only in the thirties, but the sunshine promised to warm things up.

Shurnik entered the mess hall as Mia finished her coffee. She had been brooding over unanswered questions since the early morning, getting nowhere without Farland's input. Mia noticed Shurnik and looked up.

"Good morning, Ms. Trentino. Would you like to witness our first satellite call?"

Perplexed, Mia looked at Shurnik. "Satellite what?"

Shurnik smiled. He reached one arm out to assist her. "Here, let me help you with this." Before Mia could protest, Shurnik had taken her coat of the back of the chair and offered it to her.

He went on. "We installed the stationary satellite communication unit yesterday. Mr. Farland and the engineer worked on it all day. I thought you were aware of it." Shurnik's voice changed. He wondered about Mia's lack of involvement in such a serious matter. To him it had been only a matter of time before the woman proved herself unfit for this kind of responsibility.

She realized why Douglas had been missing last evening when she'd wanted to go over today's tasks. Had he kept her out of the loop intentionally and used Mia's absence to take over? Farland, you…Mia thought angrily. At this point there was nothing she could say to Shurnik. Instead she looked up at him, trying not to show her irritation.

Shurnik motioned toward the open. "Follow me. I will explain it on the way."

Of course Mia had known about the plans to rig up a satellite communication unit. She just hadn't realized it would happen so soon. The unit sat on the west side of the four hundred and fifty acre field. Once the executive offices had been built, the communication unit would be integrated into the new complex.

It consisted of a gray, two-hundred-square-foot movable metal container about ten feet high and came with its own generator. A huge satellite dish had been installed, and there were cables and equipment everywhere. Shurnik had explained the operation to Mia during their short drive, but she hadn't been listening.

Douglas stood between two men with his back to Mia as she climbed out of Shurnik's truck. When he heard them, he turned around and beamed at Mia.

"Well, good morning. How was your trip to Irkutsk?" He asked innocently.

Mia was furious. She bit the inside of her cheek and worked on keeping her composure. She buried her fists into her coat pockets and stared at him. Apparently these men spoke English, so she dared not confront him right here.

"Isn't this amazing? One step closer to civilization." He didn't wait for her answer. "I already had a quick talk with Seattle this morning. Once we have it all hooked up, we'll be able to receive e-mail and fax."

Mia could not believe it. While she'd been on a day trip to the city, enjoying her sudden fame at saving a man's life, Farland had been out here taking charge. Her rage was a burning fire in her chest. She felt betrayed and deceived. This was not what she considered teamwork.

"Congratulations. What a success," she managed. Realizing her control on her temper wasn't going to last, she deliberately turned away from Douglas and focused on Shurnik.

"Mr. Shurnik, I have several important things that need to be done at camp. Would you mind giving me a ride back? Or may I drive myself?"

Shurnik crossed his arms in front of his wide chest. "If you feel comfortable driving yourself," he motioned his chin toward his truck, "I will stay behind to monitor the development here."

"Of course." Mia turned to walk back to the off-road vehicle. From there, she pierced Douglas with dark, livid eyes.

Chapter 15

Mia slammed the truck door.

What in the hell was he thinking? She had worked so hard to gain the acceptance of the Russians. A woman out here was looked upon as fresh meat—an opportunity. She had earned respect through her work, and now she was afraid she was going to lose it thanks to arrogant Farland's hotshot behavior.

God, she was mad!

I need a run, she thought. She stood in her barracks, undetermined what to do. She wondered if she could sneak away for a while. The men would probably be preoccupied out there for several hours this morning. She had planned on setting up the printer and working on putting her notes into the computer to be printed out.

What the hell—she deserved a little time alone. Maybe the sweet pain of aching legs would calm her down.

She always packed a few sets of running clothes and her Asics shoes. She found her sports bra on the bottom of her duffel bag and picked out a long-sleeve shirt and a periwinkle windbreaker. Looking for her iPod, she gathered her hair in a ponytail and adjusted the ear protection. It sure was nippy out there.

After a few stretching exercises, she stepped out of her tent, praying nobody would be around. She walked the first few hundred yards and then took off. The Red Hot Chili Peppers jammed something about California into her ears. She hadn't exercised since she left home. After the first few miles she could feel her inner core opening up and her irritations being flushed away. This felt good and was long overdue.

The further she got away from the oil field, the cleaner the air smelled. She took deep, satisfying breaths until her lungs burned. The terrain was a bit ragged, and she needed to be careful where she stepped. The beat of the music in her ears was hard and loud. She would turn it down after a while, but needed this aggression to start out a long run.

The thought of what danger might await her crossed her mind. It felt a little spooky out here in these woods once she could not see the camp anymore. It was just her, the taiga, and a mountain range to the east. She could feel the wind coming from the North—not a promising sign for a warm up.

Her thoughts traveled all over, but no matter where they wandered, they always came back to Farland. Until a week ago she had been doing just fine on her own. She was certain that she would have managed this assignment by herself as well. He had been a huge help, though—she had to admit it. Especially with the rather uncultured Russians out here. Besides herself, Helena was the only woman. Mia had counted over twenty-five workers, and that included ominous Shurnik and bald-headed Oleg.

Well, and of course Farland. But Mia was not sure she favored his demeanor over the other men's.

Now that she thought about it, she was surprised by how much he had influenced her in just the few days she'd known him. They worked well as a team, and the natural competitiveness between them had brought out the best in her. Sometimes he seemed to be a step ahead, and that had kept her on her toes, but his confidence was borderline cocky.

His image popped up in Mia's mind. She recalled the way he had looked this morning—towering in front of her and dressed in work clothes, covered in dirt from head to toe. He had grown dark stubble over night, and the flash of his Pierce Brosnan smile and the unruly state of his almost-black, wind-tossed hair had definitely had an effect on her. His presumptuous ways undeniably pushed her buttons. If only he wasn't so damn charismatic!

Mia realized now that her defensive reaction had been in part to shield herself from his affecting her like this. She had to smile as sweat started to build on her face. Good looking with a mean streak, Mia thought.

There had not been a man in her life since her divorce. She had liked the independence of being a single woman and had not missed intimacy much. The people surrounding her in Stoney Creek she called friends, were like family to her, and gave her a sense of security and warmth. Douglas woke up emotions in her she had no clue existed.

His sexy drawl especially seemed to have a hypnotizing effect on her. After that incident with the injured worker, Mia hadn't been able to do anything but sit there feeling distraught. If it hadn't been for him, she was certain she would have lost it. He had talked to her in his low, masculine voice and soothed away the effects of the grueling images she had just witnessed.

Damn. He was able to get under her skin with such ease and intensity! Her instincts told her that Douglas Farland was trouble, and she most certainly didn't need trouble of this kind in her life. She decided that her feelings for him needed to be suffocated in their seedling stage. Be professional, she told herself. You've got to stop letting yourself go.

Anger began to rise in Mia like a bad storm, and it was not anger against Douglas. Self-discipline was one of her strong traits. Well, it had been before she met him, anyway. Now that self-discipline seemed to be going straight to hell. Her anger grew at herself, and she lengthened her stride and picked up speed. Her hamstrings and calves protested with a sharp pain. Mia used it as a stimulant.

Oleg had been watching Mia.

He was on the bottom of the heap out here, his duties simple and low after Shurnik had taken the task of researching Farland away from him. He constantly tried to stay out of Shurnik's way. The mean bastard—he always found a reason to punish him. His life was miserable, and there was no improvement in sight. He had worked as a pickpocket at the train stations of St. Petersburg until he had made the mistake of trying to steal Shurnik's billfold. Before he could even pull his hand back, his right wrist had been broken.

Shurnik had snapped it in a blink of an eye, without any effort or drawing any attention to himself in the crowded train station. He had taken Oleg by the arm and guided him into a dark corner. He was promised medical aid and no police report in exchange for his services. Not having much of a choice, Oleg had decided to look at his recruitment as an improvement in his career.

He lit a cigarette and thought about the highlight of his day: when he bumped into the woman. Sometimes it was by accident, sometimes because he had stalked her. Because he was friendly to Mia, she pretended to respect him. He knew better. That kind of women didn't respect anybody but herself, and sometimes he sensed her apathy toward him. She was beautiful and smart, but she never gave Oleg a second look or any of her time other than what was necessary for her work.

The few women who'd been part of his life hadn't had attitudes like that. His mother had been beaten by his ruthless father until he'd drunk himself to death. His only sister had married some loser who had treated her like their father had treated their mother. He'd never had a relationship with a woman. The only sexual encounters he'd had in his life had been with cheap streetwalkers in the St. Petersburg's dark and lonely nights.

No—there had been a young girl in his shabby neighborhood who he'd tried to get close to when he was in his late teens. It had almost slipped his memory, even though at the time the girl's father had made sure he would never forget what he had done.

Hiding in the shadows, Oleg observed Mia when she had stepped out of her tent wearing black exercise tights and a blue jacket. Excitement spread through him as he felt like a predator watching his prey. He moistened his lips and could hardly wait for his chance to get her full attention.

Chapter 16

THE RUN HAD FELT great, and was just what she had needed. The endorphins her body had produced during the exercise had given Mia a natural high. Now that she was approaching the camp again, her mood sank.

She turned her music off and thought about how she needed to address Farland about his behavior. Rather than trying to figure out how to go about that, she had wasted her time mooning over his good looks. She felt disgusted with herself.

Resting her hands on her hips, she walked back to her yurt. She needed to turn on the electric heater before she took a shower and finished up her papers for the day. She decided not to share the new ideas she had come up with after yesterday's meeting with the Yukoil execs with him.

Breathing hard and drenched in sweat, she held on to the top of a bench outside her barracks and went to her knees to stretch her back. She closed her eyes and focused on bringing her heart rate down. She had not walked long enough after her run to get it under control. Now she felt a bit dizzy.

"I'd like to know the secret to your motivation."

Mia shot up. Douglas stood behind her. She held a hand to her chest above her pounding heart.

"Are you out of your mind?" she gasped, looking incredulously at him. "You scared the living daylights out of me! What in the world were you thinking?" Her temper was quickly rising.

Douglas held his hands up defensively before him. "Whoa, easy. No need to shout," he laughed.

Mia just stood there for a long moment, bewildered. It was all a joke to him, wasn't it? While everyone else worked hard, Mr. Macho just walked through life like it was a breeze, not worried about consequences whatsoever. Mia could and would not tolerate it. Until she got notice from her boss in Seattle, she was still in charge. And she was about to make that very clear to him.

She took a breath to unload on him, but he interrupted her before she could even start.

"I'm sorry. I apologize." He tried to sound sincere. When there was no reaction from Mia, he tried again. "Really, please forgive me."

"What, exactly, am I supposed to forgive you for?" Mia asked sarcastically. "You overstepping your boundaries? Or maybe for not giving a damn about the definition of team and for compromising every effort *we* have put into this project to get these people taken care of." She stabbed a finger out toward where Yukoil's complex would be built.

Surprised by her anger, Douglas took a step back. Before he could apologize again, she continued to unload on him.

"Or were you just apologizing for sneaking up on me and scaring me half to death?" Mia had a knot in her throat, but she was damned if she was going to cry, even if it cost her every last bit of her energy. She wanted nothing more than to send him straight to hell. But instead of letting herself get carried away and saying something she might regret, she turned around and walked away before he could respond.

"Ms. Trentino," he continued doggedly, following her inside her barracks. "Please give me a minute—"

"Mr. Farland," she cut him off. "If you don't get out of my room right now, a minute is all you have left."

She stared at him with a dangerous glare, and Douglas realized he had gone too far. Finally he left the room silently.

Mia began to shake. It was as much pure irritation as it was exhaustion from the run. She just could not deal with him at this moment. She needed a hot shower and a meal. Maybe then she would be ready to face him.

She knew there was no way she could avoid him for long. The whole situation seemed so ridiculous, so unprofessional. She felt like her control was slipping through her fingers. Besides that, never in her life had anybody humiliated her like this before, not even her ex-husband's mother. But she had just shown him her claws, and he had backed off. She wondered how long it would take before the warning wore off.

Dressed in a purple, cashmere sweater and jeans, Mia went into the mess hall hoping she'd find something edible. The hot shower had helped her to calm down, and she felt ready to fight her dragons. Douglas was waiting for her. She had expected that.

He got up when she entered the room and looked very remorseful. She stood, leaning with one hand on the backrest of a chair, watched him, and waited.

"Ms. Trentino," he began in his irresistible, warm tone, "if you would let me explain." For a second Mia thought he was going to reach out to her.

She squared her shoulders and interrupted him. "Fine. Have a seat. I'm interested to see how you talk yourself out of this." Mia knew he was aware of his screw up. She studied his face and almost felt bad, but she could not give in this easy.

"I was hoping I would not have to do it here." He sounded sincere.

Mia was puzzled—what was he saying? "You have some place you need to be?"

Douglas sat on the edge of the table to be eye level with her. "Well, I was hoping you would agree to go for a ride."

Mia was speechless. Was he out of his mind? She crossed her arms in front of her chest. "A ride? Why would I want to go on a ride?"

Douglas shrugged and said honestly, "Because it will take me a while to apologize." He paused and added, "And I think you would like the destination."

I don't trust you, Mia thought. Unconsciously she began to bite her lip as she studied his face.

"Where would we drive to?" Her curiosity made her ask.

"It's a surprise." He was getting braver and gave her a teasing smile. Come on, girl; say yes. He added in his mind.

Mia shook her head. A surprise? This guy was impossible. "We still have a bunch of work left to do." She was trying to maneuver herself out of this.

"No more work for today. We are ahead of schedule as it is." He knew he was right.

Dammit, her common sense was leaving her, if she was even considering this. But she was not quite convinced. "I need some food," she pointed out, putting her hands in the pockets of her jeans.

Her body language relaxed and Douglas smiled. He knew he had almost talked her into it. "Of course you do. Here is lunch." Douglas pointed to the cardboard box on the table next to him. There were several food items neatly wrapped in cellophane and bottled water. "You must be hungry. I thought we'd eat on the way."

Mia was suspicious—he was prepared. Another moment of silence, and then she thought, what the hell. What could it hurt? Her curiosity won out and she agreed to his idea.

"You might want to take a coat," he suggested. Mia went back to her room to grab her quilted zip jacket, twisted her shower-damp hair into a knot, and laced up her leather boots.

For a moment she stood alone, trying to figure out where this could lead. Her common sense told her to stay here and get her work done, regardless of the schedule, but her intuition told her to take a risk for once and let him take her for a ride.

"I need to know where we're going," Mia tried again when she met Douglas outside.

"That would interfere with the concept of a surprise," Douglas countered. He thought about it and gave her a hint, "I can tell you this much. The distance is about sixty miles and we're headed northeast."

Mia forced herself to pull a face at him. She was surprised at how fast her mood had improved. She was still trying to be mad—unsuccessfully.

Mia walked up to the 4x4 truck Douglas had parked in front of the mess hall. He had borrowed it from someone. It was an extremely uncomfortable ride, but the only way to travel on these dirt roads. Mia held on to the handle above her head.

"Please remind me why I agreed to this?" she asked, looking straight ahead.

"Because I have food." Douglas grinned and handed her a sandwich.

Mia unwrapped it and took a bite. She thought about how he had organized lunch and transportation. He must have been planning this for a while. Satisfied, Mia knew that the look she had shot at him this morning had hit the bull's-eye.

Douglas watched her out of the corner of his eye. "How far did you go, ten miles?" He couldn't hide the admiration in his voice.

Chewing, Mia checked her watch. "Probably. That's about what it felt like."

"Tell me, is it easier to knock down that kind of distance when you're upset about something?"

Her anger had propelled her into a good performance. But for him to ask that was weird, and she wasn't sure where he was going with it.

"I guess aggression is a good motivator."

Douglas seemed pleased. "So I get the credit for your effort today?"

Mia put down her sandwich and looked at him, exasperated. "That's not really something you should be proud of."

"I know, I know," he laughed. "I'm just trying to make it up to you!" He sobered and continued "Listen, I know I've made a mistake by not waiting for you to work on the satellite phone. It didn't occur to me until later on."

Mia turned her head to him. Should she believe him? She wanted to, but he was not really trustworthy yet. But he apologized again, looking at her with puppy eyes. "I'm sorry, Boss."

Mia laughed. "Enough already. Apology accepted. I just hope the damn thing works."

"There is one more thing," Douglas added. Mia continued to work on her sandwich and waited.

"I guess I have been ignorant because I felt intimidated." Douglas looked straight ahead. "There aren't many women like you out there in the business world."

Wow, she thought. It must not be an easy task for a guy like him to be so honest about something like this.

She waited a little bit to answer, then looked at him and said, "I gladly accept your peace offering." Mia smiled to herself, feeling very gratified.

The scenery changed quickly. They had left the oilfield behind them, and Mia could make out the dark green of an approaching forest.

The dirt road turned into a steep, narrow path. Douglas tried to chose the smoothest part of the road, but the truck bounced all over, and Mia had to hold on to her handle. He's gonna get us killed out here, she thought a little desperately. She was already a bit nervous about this ride to begin with.

After a while they found themselves in the midst of old larches and cedar trees. They were big, some of them over five hundred years old. The soil was very sandy, and sometimes the wind would blow the sand from underneath them, exposing the four-foot-high jumble of roots the trees stood on. Mia had never seen anything like it.

She felt Douglas growing anxious. She would have liked for him to stop the truck so they could have a look around, but it was apparent he was on a mission. He checked the GPS and headed further east. Suddenly there was an opening in the trees in front of them.

"I think this is it," Douglas said and stopped the Jeep.

"Well, what is it?" Mia got excited herself and jumped out.

"Wait!" Douglas yelled after her. "We don't need a broken ankle out here."

But Mia had already started to climb up the hill where she could see the opening in the trees more clearly. When she got on top, she held her breath. She could not believe her eyes.

A few hundred feet below her, Lake Baikal stretched in a spectacular blue all the way to the horizon. The clouds were mirrored in small white puffs on the crystal-clear water. She had never seen so many different shades of blue before. Closer to the shore the water turned softly into a turquoise while it remained a deep, royal blue toward the middle of the lake. No wonder they call it the Pearl of Siberia, Mia thought.

A pelican glided majestically through the air, and Mia thought she'd just seen a whitetail disappear in the woods. The cliff in front of her was too steep for her to see the shore. On both sides the lake was rimmed by a deep forest of hundred-year-old trees.

The pine scent was almost overwhelming, but after a while Mia was intrigued by another familiar smell. She stood far above the very southern end of the lake, and when she let her eyes travel due west, she could make out a violet-colored meadow far below.

Mia didn't know how long she stood there. Her admiration of nature's beauty was endless. She was still in awe when she sensed him standing behind her.

"Magnificent, isn't it."

Mia nodded. She didn't have words to describe this incredible view.

Douglas lifted his arm and pointed above Mia's left shoulder into the distance. "Do you notice anything familiar?" he asked knowingly.

"That big, blue field? Looks like Russian sage," Mia observed as she looked out to the soft flowing meadow in the distance.

"Lavender." Douglas let the word melt on his tongue.

"Breathtaking," Mia exhaled.

Then she thought about what Douglas had just asked her. Her eyes narrowed, wondering what he could mean.

"Why would I recognize a lavender field?" Mia asked curiously.

"Well, don't you love it?" Douglas asked back. He moved a bit closer.

"Yes, but how do you know?" Mia felt a little exposed that he could read her like an open book.

"Maybe because you always wear something purple," Douglas spoke softly as he took the clip out of Mia's hair and let it drape over her shoulders. "Or maybe because it is your wonderful scent."

Chapter 17

MIA'S BACK STIFFENED INSTANTLY. She held her breath and did not move. But before she could react, Douglas had walked past her and said, "Let's hike down there. It shouldn't be too far."

Mia looked after him, puzzled. What was that? He was mocking her, was that it? And now he was just going on a hike? She wanted to tell him not to touch her again, but felt it would be a ridiculous thing to say. He hadn't really touched her—or had he? Should she get upset about it? Her common sense told her yes, but her body told her no.

She decided not to make a big deal out of the situation and told her worried mind to ignore what had just happened. Silently, she walked behind Douglas, trying to convince her tingling body to ignore it, too.

Douglas was chatty. He seemed to know a lot about this area. Pointing out several native trees he knew by name, he explained the biological diversity of the natural treasures. A few times he knelt down to pick up a blossom to show Mia the many species of alpine plants the region contained.

Douglas' way of sharing his knowledge was not annoying at all. He was a good teacher, and Mia started to relax and enjoy her private tour of southern Siberia's natural wonders through the eyes of Farland wisdom.

One thing irritated her a little, though. He had fastened her hair clip on his right index finger and was using it as a pointing device.

Following a trail clearly not marked on any map they had to climb over dead timber and duck through thick brushes. Mia was glad she had chosen her boots for the trip.

They watched busy squirrels climbing up tall trees, and there was a woodpecker somewhere in the distance working on a new construction.

As they descended the hill, Mia noticed the aroma of lavender intensify. The wooded area became sparser as the huge old cedar trees thinned out. Mia was glad to get out of the woods. Not that it mattered; there was not another human soul around. She trusted Douglas not to do anything stupid. She was not afraid of him. On the contrary, Mia could feel anticipation growing in her.

Wondering what would come out of this little adventure, she figured a harmless conversation might break the tension.

"It is colder down here," she said.

Douglas nodded. "The temperature close by the lake is a lot cooler through out the summer. The huge volume of water is responsible for that."

Mia remembered reading in a brochure at the hotel something about Lake Baikal being the deepest lake in the world.

"How are your legs holding up?" Douglas wanted to know. "Do you need to rest?"

Mia liked that. "No, I'm good. Thanks, though."

Lower growing bushes and small junipers dominated the landscape now. Suddenly Douglas stopped and ducked. He stretched one arm out behind him to stop Mia. He didn't move at first, and then very slowly and quietly he crouched down. He turned around and laid a finger on his lips to signal Mia to be silent.

She tried to catch a glimpse of what seemed to be so intriguing. And then she saw it. A huge moose stood in the distance, belly high in grass. Its coat was shiny and dark, almost black, and its antlers were covered in velvet.

"It's a bull. He must be standing at least six feet high," Douglas whispered.

Mia held her breath.

As sudden it had appeared, the big animal took off on his long, lanky legs.

"Extraordinary." Douglas straightened back up. He turned around, "You okay? He didn't scare you, did he?" She just smiled with excitement glowing on her cheeks.

They kept walking on a narrow, single-track trail and soon reached one end of the lavender field. An unbelievable mixture of a pale violet and a bluish gray stretched out in front of her. Back home in Montana, she was nursing a little lavender bush in the front yard of Zulu's house. Its blossoms would bring her joy in early July. But this was a different world.

"Oh my God, how beautiful," Mia whispered as she took a few steps into the almost hip-high bushes. She had never seen lavender of this size before. The smell was sweet and almost overwhelming but wonderful to her senses. She walked deeper into the field, mesmerized by its size. Finally she forgot about Douglas and twirled around like a young girl. With closed eyes she ran her hands through the blossoms.

Douglas watched her as she inhaled the scent she found so much delight in. Lifting her head toward the sky, she let the sun warm the skin of her beautiful face. He had never seen a woman more sensual. Her eyes would darken with her mood, and her movements were as smooth as a cat's. Her skin was like alabaster, and he wanted to run his fingers through her silky hair.

When he thought about the fire in her attitude she had shown him earlier today, he grew excited. He was aware of the effect he had on her, but he still would have to use all his finesse in order to manipulate her into the direction he needed her to go. He had to be careful not to scare her off, but Douglas could hardly wait to lay his hands on her.

Deep in her thoughts, Mia picked a few blue tips and let their small individual blossoms roll through her hand and wandered around like she was in a dream—a wonderful, lavender-scented dream.

"And?" Douglas drawled in his deep voice. "Tell me—am I forgiven?"

Mia stood still and looked at him. How in the world had he known about this place?

"All this to make it up to me?" Her voice was very quiet. There is got to be more behind this, she thought. Mia had an idea about what he had in mind, and it did not scare her.

Douglas walked up to her and looked down into the captivating depths of her dark eyes. She did not move away. He slowly raised one hand and parted her open jacket carefully. Touching her side, he laid one hand on her waist and gently pulled her toward him, knowing she would not resist.

Mia's heart raced. She could feel the strength in his hand, and her body absorbed his warmth. She was losing herself in those blue eyes and felt them as they left hers to wander to her lips. She felt his hand gripping tighter, sliding up her side and pulling her closer to him. Mia rested her hands lightly on Douglas' strong forearms, wanting to keep distance—she was not yet ready to be too close. But the intensity he radiated weakened Mia's knees, and she tightened her clasp on his arms. Finally, after what seemed to be an eternity, he slowly lowered his head. She parted her lips slightly to welcome his. Douglas kiss was tender at first, not probing, and Mia felt how he held back.

Warm lips just touched for a while, but when his tongue dared to enter the sweetness of her mouth, her mind stopped. She leaned into him, and her hands reached up over the tops of his muscled shoulders. Her fingers combed though his dark hair, and as he felt her nails gliding down his neck, he dared for more.

One hand left her side, and as he lifted it in search of the delicate skin of her neck, he let it lightly brush against the bottom of her breast. A jolt went through Mia's body like electricity, and Douglas regretted his touch instantly.

"We need to go." Mia's voice was just a breath on his lips, but to Douglas' surprise, she didn't break free.

Douglas lifted his head and his eyes found hers yet again. "I guess we do." He very softly rested his lips on her forehead. He held her for a little while longer, and when he reluctantly let go of her, Mia swayed.

Chapter 18

Shurnik smiled.

The cliff high above the meadow offered perfect concealment. He was lying on his stomach behind a bush holding his Steiner binoculars to his eyes. His discovery amused him. Actually, it amused and relieved him both.

The last couple of days Shurnik had narrowed his focus on Farland. This morning Shurnik had laid out bait by arranging for the camp to be completely empty and had made sure the American was aware of it. Shurnik had expected Farland to nose around after he had followed the woman back to the base. Farland had used a plausible explanation for leaving the communication unit, but Shurnik was suspicious.

He had followed at a safe distance. Shurnik was prepared to interfere with Farland's search before he could discover anything. To Shurnik's surprise, Farland did not attempt to rummage through the camp look for whatever he might be searching for. He seemed to be concentrating on the woman.

Behind a thin canvas and a palette of kitchen supplies, Shurnik had positioned himself to be unseen but able to listen to their conversation in the mess hall. He was aware that there might be something happening between the two, but he hadn't thought it would be Farland's main focus.

Farland had talked the woman into heading out for a drive. Whatever he was up to, it had nothing to do with searching the camp, Shurnik had been sure of it by then.

After they had left, Shurnik had followed in a safe distance in his truck. The road leaving the camp had not offered much cover, but it had been clear to him where Farland would take her.

Once they had disappeared into the woods of Lake Baikal, Shurnik had continued his pursuit on foot. Staying behind and above them, he used the thickness of the forest as concealment. A few times his silent stalk had allowed him to get close enough to overhear bits of their conversation. They did not talk about anything suspicious. In the contrary, Shurnik wondered about Farland's meaningless chitchat about trees and plants. Shurnik felt like he had accidentally put a tap on a Boy Scout troop.

Knowing the area well, Shurnik was able to cut the distance of their hike several times as he was able to anticipate their destination. Now that he had been following Farland's tracks, Shurnik had concluded that the American wasn't much of a threat. To his amazement, Shurnik realized he had been wrong all along. Yes, he would keep watching him—because suspicion was Shurnik's second nature—but it seemed highly unlikely that either one of the Americans presented a hazard to the op.

Shurnik smiled again. He couldn't wait to brief Lagunov about his findings. He focused his high-tech binoculars again and watched as Farland made his move. With a touch of a button Shurnik froze the image of Farland and the woman kissing in his viewfinder. He would download it later and send it to command so they could relax.

Shurnik carefully retreated by crawling backward until he was certain he was out of their range of view. As he jogged down the other side of the cliff, back to where he had parked his vehicle, he had to laugh out loud. Instead of snooping around at the base, Farland had taken the woman to the lake like some lovesick teenager.

Chapter 19

THREE MEN IN WHITE protective gear worked fifteen feet beneath the mechanic's barracks. Wearing gas masks, their gloved hands measured and mixed different kinds of chemicals together. Propane cylinders were connected to hot plates and several five-gallon plastic bottles with rubber tubing inserted sat on the tiled floor. A shiny, stainless steel shelf held a large number of chemical glass cylinders containing a clear liquid with red solids on the bottom. Neatly labeled jars had been alphabetically organized.

Oleg studied the glass jar containing kerosene. Silver chunks of metallic ribbons were stored in it. He had no idea how things were done, but Oleg just liked to come down here and follow the process. Not wearing a mask to protect his face and lungs, he could only take the ammonia stink in the lab for a short amount of time.

In the need of fresh air, Oleg climbed the stairs and carefully observed the monitored area outside on a TV screen before he opened the trapdoor. He wanted a cigarette, and it was too dangerous to light up a smoke down there.

With growing despair he looked at the amount of antifreeze containers and gallon-sized plastic bottles he had to get rid of. There was a deposit site fifty kilometers away where they buried evidence. Usually he took one of the dump trucks and used the darkness of the early morning hours to drop this stuff off.

But today he had woken up in a daze with a tremendous headache. He had felt hung over, even though he hadn't touched a drink. It must have been the smokes from last night. They had told him it was a new design, and he willingly played the guinea pig. Whatever it was, it had worked.

It had hit him as soon as he inhaled the first drag. Oleg had felt like he was getting sucked into a tunnel—his body became weightless and detached from him. Sitting in the cab of a broken down tractor trailer he had taken out his pocket knife and picked his finger nails—for hours.

He had not felt either hunger or thirst.

Compulsively scraping the dirt from under his nails, he had watched the pattern of his work shirt circling in imaginary swirls all over him. It had been a wonderful, soothing feeling at the time. He had been aroused by it. Then he had passed out. Shaking from the freezing temperature, he woke up several hours into the night. He had climbed out of the tractor and barely made it in his yurt. That had been at about the time he normally got up to do his filthy chores.

He needed to get to it before Shurnik returned. He was aware of the dangers of being discovered. The lab was located in an underground, ex-military facility. During the cold war the structure had been used for weapon storage and for the research and development of biological weapons. Its several-feet-thick, cement walls and ceilings had been constructed to withstand large explosions. It was indestructible. Neither an accident within the facility nor an attack from outside could harm it. Connected by a labyrinth of narrow, dimly lit corridors, the whole complex had been the size of several football fields.

During the existence of the Soviet Union, people who had worked in that environment had not been allowed to surface for weeks at a time. The facility had functioned completely self-sufficiently with the exception of supply deliveries.

Yukoil's oilfield and adjoining properties bordered this underground structure to the east. Prior to the construction of Yukoil's project, the military had been out here to seal up the old storage facilities. A rather substantial amount of European currency had exchanged hands for a few units to be excluded in this task.

Today, the maintenance garage for the heavy equipment was located conveniently above one of those units. With a working crew of two men, the garage was always busy, and an onlooker would not suspect anything suspicious.

Oleg lit a cigarette. He nodded to the mechanics, who were busy changing a transmission in one of the big trucks. He grabbed an empty bucket and turned it around to sit on it. He was plagued by paranoia lately. Unconsciously he scratched his arms and repeatedly wiped his face.

A truck pulled into the tent. There was his reason for his paranoia. Shurnik glared at Oleg as he exited his vehicle. Shit, Oleg thought and stomped the cigarette with his boot. His heart rate skyrocketed as he feared what the consequences of his negligence might be. He turned his face to seek help from the mechanics, but they had silently disappeared.

Shurnik approached Oleg, who could not bring himself to look up at him.

"Taking a little break?" Shurnik asked, dangerously calm. He slowly circled Oleg like a predator and stared at him with eagle eyes. With defensively hunched shoulders, Oleg stood, his view focused on his shoes, twitching nervously. Despite the cool temperature in the shady garage, sweat started to poor out of Oleg's pores. His stomach twisted into a knot and he didn't reply to Shurnik's question. Oleg knew that there was nothing in this world he could do or say to save his skin.

"Been busy with the clean-up?" Shurnik asked sarcastically and looked over to the pile of garbage Oleg should have taken care of that morning.

He positioned himself in front of Oleg, slightly spread his legs, and crossed his hands behind his back. Shurnik took a deep breath and exhaled as he straightened his broad upper body to fully intimidate Oleg.

"I'm sorry," was all Oleg had time to say before a hand as strong as a steel clamp grabbed his right arm with lightning speed. The twist came so fast and hard that it threw him to the ground, face first, with tremendous force.

Shurnik stepped with his heavy boot on the back of Oleg's neck, and his left cheekbone felt like it was getting crushed. Oleg's right arm extended straight up behind him, and Shurnik held on to Oleg's hand, not letting go of the agonizing sprain. Shurnik said in a sweet voice, "Oh, I'm sorry, too."

Then Shurnik continued in his distinctive, harsh tone. "Would you like to keep the full range of motion of your arm and get this shit cleaned up, or would you like for me to find someone else while Helena hand feeds you for a month?"

Oleg, unable to breath, answered in a helpless whimper. Shurnik stepped back and watched, smiling, how Oleg tried, coughing and wheezing, to get to his knees. It took him a while to realize that Shurnik had spared his arm, and when he finally got up he shook all over.

Shurnik grabbed him by the throat and brought his face within inches from his. Oleg had to look into Shurnik's cold, gray eyes, and there he saw joy.

"I know you have been dipping in the cookie jar downstairs," Shurnik spoke very quietly. "I really don't care if you destroy the very last of your pigeon brain with this shit, but as soon as you shirk your responsibilities, your replacement will get rid of the garbage *and* what's leftover of your body. Is that understood?"

With this warning in the open, Shurnik let go of Oleg, went back to his truck, and sped off.

Oleg allowed himself to breathe. His legs buckled, and as he knelt in the dirt, he tried to control the shivering of his body. He knew Shurnik was in charge of the production. He didn't know who else was involved. He didn't care to know. It seemed to him that the more he knew, the more vulnerable his life was becoming.

Shurnik was fed up with Oleg. This had been Oleg's last mistake. Another one was not going to be tolerated. On top of that, Shurnik had no room for an addict. Their first delivery over the Chinese border was planned for Friday, only three short days away.

Shurnik knew he could count on his crew downstairs as long as that dumbshit Oleg didn't use up the whole damn stash before they'd made the transfer.

Chapter 20

Mia felt uncomfortable.

Hiking back up the trail, her mind raced at a hundred miles an hour. What had happened? Farland had taken her out here after she had butted heads with him about that stupid communication unit. She had been trying to talk herself into withstanding his charm. But after enjoying the breathtaking beauty in this lonely area, and after seeing this lavender field he had somehow found, she'd let him kiss her and fallen to pieces.

She was certainly aware of the consequences if she continued this. It would harm the project and all the ones to follow, wouldn't it? How could they work side by side as professionals and have a thing going on? On the other hand, how could they not have a thing going on when their feelings were obviously so mutual and strong?

She wondered if Farland had been plagued by the same mind game. His fast tempo hiking uphill, sometimes crawling through underbrush, was almost too much for Mia. Her legs were achy from the early morning run, but she was glad that there was a little distance between them.

Arriving back at the truck, Mia realized that not one word had been said by either one of them since they'd left the lavender field.

Douglas retrieved the keys from under the left front fender where he had hid them before they had taken off on foot. "Security measure," he had said. "I break a leg, you take off running back here to get help, and I'm lying out there miles away with the keys in my pocket." It had made sense.

With his eyes on Mia, he stepped around the truck. She did not look up as he opened the passenger door for her.

"Thank you," she said softly. Her words were the first ones since their little encounter.

Mia was going to step into the truck, but Douglas stopped her by taking her arm.

"Listen," he started to say.

"We shouldn't have...I'm sorry," she interrupted.

Douglas raised his eyebrows. "Sorry?" he asked surprised, then continued. "I'm certainly *not* sorry..."

Mia looked up to him and she saw the same intense look in his eyes that she'd seen a while ago. With her back against the truck and Douglas close in front of her, Mia had no place to go. She swayed between calmness and panic.

Douglas sensed her uneasiness and backed off. He slid his hand from her elbow down her arm and found her hand. "I understand the problems this could create," he said in a serious tone, watching her closely. "But I am not sure that I can behave myself." One of his bright, sparkling eyes winked at her.

Mia had to laugh and the tension drained away from her. Douglas took Mia's hand in his, and she said quietly, "Well, we'll have to see about that." A strange calm had overcome her. Douglas just smiled and lifted her hand to his lips. He brushed a soft kiss onto the back of her hand and gave her a deep, promising look.

The weakness in her knees returned, but only for a second. He let her go so she could finally step into the truck.

As he started the engine, he chuckled, "Let's see if we can't find our way out of here."

Being the woman she was, Mia analyzed the situation. He is quite the guy, she thought. She was fully aware that Douglas observed her and adjusted his manner depending on her reaction. Yes, he probably should have never kissed her in the first place, but she was glad he had. Now she just needed to handle the situation right.

After they had been driving for a while, Mia tried to think about the work they had to do this afternoon. Wondering why she had difficulty concentrating, she realized that her heart was still pounding hard in her chest and it was not a result of the hike.

There was nobody in sight as they arrived back at the camp, and Douglas was glad about that. It didn't matter to him, but he needed Mia to be comfortable, and he knew it would have bothered her. Someone watching them pull up in the truck would not have given away their little excursion—they worked together all the time—but he knew how women thought.

His manipulative game had worked out better than he had hoped. By applying a little reverse psychology he had her wound around his little finger. Douglas knew to what extent he affected most women. Usually well enough to easily persuade them, if necessary. Mia was different, though. She was smart and tough in her business, and she had surprised Douglas with a rare enchantment that had a great effect on him. He needed to be careful and keep a clear head. Easier said than done, though. She was definitely a one-of-a-kind woman.

Things were going smoothly so far, and he wanted to keep it that way. Even Shurnik had reacted the way Douglas had anticipated. He was anything but easy to size up, though. His background was hardcore and his training excellent. If Douglas had not been expecting Shurnik to follow them, he might have missed him. He'd only been able to catch a glimpse of Shurnik's presence a few times. He almost admired Shurnik's ability to keep a low profile. Douglas could appreciate a worthy opponent and knew it could be a deadly mistake to underestimate the enemy.

Chapter 21

There was still a lot of work to do.

Mia and Douglas were sitting in the mess hall. Earlier, Mia had installed the printer software on her laptop and watched, satisfied, as the HP model spat out page after page of diagrams they had designed.

She was switching her keyboard from the Latin alphabet back to Cyrillic when Helena entered the dining room. She smiled at them shyly and went into the kitchen to prepare dinner. She tried to work quietly without disturbing the Americans, but once she accidentally dropped a heavy pan, and Mia startled at the sudden noise. Helena gave Mia an apologetic look, and Mia told her not to worry about it and to go on with her business.

"It's certainly not quiet in my house when I cook," Mia said to Helena in Russian. The older woman nodded and smiled.

Douglas gave Mia a look like he wondered what she had just said. "Girl talk," she said, smiling. He nodded and smiled, too. Suddenly she wondered if she'd get to cook for him some time. Better concentrate on your work, she warned herself.

Mia focused back on her laptop and forgot all about Helena until the smell of pan-fried onions, fresh mushrooms, and herbs filled the room. Douglas dropped his pen onto his notepad. "I give up," he said. Leaning back in his chair, he folded his hands behind his head.

Mia looked up. "Why? What's wrong?"

"It's impossible for me to think with this fabulous aroma in my nose." Douglas turned his head toward the kitchen and inhaled deeply.

"I know," she agreed. "I'm hungry, too." She thought about what she had had to eat today. A sandwich on her way out to Lake Baikal and a small breakfast very early in the morning. No wonder I'm starving, she thought.

"Why don't we call it quits for today," she offered. "I wouldn't mind meeting with Shurnik, though." Mia paused, remembering that this was a sour spot, but continued. "I'd like to find out if the comm system works by now."

"You are asking for me?" Shurnik's voice startled Mia from behind. He must have come out of nowhere, she thought. Douglas hadn't even had time to greet him, which would have let her know he was there.

In the meantime, Douglas was wondering why Mia startled so easily.

"Mr. Shurnik! You certainly know how to sneak up on a person," she exclaimed while she tried to cover her surprise.

Shurnik couldn't suppress a grin at the double meaning behind her words she was oblivious to. The irony wasn't lost on Douglas either, but he managed to keep a straight face.

Shurnik had stepped around the table and stood next to Douglas. Usually only his pants were camouflaged, but today he was fully dressed in fatigues. He was dirt-covered and had probably just returned from the oilfield. Even his face had traces of soil and grease on it.

"I am happy to report to you that our communication unit is fully operational. Our engineer informed me that it would have been a much more difficult task without Mr. Farland's assistance."

He laid one hand on Douglas' shoulder, patting him twice in appreciation of his accomplishment.

"At your service," Douglas replied, trying to stay cool. "I'm glad to help."

Finally Shurnik took Mia's invitation and sat down on the head of the table. He asked Helena how long it would be until dinner. She timidly replied that it would not be very long at all. Mia could hear a tremor in Helena's voice and it saddened her. How awful it must be to live in constant fear of the people surrounding you, she thought. Then she wondered what had initiated Helena's anxiety besides the painful cause of her husband's death.

Later they sat over Pelmeny, a dish similar to minced meat, while Shurnik discussed the usage of the satellite comm unit. In her last meeting with the Yukoil board, Mia had been able to talk the Russians into setting up the new school with Internet access for the students. It certainly was not common in these parts of Siberia.

Mia asked after the injured worker, and Shurnik told her he had not heard any news from the hospital. For some reason Mia knew that Shurnik was not the kind of man who would go out of his way about an inquiry to the hospital.

"That reminds me, I have a proposition for Mr. Farland." Shurnik's eyes went from Mia to Douglas.

Douglas paused his eating, used his napkin, and had some water without ever dropping Shurnik's gaze. Mia could not read Douglas' expression. The two men seldom talked to each other directly. Usually it was Mia's job to communicate. There was tension—Mia could feel it—and she wondered why.

"Petronovich, our man in the hospital, had brought his own trailer from his home in Ulan Ude to live in when he began working here." Irritated, Shurnik stopped. A group of workers had entered the mess hall and were noisily going about their dinner. Shurnik got their attention with a loud, sharp command for silence and they obeyed.

"Please excuse them, they don't have any manners." Shurnik stared at one worker, who immediately averted his eyes. It was bizarre, but the entire scene reminded Mia of a pack of wolves and their pecking order.

Douglas had been watching Shurnik closely. "You were saying?"

"I was going to offer you Petronovich's trailer. He will not be back for a long time, and you cannot possibly be comfortable sharing space with them." Shurnik lifted his left arm and pointed his thumb toward the workers. He looked at them disdainfully, like they were infected with some awful virus.

Douglas evaluated the offer quickly. He knew what trailer Shurnik was referring to. There would be both advantages and disadvantages to being cooped up in there. But first he needed to see how bad Shurnik wanted him out there.

"I appreciate it, Mr. Shurnik, but I am just fine—"

Shurnik raised one hand. "Mr. Farland, I will not allow 'no' for an answer. Ms. Trentino and you have been inconvenienced long enough without the hotel amenities. I truly believe this would be to your benefit." Shurnik paused, looking between Douglas and Mia as if he was trying to figure out who was easier to persuade. He continued, "There will be more comfort, and you will have additional space to meet over your papers." He took his eyes off Douglas and looked at the stack of documents in front of Mia's plate.

Mia knew Farland would be too modest to take the offer, so she stepped in. She was tired of organizing her work here in the mess hall, anyway.

"If I may interrupt." Mia shot Douglas a warning look. "If it is agreeable with Mr. Petronovich, I would like to thank you for your kind offer and accept it."

Shurnik turned his head to Mia. He gave her a boyish smile. "I am pleased, Ms. Trentino. Please forgive me for not offering this accommodation to you, but I am afraid there is no plumbing available. Mr. Farland will still have to use the washroom in here."

After dinner Mia gathered her papers.

They had agreed to look over Petronovich's trailer to see if it would be suitable.

Approximately four hundred yards from the main tent, close to the Helicopter pad, stood a twenty-five-year-old travel trailer on wheels. Man, look at this thing, Mia thought. She had never seen anything like this old treasure. It had a flat front and reminded her of a huge shoe box. Whoever had designed this thing had not been introduced to the concept of aerodynamics.

Exposure to the elements had faded the light green exterior over the years. The thin, plastic paneling was chipping off, especially at the corners. It was twenty feet long and a little over eight feet wide. The left side of the front window was shattered but in place. There was an entry door on both sides, but only one window on the right side and one in the back. It didn't seem to be higher than seven feet, and one set of the tandem tires was flat.

As Shurnik opened the door, Mia felt she was intruding someone's space, but Shurnik assured her that it had been Petronovich's idea to offer his trailer to them.

The inside was as old as the exterior but surprisingly well kept and clean. The wooden cabinets had been handmade and displayed love in the detail. The cream colored carpet seemed to be a newer replacement. A beige couch sat alongside one wall, and as Mia looked closer she noticed a neatly folded quilt, similar to one she had received from her grandmother.

Located across from the couch was a pretty cherry wood table with two chairs. There was a narrow floor-to-wall cabinet, and all the way at the end sat a twin-size bed with more cabinets above it. Several pictures of smiling children, at different ages though accompanied by the same woman, hung on the wall. Petronovich's family, Mia thought.

The trailer looked lived-in, with a few pieces of clothing laid out and some newspapers littering the narrow counter, but Mia had seen so-called freshly cleaned hotel rooms that had looked much worse than this trailer.

He loved this place, Mia thought gloomily. Petronovich's accident came back to her mind in vivid detail. How worried his family must be about him. And how lonely he must feel without them.

Her stomach cramped up.

"Helena will have this cleaned up by tomorrow," Shurnik noted. Ripped out of her thoughts, Mia suddenly felt crowded standing close to the back wall with the two men between herself and the door.

Squeamish, she looked up to Douglas, who was pointing at the table. "There is a lot more room in here to work." He paused, noticing Mia getting pale. He turned his back to Shurnik, looking at Mia, and his lips formed a silent question, "You okay?"

Mia shook her head as a wave of nausea rolled through her. Douglas turned back around, facing Shurnik, and felt Mia lean slightly against him.

Mia raised one hand to take a fistful of his denim shirt, and at the same time she closed her eyes to suppress the sickness crawling in her stomach. Her forehead rested against his left shoulder. Tiny pearls of sweat were beading above her lip.

At that moment Mia would not have cared if Shurnik had turned around to see her that close to Douglas. But Shurnik seemed to be satisfied with his tour of Petronovich's trailer and was heading toward the door.

Douglas waited a moment to give Mia a few extra seconds to compose herself. He did not want Shurnik to see her like this.

Mia swallowed. "I'm okay," she exhaled quietly, and Douglas moved to follow Shurnik outside the trailer. By the time Mia took the low footstep, she had regained her color.

"Mr. Shurnik," Mia said. "Again, we appreciate the offer. Please forward our deepest gratitude to Mr. Petronovich and his family."

"Very well." Shurnik seemed almost serene. "As I said, the trailer should be available to you by tomorrow."

He nodded to Mia and Douglas and walked off.

Chapter 22

Douglas watched Shurnik leave.

He surveyed the area in front of the trailer, which faced directly to the north. The helicopter pad was only about four hundred feet to the southeast. The pad was located on the southernmost point of the camp.

A group of trees and thick brush on a downward slope due northeast blocked the view of the men's sleeping quarters next to the mess hall. The bottom of that hill was not visible from Douglas' position. Further north of the sleeping quarters was the area where the heavy equipment parked and the mechanic's garage. The men's washroom sat exactly between where Douglas stood and the mess hall.

Douglas estimated the distance between the helicopter pad on the south and the garage on the north end of the camp at three quarters of a mile.

The entire area sat on a flat between rolling, forest-covered hills. The immediate center of the camp had been cleared of timber and other growth.

He did not like the fact that the trees to his right prevented him from observing the incoming and outgoing vehicular traffic to the oil field. That must have been Shurnik's main reason for offering the trailer to Douglas. He still wasn't quite sure if Shurnik suspected anything or if he still believed Douglas to be Mia's partner.

The fact that Shurnik had been following him and Mia this morning spoke for itself, but Douglas had expected that. People like Shurnik would tap their own mother if she came to the camp to visit.

Douglas was aware of Shurnik's past and knew that the Russian was extremely careful. He took all the precautions necessary and only allowed low risk.

Mia watched Douglas as he stood with his hands crossed behind his back, looking toward the camp, and wondered what he was thinking.

"I really feel bad for the man," she commented, still feeling a bit queasy. Douglas did not move. Focused on the direction Shurnik had disappeared in, he asked, "Who, Shurnik?"

"No, Petronovich, of course," Mia said, confused. "Why would I feel sorry for Shurnik?"

Mia's statement had caught Douglas off guard. He'd just been visualizing applying a little pressure on Shurnik. He ignored Mia's question and turned his head over his shoulder. "Do you feel better? For a moment I thought you might pass out."

Mia grimaced and said, "Yeah, well, I'm glad I got a hold of you, otherwise I would have."

Petronovich had cut the trunk of a thick pine tree in two-feet-long pieces to use as seats around a fire pit. Mia sat down, crossed one leg over the other, and said, "So, this trailer should work out nice."

"Indeed. A little lonely, maybe, without all my Russian friends around," Douglas said sarcastically. "But I'm sure I'll manage."

You can always drop by and finish what we started earlier today, Douglas added in his mind.

He had turned his head forward again, focusing once more on Shurnik's disappearing image.

Douglas was getting edgy. His eyes narrowed and the palms of his hands got a bit sweaty. His breathing quickened, and adrenaline sweetened his blood. It was a very familiar feeling. The anticipation of combat—that's exactly what it was.

He knew all too well that this situation would not end peacefully. That fact did not scare him. As a warrior he yearned for it. He also needed to be level-headed and keep his cool. Most importantly, he needed to keep Mia unaware.

Douglas almost had to force himself to move. As he turned around to take the few steps back to Mia, his expression softened and the readiness in his trained body was just a memory.

Mia gave him a questioning look but did not say anything.

"What's that look for?" Douglas smiled at her as he took a seat next to her on one of the wooden stumps.

"I'm just wondering…" she trailed off and looked down to the tip of her boot, fidgeting.

"Tell me what worries you." Douglas was his old, charming self. Mia opened a plastic bottle of water she had carried with her and took a few swallows. She thought about Douglas' question and was not sure what to say.

"You," she finally said, still fidgeting.

Douglas looked surprised. "Me? What did I do to make you worry?" He knew the answer.

Mia continued to study him. "Can I be honest with you?"

"By all means." Now Douglas was curious to see how honest she'd be.

"I'm worried that you don't like Shurnik. That it will interfere with our project, maybe damage the relationship between Yukoil and Worldmove." There, take that, Mia thought, hoping she'd done the right thing by being so candid.

Douglas nodded. He had to give in and reestablish her trust. "You are right," he admitted. "I don't like Shurnik, but I will not let that influence my work."

Mia looked very skeptical. At least he didn't deny it. She had stopped fidgeting but was now gnawing on her lower lip.

Douglas saw she wasn't convinced. She was very bright, and Douglas had to remind himself again to be more cautious in the future.

"I'll be nice, I promise," he said, then added, "regardless if I like the man or not."

Mia sighed. The cold dampness was starting to get to her. She zipped up her coat and stuffed her hands deep into the pockets. It had been a long day. She wanted to go back to camp and sit in front of her electric heater, but it was too beautiful out here to leave just yet.

She turned her head due west. The sun was setting over the black of the Siberian taiga. All kinds of reds and oranges painted the darkening sky like brush strokes. It was one of the most colorful and amazing sunsets she had ever seen. Too bad she could not fully enjoy it. She had to take care of business. She needed to stay in charge and not let Farland's attitude toward the Russians hinder the success of the task. She thought about the promise he had just made.

She had to believe him, she had no choice.

Chapter 23

THE PHONE RANG.

Markovich startled awake. Big Ben had just rung three times. Had he had a bad dream? Trying to focus, he lay in his bed holding his breath.

The phone rang a second time. Christ, it was three o'clock in the morning. Wondering who in the world it could be, he picked up the receiver.

"Is it secure?" a familiar voice asked in Russian.

Markovich squinted his grainy eyes into the darkness.

"What? Shurnik? What the hell..." Markovich was still trying to wake up.

"Is it secure?" Same voice, same question, more emphasis.

"Yes, yes, it's secure." A healthy dose of adrenaline rushed through Markovich's system when he really recognized Shurnik's voice. It helped him to finally wake up completely. He sat up in his bed.

"Did I get you off a British whore?" Shurnik laughed.

"I wish," Markovich yawned. "They don't make them like they used to," he complained. "These days you've got to pay *and* seduce those bitches."

Shurnik laughed again. It was good to hear his old friend's voice. He imagined him in his comfortable, downtown London apartment in a plush bed of red silk linens.

"What can I do for you, my friend?" Markovich wanted to know. He smiled. If Shurnik had called yesterday, he would have actually caught him with Kalinka, one of his regulars and probably his favorite. Expensive, but she treated him well. But not tonight, and he was glad about that. He would have hated to kick her out in the middle of the night, having to miss out on early-morning sex, just to talk to Shurnik.

"I got you all I could find on the Americans," Markovich continued.

"Yes, I received your brief," Shurnik said. "I need to know what your accessibility to bugs is."

Markovich scratched his jaw. "What do you have in mind?"

"Wireless, infrared, open circuit."

"What's the location?" Markovich leaned over to his nightstand to grab his pen and notepad.

"Only fifty-five square meters," Shurnik said and went on to describe the inside of the trailer Farland would be living in.

"Got it." Markovich visualized the trailer and the necessary places to bug for surveillance.

"I believe you should receive the new bearings to gear the truck within twenty-four to thirty-six hours." He described the package the surveillance equipment would be shipped in.

"Put a rush on it," Shurnik said and hung up.

Balding and overweight, Markovich sat on his bed. He yawned again. There was physically not much left of the soldier he'd once been. He had not seen Shurnik in many years, but he was convinced that Shurnik was in the best shape possible. He thought about old times and melancholy swept through him.

Damn it, he wasn't just fat, he was also turning into a spineless crybaby.

Every time Markovich talked to him, a feeling of embarrassment crawled up his neck. He hoped Shurnik never found out that his friend had become a helpless victim of western civilization's overindulgence.

Patience was not one of Shurnik's strongest characteristics. But he had to have it until the equipment arrived. After what he had seen, his suspicions about the American had weakened, but he still found it necessary to keep tabs on him.

It had been good to hear his old friend's voice. Funny, though they talked to each other very rarely, they never wasted a breath with insignificant chat. Markovich had asked Shurnik about the phone line and Shurnik had told him about the new communication unit. He had made sure the engineer installed a modern phone tap detector, protecting against eavesdropping attempts.

He checked his watch—it was almost noon.

He would be surprised if the delivery from Britain really took twenty-four hours. Markovich had his ways. There was a lot to be done in the meantime. He had to check the status of production downstairs and make final arrangements for the transport.

He had received a message from headquarters earlier today. Somebody from the Irkutsk environmental office would arrive in the next few days. The removal and deposit of the oil discharge from the field had to be inspected. An impact analysis had to be done.

Shurnik mentally prioritized.

The security of the operation was clearly on top of his list. Once the surveillance equipment was in place, he would feel better about it. He would worry about the scientist from Irkutsk when he got here and prepare his crew and the drill equipment on short notice.

Shurnik had been out on the field since very early that morning. It was time to drive back into camp and check on the Americans. He had told Oleg to keep an eye on them, but he could not count on that dope-head anymore.

The temperature had dropped over night even lower. Snow would arrive soon. Sharp wind gusts cut into Shurnik's face, but he did not care.

As he took his leather work gloves off, he noticed an approaching vehicle. Shurnik squinted into the dusty wind and tried to make out the driver. It was one of the chemists from the lab. He parked his truck next to Shurnik's and turned the engine off.

He signaled Shurnik to get into his vehicle. Shurnik wondered what was going on. He would not tolerate any delays.

"We are finished," the man said as Shurnik sat down in the passenger's seat. "We worked through the night and are packaging now. The first batch of merchandise will be ready for shipment sometime today."

"Excellent." Shurnik was satisfied with his crew.

The chemist nodded and Shurnik stepped out of the truck. He stood for a moment and gazed into the distance, watching a coyote trotting along the horizon.

Mia had not slept well. She had worried about Douglas' attitude. And the weather was getting to her. Two days ago it had been so beautiful, and the afternoons had warmed up nicely. But last night frost had covered the ground, and Mia's electric heater had given up on her. Shivering, she had huddled under her covers and replayed the last days in her head.

The assignment continued to go well, that was not a problem. Farland's disposition toward Shurnik certainly was, though. She had never before experienced such hostility between two adults who didn't even know each other.

She had tried to figure out the reason for that. Farland had promised to not let his dislike for the Russian get in the way. But why *did* he dislike him in the first place? Whenever she stood between the two men, she felt like a referee in a ring, and all she had to say was 'fight' and they'd go at it.

She knew Farland had been in the military, and she suspected the same of the Russian. Was that it? Was their love for their countries the reason for the grudge? Good God, the cold war was long over!

But just because the political standpoint of a country changed didn't mean its people's opinions changed as well. She had thought about that pretty much all night. Her own reaction to Farland had not helped the sudden attack of insomnia, either.

Every intelligent cell in her brain told her to not let this thing go any further. It was not her normal behavior. But the environment she had to function in was not normal either. The Russians had tried to make her stay as comfortable as possible, but in the end she had to sleep in a tent, for Christ's sake.

She had exchanged her business attire for jeans and work boots, and a few days ago she had even quit applying makeup. Instead of researching important landmarks or the school system of a modern city and discussing those things with clients in proper meetings, she had been ankle deep in dust and mud.

This assignment certainly tugged at the roots of her natural survival instinct. Did that not include allowing male contact, which brought a sense of security she usually would not need? Her common sense screamed no, but every cell in her body screamed yes.

Mia had been wracking her brain over those issues when she had finally fallen into a shallow unconsciousness in the early morning hours.

She woke up aching. Muscle pain from her run the day before and sleep deprivation were taking their toll on her body. A hot shower should help jumpstart her system. Just as Mia went to swing her legs out of her bed, she heard Helena quietly call out her name from the outside of her yurt. Panic flushed her body. For an instant she thought she had overslept, but then she noticed there was not yet any light penetrating the heavy canvas. It was still dark outside.

"What is it, Helena? Are you okay?" Mia asked.

"Yes, but the propane is out. There is no hot water. I thought you'd like to know." Helena sounded apologetic, like it was her fault.

Damn it, Mia thought and thanked Helena for letting her know.

She stayed put, pulled the covers up to her chin, and closed her tired eyes. Feeling sorry for herself, she wished she was anywhere else than this god-awful place. Then she realized that the sooner she finished up this assignment, the sooner she'd get back home. Finally, some inspiration to start her day.

She tamed her hair into a knot, slipped into a fresh pair of jeans, and stepped into the washroom. She splashed cold water on her face and it took her breath away, but it woke up her senses. While she brushed her teeth, she studied herself in the small mirror she had taken out of her cosmetic bag and hung up by a shoelace.

Her eyes looked puffy and had shadows beneath them. But her usually pale skin had begun to show some color from the intense autumn sun.

She dressed in layers—a long-sleeved garment and a white turtleneck sweater. When she grabbed her favorite purple fleece shirt, she had to smile. All these purple colored clothes Farland had pointed out were really turning into a tick. She made a mental note to order something green out of the next *Sundance* catalog.

Mia stepped into the cold darkness of what would be considered a hallway, if it were a real building, and walked over to the main barracks and the brightly lit mess hall.

Several workers were having their breakfast and looked at Mia when she entered. She could feel their eyes undressing her and it repulsed her. She knew quite well what they where thinking, smiled at them out of spite, and wished them a good morning.

Farland sat on a bench by himself, studying papers. He looked refreshed. Helena went over to refill his coffee cup and he lifted his head to thank her. He noticed Mia, put down his pages, straightened his back, and smiled.

"Good morning, Boss." Douglas threw his charm at her.

Mia ignored it. The tangy aroma of his aftershave hit her senses, reminding her of the absence of her own fresh, clean feeling.

"Do you have hot water over there?" Annoyed, she nodded her head toward the men's washroom.

"Why, yes—don't you?"

"Propane's out," Mia said briskly and sat down. She crossed her arms in front of her chest, unable to warm up.

Before Helena could serve Mia, Douglas got up to get a cup of coffee for her. Helena chuckled. Douglas had approached her with his back to Mia. He had pulled a face at Helena and then winked at her. His grimace did not need to be explained in the Russian language for Helena to understand what he meant. Helena had picked up on Mia's mood, but she was also aware of the chemistry between the two.

Helena filled up a coffee cup. "Spasibo," Douglas thanked her in Russian.

Mia took the cup from Douglas. She looked suspiciously at him, wondering why Helena had laughed.

"Something the matter? You don't look like you've had a good night," he observed.

"You don't want to know," Mia answered, thinking of her heater breaking down in the middle of the night. She held her cup in both hands, trying to warm them with the hot, steaming liquid.

Douglas imagined it was partly his fault that Mia did not have a good night's sleep.

"I can certainly offer you the men's washroom" he said, trying to lift her spirits.

"You must be joking."

"No, I'm not. In addition, I would be honored to stand guard while you shower." He was kidding, and the corners of his mouth gave it away.

Mia's mood lightened a little. He always tried to comfort her with his easy demeanor, and she could appreciate that.

"I'd rather jump into Lake Baikal for a bath before taking a shower in the men's locker," Mia responded.

"Really?" Douglas smiled. "You just let me know when you are ready. I'll arrange wheels to get you there."

The conversation then turned to the day's tasks. Douglas planned on moving into the trailer as soon as Helena had finished her work inside. Mia would take the opportunity to reorganize their documents and prioritize the agenda for the following days.

"I need to call Seattle before they go home for the day." Mia checked her wristwatch. "Would you like to be there for it?"

It pleased Douglas that she included him. "Only if you need me to," he hesitantly answered. "Otherwise I'd like to get things settled in my new home." Douglas hoped for the latter.

"Go ahead," Mia decided. "That way I can tell the boss how difficult you've been."

The joke surprised Douglas. He looked up at her, and her dark eyes sparkled mischievously. She had an unbelievable smile and had laughed out loud at his attempts to be funny in the past. But until now she had not shown Douglas her own humorous side.

He got up. "Well in that case, I better go and save the day."

Mia nodded. Unaware of the significance in his words.

Chapter 24

SHURNIK PUSHED THE KILL SWITCH.

He had parked his truck in the mechanic's garage and ordered a technician to do a thorough service. This Kamaz truck would be Shurnik's livelihood, and he had to make sure it was properly cared for.

The mechanic went right to work.

Shurnik leaned his seat back and reached behind it to retrieve a black, metal briefcase. It was a heavy steel safe box, made to withstand extreme temperatures in case of a fire. It contained everything important Shurnik needed for this coup: maps, time schedules of the border patrols, and a fake Russian and Romanian passport. Most of his mission was embedded in his brain, though.

He took the briefcase and stepped out of his truck. Shurnik took a full minute to observe the garage. He walked toward the opening which faced the woods due north and scanned the area, first with eagle eyes, then with his powerful binoculars.

Nothing—not even a bird in the sky.

A faint smile appeared on his thin lips He seemed to intimidate even Mother Nature and her creatures badly enough to stay away. Satisfied, he turned toward the hermetically sealed hatch. It opened with a faint swooshing noise and he let himself in.

A blanket of heavy ammonia stench bit his face. Shurnik immediately grabbed a towel, held it over his nose and mouth, and stepped back. Something must have happened. There was always a smell like cat urine in the air, but this was unusual.

Halfway down the steps hung the protective jumpsuits and respirators on the wall. He took one mask and pulled it over his face.

One man lay unconscious on the floor and another one was on his knees, his head close to the ground, blood spurting out of his nose and mouth as he gagged violently. Shurnik checked the vital signs of the man down. The pulse was a bit slow and his breathing shallow. He still had his mask on, but it seemed to have malfunctioned.

He knew right away what had happened.

The other guy would not be able to stop vomiting until he got out of this ammonia cloud. Shurnik had to react fast. The conscious man was in severe pain and scrambled to climb the stairs, but Shurnik could not allow him to reach the trapdoor. Unable to breathe and panicking, the man would open it before checking the monitor. Shurnik threw himself between the man and the stairway, knocking the lab technician off balance. He fell back heavily onto his knees gasping for air, one hand on his throat. Starting to turn blue in his face, he finally passed out. Shurnik rolled him onto his side and hyperextended his neck so he would not suffocate on his own blood and vomit.

He got up and hit the switch for the emergency exhaust.

Shurnik was taking a risk by allowing the contaminated air to flow outside. The end of the air shaft was located just outside the garage, concealed. But if someone was close to it, they could still detect the smell.

He looked at the two men lying on the concrete floor. They were lucky to be alive.

Shurnik had studied the production thoroughly, and he knew about the chemical reaction they called Birch reduction. He'd had one of the scientists explain it to him. The method consequently released anhydrous ammonia.

Usually the extremely toxic gas would be slowly freed with no immediate danger. Something must have happened for the reaction to have escalated this much.

They could have blown themselves up.

Shurnik was infuriated. Lagunov had paid a huge chunk of money to get the best chemists he could buy. They were supposed to be experienced and efficient. Now they had almost killed themselves. And worse, they could have compromised the operation.

There was nothing he could do for the two men.

Shurnik would have to wait until they'd come around and escort them out to make sure everything was secure.

The air should be breathable again. Carefully he lifted the mask of his face and took a shallow breath. It still stinks like cat piss, he thought, but the immediate danger was over.

He sat on a step and placed his heavy briefcase on his knees. He dialed the numeric lock and it snapped open. Shurnik had come down here to see the finished product. He had to get an idea of its size so he could work on proper concealment for the transport.

Just then it occurred to him that the other chemist, who had driven out to the oil field, had said production was completed.

Again, he studied the knocked out men. He wondered if they had tried to cook some of this stuff up for their own little enterprise after they had finished the big load. Shurnik would have to investigate and react appropriately. The usage of the lab and production for private distribution was clearly prohibited, and to disobey this rule would carry consequences for both men. Especially after provoking an accident.

The situation had pressured Shurnik's instincts into reacting fast. Now he had to stand by in here and babysit the idiots until they regained consciousness. He needed to concentrate on the transport and make some vital decisions. He had looked forward to doing so in his office, accompanied by the bottle in his desk. But now he had no choice but to arrange his documents sitting on these damn stairs.

Shurnik studied the detailed map of China. He had it memorized by now, but needed to eliminate any room for error. The border between Russia and China was over 4300 kilometers long and heavily patrolled. He knew a few places they could get through undetected—he had been to those parts of the border before. What a miserable place. The attitude amongst the Chinese close to the far eastern Siberian border was bad.

Shurnik had been to China many times. He had traveled through it on his way back and forth to Russia's only eastern port, the city of Vladivostok, when he was still employed by the Russian Mob.

Shurnik knew the Red Mafiya well. He had belonged. Once one belonged to the organization it was eternal. The Mafia was a family, a big happy family. It would take care of you, feed and nurse you, and if needed, bury you. Shurnik had witnessed a few suicidal souls who tried to untangle themselves from the Russian Mafia's spider web without success. The organization's sticky tentacles could reach far beyond this country's borders if necessary. Very few members who had made the deadly decision to leave had actually made it out of Russia.

Usually traitors fled into what was then East Germany, still led by the Communist Party. The really lucky ones made it even deeper into Europe, seeking refuge and trying to enlist with a rivaling organization.

The Russian Mob had ties with its archenemy, the Italian Mafia, for just that reason. The Italian cartel would often employ the betrayer, shield them from harm, and make them feel safe for a while, just to spit them back out, selling them back to the Red Mafiya, who would seek revenge.

After the end of the cold war, some of the traitors went to the United States, only to be tracked down and killed by the Russian Mafia's affiliates. The Mafia's retribution did not stop with the punishment or murder of the individual who had committed betrayal, but also included their family members as well.

Shurnik had needed to get out of the Mafia's tight claws. He had been a loner all his life. Yes, he had developed a deep brotherhood with a few people during his deployment in the Middle East, but for the most part he functioned best on his own.

The Russian Mob had been a jump start for him, like for so many others, after the war. And he always would be loyal and appreciative. However he had needed to gain back his independence. To his advantage, he was much more intelligent than the average person. He had known how to save his skin in the process of leaving the pecking order of the Red Mafiya.

To succeed, he needed to get closer to the leaders.

Shurnik had worked his way into the inner circle of the bounty hunters. He had become one of those feared men who went after the traitors within the mob. Doing very well in this position, he very quickly had become known as one of the most ruthless hunters within the Russian Mafia.

His work and reputation had earned him close relationships with leading Russian mobsters, like Victor Ivankovich and Sergei Selkin, who resided for a while in the same neighborhood as Shurnik in St. Petersburg.

During his career with the mob, Shurnik had enjoyed a relatively luxurious lifestyle, including imported sports cars and other nonessential items. He was constantly surrounded by beautiful women, and his indemnities had been wired into a secret bank account in Switzerland.

Shurnik had not cared much for the extravagances. What he yearned after most was his freedom, and he had come up with a plan. He was going to convince the Mob to arrange for his financial support until he reimbursed them with huge profits.

During his travels to Vladivostok, he had discovered many advantages that China had to offer. Low labor, and therefore low production costs, had opened the borders for Western businesses. Over the years Shurnik had watched how China's economical growth had turned into a miracle.

However, environmental disaster and rural unrest due to overpopulation started to make the country more vulnerable to corruption. Several of Shurnik's dependable resources in the corrupt political world predicted China's unemployment rate to quadruple by the end of this decade. Droughts had caused the already scarce land to be too exhausted for agriculture, resulting in declining harvests. China's political safety was nonexistent, and officials predicted its economical liberalization process to deteriorate.

Shurnik had expressed to his leaders that China was the perfect breeding ground for a new ring of crime and profit. There had been opposition to Shurnik's idea. The existence of China's own criminal cartel had been discussed, but Shurnik had explained the work of the Chinese underground society, the Triad.

"Their focus lies on illegal gambling, money laundering, and prostitution," Shurnik had told his bosses. "The main income is made on the black market, selling counterfeit computer software, entertainment items, and other intellectual properties," he had gone on. "There is room for expansion on the Chinese market."

The Russian Mobsters had still been skeptical, until Victor Ivankovich had asked the right questions, "Shurnik, tell us what you know."

"The Chinese Triad has some drug trafficking activities as well, but mostly just opium and heroin. Nothing has changed much in two hundred years. We have been expanding into the West to Europe and the United States. But China is the *new* land of opportunities. It is a virgin country to chemically manufactured drugs. And if you give me free rein and let me handle the production and distribution, I will guarantee a profit never before seen in this organization."

They had known Shurnik. He would have never proposed something he couldn't back up. And after he had promised a substantial capital gain, they had become curious. Ivankovich had stood up, faced Shurnik, and placed both hands on his shoulders.

"I believe I speak for us all when I say that you have proven yourself in the past, and that you have our attention, trust, and our permission to operate independent from the organization. But please satisfy our curiosity and share your idea of breaking into a new market. Tell us, what is the product?"

Shurnik had been pleased.

Smiling he had answered, "Philopon, or as it is known in the West, Methamphetamine."

Chapter 25

DOUGLAS SAT MOTIONLESS. HIS legs tingled from the lack of circulation, but he did not even notice. Fully dressed in fatigues, he sat hunched up in a tall pine tree. From twenty-five feet above the ground he was able to observe the area between him and the mechanic's garage. He wore hands-free binoculars. Integrated in the digitally enhanced field of vision was a little internal screen. It displayed date and time, the heading, and distance of the object focused on.

Douglas had watched Shurnik arrive and how he had observed the premises. He had zoomed in on Shurnik and seen that he was on the lookout. He had taken his time inspecting his surroundings before collecting some sort of a case from behind the seat. Douglas had been unable to identify the case. The mechanics had been interrupting Douglas' focus on Shurnik by walking in and out of it. Within a few minutes Shurnik had disappeared through a very smartly concealed trapdoor. After a while one of the mechanics had left as well, driving off in an excavator.

Douglas had been sitting quietly on a thick branch with his legs bent and his back propped up against the massive trunk of the old tree. He was not carrying his M40 high-powered sniper rifle. Today's mission was to observe, not to kill. But he had decided to pack his FN Five-seveN, just in case. He would feel naked without a firearm, and he loved that gun. It held twenty rounds and, with a weight of not quite eight hundred grams, was extremely light, comfortable to carry, and easily concealed.

Douglas had not seen anybody for at least forty minutes. He had been sitting in this tree for almost two hours without shifting. He decided it was safe to relax a little. Allowing himself to move, he very slowly lifted his hands to take off the goggles and carefully stretched his legs out as far as the tree branch would let him.

The wind picked up and rocked the tree, including Douglas, from side to side. It was cold. The temperature had continued to drop throughout the day and was now below freezing. The sun hid behind a thick cover of gray clouds which promised snow very soon. But all that did not matter. This was what he had been trained for. If he had to sit here all day, so be it; combat readiness and patience was his strong suit. He quietly observed and gathered information and rapidly processed it to make vital decisions. Finally he would react quickly in the most appropriate and efficient way.

The garage's location did not allow any other way for Douglas to keep an eye on the place. He had followed Shurnik's every move throughout the day and had prepared for the examination of the garage and consequently the meth lab.

Douglas had received a notification on his wireless. His equipment had arrived. With one of the rarely used small trucks he had driven to Irkutsk the night before to meet up with one of his European counterparts to exchange intelligence and to collect his package.

He had been informed that someone would contact him to join the investigation on-site. Douglas had not liked the idea, but agreed that backup would be necessary once Shurnik was on the move.

"Who is it? And how is he going to contact me?" Douglas had asked his informant, a young man from Poland disguised as a locomotive engineer for the Trans-Siberian Railway.

"I don't know. They didn't tell me anything," he had answered.

Douglas had not been surprised. The Acronym's secrecy sometimes got in its own way.

Hiding in the darkness of the very early morning hours, Douglas had returned back to the camp. With killed headlights he had quietly idled down the hill into the area where the excavation equipment was parked. The engine of the small work truck had barely made a sound. Douglas had only detected a quiet crunching noise from the tires rolling over dirt.

After his return from the city, he had observed Shurnik for a while until he was assured the Russian had not been aware of Douglas' little excursion. The overcast weather had benefited Douglas. Without a moon in the blackness of the night, Douglas had been able to move around undetected. It had allowed him to deposit his gear into the woods not far from Petronovich's trailer. He had found a low spot in the thick underbrush, perfect for concealment of his equipment and weapons.

Still on the lookout in his tree, Douglas thought about the situation. He knew he needed to stay put in his location until Shurnik reappeared. It was relatively safe, and Douglas was unlikely to be discovered. But he was also pressured in time. He still had work to do, and he was supposed to move his belongings into Petronovich's trailer. He was sure Mia would want to meet up with him after her phone call with Seattle.

Mia needed to be unaware of this op as long as possible. Preferably she should not be involved at all. No, he thought, she can't be involved. A smile came over Douglas lips, thinking about her healthy dose of curiosity. She was nosy, and it would clearly compromise the mission but also her own safety, which was steadily climbing higher on his priority list.

A sudden, deafening screeching noise startled Douglas. One of his legs slid off the thick branch and he almost lost his grip. Adrenaline flooded his body, and he realigned himself in the tree.

Douglas held his breath, trying to figure out what this sound was and where it had come from. Slowly he raised his right arm and deployed his gun. He tried to hear over the sound of the strong wind through the trees, but could not detect anything. All his senses were armed for combat, his nerves taunt, and as he scanned the distance, he did not even blink his eyes.

Then, unexpectedly, the source of the noise jumped onto Douglas' branch. A squirrel, standing approximately five feet away from Douglas, let out another high pitched shriek in complaint of the intruder. His brown, furry body quivered when he opened his little mouth to scream yet again. Now he sat upright on his hind legs, his tail twitching nervously. Douglas could make out the lighter colored fuzz on the critter's belly and the shine on the tiny, black claws of his little front paws.

"Well, you little stinker," Douglas lifted his weapon very slowly and aimed. Too bad, he thought. Where is my silencer when I need it? Instead of wasting the squirrel and potentially orphaning a squirrel family, he decided to shoo it away with a quick throw of a small pine cone.

The critter let out one last cry as it disappeared. Relieved and somewhat amused, he thought about his comrades back home bending over laughing if they ever found out Farland, the master of disguise, was almost exposed by a squirrel.

Douglas showed white teeth against his olive green- and black-painted face as he grinned. Mia would be proud of him for sparing the little creature's life.

Douglas regained his motionless position and his focus went back to the garage. His thoughts, however, stayed with Mia. Their job was almost complete. As far as he understood, there were a few tasks leftover and another meeting was planned at the main office in Irkutsk. He would have to persuade Mia to let him get around attending it. How he would do that wasn't a concern at the moment. He would worry about it when the issue arose. The risk of Shurnik moving out while he attended some meeting with Yukoil was too great.

Douglas readjusted his binoculars. It had been over an hour since Shurnik had entered the lab. Still no sign of him. Douglas had followed Shurnik in the past, and the Russian had never been longer than a few minutes down there.

Shurnik did not seem like the kind of guy who would spend more time than absolutely necessary in a meth lab. He would be aware of the dangers. Douglas was certain the lab here was as modern and safe as possible, but the chemical reactions still posted a hazard. Douglas had searched the garage, but the busy foot traffic of lab technicians had not allowed him to investigate the lab itself.

Suddenly Douglas became very uneasy. Had something happened that Shurnik wasn't returning? Apprehension built up. There was one important point he had not considered, yet. A second exit. Shurnik might have been long gone out the other side of the garage, not visible from Douglas' location.

Douglas' mind began to ponder over the possibilities. Had Shurnik been aware of Douglas' observing him all along and outsmarted him?

Impossible—wasn't it?

It took all his self-discipline to stay calm. He could not allow himself to doubt his own competence. He forced himself to slow down his breathing and concentrated on reducing his quickened heart beat.

Stay put, dammit. Don't let that son of a bitch get to you!

Douglas calmed down a bit. Still anchored in his position, he suppressed his worried mind back to rationality. In his head he went over his past actions in the last few days, and even though he was self-critical, he could not find any mistake he could have possibly made.

An approaching van brought Douglas back to the present.

He zoomed in and saw the van pulling into the garage. The driver backed up and pulled forward again, navigating the van's back end close to the trapdoor. They were getting ready to move the drugs, Douglas was sure of it.

The wind had become even stronger in the last hour, and several branches swayed in front of Douglas, obscuring his vision. He held his breath to better concentrate on what he was watching.

The van's back doors swung open and so did the hatch of the lab entrance. Shurnik appeared from underground, but to Douglas' astonishment, he was not carrying any kind of package that could conceal the drugs. He had a man in a white jumpsuit over his shoulder.

The man was either dead or unconscious. He did not seem to be shackled.

Shurnik leaned forward and deposited the body into the back of the van. He said something to the driver, who shook his head. He disappeared again into the lab, just to return momentarily with yet another body draped over his shoulder.

"Holy shit," Douglas murmured. It didn't take a rocket scientist to figure out that there had to have been an accident, or Shurnik was involved with disposing of the witnesses.

Through swaying tree limbs Douglas could make out that the driver and Shurnik were arguing. The driver had to be in a state of shock to be talking back to Shurnik. Douglas had not seen anything else but total obedience from the crew toward him.

Finally, the driver climbed back into the van and took off. Douglas watched as Shurnik stayed behind. Again, Shurnik raised his binoculars to his eyes and looked around.

For an instant the two men seemed to stare right at each other, and Douglas' heart stopped.

Chapter 26

SHURNIK SHUT THE VAN doors.

His cold gray eyes penetrated the driver. "You will do as I say," Shurnik demanded. He stood close to the man, who clearly was frightened to death.

"You will do as I say." Again, his voice was strangely low, and with such emphasis, it sounded like a fact.

The driver lifted his head up to Shurnik. His face was snow white and sweaty, the pupils of his eyes were dilated from stress. Shurnik applied just a bit more pressure by saying, "You understand the consequences if you fail."

The driver nodded. He looked like he wanted to say something, but was unable to speak. A frightened, almost childlike noise escaped his throat and he turned around to get back into the van and drove off.

Amateurs, Shurnik thought. Despicable.

He had been sitting in the lab longer than he had wanted to. Both injured chemists had remained unconscious, and as one of them began to have convulsions, Shurnik had had to make a decision.

First of all, he could not sit there any longer. Markovich's equipment had arrived and Shurnik needed to bug Petronovich's trailer before the Americans used it. Furthermore, he could not let the two men's injuries draw attention.

It was clear that they would need intensive medical care in order to survive, and Shurnik could not risk that kind of exposure to either Helena or the hospital.

He'd had no choice.

He'd stood behind the first unconscious man, propped him up against his leg, and bent down. His left hand had slipped around the man's throat and got a hold of the jaw while his right hand held on to the top, left side of the head.

Shurnik stood motionless for a short second, inhaled, and with one quick and very strong move, the man's cervical vertebrae broke and severed his spinal cord.

After applying the same method to the second man, Shurnik got out his handheld radio. He used a coded message to order the van into the garage.

As he had waited for the van to arrive, he had gathered the contents of his briefcase and sat in one of the chairs. Looking at the two dead men, he did not feel anything. Shurnik had killed with his bare hands before, but only in a combat situation. This had been the first time that he had had to end an unconscious man's life.

He had thought about it and decided it didn't matter. In Shurnik's mind, these two men had not been victims, they had been an inconvenience.

Now he stood in the garage, watching the van leave. There was no assurance that the driver would not fail, but it would surprise Shurnik if he did. He was able to put a man into state of mind that was more terrifying than the simple fear of death alone.

Observing the premises thoroughly with his field glasses, he did not see anything suspicious. In the near distance, the group of tall pine trees was swaying in the wind. The weather had worsened. He needed to take care of Petronovich's trailer, and he needed to do it fast.

The delivery from his friend Markovich in Britain had been sitting in the garage. Shurnik retrieved the package, snapped open his switchblade, and carefully cut the bundle. He took the shrink-wrap embedded Styrofoam box out of the package and opened it.

In it was a shiny, stainless steel bearing, used as a replacement part for heavy equipment. Shurnik carried the bearing to the workbench inside the garage. He looked around for a minute and found two screwdrivers. He closely studied the ribbing in the metal until he saw what he was looking for.

He wedged the two screwdrivers in a tiny slot and cranked it open. As it popped, Shurnik grunted, satisfied. He removed the top part, and in front of him lay the very latest in modern surveillance equipment.

He didn't know how Markovich had done this so fast, but he probably had parts like this one lined up, ready for usage. The delivery of it had taken exactly twenty-two hours from when Shurnik had phoned him.

Shurnik turned back to his truck and opened the hatch behind the driver-side door and stowed the equipment and his metal briefcase in it. There was not much in the world that could get Shurnik excited, but installing and using this new equipment would certainly do it.

Sitting tight in his tree, Douglas felt his heartbeat returning.

For an instant he'd thought Shurnik had spotted him, but it was not so. Shurnik had been rummaging in the garage for a while. Douglas thought he had watched as the Russian handled some sort of a box or package, but he could not say for sure—it had been impossible to identify.

After Shurnik had driven off, Douglas had waited for a while until he believed it was safe to repel himself out of the tree. He landed on his feet and immediately went into a crouched position, waited, and listened.

Nothing but the wind.

He wound up his black nylon rope and gathered his equipment. Using the low end of the hill for cover, he ran back to his hideout. He kept his head down and twice he disappeared into some bushes to observe his surroundings.

Douglas had scouted out the wooded area close by Petronovich's trailer. At first he had not been happy about how little he was able to observe from there. But then it had come to mind that if he could not see them, they could not see him—especially hidden by thick underbrush.

Three very tall trees stood close together, and in the midst of them grew a five-foot-high cypress brush. Snow would come soon, but for now he had found a perfect hiding spot to conceal his gear.

The cypress brush formed a wall-like barrier between the trees. Several feet in diameter, they had grown in a tight formation. A person would have to be very close by in order to notice anything.

Early that morning he had moved some of his personal belongings in the trailer, before Helena had been there to clean up. It had been a precaution rather then a necessity. Douglas knew Mia could not wait to use the trailer as an office. She would find evidence that he had been working on moving in. She would not question where he might be and possibly go looking for him. He had told her a lie about one of the English speaking engineers asking for his assistance out in the oil field. That excuse had have given him a few additional hours to investigate.

Douglas was tempted to search the lab. He was certain that after Shurnik had carried out the two men, it was empty. But he had to catch up with Mia. Sweet Mia, how much trouble she was.

If it wasn't Shurnik, with his meth lab and probable double homicide offense, it was Mia and her sharpness who kept Douglas on his toes.

He smiled at that thought. The awful awareness of evil was always apparent, so one had to focus in on the pleasantries.

Suddenly a sharp, burning pain beneath Douglas left shoulder blade stopped him in his tracks. For a peculiar second, Douglas thought he'd been shot.

Impossible, he could not have been shot—he was leaning his back against one of the trees, changing his shoes.

Slowly, he turned around and looked at the huge tree trunk, trying to find the source of the sudden pain. Ivy-like plants snaked up the tree. He looked closer and saw thorns, about three inches long, blending in perfectly with the rest of the vine. Mother Nature and her own weapons.

By moving his arm, Douglas could feel that an object had penetrated his muscle. He did not know if he would be able to reach it, but decided to take his first aid kit back to the trailer with him.

Douglas pulled his field boots off and stood upright. He thought about his mishaps that day.

Earlier he'd almost fallen out of the tree because of than damn squirrel, and now he had to deal with a thorn stuck in his back. It seemed like every time his mind wandered off to Mia, his safety was endangered.

She's cursed, he thought, and grinned.

Trying to ignore the pulsing heat on the left side of his back, his focus went back to his gear. He had brought a change of work clothes and whatever his very dependable partner back at the Acronym had anticipated Douglas would need.

He found everything this op called for, including a pack of face paint removal wipes to get rid of his greasy camo paint.

After Douglas changed his clothes, he made sure his equipment was undetectable. Satisfied with his mission, he continued his way to Petronovich's trailer.

Last night he went to Irkutsk, and Douglas knew that he had yet another investigation to undergo through the coming night. He was trained to function with sleep deprivation. As long as he could get an hour or two, he'd be all right.

Tonight would be crucial. If Douglas could find the van, and eventually two bodies, Shurnik could be taken in.

Never assume, he reminded himself, but his instincts told him the two men were dead. The mission was to find and eliminate the drug ring in China, and with Shurnik out of the picture, they would be more vulnerable and easier to expose. Douglas liked his theory.

He would brief the Acronym about what he had seen and negotiate the proceedings. He only had one problem—the damn thorn in his back was killing him.

Chapter 27

"Ms. Trentino! Excuse me!" someone hollered in Russian.

Mia was on her way to the mess hall and turned around when she heard her name. It was Shurnik, jogging after her.

An icy wind lashed her face and she turned her back to it, trying to protect herself from the unfriendly element.

"Please forgive me for shouting," Shurnik switched back to his accented English and took her by the arm, as if he could shelter her from the cold. "May I carry that for you?" He didn't wait for an answer and took the empty cardboard box from her.

Mia kept walking and asked without lifting her head to him. "What happened to your beautiful weather out here? Are we supposed to get snow?" Mia had to speak up so Shurnik could hear her against the wind.

"I believe there is some on the way, yes," Shurnik answered. "But it will not stay. It is too early in the year."

"That's what the forecast always says at home in Montana, and then we're snowed in until May."

Mia was glad Shurnik had shown up. This morning she had been organizing documents in Petronovich's trailer. She had found room to set up her laptop and the printer permanently. Farland must have been in it earlier to drop off some of his belongings, but Mia had not seen him at all today. Yesterday he had mentioned something about one of the tel comm engineers asking him for help. He must be out in the oil field avoiding paperwork.

Mia could not blame him, but she could have used his help.

She had been back and forth between the trailer and her barracks several times carrying that cardboard box filled with papers. At times it had been a challenge. The wind gusts had become stronger throughout the morning, and twice Mia had had to run after some stray pages, carried away by the wind. Not her usual way—storing important papers and research documents in an old box—but that's all she'd been able to find.

There is certainly no Office Depot around the corner to get some file folders, she had thought sarcastically.

The more the wind had picked up, the more her mood had sunk.

At least they had installed a second phone closer by that picked up a satellite signal. Now she did not have to drive out all the way to the comm unit for her calls.

She had phoned her boss at Worldmove first thing that morning. He had been satisfied with her and Farland's work. Scott had inquired about him, and Mia had spoken positively for her colleague.

Scott and Mia had discussed the day of her and Farland's return. She had suggested Friday, which would have been in two days.

"I understand the circumstances out there, Mia. And I am sorry you have to live like a bunch of tree huggers at a survival camp. But you are going to have to stay until the environmental survey is done," Scott had answered.

"What survey?" Mia had asked, surprised.

"I just got the word on it a few hours ago. Shurnik is supposed to inform you about it," Scott had said. "Call me tomorrow and we'll figure out when you guys fly back to Seattle."

The situation had brought the phrase "not a happy camper" to a totally new dimension. Frustrated about not being informed to the fullest extent, Mia had walked over to check on the status of the trailer.

Helena had outdone herself. The trailer had looked acceptable to begin with, but she must have spent all morning cleaning the place. To open a door and step into a room with real walls was a very nice change from a canvas enclosure.

Now that Mia had run into Shurnik, she thought about the survey Scott had mentioned. She wanted to bring it up, but than changed her mind. It was Shurnik's job to keep her informed, and she was curious about how serious he took her.

Together they stepped into the mess hall, and Mia took off the hood of her coat. The warmth of the inside soothed Mia's mood, and she could feel her cheeks tingle.

"Unbelievable. I have never seen anything like this." Mia was referring to the drastic change in the weather.

"I am really sorry, Ms. Trentino. I wished I could offer better accommodations for you." Shurnik sounded sincere.

"Thank you, but I can manage. It looks like we are almost finished, anyway. Mr. Farland and I will have to meet with the management in Irkutsk, but I think we'll be ready to leave by Friday." Throwing him the bait, Mia eyed Shurnik as she took off her coat.

It was almost time for supper, and Shurnik walked over to the kitchen area where Helena was cooking. He took a beverage and turned back to Mia and asked if she would like something. Mia declined graciously. She had the feeling Shurnik was trying to make up his mind about something.

He returned to the table were Mia was sitting, placed his drink in front of him, and took a seat. He studied Mia for an instant and then smiled apologetically.

"Ms. Trentino, headquarters have informed me that the government of Irkutsk is requiring an observation on our environmental safety." Mia's face did not give away that she had known and Shurnik continued. "A scientist is going to inspect the deposit of our soil we have been excavating from the oil field."

"I am not sure if I understand the relevance to our project," Mia said.

Shurnik nodded. He was just starting to explain further when he lifted his head. Mia followed his eyes and watched as Douglas walked into the dining room.

"Good afternoon," he said. "I'm sorry I'm so late. I wasn't aware that we had a meeting scheduled."

"We didn't," Mia said briskly. "Mr. Shurnik was just telling me about this environmental issue. Why don't you have a seat?" Mia noticed tiny white droplets sparkled in his dark hair. It must have just started to snow.

He wore his usual work attire and an old parka. Mia noticed a Russian military emblem sewn on the left shoulder. Douglas must have run out of layers and borrowed this coat from someone.

He saw Mia looking at his jacket and said, "I should have done more research about the weather conditions in this country. So, what do I need to know about this environmental issue?"

He looked straight at Mia, ignoring the Russian.

Before Mia could say anything, Shurnik answered instead. He patiently repeated what he had just told Mia and then continued. "Yukoil's management would kindly ask you to stay until such investigations have been completed, in case re-structuring is necessary."

Mia's heart sank. That would mean she'd be stuck here for several more days.

"Mr. Shurnik, please explain how that would happen," Mia requested.

Shurnik shrugged. "I am just the messenger. To have your question answered, you need to talk to Irkutsk."

Shurnik knew more, but was not going to share his information with them. This morning he had spoken with Lagunov. He was the leading executive of Yukoil, but all decisions were made through voting by all seven board members. Only one other man had voted in Lagunov's favor. Yukoil had decided to have the Americans stay until the oil field was cleared and a go ahead was given by the scientist.

Shurnik looked at Mia and said, "I wanted to apologize for your dilemma with your heater. It has been replaced with a new unit. You should be comfortable in your sleeping quarters."

His clumsy attempt to change the conversation didn't fool her. Annoyance rose in her once again. She withstood Shurnik's gray, probing eyes but did not dare to pressure him further about the environmental issue.

"I appreciate it," she said.

Douglas turned his attention toward Shurnik and asked him directly, "Do you know when we can expect the scientist?"

"As far as I understand, sometime tomorrow." Shurnik's gaze went from Douglas back to Mia. "Is there anything else I can do for you this evening?"

Mia took a deep breath. "No. I think after dinner Mr. Farland and myself are just going to finish up in Mr. Petronovich's trailer. We need to sort through all the documents I took over there today."

"Very well," Shurnik replied. "Please enjoy your dinner, and excuse me for not keeping you company. I have business to attend."

I'm sure you do, Douglas thought, watching Shurnik getting up, gather his coat, and leave. He would pursue Shurnik later. For now he had to stay with Mia.

"So what's the plan?" Douglas' eyes went back to her after Shurnik had left. She was sitting hunched over, gnawing on her lower lip, looking miserable.

"Maybe if we can provide additional information for that scientist, we could speed up the process." Douglas detected a tinge of hope in her voice.

"You really had your mind set on going home on Friday, didn't you?" Douglas had needed to stay beyond Friday. Now that they would, he was glad he did not have to come up with a wild story about why he could not join her going back to the U.S. But he felt bad for her. This was probably turning out to be one of those jobs she'd want to forget about once it was finished.

Mia looked at him. Suddenly her expression softened and she smiled. "Yes, I was looking forward to leaving this place in two days, but this is what I do. And if we're flippin' stuck here until Christmas, I'm gonna get this job done!"

Her sudden determination surprised Douglas. "All right then," he said. "But let's eat first."

Chapter 28

Eyes are more important than ears, Shurnik thought. He had an hour.

He was positive that he had time enough to plant the surveillance devices in Petronovich's trailer. At least some of them. He would get to install the audio surveillance some other time.

The Americans were having dinner, and he had positioned Oleg outside the dining room to give him a heads up via radio when they were on the move.

He drove his truck across the camp due south and parked it by the helicopter pad. If Oleg couldn't radio him in time, at least his truck was parked inconspicuously. Shurnik stepped out of his vehicle and retrieved the devices from the hidden compartment. Wanting to spend the least amount of time possible in the trailer, he sat in his truck studying the equipment. Markovich had briefly explained how the system worked. It was fairly simple.

The layout of the trailer called only for two cameras. Installed on either side of the trailer, they observed the entire room. The cameras came with a wide angle lens, which wasn't even necessary since the trailer was fairly narrow.

The first camera was concealed in a wall clock. Shurnik thought about this for a moment. As far as he remembered, there had not been a clock hanging on the wall. He wondered if either of the two Americans would notice.

The chance was small. He did not think the woman was that observant, and Farland had only been in the trailer for a very short amount of time. He decided that it was not worth worrying about it now; he had to use it.

The second camera was the newest device on the market. Markovich had asked Shurnik what the light switches in the trailer looked like. As far as Shurnik knew, there were just the regular beige colored knobs which switched left to right or vice versa.

Shurnik examined the beige light switch he'd pulled out of the box and could not detect a camera. Then he found it. There was a tiny hole, no bigger than a grain of sand, in the switch itself. The camera lens was tucked away behind it. If the light switch was flicked, the camera automatically readjusted to the new angle of the room. Shurnik had never seen anything cleverer. Fascinated, he studied the equipment.

Suddenly the radio crackled. It was Oleg. "I'm on post and the man just stepped out. He is walking north to the sleeping quarters. The woman must be still inside. I have not seen her."

Shurnik pushed the button on his hand-held radio. "Roger that. Stay at location."

Damn, he had to move quickly, now. Farland was probably getting his belongings out of the men's sleeping barracks. There was not much time.

He gathered a few tools and put them in the pockets of his olive cargo pants. Getting quickly out of the truck, he ran the short distance to the trailer and opened the door. Several stacks of paperwork sat on the table and on the narrow counter. Shurnik stared at a suitcase and the few items of men's clothing lying on the bed. He had not considered this. Farland had already been here. He was more familiar with the trailer than Shurnik had thought.

He reassessed the situation. There was no turning back—he had to hang up the wall clock. If he wanted full surveillance of this room, he had no choice.

He hurried as he inserted the small battery to activate the camera and used his needle point to set the channel. He set the clock and hung it up. He positioned the wall clock closer to one corner, hoping it would be less obvious.

He found his small Phillips screwdriver in his left pant pocket and unscrewed the light switch close to the bed on the other side of the room. He needed to cut the wires in order to install the surveillance light switch.

Looking for the breaker box to turn off the main power supply, he had the urge to check in with Oleg. Shurnik knelt down, went through the cabinets, and finally found the breaker box behind one of the handmade cabinet doors.

As he flipped the switch to the main power, he thumped the button on his radio.

"Oleg, status," he commanded. "Same," Oleg whispered back.

Relieved, Shurnik got up and retrieved the wire cutter out of his pocket. After he cut the power supply to the original light switch, he twisted the wires of the new switch and the power supply together. The old light switch went in his pant pocket. He inserted the battery for this camera as well and went through the same process as before.

Carefully he set the casing back against the wall and fastened the screws to hold the replaced light switch in place. He flipped the switch several times, and it sat snug against the wall. He was satisfied. Markovich could not have found a better system. He still had a little concern about the wall clock, but the light switch was almost identical to the old one.

Calm but efficient, Shurnik collected his tools and double-checked the premises. He could not see any evidence of his being there. Time was running out, and he could not wait to see how well this wireless video surveillance system worked.

He had to program the receiver, but that was an easy task. The range on this unit was supposed to be over a thousand meters—plenty of distance. It was only eight hundred meters to his office by the mess hall.

Just as he stepped out of the trailer he froze in his tracks. He turned around and stepped back into the trailer to switch the main power supply back on. He cursed as he shut the cabinet door. He had almost made a crucial mistake.

Just as he was arriving back at his truck, Oleg's voice came back on the radio.

"On the move," he said. "I'm out," Shurnik answered.

He knew he would not have enough time to drive off unseen. He took his metal tool box out of his truck to make it look like he was working on his helicopter. Although, since he was already there, he decided to check on Charlie. He needed to service the rotary-wing shock absorber, which seemed to be having some trouble.

As he topped off the hydraulic fluid, he watched the two Americans approaching the trailer on foot. The woman was carrying a box and the man had a suitcase in one hand and a duffel bag in the other. They were chatting with each other and weren't paying any attention to Shurnik doing maintenance work on the helicopter's rotor.

He had been worried about using Oleg to be on the lookout. It had seemed like too important a job for a junkie, but there had not been anyone else available. He'd had to send his whole crew out to the field to prepare for the environmental scientist's arrival.

That thought brought him back to his conversation with Lagunov.

Lagunov had explained to Shurnik the different scenarios they might have to deal with, depending on the outcome of the environmental scientist's investigation. If the scientist didn't approve of Yukoil's safety measures, they would have to remove the excavated soil and move it, and that would have consequences.

The planning stage of Yukoil's small city was complete. However, if the soil tests showed a positive reaction to contamination, they would not be able to begin with the construction of the housing. That brought them back to the problem with the Americans. Despite Lagunov's pressuring and influence, the company had still decided to have them stay on in case something went wrong with the inspection.

Of course none of the other Yukoil execs were involved in the drug coup and didn't care if the Americans stayed. Shurnik had understood. The environmental scientist would probably arrive tomorrow, on Thursday. He would not complete his work in time for the Americans to leave by Friday, even if everything checked out okay in the oil field.

Therefore, if Shurnik still planned to move the drugs on Friday, Farland and the woman would still be present. And after considering, he thought that seemed very risky. He had discussed the issue and his concern with Lagunov. He did not want them to be in the area when he left for China. Lagunov had agreed that it posed a risk, but every day they held on to unsold merchandise was a day without profit. Shurnik's men had already been notified and were positioned in China, waiting for delivery and ready for distribution.

"Find a way," Lagunov had told him. "I have Sergei Selkin in St. Petersburg breathing down my neck. You promised fast profit. You better make it happen."

Lagunov had made it clear that even though Shurnik was working as an independent, he would still be within the Mafia's reach if the mission was not completed as promised.

Chapter 29

Douglas zipped up his suitcase.

After dinner he had gone to the men's sleeping quarters to collect his belongings. It was time for him to move in to Petronovich's trailer. He had also needed to brief the Acronym and had called his partner in Ocean City, Maryland to do so.

"Mr. Secona has stepped out for a moment," somebody at the Acronym had told Douglas. He wanted to call Brian on his cell, but that kind of connection wasn't secure.

He had to wait until his partner returned and use the secure landline at the Acronym that would scramble the signal. Douglas just had to keep packing. His partner would call him back, shortly.

The Acronym was a private organization supported by the United States, Great Britain, and a few other allied European countries' governments. Established by the U.S., the Acronym had been a top secret intelligence and investigative agency, a mixture of the CIA and FBI both.

The Acronym had been designed to support and assist, but also to interact and overrule any other American law enforcement, military, or intelligence organizations in every jurisdiction within the United States and on foreign soil.

Very few outside people had known of the existence of the Acronym and those who had had been critics right from the start. But the

Acronym had proven itself to be a very efficient and inventive configuration. At least until a news reporter had been able to uncover an incident involving a Middle Eastern detainee, who had been linked to Al Qaeda.

The news reporter's article had included a description of an illegal interrogation technique used by officers of the Acronym. During this incident the potential terrorist had been killed. The Government had been forced to react quickly after its classified agency had been exposed.

Through intensive investigation, the Acronym had been able to expose the leak, and the individual from the press who had featured the story. Both men had to deal with the consequences.

The Acronym had tried to save itself by freezing all ongoing tasks, and the government had denied on all levels the existence of such an agency. However the risk of total exposure to the public had been too great and only one solution had seemed to be in reason. After almost a decade of working hand in hand with other agencies and the military and succeeding in a very high percentage of its missions, the Acronym was disbanded.

A very secret meeting took place in an undisclosed location somewhere in the Washington D.C. area. A few high-ranking military officials, the heads of the federal agencies, three extremely wealthy politicians, and one business man whose son's murder had been brought to justice brainstormed for a few days.

To protect the assets and the wealth of intelligence belonging to the Acronym, only one solution had made sense. The end result of the meeting had been the privatization of the Acronym. It had been decided to combine the intelligence of two additional agencies for further growth.

The president of Great Britain's MI6 and Interpol's secretary general both willingly agreed to share their extensive databases with the Acronym in exchange for its assistance on an international level.

When Douglas had been first introduced to the Acronym, he had been a member of the FBI tactical branch. He had joined the feds shortly after he got out of the Marine Corps. His combat experience in the Middle East had helped him to climb the career ladder at the FBI rather quickly.

Douglas had been involved in several hostage rescue missions. One of them had been California's former governor's wife. A group of illegal Cuban immigrants had snatched her during one of her kid's baseball games and had held her for ransom. Against the FBI's advice the governor had agreed to pay the ransom. He had not cared about hostage negotiations and wanted to buy his wife's freedom.

During the exchange, Douglas' team managed to rescue her unharmed, but three of the kidnappers had been shot. The story had hit the news nationwide. Instead of praise for the agent's bravery and the success of the mission, they had been slaughtered by the mainstream media for weeks for the so-called unnecessary shootings and the killing of a fourteen-year-old Cuban gang member.

This event had shattered the morality of Douglas' team and two very good agents had left the FBI, not being able to withstand the public pressure and the consequential psychological stress. Despite the successful rescue of the Governor's wife, the FBI had put Douglas on a leave of absence—he had been the one who had shot the Cuban boy.

During that time, he had been contacted by a recruiter of the Acronym. Douglas had met the man on several occasions, and it had been explained that the offer would expire very soon. At first Douglas thought someone from the bureau was playing a sick joke on him. He had never heard of an agency named the Acronym before. But the recruiter had been extremely convincing.

The proposal had sounded very intriguing to Douglas, but he was uncertain. He had learned loyalty in the Marine Corps and his allegiance to the agency was unimpeachable. The recruiter had explained to Douglas that there was no question of disloyalty since the Acronym was in close contact with all federal agencies, including the FBI. And the pay would be more than double his income with the government.

"Being an agent with the Acronym comes with disadvantages as well," the recruiter had told him. "The privileges that come with being a sworn U.S. Government agent will be revoked. There will be no benefits for your family in the event you get KIA."

Douglas understood. It had not mattered to him. There was a brother somewhere in Texas, but he had no family on his own.

"Also," the recruiter had continued, "if you get captured by the enemy, there will be a complete denial of our existence. You will have no record beyond your service with the Marine Corps. The FBI would have no recollection of your employment." He had looked very hard at Douglas. "If you want my advice, sir, if you decide to work for us, whatever your mission might be, do not, under any circumstances, get caught."

Right from the beginning of the negotiations Douglas had been sworn to secrecy, even if he ended up declining. He was told that he would endanger his own kind if he breached secrecy. He'd been given a time and a location to meet, in case he decided to accept the offer.

The following days, Douglas had been more restless than he had ever been before in his life. Finally, he had made his decision. The 250-mile drive from his home in Louisa, Virginia to Ocean City, Maryland had taken him three and a half hours. To this day he still remembered every minute of it.

During the drive he'd had the feeling of being tailed, but had not detected anyone. He'd circled the neighborhood of the address given to him, then had staked out the building for some time, but had not seen any movement.

Finally he had parked his black Ford Mustang a few blocks away. As he had walked up to the Victorian style bed and breakfast he'd wondered if he had misunderstood the address. But when the wooden front door had opened and Douglas had seen his old friend Brian Secona standing in the door way, he had instantly known that this was the right place.

Throughout his career with the FBI, Douglas had kept in touch with his longtime friend and fellow Marine, Brian Secona—BS to his friends.

After the Gulf War, Secona had worked first for local law enforcement in his hometown and had later gone to the Pentagon. Together they had been recruited by the Acronym.

The vibrating cell in Douglas' pocket brought him back to the present time. The past had flashed through his mind in minutes, but he felt like he had been thinking about it for hours.

He took his phone out and picked up the line. It was Brian. Douglas briefed his partner on Shurnik's situation.

"I guess you need to trust your instincts about Shurnik," Brian said. "We have dealt with him in the past. From what you're telling me, it looks like he's showing the same pattern of behavior."

"I agree," Douglas said. He sat down on his bed and rubbed his tired eyes. "He seems to be rather predictable. So tell me, who is my backup?"

Brian told him and Douglas was speechless.

"Hey, Doug, you still copy?" Brian listened hard for a respond.

Douglas stood, motionless, staring at the green canvas of the barracks. "Yes, yes, I'm still here," he said quickly. He pressed his cell phone close to his ear, not wanting to believe what Brian just said. He switched hands even—like it could make a difference.

His eyes went to the entry to make sure nobody was there to overhear his conversation.

He heard Brian ask again, "Doug, what's the matter? Are you still there?"

"Yes, I hear you fine. I'm just in shock," he said, rubbing his forehead with one hand.

"And why is that?" Brian innocently asked. He knew exactly what Douglas meant.

Douglas took a breath and said, "Come on, man. There's got to be somebody else."

"Not at this time." Brian said, amused. He knew Douglas had to be sweating bullets. "Haven't you and Ludvika Bogdan worked well together in the past?"

"Yes, but why someone from Interpol?" He sounded like somebody was putting thumb screws on him.

"Because of the jurisdiction. Come on man, you know that." Brian was starting to feel bad. "Listen, Doug," he tried in a mollifying tone. "She speaks the friggin' language—all of them, as far as I know. Place her somewhere in Eastern Europe or Russia and she gets along. On top of that, you have to admit she'll be perfect to keep Shurnik and his fellows in check."

Douglas gave up. "Yes, I agree..."

"Well then. We set her up with the Irkutsk chief of police. Bogdan will pose as the environmental scientist they're expecting. She's knowledgeable in that field and has plenty of combat experience. But you know that, too."

"Yes, I know that," he replied, annoyed.

"There is one more thing, my friend," Brian said sympathetically.

"And what is that, BS? Am I supposed to be thankful for my backup?"

"Sure, why not? But you might like to know that she volunteered."

When Brian hung up, Douglas stowed away his cell. Ah Christ, he thought. Now he'd have Bogdan to deal with.

He checked his watch and sat back down on his bed to wait for Mia. After dinner she wanted to gather the rest of her papers and meet him here to walk down to the trailer. He had a few minutes to think about the phone call.

He had to expect Bogdan to show up at any time. She was one of Interpol's best agents, but at times she could be extremely eccentric and difficult. Actually, she really was a pain in the ass. He did not want to think about her.

He had never regretted the move from the FBI to the Acronym. There, he had the best of two worlds. Technically he was a civilian, and he had had to get used to the idea, but thanks to a generous budget, he enjoyed the very best of equipment. The mutual agreement between the Acronym, the military, and the federal agencies stated that agents employed by the Acronym would take advantage of the newest training methods in every aspect—including the provision of gear and weapons.

When his partner Brian, Douglas himself, or any other officer was not on a mission, they either stayed low in a very sophisticated hideout in Colorado, or they continued their training. Depending on the agent's field, one would train with special ops at Fort Bragg to fine-tune combat readiness. Other times they would crawl through parts of hell week with the Navy Seals. A challenge, if one considered the age of most of the Acronym's agents.

For further schooling in the wide field of international intelligence, they visited Langley. And the forensics unit at the bureau in Quantico provided continuing education on evidence collection and examination. In the end the Acronym offered the individual agent a career shaped to their background.

Douglas was aware that no one would come after him if he was captured. That was certainly a change from the past, but as bizarre an idea as it had been to get used to, he enjoyed the extra thrill of being totally on his own.

There was one huge advantage compared to the work of a government employed officer. Since the Acronym was a privately owned enterprise, the rules and laws of the entire game could be bent and stretched a little.

Depending on the severity of a mission, certain agencies in need of assistance contracted the Acronym for just that reason.

Chapter 30

"DOUGLAS, ARE YOU READY?" He could hear Mia's muffled voice through the thickness of the canvas walls.

"Yep, I'll be right out." He had to smile. Sometime in the last two days Mia had started to call him by his first name. He knew it was against her principles, but it was amazing what a little kiss could do to principles.

For the operation Douglas needed her to be comfortable around him and trust him. He had to do everything he could to deepen that trust. If Mia found out about this mission and panicked, things could end in a disaster.

He picked up his luggage and walked outside. Dusk had already begun to set in. Mia stood to the side of the tent holding her cardboard box. She had taken a shower right after dinner since the empty propane bottle had been replaced and the women's washroom once again had hot water.

She felt refreshed and ready to conquer the project of reorganizing. She was determined to work as long as it took this evening to be able to provide everything necessary for the environmental scientist tomorrow.

Douglas' eyes went over Mia. She looked nice tonight in an ankle-length, black wool skirt and lace up Tori boots. She had not bothered with her hair after her shower and it lay in soft waves over her shoulders. She was wrapped in an oversized, knitted sweater jacket, and a pale blue cashmere scarf hid half of her pretty face.

Douglas laughed. "Are you freezing?" Mia stretched her neck a little to uncover her mouth to speak.

"Not too bad. I turned the heater up in your new house earlier."

"I was hoping we could use half of those to start a fire," he said as he looked into the box.

"Not funny, let's go and get this done."

"Do you want me to get the truck for all this?" He asked, nodding at her box and his suitcase.

"Not for me, but if you don't want to carry your things, you can get the truck," The air was crisp and the wind had calmed down. It was a beautiful evening.

Douglas did not need the vehicle. He was glad to get a chance to observe the premises.

Together they walked the few hundred yards south. The wooded area where he had hidden his equipment earlier today was to his left. No movement out there. Everything seemed clear as far as he could tell in the quickly encroaching darkness.

Mia was walking to his right. He turned his head slightly toward her and could see Shurnik working on his helicopter a ways beyond her.

He was relived that he had a visual on Shurnik. He had wondered where the Russian had gone to after leaving him and Mia during dinner.

"Are you listening?" Mia asked. She had said something, but Douglas had been concentrating on Shurnik.

"I'm sorry, what? You need to speak up when you're hiding behind your scarf," Douglas teased as an excuse.

"I asked you what you have been doing all day."

He hoped she hadn't checked with the engineer. He took a chance and lied. "I spend several hours on the oil field. They had asked me for help, remember?"

When Mia didn't reply he tried for humor. "After that I was hiding from you and took a really long nap."

Mia laughed. "I certainly believe that you have been hiding from me, but I don't know if I believe the nap."

They arrived at the trailer, and Douglas quickly opened the door to let Mia in. He did not want to give her a chance to investigate deeper into his day.

Mia stepped into the trailer and sat her box on one of the chairs.

"Look at this mess," she said. We'll be hours organizing." She took the stack of papers out of the carton and added it to an existing pile.

Douglas looked in dismay at the work to be done. He hated duties like this—he was a man of action.

"I have to go back and get one more stack," Mia said. "I'll be right back."

"Would you like me to go with you?" Douglas asked, looking out the window. It was almost dark.

Mia shook her head. "Thanks, but you can take time to get your personal things arranged."

When she'd left, Douglas looked around. There was only a little room. He decided to not waste any of it by unpacking his clothes.

Scanning the inside of this trailer, a funny feeling started to creep up in him. He sensed somebody had been in here today, and he knew it had been someone besides Mia. He took time to observe, visualizing the interior from the time he'd been in here before. His trained eye could not detect anything, but the feeling would not leave him.

His eyes went back to the piles of papers Mia had stacked up. For now he had to put the mission on hold and work with her.

When she got back, Douglas was sitting on the couch leafing through documents.

She looked at his luggage sitting on the floor. "You're not unpacking?"

Douglas looked up. "No, I'm like you and hoping we get out of this place soon."

Mia grimaced as she slipped out of her thick, knitted sweater. "Nice and warm in here." She noticed Douglas watching her and was fast to add, "Okay, let's see what could possibly be important to an environmentalist."

She took a seat in one of the chairs across from Douglas, crossed one leg over the other and smoothed down her skirt. She had been thinking about spending time in this trailer with him. It was the same size as a good sized office cubicle, which could easy accommodate two people. But living quarters like this had a different atmosphere.

Instead of a desk with a computer and a fax, there was a bed at the end of the room. In her imagination it had not been a problem to work in here. But now she felt a bit fidgety. She hoped her thin silk blouse would hide the goose bumps Douglas gave her.

During the last two days, she had been relaxed and comfortable around him. Both of them had been friendly but somewhat reserved with each other, and Mia had successfully been able to ignore their little episode in the woods.

But being close to him in the small of this trailer brought back what she had felt in the lavender field. The memory of his kiss made her lips tingle, and she remembered his intoxicating, masculine scent. Damn, he was sexy. There hadn't been anyone in her life who had had such an impact on her.

With effort, she forced her libido back under lock and key and concentrated on the job. She watched Douglas as he read several pages and relaxed. He was focused on what needed to be done, and she would try hard to do the same.

Over the next two hours they worked on a plan to influence the environmental scientist, if that was possible. Mia knew that the decision was not up to them, but she would try anything in her power to avoid a negative outcome. Adding on another week to overhaul this project did not seem to be in anyone's interest.

Douglas felt like he had never wasted more valuable time in his life. They were sitting there working on an unnecessary plan. The scientist from Irkutsk was going to be a planted Interpol agent. She would make a "scientific" related decision on the goddamn dirt based on whatever he told her needed to be said.

He should be out there spying on that rat Shurnik's every move. Getting frustrated, he got up and began reading a page as he walked up and down the short length of the trailer. His objective was to manipulate Mia into a recess so he could at least step outside for a while and check on the scene.

It didn't take long for her to notice. She'd been a bit fidgety all evening, and Douglas' pacing wasn't making it any better.

"I think we should take a break," she said finally. Satisfied that his move had worked, Douglas stopped and looked at her.

"Sorry I've been pacing. Nervous tick of mine. You are just so much better at all this paperwork than I am."

Mia smiled. "It's okay. I think we're almost done, don't you? Let's take a little break and finish up in a while." She got up as well and looked around, satisfied with the progress they had made.

Facing each other, Douglas smiled down at Mia and said, "I will be back shortly. Just need to stretch my legs."

Mia nodded, and as Douglas turned around, she raised one hand to gently push him toward the door—except she happened to push right against the thorn in Douglas' back.

"Go ahead—" She paused as Douglas moaned and almost went to his knees.

She pulled her hand back as though she'd touched a hotplate. Alarmed and confused, Mia watched Douglas recover and sit back down on the couch.

"Wow," He said. "That takes a guy's breath away."

"Oh my gosh. Are you okay?" she asked anxiously. He was in obvious pain.

Douglas knew he could not play it off. He had been able to ignore the constant throb in his back throughout the day, but he hadn't been prepared for the sharp pain when Mia had pushed on it.

He had to come up with an explanation. "Yes, I'm okay. I had a little mishap earlier." "Let me see." She anxiously nudged Douglas to get up and expose whatever it was that was hurting him.

"Really, it's nothing," he lied and got back up on his feet.

"Right; let me see." She sounded more demanding now.

She looked at him intensely and Douglas knew that she would not let it go. He took a breath, wanting to reject her, but was smarter than that. He stood, pulled his black cotton shirt out of his blue jeans, and started to unbutton it.

"This is embarrassing," he said with his head down, looking at his buttons.

"Yes, well, I really don't care." Mia was not in the mood for his jokes. A guy like him would not be forced to his knees by anything small.

Douglas took off his shirt, undecided what to do about the sleeveless shirt he wore underneath. "Turn around," Mia commanded, and he obeyed.

For a second her eyes focused on Douglas' muscled arms. She noticed an old, long scar following his left triceps. As he turned his back to her, she instantly saw what was bothering him.

Approximately three inches to the left of his spine, below his shoulder blade, was a hole in his white, ribbed shirt, circled by a bloody spot.

"How did that happen?" she demanded as she pulled his shirt out of his jeans. "Here, take this off, too, so I can examine this better."

"It happened earlier today out on the oil field. I stepped over some timber and slipped. Hit the ground pretty hard on my back."

He hoped it sounded more believable in Mia's ears than his own. He slipped his white shirt over his head and stood there naked from his waist up.

"I don't see any bruising," Mia observed. She had to swallow. Damn, he looked good. She glanced down over his sculptured shoulders and noticed more scars on his lower back. There was a semi round one, the size of a silver dollar, circled by a few smaller ones. For a moment Mia wondered what injury could have possibly inflicted a scar like this. She'd never seen anything like it. They had healed completely, but would be there for ever.

Her focus went back to the fresh wound. She could see the fragment poking out of his flesh. The skin close to the splinter was crusted with dried blood. Her stomach got weak just by looking at it.

"I have no idea how to get it out." Mia said. She swallowed hard. "This is gonna hurt." Her fingertips lightly touched Douglas' skin around the thorn. He did not flinch.

"I have a small first aid kit," Douglas said. "Maybe it includes some tweezers." He took a few steps forward to his bed and unzipped the front pocket of his suitcase.

He retrieved an olive green pouch, opened it, and immediately found what he was looking for. He handed over a pair of metal tweezers and some gauze and turned his back to her again.

"Dig it out," he said briskly.

"I don't think so," Mia was getting nauseous. "Why don't we have Helena take a look at it?"

Douglas grew impatient. "Because it's no big deal. I know you can do it."

"Man, I really don't know. How come you carry a first aid kid around with you?" Mia asked, confused.

"So I can have a pretty lady dig a piece of lumber out of my back." Douglas was not laughing. "Go ahead, do it."

Mia took a deep breath. "All right, sit on the chair and lean over the back rest so I have more light."

He did as he was told, angry with himself that it had come to this.

Mia's right hand trembled lightly. She wiped her sweaty hand on his shirt hanging over the chair and held on to the tweezers with a firm grip.

Suddenly she made up her mind that this was going to be fine, that she could deal with this. She used the thumb and index finger of her left hand to spread the skin tight. Then she used the tweezers to get a grip on the very end of the splinter.

She bit her lip as she carefully but firmly pulled it out of his back. To her surprise, it came out relatively easy, and Douglas' only sign of pain was when he quickly inhaled. A small trickle of blood followed, but the cut looked clean.

Mia unwrapped the gauze and gently pushed it against the small wound. She sat the splinter on the table next to Douglas and said, "Look at this thing. It has to be at least two inches long. I'll need to disinfect this. Do you have some peroxide in the kit?"

"No, it'll be all right, thank you. It already feels better."

"It's going to get infected," Mia argued.

"It's going to be okay," he countered. He stood up and turned back around to face her. She took a step back, feeling suddenly overpowered by his masculinity.

Douglas could feel heat on his skin everywhere Mia had touched him. He stood close to her and she looked up to him and said, "Let me at least put on a bandage."

"Do you always have to have the last word?" His voice was getting raspy.

Mia's stomach had recovered from the sight of the wound, but now as he intensified his look into her eyes, the insides of her belly started to flutter and she gnawed her lower lip.

"I have been wanting to try that habit of yours for some time." His intense blue eyes left hers and moved to her mouth.

"What habit?" she asked nervously.

Douglas raised his right hand lightly touched the soft skin of her cheek with his knuckles. He lowered his head, and his fingers gently slid down her jaw line to her chin. He lifted up her head for his lips to greet hers.

For a moment he replayed the same tenderness in the kiss as the one before. But as his warm mouth parted slightly, his teeth found Mia's lower lip and he bit it ever so gently.

A shudder went through Mia that Douglas could feel without touching her body. He released the bite just to let his mouth caress hers yet again. Then he drew back and said in his sexy, deep voice, "That habit. It has been driving me crazy for a while now."

He tasted his lips as though he'd just tried the sweetest of treats. "Hmm," he murmured, "and it will be a hard one to break."

She took his hand from her face and placed his palm directly above her heart, taking him by surprise. "This is the habit you have given me," she said. He felt her heart beating fast and strong, echoing through her chest. "And I don't know how to stop it."

She looked into his eyes with such honesty, he was genuinely touched.

"Then don't," he said simply. "Don't try to stop it."

With those words he lowered his head again, and this time he did not need to help her raise hers. Their lips met again, but this time the kiss was more intimate and probing.

In silent understanding they let themselves go a bit more. Embracing each other almost felt like a reward. They had been waiting to do so for a long time.

His hand slipped under her blouse and found its way to the wonderful smoothness of her skin. As Douglas let his hand glide up Mia's beautifully flat stomach, she leaned into him and a moan escaped her throat. The way she was pushing herself against his groin was driving him crazy, but he had to hold back. Not here, not now, he told himself. No matter how badly he wanted her.

Douglas slowed down the hungry kiss and finally stopped. His breath caressed the sensitive skin by her ear, and Mia moved her head slightly to one side, offering him the nakedness of her neck. Her fingertips left hot trails as her nails dragged from his naked shoulders down to his lower back, carefully avoiding the injured spot.

As his lips went down the side of her neck she whispered, breathless, "We ought to stop."

"Hmm," Douglas mumbled, not wanting to. He continued to tease her neck and throat just a little while longer, and his wonderfully warm mouth found its way back to Mia's lips. She responded to his kiss with the same intense passion, letting her tongue playfully explore his, and eventually slowing down, finally separating. Mia rested on his strong chest, indulging in his deliciously masculine fragrance. Dazed, she combed her fingers through his hair, letting the rush of the moment ease out of her body.

She wanted to be held and he knew it. He had his arms wrapped around her tender body, holding her tight. He was amazed he'd been able to hold himself back. He didn't think Mia knew the power she had over him. He tipped his head a bit to one side to rest his cheek lightly on top of her head and inhaled the lovely scent of her hair.

In deep thought, he stared at the wall. It took him a while before he realized what he was looking at. His eyes narrowed and he lifted his head, puzzled. He thought about it for a moment and then was absolutely certain. The clock on the wall had not been there before.

Chapter 31

DOUGLAS AVERTED HIS EYES. If the clock was what he thought it was, he did not want to be caught staring at it.

He quietly cleared his throat and said gently, "Hey, are you still with me?"

Mia lifted her head and he loosened his embrace. She looked at him with deep brown eyes. "I'm sorry, I—"

"Shh, don't say it. I feel just the way you do," he assured her.

Mia lowered her eyes. "Thank you for not trying to, you know…" She was a bit embarrassed.

"I tell you one thing, Kid," Douglas replied. "This is not the right place, but I can't promise that I won't ever—" Mia did not let him finish the sentence. She quickly brushed a kiss on his lips and said, "I know."

She moved to get away from him. Suddenly, she felt a bit claustrophobic.

"Do you still want to go outside for a while before we finish this project up?" The magic was suddenly gone, and Mia was all business again. Douglas was glad.

"Absolutely. I will only be a moment. Are you leaving?"

She nodded. "Yes I'd like to go up to the ladies room, but you don't need to accompany me on the way."

Douglas smiled, "Of course not. But here, take this." He stopped to grab his flashlight and handed it to Mia. "So you see where you're going and don't end up with a splinter in your back."

Mia pulled a face, took her sweater jacket, and disappeared into the darkness.

Douglas did not have much time. If he wanted to check out the clock he had to hurry. He knew that it was risky to run to his hiding place and get the necessary equipment. He had not observed the premises and might be under surveillance. But he had to take that chance.

He slipped his shirt back on and took his jacket. His back actually did feel a lot better. He didn't take time to think about Mia—he wanted to but couldn't.

Douglas opened the door and silently stepped outside. He casually took a few strides into the black night, stopped, and listened for anything.

When he couldn't detect any movement, he took off running. He made his way to the group of trees in a roundabout way in case he was being followed. He knew the area well by now, and the faint moonlight was just enough to help him find the spot where he hid his gear very quickly.

The unbelievable rush Mia had given him had ebbed away. Now his senses were armed for combat. He had to expect unwanted company and was ready for it.

With a small pen light between his teeth, he dug through the brush and recovered the smaller of his duffel bags. Being as organized as he was, it took him only seconds to retrieve what he was looking for.

He stuck the device in the back of his pants and took his time concealing his bags. He stayed in the crouched position and listened intently to the darkness. He could hear the top of the pine trees swaying lightly in the wind and a hawk cried somewhere in the distance. But he felt secure. There was no one out there watching him.

The last hundred feet he slowed his jog to a walk to bring his heart rate back under control. He approached the trailer slowly, looking for anything suspicious. He stepped up to it and glanced through the window. All clear—Mia had not yet returned.

In the faint light shining through the window, Douglas inspected his high-tech equipment, no bigger than a deck of cards. It was a Camera and Bug Detector. It came with a digital display and had a sweep area of 3.5 GHz, much more than what he needed here. Douglas programmed it for a silent alarm. If it detected any kind of surveillance equipment, it would signal with a tiny red light.

Equipment similar to this had been available for years now, but the device his partner had sent Douglas with his gear was completely new. The detector came with a receiver. It tapped into the frequency of both wired and unwired cameras. On a small, two by two inch monitor it displayed the same pictures being captured. Douglas could see what they could see.

He stepped back inside of the trailer. Suspecting that spying eyes lay upon him, he sat down on a chair and picked up two pages of paper. He slipped the device between those pages and flipped the tiny switch into the on position.

By the way the small bars on the digital indicator ran up and down the scale, Douglas could see that there was indeed at least one surveillance camera in this room. The frequency was clear, and within seconds Douglas watched himself sitting in the chair on the tiny black and white monitor.

So far there was one camera active. A second one had been detected but did not show activity. It either had not been turned on or it had malfunctioned.

Douglas watched his own back on the display. He turned his head as if he was reading from a page, his image turned its head after a two second delay. The camera had to be behind him, but he sat in the chair, facing the wall clock.

He wondered where the hidden second camera might be. He went through the options in his mind, visualizing the room behind him, but he could not think of anything.

It would be very difficult to investigate without looking suspicious. Douglas decided that it really didn't matter if he knew where it was. He could not do anything about it, since he was being watched.

Suddenly the screen split into two scenes, and Douglas watched live on the little device as the second camera got activated. He could now see the entire room and his own image from the front and the back. Someone must have just now turned on the receiver for the second camera.

Douglas thought about the lie he had told Mia. That he had been working out on the oil field today. Whoever had spied would follow up on it. But then he saw that there was no need to worry. The scale indicated the cameras did not have ears. They had not been listening to Mia and his conversation.

Anticipating Mia's return, Douglas moved sideways and dropped a page of his papers to the floor. As he bent forward to pick it up, he nonchalantly let the bug detector disappear in his pocket.

Thinking about what they had seen so far, Douglas felt very guilty about getting close to Mia. She had seemed so incredibly innocent with her honesty about her feelings. It certainly had not been purposely subjected to Shurnik or whoever was watching. His eyes wandered over to the luggage lying on the bed. He could not handle the thought of them being observed while in a more intimate situation than they had been in earlier.

Douglas grew more irritated. For some reason it bothered him more that whoever it was had spied on Mia in her tenderness than he was worried about the security of the op.

Chapter 32

You're gonna get your heart broken, girlfriend, Mia thought.

She took long strides running toward the sunrise. It had been still semi dark when she had gotten up, but she wanted to enjoy the early morning. She had slipped into her workout gear. And even though she did not dare run before it was lighter outside, she wanted to get some air and sort through her thoughts. She had been walking for a while, and now that the night was beginning to disappear, she picked up her pace to run a few miles.

The air was sure cold. Frost covered the ground but there were no clouds. Out here, far away from any city lights, the stars stayed visible a lot longer. When the sun crawled just above the horizon in the east, the sky in the west still flickered of stars. It was incredible.

Mia inhaled the pine-scented air, and when she exhaled, she could see her breath in front of her face. She wanted to think clearly about her situation with Douglas.

Opening up to him had felt so natural. She was aware of the danger but plainly did not care—not anymore. She hoped her heart would stay intact through this. She was an adult; she knew which direction it could go. Mia decided it was worth it to give it a try. Obviously he felt the same way and was not hiding it, either.

People fell in love all the time in all kinds of situations, so why not during a work assignment in Siberia? She knew she could not call what was going on between Douglas and her love—not yet anyway. But she was falling for him. And she felt that there was more than just pure physical attraction on his side as well.

To her surprise, Mia felt very content. She would keep her head on her shoulders while she accepted her feelings for Douglas. Mia would not let it cloud her mind for the rest of her days here. She knew she was right, she had proven it last night. The experience with Douglas had been like nothing she'd ever known. Just his kisses and his touch had been incredible, and she had wanted so much more. But as exciting as it has been, she had been completely composed when they'd returned to their work.

Mia returned from her run to the camp. It was still too early for breakfast, but she walked into the mess hall to see if Helena had coffee ready. To her surprise Douglas was already up as well. He sat at a table with shower-damp hair talking to Shurnik. Mia's stomach cramped for a second, but she had to trust in Douglas' promise to get along with the Russian.

"Good morning," she said to both men.

Douglas just winked at her, and Shurnik's eyes went over her attire. He looked up at her and responded, "Good morning. I wished you would not go out there in the wilderness by yourself. It can be dangerous."

Mia took a seat next to Douglas and looked at Shurnik. "I understand. But I have been careful and I stay close by. No need to worry." When she saw that he wasn't convinced she added, "You are more than welcome to accompany me during a workout."

Shurnik's gray eyes lightened up as he laughed. "I am an old man, Ms. Trentino. I am afraid I could not keep up."

He knew that was not true. If needed he could still perform quite well, but he never worked out for fun, there was always a combat situation in mind during his physical exercises.

Mia peeled herself out of her windbreaker. The heater system in the barracks worked well, and she needed to cool down before she took a shower.

"So what is on today's agenda?" Mia looked at Shurnik. "I supposed the scientist will come today from Irkutsk?"

He nodded. "Yes, we expect him to be here some time this morning. I would like for you to join us out in the oil field during the examination."

Mia looked at Douglas and then back at Shurnik, "Of course. We will be available for whatever is needed."

"Very well. I will find you when the scientist arrives." Shurnik got up and left.

"Well, good morning to you," Douglas said to Mia after the Russian had walked out. "How did you sleep?" They sat close but did not touch.

Mia turned her head and looked into Douglas' blue eyes. They looked glassy and showed dark circles beneath them.

"Apparently better than you."

"I had you on my mind." Another lie he had to tell. Mia had only periodically crossed his mind during the long hours of last night's tasks.

He had tailed Shurnik to his office, hoping he would lead him to the two men from the lab, dead or not. But no such luck. He had not been led to any bodies, a van, or any other evidence hard enough to take Shurnik in.

But he was able to investigate the garage closely after Shurnik had retired to his sleeping quarters. It had been a difficult investigation. He had been going without sleep for thirty-six hours and his focus and concentration had suffered.

He had hoped to be able to get into the meth lab, but it was occupied. A few times somebody had opened the latch to exit or enter and Douglas had been able to catch a whiff of the distinctive smell of an active lab.

He had been hiding between two vehicles on the oily dirt floor for hours observing the activities. His endurance had helped him to stay focused but long after midnight his body temperature had dropped and he had begun to shiver. First he thought it had just been the night's dampness. But the effects of the cold and the sleep deprivation grew and he had shaken uncontrollably.

He had known it made him vulnerable in case of an attack. During his time with the Marines and after, he had been in his prime.

Having to go days without sleep and minimal food intake had been on his plate many times, and he always had handled it well. *You're not twenty anymore, old buddy,* he'd reminded himself.

Shurnik had been out of the picture for the night, and Douglas had not anticipated the drugs being moved any time soon, so he'd voted for a few hours of sleep.

Using the concealment of the night he had made his way back to the trailer.

He had been thinking about Ludvika Bogdan joining in the investigation. She was a damn good agent. When he had spoken to Brian, he had not been thrilled about her showing up here. Now Douglas was glad to get backup. Ludvika had been quite capable in the past. Her investigative skills were trustworthy enough to share the op with her, so he could get some serious shut-eye.

Douglas had thought about their problems in the years before. Damn it, he could not let the past influence this mission in any way. He just hoped that agent Bogdan had the same attitude about it.

Too exhausted to sleep, he had stretched out on the bed, stared into the darkness, and had smelled the sweet scent of Mia lingering faintly in the air.

"All night?" Mia asked, bringing Douglas back to the present time.

Douglas looked confused. "Excuse me, all night what?"

Mia frowned. "You just said I was on your mind. I asked you if that was the case the whole night? Because you don't look like you slept much." Mia was worried about him. He really did not look very good this morning.

"No, I did get a few hours." Douglas got up to get some coffee for them. The smell of breakfast filled the air, and after a good bite to eat, he'd feel like brand new.

He turned to hand Mia her cup, but she had already left the room.

Ludvika Bogdan yawned. She sat in the police chief's office. Early that morning she had arrived in Irkutsk from west Russia. The Interpol field office in Moscow had briefed her on this assignment. It was a top secret operation; they had not disclosed any information other than the location to her.

Her superiors had made her travel light. She had been ordered not to bring any of her own gear or her handgun. No government ID, either. If the people she'd have to mess with revealed her identity, she would be killed. Probably tortured first, then killed.

The police chief watched her curiously as Ludvika talked to her superior in Moscow over a secured line in a language he could not understand. Dressed in jeans and a brown leather jacket, she leaned back in her chair and had her long legs casually stretched out in front of her, one ankle over the other. Her arms were crossed in front of her chest and she held the phone receiver between her cheek and her neck.

She eyed the police chief, who stared at her large breasts. She wondered if he was a fast draw, if he'd be able to get to his side arm in time if she were to jump up over his desk and kick his teeth in for staring at her chest.

Ludvika's superior had just outlined the op. "Apparently there have been two murder victims, but that has not yet been confirmed. The agent has witnessed the disposal of two bodies into a vehicle, but as I said, from his position he could not tell if they were dead."

"Who is it?" Ludvika wanted to know. "Who's the agent in charge?" She was certain the American feds were in control.

"It's Farland," her superior told her. Ludvika's bright blue eyes went wide. "As in Douglas Farland?"

"Affirmative," her superior said without emotion.

"What the hell is the Acronym doing here? Isn't this coup the FBI's cup of tea?" "That's exactly why. The Acronym is just doing the dirty work," her superior said. "The FBI wants to be in charge but has no official jurisdiction because there aren't any Americans involved in the crime."

Ludvika smiled. She had not seen Farland in years. This should be interesting. After a moment she asked her superior, "Does he know who to expect? And what about equipment?"

"We imagine he has been briefed by his partners. And as you should know, Agent Bogdan, whatever gear and weapons he has, it is probably more sophisticated than ours."

Ludvika had to agree. She hung up the phone and stood. The police chief got up as well. He gave her a file folder. "Here are the test sheets from the Irkutsk environmental office to take with you. They look real to me. Would have fooled my ass."

Ludvika looked down to the chief. He was at least five inches smaller than her. "Yeah well, I don't know if it would take much to fool you." First she sounded arrogant, but then she smiled and winked at him.

She had an incredible impact on people. With her six-foot height and her athletic frame, she intimidated most men. And her blond mane and those baby blues provoked most women into defensive jealousy. She was one of those few people who left a permanent imprint in one's mind even after just a short encounter.

She had been a product of the destruction her homeland, Yugoslavia, had suffered during its bitter ethnic conflicts in the past. She remembered the economical boost the Republic of Bosnia and Herzegovina had experienced during and after the winter Olympic games in Sarajevo. Then a few years later the Wars of the Yugoslav Secessions began and all hell broke loose.

When she was only eighteen years old Ludvika joined an underground group fighting the Communistic regime. They had set up training camps in Turkey teaching young Bosniaks like Ludvika, everything they needed to know about survival and weapons.

The camps were financed through an eastern European drug ring which had expanded its business into western Europe through its lessened border security. In exchange for the financial support, the young survival camp trainees were recruited to work the streets and introduce harder drugs to Warsaw, Berlin, Prague, and other European cities.

Politically motivated Ludvika had no interest in organized crime, and as a liberated East European she went to the United States to study political science at Columbia University.

With a bachelor degree in her pocket Ludvika had knocked on the FBI's door in Quantico, but they had turned her down. Disappointed, she left the U.S. to work for Interpol in Lyon, France.

Officially Interpol did not have law enforcement officers working in the field, but the fast growth of international crime overlapping several countries had called for a reinvention of the organization a few years back. After the privatization of the Acronym Ludvika had been one of the first agents to be involved in a joint investigation.

She had met Douglas in Paris as they both had been assigned by their agencies to partner up on a mission. Interpol had been on the tracks of a ring of Croatian thugs specializing in money laundry. During the hunt Farland and Bogdan had crossed several European countries. The investigation had been dangerous, and the agents had worked together closely. Too closely actually, if one played strictly by the rules. Interpol's covenants prohibited any kind of personal relationship between its own agents and other bureau's officers.

The affair had been short, intense, and based exclusively on sex.

The mission had been a success for both agencies. They had been able to crack down the Croatian organization and arrested several members who then faced high-profile prosecution in three different European countries. And with the Acronym's top secrecy, Interpol had been given all the fame.

After the conclusion of the assignment Douglas had left Europe literally over night. Because as good and crazy as the affair with Ludvika had been, she was just as crazy.

Her possessive behavior had drastically complicated Douglas' life in a very short amount of time and he'd reacted to it. And when Ludvika found out that the American had dumped her, her rage had been felt thousands of miles away across the Atlantic Ocean.

For a while she had tried to make his life miserable—phone calls, threatening letters, and damaging gossip within the circles of the agencies. Douglas had ignored it. The incident never got the attention of the higher ranked officers in either agency, and after Ludvika's hot-blooded wrath had eventually died down, Douglas had forgotten about her.

Until now.

Chapter 33

"You wanted to see me, boss?"

Oleg stood in the door of Shurnik's office. His eyes were glazed and he looked like he had aged ten years in a week. Red spots marked his cheeks and forehead, he kept rubbing his hands, and he seemed very nervous.

"What the hell happened to you? You look like shit," Shurnik asked when he knew very well what had happened. The meth Oleg had been smoking for a while now was destroying him. It would not be long before Oleg was completely useless to him. Damn it, he'd had to get rid of more men lately than he wanted to.

"Uh, I haven't been sleeping good, boss," Oleg lied. He had not slept at all in several days. Busy thoughts had kept him awake. There was so much to do and than all these noises...

"Shut up," Shurnik yelled, and then he went on in a dangerously low voice. "Tell me what happened to the van."

Oleg nervously lit a cigarette and inhaled deeply. "They drove it to Irkutsk and sold it to a group of visiting teenagers." Unconsciously he scratched his forehead again as he continued. "The men...the interior was taken care of at the dump site. They buried them, as far as I know. And then they got rid of the van in Irkutsk," he repeated.

The van had never been registered and the metal plate with the vehicle identification number had been pried out. The kids who bought it must have been visiting foreigners and would not care. They would have been happy to find a decent ride for a few rubles. Within a few days the vehicle could be anywhere in Russia or even on its way across the border.

"Did you witness the deposit of the bodies?" Shurnik demanded to know.

Oleg cringed. He knew he should have been there, Shurnik had told him so. But he'd been too doped up to pay any attention.

"Well, not exactly. But they guaranteed me it had been done." Oleg watched Shurnik approach him through a thick fog. From past experience he should have known what was coming, but he was too dazed to react.

Shurnik's right fist exploded in Oleg's stomach. He wanted to turn the goddamn dope-head's face into pulp, maybe even turn his lights out for good. But he still needed him, just for a little while longer.

Agent Bogdan drove herself from Irkutsk. She had talked the police chief into using one of their unmarked vehicles. It was a 4x4 truck. Nothing too fancy, but it would get her places in case she had to pursue someone.

She had left Irkutsk early, right after her meeting with the chief. He had done an outstanding job at setting her up as the environmental scientist. The chief of police himself had posed as the messenger to Chairman Lagunov at Yukoil, so there would not have been the slightest doubt of her legitimacy.

The truck bounced all over the road and Ludvika had to focus on her driving. But she enjoyed the feeling of freedom the Siberian taiga gave her as she raced toward the Yukoil camp. The big silver metal case lying on the backseat bounced as well. It contained her testing equipment, including glass test tubes and a microscope from the University in Moscow. There was no worry about it getting destroyed. They had explained to her that the metal case was designed to be dropped out of a helicopter and still keep its contents safe from a fifty-meter fall.

It was a sunny morning and she shielded her eyes behind a pair of mirrored shades, the kind the cops wore in American movies. She loved American movies. Despite the biting temperature she had the driver-side window rolled down and her blond hair was flowing in the wind. The truck kicked up dust, which covered the interior and smelled like century old dirt. She didn't care. With both hands on the steering wheel and her beautiful face hard with determination, she thought about the task at hand.

She knew about Yukoil's expansion. There had been a story in the news a few months back. The Russian government had given Yukoil some sort of tax break for their effort to provide housing to their employees. She also knew about Shurnik. Her superior had mentioned his name during a meeting back at the field office in Moscow.

He was bad news. Of course she never had met him in person, but one of her partners had been shot by him during an unrelated investigation in St. Petersburg. Her partner had been a good agent, but the Russian mafia had been on his tracks and Shurnik had taken care of him personally.

When Interpol had briefed a group of agents about a case in Irkutsk involving Yukoil, Ludvika had volunteered after hearing Shurnik's name brought up. She had been warned by her superior not to let this mission become personal, but they knew she was just the right person to get the job done.

"Get in, get out," is what her superior had told her. "Gather evidence as quickly as possible. If they don't get to move the drugs, that's even better." Interpol's intelligence had reported a possible connection to China. Ludvika was not looking forward to a chase deeper into Asia at all, but she would do it if necessary.

And then there was Farland. The hell with him. There was no time to brood about the past. She would have to accept him as the agent in charge and hope he had not lost any of the sharpness she had once so admired. She did not know what he was posing as or who else was involved, but soon enough she would find out.

Ludvika was thirty minutes away and the senses of a warrior began to heat up in her. All her focus was on the mission. Shurnik's involvement alone made this case extremely dangerous.

Shurnik scanned the horizon. A faint dust trail followed a small black dot. Someone was approaching the camp at a very high speed. It must be the scientist from the city, Shurnik thought in dismay.

The operation had not been going as smoothly in the last few days as he would have hoped for. First he had been unable to dig up anything about Farland, then he'd had to get rid of two dead bodies, and now he had to satisfy Yukoil by accommodating this damn scientist. All the while Lagunov was threatening him with Sergei Selkin and the Mafia's long reach.

He had to move the drugs, and he had to do it soon.

Yesterday he was able to buy himself some time. Lagunov had experienced first hand the complications the environmental scientist's visit would bring. Since Lagunov himself had not been able to talk the Yukoil board into letting the Americans leave before the survey was finished, ultimately Selkin and his group in St. Petersburg had allowed a few extra days for the delivery.

"A few," Lagunov had warned Shurnik. "Just a few."

Shurnik narrowed his eyes. He should go and find the two Americans to meet the scientist as soon as he arrived. He checked his watch; it was only nine o'clock. He did not want to loose any time this morning, but this was fascinating to watch.

The truck had just pulled into camp, and the driver apparently knew how to navigate on this terrain. He had to have been going at least a hundred kilometers an hour when the truck had come down the hill on the narrow, winding dirt road. The truck came to a stop, and for an instant Shurnik could not see it—it was completely swallowed by a huge dust cloud.

The engine stopped and the driver's door swung open. The second Shurnik saw those long legs step out of the vehicle, he knew it was a woman.

She wore heavy work boots, jeans, and a man's shirt underneath an open leather coat. A baseball hat and glasses disguised part of her face and blond hair was gathered in a pony tail that reached down to her waist. The way she shouldered a big metal case on straps on one arm and a duffel bag over the other told Shurnik that she was a woman who took matters in her own hands.

He walked up to her and noticed that she was almost as tall as him.

"Shurnik?" she asked briskly.

"Yes, you must be the scientist the environmental office sent?" Shurnik offered her his hand.

"Right. I'm Yeltsin, Doctor Ludvika Yeltsin." Ludvika had used that cover name before. She liked fooling with political figures.

As she shook Shurnik's hand he asked her, smiling, "As in Boris Yeltsin?"

"Yes, but there is no relation." She smiled back at him. Funny, she thought, it works every time.

She took her shades off, folded them, and stuck them into the front of her shirt, making sure Shurnik got a glimpse of her cleavage.

"Please follow me, Doctor Yeltsin. Why don't you give me one of those?" He pointed at her duffel bag and Ludvika gave it to him, plus an extra second of her amazing blue eyes.

As they walked toward the mess hall, Shurnik let his eyes run over Ludvika's body. She looked very athletic to him, her long strides powerful and confident. He could make out the muscle of a well-defined hamstring beneath her jeans.

The heavy case she was carrying did not seem to bother her at all. Her hands were like a man's—strong and big—yet she had long, feminine fingers and wore several wide, silver rings.

Shurnik retrieved his handheld radio out of his back pocket and spoke in an east Slavic dialect. "Oleg, find the Americans and send them into the dining room. The scientist has arrived." Ludvika understood but didn't let Shurnik know.

She asked him in her perfect Russian, "I have never heard that language before. What did you just speak, if you don't mind me asking?"

"By all means. It was a Rusyn dialect. Not many people speak it anymore."

When Mia returned from her shower, Douglas was in the middle of a huge breakfast. Somehow he had explained via sign language to Helena that half a dozen scrambled eggs and fried potatoes would make his day. Helena had understood and spiced it up with something that tasted like Mexican jalapeños. She already had Mia's portion of beloved cottage cheese and fruit sitting on the table, waiting for her.

Mia had anticipated a day out on the field. She wore her boots, a simple blue turtleneck sweater, and carried her coat over her arm. She had chosen a pair of black cargo pants she had found during a quick shopping spree the last time she had gone to Irkutsk. With her chestnut hair braided at the back of her neck, Douglas thought she looked like a female construction worker. Adorable, but ready to get down and dirty.

Mia looked at Douglas' plate and wrinkled her nose. "It's fascinating to watch a man shorten his life by simply having breakfast."

Douglas chewed happily and grinned. "Oh yeah? Why's that?"

Mia took her breakfast bowl, thanked Helena, and turned back to Douglas. "There is no such thing as a cholesterol-free egg," she said dryly.

Douglas laughed. "I wouldn't want those, anyway." And when Mia sat down across from him he leaned forward, raised his coffee cup to his lips and drawled quietly, "You never know, Kid. The way things are going I'll need all the protein I can get." Then he winked at her.

All those butterflies returned to her stomach from out of nowhere, but Mia held his gaze and said, "You better be careful not to hurt yourself in the meantime."

A few minutes later Shurnik walked in with a woman carrying a metal case. After they had finished their meal, they had decided to wait for the scientists to show up. Now Mia was glad that someone had arrived already. The woman beside Shurnik did not look like an environmentalist at all.

Mia had envisioned a thin, older man standing in a laboratory holding some sort of chemical apparatus that would measure the contents of the soil. The woman approaching her was tall, not skinny, and looked like she worked outside all day. Her face was expressionless, maybe even a bit hard. There was no sign of any smile around her lips. But Mia thought she was beautiful in an unusual, a little bit rugged way.

Douglas rose to his feet. He had to admit to himself that he had been a bit nervous about meeting Ludvika again. He was not sure how she would react. He had been certain that she would not compromise the mission or do anything stupid—she was a professional. But a faint feeling of apprehension had lingered. Now that she was shaking his hand like a stranger, that feeling disappeared. She had not changed a bit. Her demeanor was fully adapted to the mission. And when he looked into her bright eyes, the feeling he was afraid of did not return.

Shurnik introduced Dr. Yeltsin first to Mia in Russian. Then Mia translated to Douglas as he shook Dr. Yeltsin's hand. To simplify the process, Douglas offered that everyone carry on in Russian and Mia could translate for him later on in a summary of the subjects talked about. Mia translated the idea to Dr. Yeltsin, and she and Shurnik agreed. They would save a lot of time that way.

Shurnik offered breakfast to Dr. Yeltsin, but she declined. All four of them took a seat and discussed the day. Dr. Yeltsin explained that she needed at least twelve hours for the test results of the soil to be available.

Shurnik asked, "Do you need to go back to Irkutsk for your procedure?"

"Not necessarily," she answered. "I brought a test kit with me, which should be sufficient."

Dr. Yeltsin opened her briefcase and retrieved a document. "Here is the order of the environmental office of southern Siberia, if you would like to review it." She handed the page to Shurnik who shook his head.

"Dr. Yeltsin, if you don't mind, we would like to begin immediately. I don't believe there is a need for us to prolong the proceedings with more bureaucratic procedures. I am sure you understand that time is money in the oil business."

"Of course, Mr. Shurnik. Now, will Mr. Farland and Ms. Trentino accompany us at the test site?" She asked, looking at Shurnik.

Mia answered for Shurnik. "Yes, Doctor, we will. Actually Mr. Farland here is a geologist, and we have put together a few documents you might find helpful in your survey."

Ludvika looked at Mia, surprised, and then nodded her head. "A geologist, I see. I am sure I can use his expertise to my advantage."
She looked straight at Douglas and smiled.

Chapter 34

DOUGLAS NEEDED A WORD alone with Ludvika as soon as possible. It would be difficult to manage, but he needed to brief her.

The group decided to take the drive to the test site right away. There was nothing else that needed to be discussed for the time being. Shurnik got up and offered Mia and Douglas a ride. Dr. Yeltsin would follow them in her vehicle. She had more of her testing equipment in it.

"Thank you, Mr. Shurnik," Mia declined politely. "But maybe Mr. Farland and I should drive out with Dr. Yeltsin. I can explain Mr. Farland's and my work to her on the way."

Shurnik thought about it and agreed. He was under a tremendous amount of time pressure and whatever saved time worked for him.

"You will find your way to the testing site if I go ahead?" he asked Mia.

"Of course. We will meet up with you shortly." Mia turned to Douglas. "We need to stop at the trailer and get the docs."

Douglas opened the passenger door of Ludvika's truck for Mia to step inside. He would have Mia get the papers and take the opportunity to talk to Ludvika in private. Mia told Ludvika the way, and when Ludvika stopped in front of the trailer, Douglas stepped out of the truck and reached into the back to give Mia a hand to climb out as well.

"Here you go, Boss. I'm not sure which pile of papers it is we need. I think it's better if you get them."

Mia sighed, "All right." And then she said to Ludvika in Russian. "Dr. Yeltsin, I will only be a minute." She disappeared into the trailer.

Douglas kept his door open and leaned against the truck with his back to Ludvika. He scanned the area where his gear was hidden in the brush. He didn't see anything suspicious.

"Getting friendly with the civilian?" Ludvika couldn't help mocking him in her accented English.

Douglas would not let her push him into the defensive.

"You will have to screw up your first test results. We need more than twelve hours. I have not been able to locate the drugs or the bodies." He spoke quietly so Mia could not hear them talk through the thin walls of the trailer.

Ludvika registered the order but decided to tease him some more. "Oh, that's right. There is no problem getting involved with a civilian since you are just a civilian now, too."

That cut deep, but Douglas would not allow it to show. Fine, she wanted to play? He'd play.

"No wonder the FBI didn't take you." He hit her soft spot right away. "As poor as your English is now, I wonder what you sounded like back then." He didn't wait for a response before adding, "And by the way, you look as good as ever."

"Fuck you, too, Farland."

"Yeah, maybe later, but in the meantime you will obey this civilian's orders. Is that understood?" Douglas' voice stayed quiet, but his tone had become harsh. He had to control her right from the get go, before she could start any trouble.

Ludvika did not answer. It didn't matter that Douglas was not with the feds anymore. This was the Acronym's playground and he was the biggest kid on the block. He would outrank any other agency officers. Ludvika knew that, of course, but apparently had a hard time accepting it.

Douglas slid back into the passenger seat. Mia would not be able to see him, even if she were looking out the trailer window. He turned his head toward Ludvika, studied her for a moment, and quickly grabbed one of her wrists. He squeezed it hard and the sharp pain took her breath away.

"Listen closely, Darling." Douglas' voice was very calm. "Ms. Trentino is not yet in the loop. We will keep it that way as long as possible. And you will obey my orders. Does that penetrate?" It did not sound like a question.

He let her go and Ludvika rubbed her numb wrist. She kept her eyes straight ahead. "Yes, it does."

Douglas knew he could keep her in check, but he had to be able to trust her, too. To smooth things over he said, "Why don't you save your claws for Shurnik? I know you want to, and I know the reason. Secona told me about your partner in St. Petersburg." Ludvika looked at him with skepticism. Douglas voice sounded more sincere as he continued. "After this task is successfully completed, you will get your chance for revenge. I will look the other way, I promise."

Ludvika studied Douglas for a long minute. She knew he was trying to manipulate her, but she could live with that if she'd get her chance with Shurnik.

Finally she smiled. "Deal."

Mia stepped into the trailer and looked over the stack of papers she had organized for the scientist. Then, as she noticed some of Douglas' personal things, her eyes went over to the bed. It was neatly made, but the pillow had a few wrinkles on it from where he had rested his head.

Mia stood still. The room was filled with his masculine presence. The fine hair on the back of her neck stood up and a shiver went through her body.

She had to smile. Damn. He was not even close to her, and she could feel him. Mia had to force herself to move. For a fleeting moment she could not remember what she had come in there for. Then she turned around, took the top pages out of a cardboard box, and scanned over them.

When she was sure she had the right ones, she opened the door and stepped outside.

Douglas had just gotten back out of the truck and was casually leaning against it when Mia reappeared.

He had his arms crossed in front of his chest and smiled at Mia. "You found everything you were looking for?"

"Sure did. Let's go."

Shurnik drove the Kamaz to the test side. The two Americans and the scientist were close behind him.

When he got there he was surprised—earlier this morning he had told his crew to clean up the area, and they had done a good job.

Shurnik was not sure if this was enough. Dr. Yeltsin would take several different soil samples and test them. As much as he hated it, the fact was that the direction the following days would take was out of his hands.

The area to test was several hundred acres big and it would take them a few hours to drive around and collect soil samples.

Ludvika had researched what she needed to do to look like she knew what she was doing. At every stop she collected a small amount of soil, put it in a glass tube, added a few drops of a chemical with a pipette, sealed the glass tube with a plastic cork, and labeled it.

Every glass tube had its spot in the thick, cushioned inside of her metal case.

Dr. Yeltsin explained in detail why the process took at least twelve hours. The chemical needed time to break down the contents of the soil, including any contaminants, which then could be examined under the microscope.

Douglas was impressed, and Mia willingly translated any dialogue between them.

Shurnik was confused. He certainly was not a man of science. He had to trust that the doctor knew her trade. After an hour he grew impatient and decided to point his focus on other things. He still had to bug Petronovich's trailer with the ears he did not get to install the other day.

"Ms. Trentino and Dr. Yeltsin, would it be agreeable if I excuse myself? I have business to take care of, and it does not look like I am much help here." He addressed the two women in Russian.

Mia looked up. She wanted to talk to her boss in Seattle today, and if she waited until the testing was done, it would be too late in the States to reach him.

"Mr. Shurnik, would you give me a ride back to camp, please?" she asked him in English. Douglas looked at her, surprised. He had been trying to figure out when he could get alone with Ludvika so he could continue his briefing. Mia wanting to leave with Shurnik was a perfect chance to do that.

On the other hand, he hated to let Shurnik out of his sight.

Shurnik smiled at Mia. "Not at all. Let me go to get my vehicle."

Mia turned her head to Douglas. "I hope it's okay with you if I leave you here to assist Dr. Yeltsin. I believe there is nothing more I need to translate to her at this time."

Douglas pretended to think it over. "Sure," he finally said. "I think I can manage. Just tell Blondie here I don't want to miss out on lunch."

Mia smiled and said to Ludvika in Russian, "Dr. Yeltsin, you will have to excuse Mr. Shurnik and myself. Mr. Farland will further assist you. If there is anything else you would like to talk about, we will discuss it over lunch."

Ludvika finished labeling a test tube and looked at Mia. "That would be fine. I'm sure we'll get along." Her eyes went from Mia to Douglas.

Shurnik pulled up in his truck and Mia stepped in.

"Well, aren't we lucky?" Douglas said to Ludvika after Shurnik had driven off.

"I'm stuck here with you, how lucky is that?"

Douglas gave her a look. "Shut up and listen."

He kept his back to the direction of the camp. Between the camp and the test field were hills and huge pine trees, but Douglas expected Shurnik to sneak back up on them and observe through his binoculars after he dropped Mia off. He told Ludvika not to look at him when she spoke.

He gave Ludvika an extensive rundown of the op. He explained the bugged trailer and the position of his hideout. Douglas went into detail about what he saw when he watched Shurnik from his location in the tree—leaving out the squirrel part. However, when it came to explaining Mia's job with Worldmove and his own disguise he only discussed the necessities.

"Are you planning on telling her the truth?" Ludvika asked. "About the mission and who you really are?"

Douglas had thought about it a lot. "Only if absolutely necessary." He did not trust Ludvika not to get him in trouble with Mia. Obviously Ludvika could sense something was cooking between them.

"She is the perfect cover for me, but if it becomes essential, you will not be the one to tell," he warned her.

"What about weapons?" Ludvika asked as they stepped into her truck to drive a few hundred yards further east to another stop.

"I've got my modified M40. It's sweet, you would love it. Unfortunately for you I won't let you touch it. But besides my Five-seveN I have a Ruger you can borrow. I guess they didn't let you come with any of your own?"

"No, they ordered me not to pack anything." Ludvika hesitated then smiled. She pulled up the right pant leg just far enough for Douglas to see a small leather holster strapped to her ankle just above her boot.

Her bright blue eyes sparkled at Douglas when she said, "But as you know, Darling, sometimes I have a hard time with orders."

Chapter 35

SHURNIK WAS QUIET.

He did not say a word to Mia while he drove from the test site to the camp. Mia was glad about that. She thought about the Doctor. What a strange person she was.

Dr. Yeltsin was hauntingly beautiful, and Mia had watched Shurnik checking her out. Mia herself had felt mesmerized by her. It was weird, though, that Douglas did not seem to have noticed Dr. Yeltsin's good looks. He had almost seemed disinterested in her. Just the opposite of what Mia would have expected from a man like him.

"Where would you like me to drop you off?" Shurnik startled Mia back to reality.

"At the main barracks would be fine. I need to update Seattle."

Shurnik stopped in front of the mess hall and looked at Mia. "Will you be calling Irkutsk as well, today?" He asked her.

"No," Mia answered. "There is no need for me to talk to Yukoil until we have the Doctor's test results. Which should be when, tomorrow morning?"

"Yes, we will know if we can let you go back to civilization," Shurnik said kindly, hoping he could be rid of them soon. With any luck the test results would be negative and the Americans could leave on Saturday. He would only be one day behind schedule.

Douglas kicked his seat back. Ludvika had at least another hour of collecting dirt left. An hour he could use to catch up on his sleep. It didn't matter to him if someone saw him like this. He would just be the lazy guy taking a nap while everyone else worked.

It only took Douglas a minute to fall asleep. Ludvika was kind enough to maneuver the truck carefully so she would not wake him up. As much as she loved to argue with him, she understood his need for sleep. They had a long night ahead of them.

She had promised herself to play by the rules, but the moment the saw Douglas, the old wounds he had inflicted years back had started to ache again. But she had been able to control her emotions once he had put her in her place.

She would let him be the leader of this task. The sweet revenge she had planned for her partner's murderer meant more to her than fighting her old feelings for Farland. He had promised assistance, and she believed him.

After she had collected the last sample of soil, she parked the truck in a low spot beneath some trees. She checked her watch—it was past noon. She would let Farland rest for another hour and then head back to camp.

Ludvika silently stepped out of the truck. She wanted to make sure the area was secure and went for a prowl.

Douglas heard gun shots.

At first he didn't see anything—he could just hear the screams of his comrades after they had been trapped in crossfire by the militia.

Two were dead, four more hit but still alive. Somehow he had managed to not get hurt. He pressed himself into the wet, soggy dirt behind the huge rock they were using as a shield. It had rained all night and the mud was slick and heavy.

He needed to think, but it was difficult with his brothers' agonized screams echoing around him. He needed to reload his weapon, and just as he rolled quickly on his back to free his hands, a snapping sound close to his right ear froze him in his tracks.

He could feel the cold steel of a knives' blade against his neck.

Douglas' eyes flew open, he was disoriented and his mouth was dry. Then he recognized Ludvika's face above his. She had snapped open her switchblade and had it pressed against his neck, right above the jugular.

She smiled. "Damn, Farland. With a reaction time like this, you're gonna get our asses in deep shit out here."

"Fuck!" Douglas exhaled and placed both palms of his hands over his eyes. "Are you out of your friggin' mind?" He tried to get his thumping heart beat back under control.

Ludvika stopped smiling. She knew exactly what he had just been through. She had her own nightmares to battle from time to time, where she relived the brutal experiences of combat.

Concerned, she looked at him. "You screamed." She paused and then smiled again. "I had to wake your ass up before you let the whole goddamn neighborhood know that we're here."

The dream had been vividly real and it took Douglas a minute to calm himself down. He had not dreamed like this in a while. He usually did not allow himself to sleep that deep. But he understood what had happened. He trusted Ludvika. Trusted her with his life as a comrade in battle. Unconsciously he had let himself go into the deep rest his body was so desperately in need of.

He felt better now—much better. She still stood beside the truck on the passenger-side door, studying his face.

"Come on," he said and put his seat back into an upright position. "We've got some serious shit to take care of."

That night, Douglas and Ludvika arranged their surveillance together.

Douglas needed to get into the meth lab; they had to find the drugs. He watched Ludvika as she armed herself with his Ruger and several additional clips. She also checked her own handgun in her ankle holster and almost drooled over Douglas' M40.

"No," he shook his head. "Not gonna happen. Be a good girl and put it down."

He loved teasing her with his rifle. He knew all she wanted to do was sit tight tonight and wait for Shurnik to come out so she could blow his brains out. But it wasn't that easy. He still needed to lead them to the drugs, and even better, to the bodies.

They were sitting in Douglas' hideout, dressed in black and waiting for things to happen. The afternoon had come and gone. Mia had told Douglas about her phone conversation with Seattle, and that Scott Hensley wanted a written report on the job before Mia and Douglas headed home.

They had to wait until the morning before the test results would conclude that report, but Mia was going to start working on it that evening. Douglas had offered her the trailer, but she had told him she would crawl under her covers for a while and maybe give one last try at beating Helena at chess later.

She would hopefully stay out of the picture for the rest of the night. He wouldn't worry about her trying to find him later on. His concentration was on the mission.

Ludvika had pretended to leave the camp and that she would return the following morning. She had left with a hand-drawn map in her pocket that Douglas had given her.

He had sent her out of the camp and up the hill, just to drive around it and to approach from the opposite side. He had met up with her several miles east of the camp and used dusk and the thickness of the tundra to reenter the camp unseen on foot.

Douglas gave Ludvika her earpiece for the two-way radio and checked the battery. He adjusted the small mouthpiece above her throat and noticed her watching him.

"Like old times," she said. Douglas finished what he was doing and gave her his equipment to assist him.

Their faces were close together, and Douglas could feel her breath on his neck. Their past flashed in front of his eyes, but just for a second. Her sex appeal was unbelievable, but he was immune to it now.

"Don't get any ideas," he warned.

She smiled. "I'm so over you, Farland."

"Good."

Douglas wasn't sure if she was telling him the truth, but the past didn't matter. The present time was important. They were comrades and that was a connection between them that reached deeper than the bond of two lovers.

Now it was a waiting game. Somebody would have to make a move, and Douglas hoped it would be Shurnik.

After the night had become pitch black, Douglas had repositioned himself in some low-growing underbrush between the garage and Shurnik's office and his adjoining sleeping quarters. Ludvika was further west on the other side of the camp, not far from Douglas' equipment hideout.

Shurnik had been in the garage earlier, but they had watched him as he went into his office. From their positions, neither Douglas nor Ludvika could see inside either the garage or Shurnik's yurt, and Ludvika was growing impatient. Finally she told Douglas she wanted to move in.

"Sit sill," Douglas barely whispered. The mouthpieces on the radio were extremely sensitive. "Did you leave your patience in Moscow?"

"This is all wrong, Farland. One of us has to move closer. We need to get into the lab," Ludvika argued quietly.

"And how would you manage that, Sherlock?"

"I have an idea." Ludvika ignored Douglas' ironic tone. "I will keep my eye on Shurnik while you investigate the lab."

"Ah, right. And if he comes out of his yurt, you're just gonna have a nice chat with him while I try to get out of the lab without someone using an Uzi, is that it?"

"Something like that. Do you trust me, Farland?"

He wondered what the hell she had in mind. "Trust you? Yes—or at least I used to. Right now you seem to have lost your marbles," he said dryly.

"Just fuckin' trust me," she said. Douglas smiled. It was hilarious to hear her curse in her heavily accented English. Then she pointed out. "I had my blade on your neck today. I could have easily slit your throat, run back home, and blamed it on Shurnik."

"Yes, but you didn't, and I know why," Douglas mocked.

"And why is that?"

"Because you still love me," Douglas sang in her ear.

"Ah, Christ, Farland—you're full of shit," Ludvika said but she had to smile in the dark.

Douglas had not ordered her to stay put. That meant he did trust her, and as she crawled backward out of her hiding spot, she explained her plan to Douglas.

When she was finished he said, "You are out of your mind, Agent Bogdan. He will wonder why you are still in camp. He watched you leave—he'll be alarmed. On top of that, it's highly unethical."

Ludvika had already changed back into her clothes from earlier in the day. She placed the thin radio in the pocket of her cargo pants and the mouthpiece underneath the wire of her bra.

She had to speak up just a little in order for Douglas to hear her. "Listen, Farland, I'll tell him some bogus story about a flat tire and he will only be alarmed for a second. You do remember my specialties, don't you?"

Douglas indeed remembered Ludvika's secret weapons.

She continued, "As for the ethical part, which agency's code are you referring to? The Acronym's? Officially, you guys don't even exist."

She had a point there. "Okay, you have my go ahead. If there's trouble, use your safe word as the signal. I should be able to move in within two minutes."

Ludvika approached Shurnik's barracks. She took her hairpiece out and shook her long, blond hair loose. Underneath the dim light outside the barracks she looked like an angel, but Douglas knew she was anything but.

She stopped and looked in Douglas' direction, unable to see him. But she knew he could see her. She said, smiling, "There won't be any trouble, and remember I'm doing this for God and Country."

"For Country? Which one?" He asked, but Ludvika had already removed her earpiece.

Douglas watched her walking casually into Shurnik's sleeping quarters. He would be able to hear bits and pieces of the conversation between Shurnik and Ludvika.

Her plan to seduce Shurnik had sounded crazy, but if it worked, it would give Douglas time to investigate the lab. Nobody besides

Shurnik had been in or out in several hours. Douglas was certain that it wasn't occupied.

He sat tight and listened. Douglas could hear faint sounds from where the tiny microphone sat in Ludvika's bra. She had switched it to permanent mode so it did not need a tone to activate the transmitting.

Suddenly Douglas could hear a male voice. He did not understand what they were saying, but the male sounded surprised, and Ludvika's voice was soothing like a cat's purr.

He was worried about her, but had to trust that she could take care of herself.

Chapter 36

THE CAMP WAS QUIET.

Douglas ran from his hiding spot around the camp to the garage. He crouched low behind a vehicle and spotted a mechanic working on something.

Damn, he thought. He would give it a few minutes, but if the mechanic didn't leave, Douglas would have to take him out. He had his wire string in the left pocket of his black BDUs, ready to be used for a silent attack.

Knowing Ludvika, and by the sounds coming from the radio, Douglas had at least an hour, if not two. He had to double task. And while he needed to keep an ear on the drama in Shurnik's sleeping quarters, he also had to concentrate on the premises around him. Getting caught would be deadly for him and Ludvika, and probably for Mia as well.

The thought of Mia being interrogated and eventually killed twisted his stomach into a knot and shallowed his breathing. But the vivid image of Mia in pain left him as quickly as it had appeared. He had to focus on the sounds in his left ear.

Douglas could not understand the words between Shurnik and Ludvika. They spoke in some weird language he never heard before. But from the sound of it Ludvika was in control, and Douglas was not surprised.

Suddenly he heard Shurnik's voice getting louder, Douglas heartbeat quickened and he listened intensely. Had he found the transmitter in Ludvika's bra?

Ludvika said something in her low, seductive voice, and Shurnik let out an animalistic moan. Douglas grinned. Hang in there buddy, it only gets better, he thought, knowing what Shurnik was going through.

For a moment Douglas thought about Ludvika's sacrifice and how repulsing it must be for her, but then he shook his head. Ludvika was tough, and it had been her choice to do it. As twisted as she was, she was probably enjoying every minute with Shurnik, knowing she'd get her chance to kill him later on.

The garage darkened. The mechanic had just turned off the lights, and Douglas watched him leave the area on foot. He stayed put for a little while to make sure the man didn't return. He took a pair of thin, black gloves out of his pocket and slipped them on. Then he made his move.

He approached the garage carefully. He had been here several times before in the dark and knew his way around. Besides the humming noise of the diesel generator in the distance, there was no sound. Ludvika and Shurnik were still in his ear, but he tried to focus on the trapdoor. The strong metal lock wasn't much of a hindrance, and he made his entry within minutes.

The electronic security mechanism on the hatch underneath the trapdoor was very sophisticated. Douglas took his black backpack off and retrieved a device. The code breaker his partner had sent him from Maryland had been tested in the modern vaults in several Las Vegas casinos. It had been able to break the combinations of all of them, so Douglas was certain it would work here as well.

And it did.

The only potential problems he might face now were a silent alarm and someone hanging around in the lab. He watched the small LED lights on his device. The code breaker wasn't registering any electronic frequencies a silent alarm would have triggered. Satisfied, he put away his equipment and shouldered his backpack. He crouched in front of the hatch and drew his gun. Very carefully he turned the handle on the hatch; it made a popping sound, as though he'd just opened a can of vegetables.

He stood in a combat ready position, pointing his Five-seveN into the opening in front of him. He listened for anything unusual but only heard the sound of his blood rushing through his body. He could almost taste the adrenaline on his lips.

He focused on the stairs, but no sounds were coming from below. Stealth-like, he took one step at a time down the stairs. His senses were armed and ready for any kind of encounter. Bright fluorescent light pierced his eyes, and he squinted a few times to adjust from the darkness outside to the well-lit room.

The distinctive ammonia smell was overpowering, and Douglas suppressed a gag reflex. He stopped and swallowed. He was aware of the toxic vapors and the chemical dust he might be inhaling. He'd brought a respirator but decided not to use it. It would decrease his field of vision, and he might not be able to fight off someone if attacked.

He waited until the nauseous feeling passed and used the few seconds to focus on the happenings in his left ear. Still the usual noises. Ludvika was murmuring to Shurnik in her caressing voice, letting Douglas know everything was going as planned. Slowly he continued until he reached the bottom of the stairs.

The lab was fully equipped and very organized. The paraphernalia he saw was on par with anything he'd find back in a high-tech chemical laboratory. The room was not very big, maybe three hundred and fifty square feet, and Douglas scanned it with one sweeping look.

He found evidence of an active lab, but all the heating devices were turned off, and the kerosene-filled glass jars did not contain any drugs for storage. This lab has been cold for at least twelve hours.

There was a metal door across from him on the other side of the room. He would have to check that first. He did a quick 360 to scan what might be behind him, but he could not detect anyone or any other openings to another room. The metal door opposite the entrance was locked, and Douglas suspected it to be a thick, fire-resistant door. The way it sat flush with the wall made it impossible to break through with the limited number of tools he had brought.

As much as he hated it, he had to let the door go and focus on the rest of the lab.

He searched the cabinets and every container he could find, moving carefully as he handled the dangerous chemicals. After thirty minutes of searching, he still couldn't find any kind of bag or package—nothing. They must have moved the drugs. But where? Was is possible that Shurnik had stayed behind while someone else took charge of the transport? Highly unlikely, he thought.

He went back to inspect the metal door one last time. Locked, the door would not budge. His instincts told him he needed to investigate whatever was behind it. His earpiece crackled. The reception was poor in the back of the room so he walked toward the entrance again.

There was nothing he could do about the damn door right now.

"Farland, do you copy?" Ludvika's voice was clear as Douglas approached the stairs.

"Copy," he said, pausing as he noticed something that didn't belong in a meth lab.

"What's your status?" Ludvika asked.

"Still in the lab. How're you doing, Bogdan?" Douglas asked, assuming she had left Shurnik's sleeping quarters and was back in their hideout since she wasn't whispering.

"Never better. He's down and out."

Douglas stared at the engine block sitting on several pieces of wood, similar to a small palette. He wondered what the hell it was doing down there.

Suddenly he realized what Ludvika had just said. "What? You didn't kill him, did you?" he demanded, panicked.

Ludvika laughed. "No, not yet. But I slipped some Luprivin in his vodka. It'll be a while before he comes around."

Douglas couldn't believe it. He tried to keep his voice down. "Goddammit, Bogdan. What in the hell did you do that for? He'll wake up and know that you drugged him. I should release you from this investigation right this minute."

"Relax, Farland. Shurnik drank a lot. He won't know the difference when he wakes up. The sedative will not affect him in any other way than the alcohol does. I just wanted to make sure he wouldn't be in our way for the rest of the night. So how should I proceed?"

Douglas thought it over. She might have done a smart thing by giving Shurnik the Luprivin, but she should have consulted with him first.

"What's your location?"

"Still looking at the bastard."

Douglas had to make a decision. Should he order her to the lab without her gear, which would save time but was dangerous, or should he send her back to the hideout to change into night camo and retrieve her weapons?

Slowly, he squatted down to look more closely at the engine block. Something about it held his interest. He raised his left arm wiped the sweat from his forehead with the back of his hand. One side of the engine was completely assembled, but the other side exposed the interior of three cylinders, and the head was lying next to it.

"Farland, do you copy?" Ludvika sounded a bit impatient. "If I have to look at this scum much longer, I will strangle him with my bare hands."

"Put a lid on it, Bogdan, and give me a minute," he drawled. He knew Ludvika was relatively safe with Shurnik unconscious next to her. She just had to sit tight for a few while he figured out the next step.

His attention hadn't left the exposed cylinders. The pistons were gone. He fished his small but powerful flashlight out of his belt. As he shone a bright light down into one of the open cylinders, he could see it. A cellophane-wrapped brown paper package the size of a small coffee can.

Bingo! That had to be it.

Douglas looked into the first cylinder and saw the very same thing. The third one, however, was empty. The piston was missing, but no package. The other side of the engine block had the cylinder head attached to it. The million dollar question was, were there more drugs on the other side, or not? And where was the package the third cylinder was prepared to conceal?

He rose to his feet and felt an immediate, painful thump in his head. He had been exposed to the drug-infested air for almost forty-five minutes. He needed to get the hell out of there before he risked any serious damage. He tried to decide what to do about his findings. The engine block would have to be moved by at least three people, and he did not want to just collect the two packages of meth and leave the rest of the drugs here—if there was indeed more hidden in the other cylinders.

He needed to brief the Acronym and ask how to proceed. He decided to meet Ludvika back at his hideout and call Brian in Maryland as soon as possible.

"Bogdan, you copy?"

"Go ahead."

"You're gonna have to kiss your new boyfriend goodnight for now and meet me back at the hideout. I've got some terrific news."

"Rodger that, asshole." Clearly she didn't like him making fun of the Shurnik situation.

Douglas held his weapon ready as he carefully climbed the stairs back up. He noticed the small TV screen showing the empty garage and its immediate surroundings.

There must be an infrared camera outside somewhere that he had not noticed before. He wondered if he had been watched by someone when he'd scouted out the garage in the past.

Nothing he could do about it now.

He watched the screen for a minute, and when nothing came into view, he opened the hatch and climbed quickly out. After closing the hatch and the trapdoor, he replaced the heavy padlock. He looked it over, but it didn't show even a scratch from his earlier tampering.

Within minutes he'd made his way back to the hideout. He was glad it hadn't rained or snowed lately. He wouldn't have to worry about leaving fresh tracks in the dirt.

Ludvika had already arrived and was changing back into her camo. He caught her literally with her pants down as she stepped into her field boots. He was not afraid to take a look at those long, athletic legs. He retrieved his flashlight again and pointed down to her boots. Ludvika almost lost her balance. "Turn the damn light out. You are going to get us caught."

"Need a hand there, Darling?" he teased. He wasn't sure how she was feeling after her encounter with Shurnik and wanted to keep the mood light.

She ignored his question and asked about his discovery. Douglas briefly explained the engine block and the two packages of what were probably the drugs.

"What about the third package? Do you think there is more?"

Douglas nodded. "I believe so."

After she finished changing she rose up to almost his height, looked at Douglas in the dark, and asked, "Do you remember my favorite movie?" He could barely see her face, but the white of her teeth was bright as she smiled.

Douglas was well aware of Ludvika's love for American movies. He thought the question was odd at this moment, but he did her the favor of thinking back on the few flicks they had watched together in the past. After a minute he remembered that she had kept talking about one film in particular. They'd seen it in a movie theater some where in Germany.

Douglas nodded. "Yes, I remember. It was the flick with that pretty red head. What's her name? Something Roberts. It was called *Sleeping with the Enemy*, right?" And as he said the name, the meaning of her question became clear to him.

Ludvika nodded, proving her mind was definitely cracked as she said, grinning, "My task tonight gives that phrase a whole new perspective."

Chapter 37

MIA STARED AT HER little, white chess pieces. Her bishops kept disappearing, and her king was in mortal danger. Helena smiled. Mia knew that the Russians had been leaders in the world of chess forever, and now she knew why.

She had been playing the game since she was a teenager. Her grandfather had taught her, and she had tried to beat him until the day he died. Once in a while he had let her win, to keep her spirits up, but most of the time she had been defeated. A "brain sport" is what he had called the game, and Mia had loved the challenge—still did.

She had taken care of her phone calls that morning. The status of her and Douglas' departure had not changed. They would have to sit tight until Dr. Yeltsin gave them the green light.

Earlier today she had told Shurnik she had no reason to phone Yukoil, but she had decided that a short conference wouldn't hurt. To Mia's surprise they had asked her to attend a meeting the following afternoon. Mia really wasn't looking forward to another drive to Irkutsk. She had hoped the next time she had to sit through the god-awful trip it would be final one out of here. But a meeting on Friday would make sense, and maybe her prayers would be answered.

It all boiled down to the soil samples, and if they showed no sign of contaminants, she and Douglas could leave by the weekend without having to wait for a meeting to finalize things with Yukoil on Monday.

Mia had summarized her work, spending most of the afternoon in her barracks. She had been able to sleep for a while, and when she was awake her thoughts had kept circling back to her situation with Douglas.

She had received a note on her mobile manager from Zulanda back home about Blue's recovery. God, it had only been ten days since the incident at Uncle Phil's barn. It seemed like half a century ago.

Zulu had written that Blue Eyes was doing well, and that Uncle Phil would have him spoiled rotten by the time Mia returned. Mia had felt lonely thinking about her dear friends at home, and she missed cuddling Blue. By the time the sun had gone down, she had become restless. Wrapped in an extra layer of clothes, she had strolled through the camp without a particular destination in mind.

The snow storm she had thought would come had not. Just a few flakes had danced in the crystal-clear sky. It was still cold, but even Montana could not compete with the freshness of the air. The sun had set quickly and within minutes she had found herself wandering around in the dark. The strong wind from the days before had died down to just a faint breeze. That kept it from being uncomfortable, and her cheeks had turned rosy.

Somehow she had ended up at Petronovich's trailer. Mia felt guilty for not calling the hospital to inquire about the status of his health.

Light had shone through the windows, and Mia had wondered what Douglas was doing. She had felt tempted to knock on his door, but didn't want to seem desperate. There was no business talk for them to discuss, and tomorrow's meeting had not seemed like enough reason to disturb him.

She thought about how tired he had looked that morning and how intense the assignment had been so far. She had napped that afternoon, and he deserved some quiet time, too. So she had walked back to the mess hall and helped Helena prepare dinner. She had declined Mia's help, but Mia had insisted. In the process she had picked up on some of Helena's secrets with the wonderful, Russian herbs she used. And now that the crew had had their supper, Mia was getting crucified on the checkered board.

"Check," Helena said in Russian and smiled as Mia tried to save her king before she lost the hopeless game.

Just then Shurnik approached them, and after a quick exchange of looks, Helena stood and disappeared into the kitchen.

He sat down across from Mia with a serious looks on his face. "Ms. Trentino, I will have to leave for several days. I am needed to accompany a truckload of equipment to Vladivostok."

Mia looked at him, surprised. "When—now? What about the final stages of this project?"

"My departure is planned for Sunday. I have to anticipate a positive conclusion from Dr. Yeltsin," he said.

Mia didn't know if it mattered, but asked, "What if the test shows contamination?"

Shurnik leaned back in his chair and removed his hat. He placed it on the table in front of him and said, "I will instruct my crew for that circumstance. And I am sure you and Mr. Farland can proceed with my absence."

Mia thought about it. "Yes, I am sure we know what to do. And if the tests are negative?"

"In that case, you and Mr. Farland will be able to leave as soon as you wish. Either way, I am certain that you will be gone by the time I return from Vladivostok. But I am sure we will have our proper goodbye." He smiled at her with the old-school gentleman's smile Mia liked.

He leaned forward and looked her in the eyes. "Ms. Trentino, please forgive me for being direct, but I must compliment your positive attitude toward our plans. Many of my countrymen and women will benefit from your hard work. I sincerely hope you will return sometime and witness what you have helped to plan for on paper."

Mia was touched. She'd had no idea he had such kindness hidden beneath all those rough layers. She did not now what to say. Shurnik got up and took his hat. He straightened his jacket, and before Mia could thank him, he walked out of the hall.

Shurnik needed to check on the status of his shipment and

headed toward the garage. The mechanic had been preparing the engine and his men had stored it in the lab.

"We will be ready to move out within twenty-four hours?" he asked when he arrived.

The mechanic assured Shurnik that they would. Nodding his approval, Shurnik left the garage to make is way back to his private quarters.

Earlier today Lagunov had told Shurnik that the Americans would leave the camp tomorrow to attend a meeting with Yukoil. Shurnik had mentioned to the woman about his travel plans to Vladivostok in the unlikely event of a positive test result, which would force the Americans to stay in the camp for several more days. Shurnik's reason for his departure was legitimate—he would be on his way to the new promised land: China.

The lab had been extremely efficient. They had manufactured the equivalent of over two million U.S. Dollars, street value, and the distribution was predicted to go safely and smoothly. The trek would leave very early Saturday morning. Lagunov had arranged for a meeting at Yukoil on Friday to make sure the Americans stayed in Irkutsk for the night.

He had told the woman he was leaving Sunday, and she would tell the other American about his travel plans. Shurnik had not found anything suspicious when observing the American over the surveillance system, but he still wanted to make sure he wouldn't be in the camp during the departure.

During their conversation today, Lagunov had pressed a vital issue upon Shurnik. If the transfer and circulation of the drugs went smoothly, the lab would continue its production, and that meant job security for Shurnik. New chemists had been already recruited and were on standby, waiting for his return. As long as the mobsters in St. Petersburg were satisfied, they would continue to give Shurnik free rein over future projects.

He was sitting in his office, anticipating a very prosperous week, when he heard a noise. He tensed, having just allowed himself to relax and enjoy a shot of his fine vodka. Somebody had come into his quarters unannounced.

Shurnik looked up. He was not the kind of man who was easily baffled, but when the beautiful Dr. Yeltsin entered his room, he was very surprised.

Chapter 38

Douglas checked his Breitling. It was seven o'clock, almost time to meet Mia for breakfast.

He popped an aspirin and stretched his back. His head was feeling the aftereffects of his exposure to the lab last night. Not too bad, though. He smiled, thinking about Shurnik. He would be in much worse shape this morning.

Douglas had been able to rest for several hours after he and Ludvika had split. She had taken her truck to a safe area to spend the night observing the camp. Douglas had provided her with his gear for a cold night's stakeout. Ludvika would need to make it look believable that she had left the camp last night after her little rendezvous with Shurnik. Douglas would notify her when the timing was right to return.

The tension of last night's task had drained out of him. He felt good but was worried about Mia. He had not seen her since lunch yesterday, and she was probably wondering why. Still, Douglas was optimistic about keeping her in the dark about the mission for a little while longer.

He had briefed Brian at the Acronym about his findings.

"We will need you to tail them," Brian had told him over the phone. "Our intelligence in China predicts Shurnik will arrive soon, but we can't rely on him not to change plans in-between Siberia and China. You and agent Bogdan are gonna have to follow."

"Tail them over a thousand miles through the fucking Gobi desert? You've got to be joking," Douglas had said.

"No, Doug, I'm not. You're gonna have to figure out how to pursue." Brian had been quick to change the subject and asked, "What about Lagunov?"

"What about him?" Douglas had asked, knowing he needed to gather evidence against him.

"Doug, you know we have absolutely nothing on the guy. If we want to make this a big catch, we need to lure in the big fish."

Douglas had been reluctant to address that subject. He did not want to leave the camp, but he was certain that there was no way around it. "Yeah, I know. There should be a meeting coming up with Yukoil very soon, hopefully before Shurnik moves. I should have my chance with Lagunov then. Bogdan will keep her eye on Shurnik while I do that."

Douglas had not mentioned what Ludvika had done last night. He would try his best to keep that between them. It had been a big aid for the op, but it was definitely not a chapter one would find in any agency's handbook on proper proceedings.

The two men had discussed Mia's involvement. Brian had voted to brief her right away. Douglas had been very emphatic with his reply. "No! Absolutely not! When she's done here, I'm going to make sure her cute ass is on a plane back to the States without ever having to know about this mess. I will come up with a story for why I'm staying behind. Maybe I'll tell her I'm quitting so I can go and live a free life with the nomads."

Brian had laughed. "Oh sure, that'll work. So tell me, how come you're so protective of her? You're not getting yourself involved, are you?"

Douglas had thought about Brian looking at Mia as possible collateral damage. Civilian casualties were not unusual in an operation like this, especially people being used as a cover. Douglas himself had been guilty in the past of endangering people who had nothing to do with the mission. It had happened before and it would happen again, but not with Mia!

Of course he could not explain to him why. Douglas was not supposed to get involved in any kind of scenario that could compromise the op. Too late for that. He already was involved, but he was going to do everything in his power to stay ahead of the problem. The success of the mission was still Douglas' number one priority. Mia's wellbeing just stood very close behind it.

Brian had offered an idea. "Just tell her you and Bogdan are FBI and that it's under control. Thank her and give her some speech about being an outstanding citizen and that she's done a big favor for her country, or whatever, and send her on her way. She'll be glad to get the hell out of there."

Douglas had agreed with Brian to keep him happy, but he knew better. He was afraid he could not shake Mia loose that easy. If he decided to tell her the truth, he'd do it right before they were to board a plane back to the States. There was much less risk to her life that way rather than involving her now. There was always the possibility of the Red Mafiya reaching her after the op was a success, the drug ring was destroyed, and Lagunov and the rest of the mobsters were, hopefully, arrested.

The risk was small. But it did exist.

Douglas had used the washroom early this morning, before anyone else was around. Usually Shurnik was one of the few men up before six a.m. Not today, though. Douglas had gone by Shurnik's yurt to see if there was any movement. There wasn't. The guy must still be out like a light, Douglas had thought.

As Douglas stepped out of the trailer he saw Mia approaching him in the distance. She did not look like she was planning on a day out on the oil field. She was dressed warmly but chic in a dark blue pantsuit and her black wool coat. It was smartly tailored and reached down to mid calf. Her hair was neatly twisted into a knot, and as she got closer to Douglas he saw that she had applied a touch of makeup.

They met halfway between the main camp and the trailer. He walked up to her, smiling. "Hey, stranger, you look like you're going to town," he said, hoping he could avoid her questions on where he had been yesterday afternoon.

"I am," she said, "and so are you. But first I had to see if you were taking today off, too."

"I'm going to town? Why and when?" Douglas looked down at her beautiful face, enjoying her scent and hating his job—at least for the moment.

Mia smiled back. She felt good today, having the end of the assignment in sight.

The collar of Douglas' gray, fleece shirt stood up on one side. Mia raised her hand to smooth it over. He wanted to take her in his arms, but didn't.

"We've been asked to meet with the board this afternoon, and I was hoping we could stop at the hotel for a fresh change of clothes."

So the meeting had come earlier than what he had hoped for. He would be able to investigate Lagunov within the next twelve hours. This was very good news.

Douglas' mind began immediately to work on a plan. "What time are we leaving?"

She looked at him dubiously. "What, no complaints about having to go back to a suit and a tie?" Then she considered. "I guess we need to wait until Dr. Yeltsin returns from Irkutsk with her analysis. With any luck we can hold our final meeting today and finish up here tomorrow, which means we could go home on Sunday." She thought for a minute and added, "That is, if I can get a hold of Simon over the weekend to find us some plane tickets."

Douglas saw the excitement in her face at the mention of leaving. His heart clenched knowing he wouldn't be able to be with her.

He might not see her again after tomorrow, but he would be glad when she was safely back in the U.S. Maybe one day he would have the chance to explain.

As they walked together toward the mess hall, Mia wanted to lean into him. She could feel his warmth just being next to him. She kept her distance, but at the thought of his touch she sighed and asked, "Tell me what you did yesterday. I missed you at dinner."

Douglas had to suppress a grin. He'd been waiting for her curiosity to get the best of her.

"I slept all afternoon. By the time I woke up it was beyond dinner time. I'm ready for a big breakfast now."

Vodka and women, Shurnik thought. That was the reason for the way he felt this morning. He never took any kind of medication, didn't believe in it. But today he wished there was something that could help his throbbing head.

He stood in the shower and let the hot stream of water massage the acing muscles of his neck and shoulders. He looked down his hard body. He was in great shape and knew how to deal with pain. Pain made him feel alive, but today he felt ill.

It must have been a combination of the Vodka and what that woman had done to him. But had it been worth it. He had not been with a woman since he had lived in St. Petersburg. Even then Shurnik had not been a man who was very much involved with women. They made men lose their focus, he believed. He had watched ruthless members of the Mafia, who dealt with cold-blooded, hard business, turn into complete idiots when surrounded by women.

In his mind the main purpose of females was to confuse and mislead a warrior like himself. Therefore, he had suppressed his feeling of need for them. Last night he had been caught off guard and let her take charge. Evaluating the situation today he had to grin. Besides his tired body, there should not be any damage as a result. He would recover quickly and focus on his work.

Sitting in the crowded mess hall, Mia looked at Douglas. They had finished breakfast, and Mia wondered where Shurnik might be. He usually had his meal long before the crew gathered here.

Dr. Yeltsin would be arriving at any time to share her test results. Mia was a bit nervous about it, but did not say anything.

"You either stop that," Douglas said leaning toward her, "or you're taking the chance of me stopping you in front of all these workers."

Mia raised her eyebrows in bewilderment. "Stop what?" But when she saw Douglas staring at her mouth, she realized she was gnawing on her lower lip again. His blue eyes sparkled dangerously, and her heart missed a beat.

She remembered what had happened the last time he had pointed out that habit and blushed. "Oh, sorry." Trying to be all business she said, "I wonder where Shurnik is this morning. I'd like to get to Irkutsk as soon as possible."

Douglas would have loved to share with Mia what had happened to Shurnik last night, and why he needed a little extra time this morning. She would have been embarrassed, but probably would have giggled, and he liked it when she laughed. But of course he couldn't.

Instead he said, "Who knows? But I think I'll run down to the trailer and change into my beloved suit so we can take off as soon as we meet with Shurnik and the doctor."

Mia nodded. She was glad Douglas was being considerate about her wish to leave. Suddenly, the memory of what Shurnik had told her yesterday went like a hot jolt through her mind.

"Douglas," Mia paused. He had gotten up and was walking toward the exit. He turned his head as he heard Mia calling his name.

She continued. "I forgot to tell you. Shurnik mentioned yesterday that he is going to leave on Sunday. He said something about taking equipment to Vladivostok."

Douglas walked back to her. Dammit, you're telling me now? his mind screamed, but he kept his composure. He placed his hands on top of the backrest of a chair and looked at Mia.

"On Sunday? That shouldn't interfere with our plans, should it?"

Mia shrugged. "I don't think so. If the tests are positive, and we have to stay longer, we'd be working without him." She paused to pull a face. "But I'm sure we could manage."

Douglas checked his watch again. Almost eight o'clock. He had to get a hold of Ludvika immediately.

"Let me go change, I'll be right back." *You're gonna get me into trouble, sweet Mia,* he added silently as he walked out the hall.

The weather had changed once again for the worse. Black clouds were darkening the sky. It was not yet windy, but a storm was brewing and it looked like snow.

Douglas had hidden his radio equipment outside the trailer. He had positioned it on the south side so he couldn't be seen by either the cameras inside the trailer or from someone approaching from the camp. The wireless receiver had a range of several feet. He had slept with his earpiece in case Ludvika had needed him, but the night had been quiet.

Douglas hoped he was not being watched as he walked around the trailer to retrieve his radio. He could see the helicopter pad from here, and Charlie was sitting on it with his rotor blades tied with long ropes to the ground.

After Douglas had returned from his observation last night, he had checked the trailer once again for bugs. Someone had indeed planted audio devices since he had found the cameras. It was Shurnik, Douglas was sure. He wondered when he could have done it. Actually, the more he thought about Shurnik's assets, the more he thought it was a shame that a man as effective as him had to be on the opposite side of the game. As an enemy, Shurnik was very dangerous and needed to be eliminated.

The radio's battery was low from being on standby overnight. Douglas had been afraid that this would happen, but he had not wanted to risk Ludvika not being able to reach him. Brian had sent a charger with the equipment but no extra batteries. How big a difference one little mistake could make.

Douglas had not been able to recharge, and he knew Ludvika's batteries would be low as well. He had to make this quick.

"Bogdan, you copy?" He whispered.

"Copy. I'm low on juice."

"I know. Listen, Shurnik is due to leave on Sunday. He told Mia. I'm sure it's a lie, but we have to—"

That was all the transmission Ludvika understood before her radio died. She cursed. She was on her stomach, lying under a brush, observing the camp approximately half a mile out. She lowered her binoculars and crawled back ward. She had not spotted Shurnik this morning, but it was time for her to change clothes and return to the camp as Dr. Yeltsin.

She thought about what Farland had just told her. Shurnik had announced his departure on Sunday. That could mean a lot of different things.

This morning, she had waited for Farland to give her orders on how to proceed today. If she wasn't able to see him alone before she met Shurnik, she was on her own. She wondered if heading to Douglas' hideout would be a good idea—he might be waiting for her there. She thought it over and decided against it. It was too risky to do it in daylight.

Yesterday Douglas had mentioned they needed more than twenty-four hours, because he had not been able to find the drugs on his own. But that had changed, and now she didn't know what else Farland had found out this morning.

She would have to go with her instincts.

Leaning against the truck, she slipped out of her night camo. The wind was getting stronger, and the temperature had not increased since the middle of the night.

Ludvika thought about Shurnik and how much she yearned for hot water to wash off the feeling he had left on her body. She was not sure if her goose bumps were due to the cold weather or last night's revolting task.

After she had braided her long hair accurately, she concealed the tired circles under her eyes with makeup. She climbed into the truck and checked her image in the rearview mirror. She did not look like she had spent the night in the open, doing what she did best. There was no doubt in her mind that Shurnik would believe that she had driven back to Irkutsk last night.

Ludvika approached the camp half an hour later.

Mia could not wait for her analysis. She had been standing outside the mess hall when Douglas returned from changing his clothes.

"You gonna catch a cold out here," he told her. He wanted her to return to the dining room so he could have a quick word with Ludvika, but no such luck. And now that Shurnik had joined them, his chances of giving his orders to Ludvika had all but disappeared.

Douglas glanced at Shurnik. He did not look too bad, maybe a little tired. There was no suspicion written on his face.

As Mia greeted Shurnik, Douglas ignored him as usual and looked toward the approaching vehicle.

"Looks like we're all a little excited about the test results." Mia pointed out the obvious.

Neither of the men said anything. Douglas stood with a cool demeanor, but his mind raced. He had to come up with an idea on how to slip Bogdan the order and he had to do it fast.

As Dr. Yeltsin arrived, Mia walked over to the truck.

"Good morning, Dr. Yeltsin. Can I help with any of your equipment?"

Dr. Yeltsin declined thankfully. She gathered a thin file and went toward the men to greet them. Douglas searched for her eyes, but she looked at Shurnik and casually nodded a good morning in Russian. She looked calm and confident. Douglas could not find anything vulnerable in her body language that could give away her cover. She was a pro, there was no doubt.

Douglas stood behind Mia and Shurnik was facing Ludvika. When their eyes finally met, Douglas shook his head almost unnoticeably. That was all the signal Ludvika needed.

In Russian Shurnik asked her for the test results and Ludvika said, "I am sorry to have to report to you that the test results are inconclusive."

Chapter 39

SNOW BEGAN TO FALL in light, feathery swirls.

Mia looked at Douglas incredulously. "So?" he asked.

Right, Mia thought. She had to translate. "Inconclusive," she repeated.

Douglas raised his eyebrows in wonder. "What does that mean?" he asked. Mia did not have an answer. Even if she'd had one, she wouldn't have been able to speak. She was disappointed and didn't want to betray it in her voice.

Shurnik's face was expressionless. He just nodded and asked everyone to step into the mess hall to discuss things. When motioning Ludvika to walk ahead of him, Douglas gave her a look of approval. They gathered around a table and Shurnik asked her to explain.

"I received mixed results," she began. "I could not measure the level of contamination of the soil properly. Therefore the environmental office of Irkutsk will not yet issue a permit for the continuance of Yukoil's project."

"Did the laboratory in Irkutsk have enough time?" Shurnik suspected she had screwed up the test because of their agenda last night. Dr. Yeltsin shook her head.

She responded calmly and looked him straight in the eyes. "Mr. Shurnik, as I explained before, the samples never had to leave my case. I took them with me to the city when I left yesterday, but there was no lab work necessary." She reached for her file, placed it in front of Shurnik and continued. "I worked on the evaluation early this morning. Please see for yourself. You will easily understand the process."

Hell of a bluff, you've got him by the balls, Douglas thought. She had pushed Shurnik into the defensive by offering him the chance to review her analysis. Shurnik would have no clue what all the chemical formulas meant and so would have to decline looking at them. It made her look very believable.

Douglas looked at her in astonished awe. Then he remembered that he was not supposed to understand the language. His look went to Mia, who had not said anything yet.

Instead of explaining to Douglas what she just heard, Mia asked, "Dr. Yeltsin, does that mean we will have to retest the existing samples, or do we need to collect new ones?"

Ludvika evaluated the question quickly and answered the way it made most sense to her. "I will have to collect a new batch of soil samples and will increase the percentage of the chemical solution. I should have clearer results for you by tomorrow morning."

That was it, short and simple. Mia sank into herself. She and Douglas would have to wait an additional day until the results would be clear. She would not go home on Sunday. Dr. Yeltsin had mentioned a "level of contamination." Did that mean the soil was definitely poisoned? How bad was it? Staring at Dr. Yeltsin, the thoughts raced through her head.

"Ms. Trentino?" Shurnik said, a bit impatient. Mia had not heard what he'd just said. She looked at him apologetically. "I'm sorry, excuse me. Please repeat your question."

Every muscle in Douglas' body tensed. He wanted to snap Shurnik's neck for glaring at Mia like that. He forced himself to stay cool.

Shurnik asked again, "Are you still planning on leaving to meet with Yukoil today? Or will you stay for the tests?"

Mia looked at Douglas. She was going to translate Shurnik's question to him, but changed her mind. She needed to be in charge and make the decision.

"We will go ahead with our meeting in Irkutsk. There will be another conference necessary depending the outcome of the tests, but they are expecting us this afternoon," Mia explained. She had already pushed today's meeting as far along as she could.

Shurnik's attention went to Ludvika. "Dr. Yeltsin, will you be needing assistance?"

"No, I know my way around, thank you."

"Very well. Will you be able to provide us with your test results by this evening?" Shurnik asked her. As much as he'd enjoyed her last night, he needed to get her the hell out of there.

Ludvika checked her watch. "Possibly, but it would be very late. After eleven at least."

She did not dare to look at Douglas for a sign. Her focus stayed with Shurnik. He got up and said to Ludvika, "If it is not too much to ask, I would appreciate the results as soon as they are available."

"Of course."

Douglas watched Shurnik closely. He wondered where the Russian was going with this.

Still standing, Shurnik turned his attention back to Mia. "Ms. Trentino, if the test results are available to us by this evening, I suggest you stay in Irkutsk overnight so you can meet again with Yukoil in the morning. I will contact you and Mr. Lagunov later this evening to report to you."

Suddenly it was clear to Douglas. To his dismay Mia nodded in agreement. "Maybe we will have to do that. I will keep in touch."

Shurnik walked off and Mia explained to Douglas what had just happened. He was not even listening. He tried to figure out how he could keep in contact with Ludvika today.

It was close to ten thirty when they adjourned their meeting. Mia checked her Dior. "Are we ready to leave soon?"

He nodded. "Any time. Did you get what you need out of the trailer?"

"No, I have to run down and get my computer and the files. Are we driving ourselves?"

Douglas saw his chance. "Yes. Why don't you walk down to the trailer? I will get the truck and pick you up."

"Do you think it's okay for us to take it?" Mia asked. "Sure," Douglas said. "They've let me use it all week. Unless you asked Shurnik to call the cab to come and get us?"

She looked guiltily at Douglas. "I forgot. I'm sorry." He smiled at her and wished she would quit apologizing for everything.

"I'll be right down," he said and headed toward the men's washroom.

Just a minute after Douglas had gone into the barracks, Ludvika whistled quietly from outside. She had watched Shurnik leave in his truck, so it would be safe for a quick briefing.

Douglas stuck his head around the corner. "Get in here, Bogdan," he said in a low voice. He retrieved his cell phone out of his pocket and gave it to her. "Here, I will contact you from a landline every so often. Keep it on vibrate and don't answer when anyone's around." It went without saying, but it didn't hurt to be explicit.

"What do the test results have to be?" Ludvika asked.

"I don't know yet," Douglas answered. "But I will let you know as soon as I figure it out."

"Will you be staying the night?"

"No, the drugs will be moved tomorrow, I'm sure of it." When he saw Ludvika's questioning expression, he explained. "He told Mia he had to go to Vladivostok on Sunday. Of course he was lying, to mislead us. I don't know if he suspects anything, but we have to assume he does. So be extremely careful."

Ludvika nodded, stepped to the exit, and scanned the area. It was secure.

Douglas went on. "The Acronym ordered us to tail them into China. How's your Chinese?"

Ludvika's eyes went wide. "Are you kidding me? It's just the two of us. How about some backup?"

"I asked the same thing." Douglas stopped. He did not have time to explain his conversation with Brian to her. "Depending on my opportunity to search Lagunov's office, you will have to delay Shurnik from moving out."

Ludvika thought for a second. "How? He will leave regardless of what the test results are, won't he?"

"Yes, you would have to sabotage one of his vehicles." He hesitated. "There is one more thing."

"Lay it on me."

Douglas hoped it wouldn't come to this. "I will leave most of my gear here. There is a second GPS in the small compartment of the duffel bag. Take it. It will let me know where you are so I can find you—in case you have to proceed without me."

"Oh, sure," Ludvika replied snottily—she was getting apprehensive about the mission. "And what will you be doing? Honeymooning with Trentino?"

Her bright blue eyes glared at Douglas. He saw fear in them. Bogdan was a fine agent, but if she had to chase after Shurnik on her own, she might be in a bit over her head. He also detected jealousy. He couldn't permit her emotions getting in the way. An emotional agent was a dead one.

He didn't have time to argue. It would be the easiest to just order her out, but instead he ignored her zealous comment, nodded his head, and said, "I'm putting my confidence in you, Bogdan. I know you can handle it."

Chapter 40

Douglas stopped the truck and got out to give Mia a hand in the trailer. He had thought about his conversation with Brian. Maybe he should just tell her the truth and get her out of there.

Dammit, he couldn't. Worldmove's innocent involvement was his perfect cover. And as much as he wanted Mia protected and someplace safe, he had to keep using her.

On top of that, it would be just another lie. He'd have to tell her he was with the feds. The Acronym had to stay, under all circumstances, anonymous—especially to the civilian population.

Douglas opened the door and startled Mia. "What is it with you?" he asked her. "How come you scare so easily?"

Mia bent down to pick up the pages she just dropped. "I don't know, I just do," she said without looking at him. He didn't believe her but let it go.

Watching her, he picked up her case with her laptop inside. "Is that everything?"

"Yes, thank you," she replied and headed toward the door.

He opened it for her and let her step out in front of him. Being that close, he could feel her tension. Wondering what she was worried about, he stepped into the truck and started the engine.

Neither one of them said much during the first half hour of the drive. It was still snowing. Nothing too serious, but the storm could intensify. Douglas wasn't worried about it. He was an excellent driver, and with this four-wheel-drive truck, he could conquer pretty much any terrain.

The road was rough, and a few times Mia grabbed the handle above her head. But mostly she sat there fidgeting, with one leg crossed over the other and her hands folded on her knee. The tip of her foot tapped the glove compartment in front of her continuously.

A few times Douglas caught her watching him. At first he thought the weather was making her a bit nervous. Then he remembered that she lived in Montana—snow should not concern her. Suddenly he considered the possibility that Mia might be starting to figure him out. The last few days had not been easy for Douglas, but he wanted to believe that Mia hadn't noticed any of his unusual tasks. Eventually, he'd had enough of mystery. "Why don't you tell me what's on your mind?"

She looked out of her window and watched a couple of native Yakutian cattle in the distance. Douglas didn't try and pressure an answer. He knew she was too polite to ignore him.

Eventually she said, "I don't know if I can."

That was not what he wanted to hear. His eyes narrowed and his mind went on overdrive. He wanted to know if she'd insinuated anything about his real job, but didn't want to say anything leading in case he confirmed any suspicions.

Carefully he said, "Why don't you try?"

But instead of doing so, she asked, "Are we staying in Irkutsk tonight?"

He was lost. Why would she ask him? She called the shots on decisions like that. "I don't know, you tell me." Douglas was getting nervous. Gripping the steering wheel harder, he waited for her to pop out some knowledge about Lagunov. He could feel how she was battling with herself. Something serious was going on.

Douglas had a hard time trying to stay composed. He felt like putting his hand on her fidgety leg and squeezing it until she told him what the hell was going on.

Mia sighed. It took courage just to turn her head to look at him. This was hard for her, but she had to ask. "Are you planning on sleeping with me?"

What? Douglas couldn't believe it. She was thinking about sex? She had to be kidding! For a second he drove silently in astonishment. Then a huge wave of relief crashed through him. He realized how bizarre and comical the situation was and almost lost it. But he kept up his guard, and instead of laughing about his foolishness, he looked over to Mia.

Her dark eyes were troubled. She was deliciously beautiful in a shy and innocent way. Douglas knew what to do to get rid of her tension. With a playful and sexy undertone in his voice he drawled, "Why, are you offering, Baby?"

Mia smiled and her eyes went back out the window. She was not sure if she was offering. Maybe. Probably not. Right—who was she fooling?

Of course the thought of their sharing the sheets had crossed Douglas' mind in the past, but today he had been too preoccupied with the task at hand to consider it. He glanced over her body; she was still jittery. Douglas felt a heat rising deep inside. It was more than just sexual excitement.

Damn. It sure didn't take much for her to get under his skin. He wanted to ask her if the thought made her nervous, but his throat felt tight, and he was afraid his voice would come out froggy croak. He had to tell himself several times to relax. After a while Douglas finally felt able to speak normally. He picked up the conversation again. He wanted her to feel comfortable and thought small talk would help her anxiety.

It worked. Mia knew what Douglas was doing, and she was thankful for the attempt to calm her down. She had no idea why she was so insecure. Usually she was quite confident around men. But then, there certainly weren't many men like Douglas around.

Their conversation turned from the job to more personal things. Mia didn't mind Douglas asking her about her family. She told him about her little nephew back east and how wonderful life in Montana was. Douglas offered some of his own history but kept it rather short and let Mia talk.

When they got closer to the Irkutsk city limits, Mia checked her watch. "We have an hour until our meeting is scheduled and I'm starving. How about something to eat?"

"You got it. What about the restaurant in our hotel? Would that work for you?"

Mia remembered the meal she had enjoyed there when they had first arrived in Irkutsk. "Absolutely. I hope they serve late lunch." She was glad to be back in civilization.

Douglas parked the truck in front of the Baikal Hotel. Mia stepped out and leaned into the backseat to collect her coat. He walked around and took it from her. She stood still as he draped it around her shoulders, trying to shelter her from the snow. Mia straightened her back and took a deep breath.

Walking across the parking lot, Mia's nervousness from earlier was gone. She felt relaxed being with Douglas and looked forward to the meeting at Yukoil.

They took the side entrance of the hotel so they did not have to walk through the front lobby. Mia felt like it had been a long time since she had been here. She thought about it. Five days was all. She had come to town with Helena the day after Petronovich had had his accident.

She turned to Douglas. "It seems to me like it's been an eternity since I've been here. Do you feel the same?" "No, but I haven't been as unhappy as you, either."

Mia raised her eyebrows and looked up to him. "Unhappy? What do you mean?"

Douglas slipped his arm around her as they walked down the carpeted hallway toward the restaurant. He gently pulled her toward him and brushed a soft kiss on top of her head.

"I know it must have been hard for you out there in the oil field. It's not really a woman's place." Mia got a little offended but allowed his arm to stay where it was.

"I think I managed quite well," she defended.

Douglas let got of her to pull open the door and to let her step inside. "I didn't say you did not manage well. I said it's not a place for a sweet thing like you to have to hang out in for a week."

She thought about that and realized he was just being protective. She liked that. "You're right. I loved the assignment but the conditions were the shits."

Douglas laughed. He had not heard her curse before and was glad that she did.

There were no other guests in the restaurant at this unusually late lunch hour. As they took a table by the window Douglas told her, "You are pretty brave, talking about the job in past tense. Depending on the test results, it ain't over."

Douglas indulged in a Russian classic, beef Stroganoff. They served it with crepes instead of the usual pasta, the way he knew it from the States. It smelled marvelous, but it would have been too rich for Mia. She stole a piece of the tender sirloin off his plate and let it melt in her mouth. It was fantastic.

She'd ordered something lighter—a vegetarian layer stew, a favorite lunch dish from Uzbek, and a small salad.

"Soup?" Douglas teased her. "You're having soup? No wonder you're so skinny. You ought to have a healthy portion of this stuff." He chewed, smiled, and chewed some more. This man could eat.

Mia was almost in the mood for a glass of wine but, of course, couldn't. There was still work to do. She watched in amazement as Douglas cleaned his plate within minutes.

"You're appetite is admirable." Douglas leaned back and took a breath "Oh yeah? What do you say, should we go and amaze the Russians some more with another mind-blowing meeting?"

He was cocky. In the past it had annoyed her, but now Mia could smile about it. She checked the time. "We're still early. What's your hurry?"

"I want to come back here as soon as possible."

Mia wondered why—he couldn't seriously still be hungry. "What for? Ah, you are thinking about desert, aren't you?" Mia smiled, teasing.

Douglas folded his hands and leaned forward with his forearms on the edge of the table. His expression changed momentarily. The way he captured her eyes took her breath away. Once again all those butterflies in Mia's stomach were released.

Douglas deep voice unraveled Mia's nerves as he said, "No, not food. But you mentioned my appetite. And since I'm such an obedient guy, I want to satisfy your curiosity about it."

Chapter 41

Lagunov sat in his office. So far, so good, he thought. Shurnik had not mentioned any problems with the process. The drugs should be moved within the next twenty-four hours. That would get Selkin off his back.

He thought about the man he was counting on. Sergei Selkin had told him about Shurnik's past—how he had lived the lavish lifestyle of a successful member of the Russian Mafia. And that Shurnik had turned down several offers to return to St. Petersburg and live a good, profitable life. He preferred Yukoil's cover to work independently in the rough climate of the southeastern Siberian Taiga.

Shurnik was an odd duck Lagunov had decided when he met him once. He had been glad not to have to interact with him on a personal basis. Lagunov very much enjoyed the lifestyle he afforded and did not understand anyone who didn't care for the finer things in life.

He drove an imported Mercedes—there was nothing that could beat the performance of a German luxury car. His two-story home sat in a wooded area outside of Irkutsk and consisted of three bedrooms and two baths. His much-younger wife enjoyed cooking so he had gotten his hands on several American-made appliances for her modern kitchen. His boys were taken care of by a European nanny, and a home-teaching program provided them with the kind of education the Russian school system could not.

Why would anyone turn this kind of life down to dig an oil well and run a meth lab?

His phone rang; it was Shurnik. Speak of the Devil, Lagunov thought.

"We are ready to depart as planned," he reported. "But there is one small problem."

Lagunov winced. "How small?"

Shurnik explained, "The scientist is still here. She has to test the soil again."

"Why?"

"She said the results were inconclusive. But that should not interfere with our departure."

Lagunov thought about it. "No, it won't. When will the new results be available?"

Shurnik repeated what he'd been told by Dr. Yeltsin.

"Sounds reasonable," Lagunov approved. "You keep your eye on her, though. We don't need her snooping around out there if she gets bored during the day."

"Right," Shurnik agreed, wishing he could keep her occupied the way she kept him last night. "Have you had your meeting yet?"

Lagunov glanced at the big, gold-rimmed clock hanging against dark-blue–toned wallpaper on the opposite side of his office. "No, but they should be here shortly. You still have not found anything on them?" Lagunov wanted to make sure.

"Negative. Besides their little love affair, they are as clean as a whistle."

He looked at the photograph on his polished wooden desk. His two children smiled at him, and his beautiful, young wife looked lovingly into his eyes. He had told them something about a business trip to Vladivostok. His kids had begged to go, but he had leaned down to his baby boy and said, "Mikail, you know how much you love your mommy?" His five year old had nodded. "That is how much I love you, and I will be back in a flash. And in the meantime you and your brother will have to help your mommy with the chores. Can you do that?" Mikail had nodded again.

Mikail's mother was suffering from a rare disease and needed constant care. They had taken her all over the country, from one so-called specialist to the next, to find a cure, without success. Medical care in Russia was not as advanced as in Europe or the United States. As an executive of an oil company, Lagunov made, compared to the average Russian, a very good income. But he had not been able to afford the advanced, Western medical technology his wife so desperately needed.

At that time Lagunov had been approached by a distant cousin on his father's side who had connections with Selkin. It had not taken the cousin very long to explain to Lagunov the financial freedom he could offer his family if he would let him work out an introduction in St. Petersburg. Lagunov had agreed. By the time he had understood the seriousness of the drug operation, there was no turning back.

He was not a ruthless criminal, and he did have a conscience. In the beginning he had felt responsible for providing people with deadly drugs, but he had eventually changed his mind about it. People who injected, snorted, or smoked whatever dope they could get their hands on had made a choice to live the miserable life of an addict. His wife didn't have a choice. She was trapped in an ill body that would deteriorate and die without proper medical help—expensive help that Lagunov could now afford. His two sons were his life, and his wife had given those lives to him. He would do anything in his power to save hers.

He lit his pipe and leaned back in his cushy, black leather chair. His eyes went from the document he was holding in one hand to the window. It had begun to snow this morning. Early for winter, he thought. But he knew how much his boys enjoyed the snow. Well if they did, so would he.

He read the paper once again. It was a proposition from St. Petersburg to enlarge the business with an unbelievable increase in cash flow. Releasing small puffs of smoke, he looked back outside. He was in deep thought. It was dangerous—very dangerous. But then, he was already in over his head in illegal activities. He was aware of the possible consequences this operation might bring with it.

Lagunov did not care. He couldn't. All he cared about was providing his wife with the very best help possible. The offer had sounded too good to be true, and he did not trust Sergei Selkin. Lagunov was a business man—he didn't trust anybody until the deal was done.

He needed to talk to the rest of the group in St. Petersburg. They had scheduled a conference with him after he'd returned from Vladivostok. They would have to confirm what Selkin had negotiated with him.

Three monitors sunken into his desk let him know what was going on outside the building and on the adjoining premises. He watched as the two Americans stepped out of a cab. The other monitors were like still pictures. There was no other movement outside.

He put his pipe down and stood. He walked into his small private bathroom to wash his hands and smooth over his thinning, gray hair. He noticed his silver tie was not quite straight and adjusted it. A few hairs lay on the shoulders of his expensive, hand-sewn suit. He brushed them away and applied just a dash of Hugo Boss fragrance. Lagunov didn't care for the scent, but he liked the name of it.

He massaged a few drops of hand lotion into his skin, paying attention to the cuticles. Looking at his image in the crystal mirror he saw his cheeks had sagged lately. His wife's fight for her life had drained him more than any difficult business project ever could. But his eyes were still as bright as those of a young man. He rubbed a hand over his chin and jaw. His skin still felt smooth—no need to worry about five o'clock shadow.

He squared his shoulders and walked to the door. Lagunov anticipated the other board members gathering in the meeting room. He could not hear them outside his door. A look through the peephole told him that the other six executives had gathered in the hallway. They all had their own offices in this building, but of course not as secure as his. His office entrance was made of steel and the inside was cushioned with a five-centimeter-thick layer of soundproof material. It was covered with dark brown leather. The same polished wood his desk was made of was installed to the outside of the door for more cosmetic than protective reasons.

Nothing went through this door—no sound and no projectiles. The glass in his windows was bulletproofed as well. There was a hidden door to a secret staircase which led to the basement of the building. A perfect escape route in the unfortunate situation that someone uninvited came to see him.

Lagunov was not paranoid, but he had listened to the suggestions of his new business partners from St. Petersburg once they had shook hands.

Just a short while after the board had gathered, the receptionist announced Douglas and Mia arriving. Douglas opened the door for Mia and she stepped into the room.

"Ms. Trentino." Lagunov approached her and smiled.

He stuck his right arm out, and when Mia shook his hand, he looked very sincere.

"I am so pleased to see you. Here, have a seat at the head of the table." He offered her his chair, let her sit, and then he greeted Douglas as well.

"Ms. Trentino, we have received your reports, and we cannot express our gratitude to you. We can only imagine the environment you had to deal with. But thanks to you and Mr. Farland, our project will be a great success." Lagunov nodded at Douglas.

The receptionist walked in and served strong Russian coffee.

"Thank you, Mr. Lagunov," Mia smiled. "These are kind words. However, you are aware of the situation with the test results, are you not?"

"Yes, I certainly am. And we will act accordingly. But please, go ahead with your current presentation at this time."

So Mia did, all the while hoping she would not have to do this again in a few days. Those damn soil samples just had to have a negative reaction.

Douglas studied Lagunov as Mia spoke. Lagunov appeared to be eating up what Mia said. From time to time he nodded his head and silently clapped his hands. After Mia was done, Lagunov rose from his chair and Douglas listened to the sincere and trustworthy tone in his voice. He seemed like a caring CEO who couldn't wait to give his employees the opportunity they so deserved. Douglas watched as Lagunov charmed Mia with his old-school and mysterious demeanor.

You slick bastard, he thought.

The meeting came to an end, and Lagunov reached out to Mia. He took her hand in both of his and looked at her, smiling. He congratulated her again, and when he took her by the shoulders to gently kiss both of her cheeks, Douglas was ready to blow the son of a bitch out of his Italian designer shoes.

Chapter 42

MIA BEAMED AND GRACEFULLY stepped down the red carpeted stairs of Yukoil's building. She stopped on the bottom and turned to Douglas.

"I could not have done this project down to the detail like this without you. You know that, don't you?"

Douglas wanted to drag her to the bathroom and scrub her face where that bastard had touched her. Instead, he smiled at her. "Well, thank you, Boss. I'm sure you would have handled it just fine without me."

He started toward the big heavy doors, but Mia grabbed his arm. Her grip was surprisingly strong, and she stopped him in his tracks.

"I mean it," she said seriously. "I want to thank you for it. I know sometimes I can be difficult to work with but I—"

"Goddamn it, Mia!" Douglas voice was quiet, but he startled her with the sudden outburst. His eyes showed hostility. "I wished you'd quit apologizing all the time!"

Then he walked on and pushed through the door. Mia stood for a moment in silent befuddlement. Her cheeks flushed hotly as though he'd just slapped her instead of rebuked her.

What in the world was wrong with him? She had never seen this side of him. Was he jealous of her? She clearly had kept the leader position throughout the job, just as she should have. Maybe he was a guy who could not handle having a woman as a superior. But it hadn't seemed to bother him before. Mia didn't understand. But whatever had triggered aggressiveness, she was disappointed in him. He had seemed like such a strong and solid man, and now he'd shown a weak side.

Mia finally walked through the door. Douglas waited for her outside, holding the cab door open. She did not look at him when she stepped into the car. She scooted all the way over to the other side of the backseat to make room for him. She did not want to be close.

But instead of taking a seat, he leaned down and looked at her through the open door.

"Mia." His voice was softer now, but his eyes did not apologize. "I'm walking back to the hotel, if it's okay with you. I will catch up with you in a while."

"Fine," she replied shortly. She ordered the driver to leave, and Douglas shut the door.

Disappointment swelled into anger. Who did he think he was? He called her boss one minute and yelled at her the next. She needed to have a serious conversation with him. She could not allow this. If they were to work together in the future, there had to be a mutual respect.

The question she had asked him this morning during the drive popped back into her head. "Stupid," she hissed to herself. The driver glanced at her in the rearview mirror, obviously not understanding the word she just said.

She turned her head and ignored him. I'm so stupid, she thought. The feelings she had developed for Douglas during the last week seemed a million miles away. This was exactly why she had not been looking for any kind of male companionship since her divorce. Her ex-husband had behaved like an idiot, and now Mia was convinced that even the nicest guy had his belligerent side. And she would not put up with it.

Douglas stood with his hands in the pockets of his trousers. He watched as the cab disappeared around the corner and said, "I'm sorry, sweet thing."

He had to make his calls. Mia had been on such a high after the meeting, deservingly so. Douglas had been afraid he wouldn't be able to find time to contact Ludvika. He had to be alone to find a landline and to make sure nobody was following him.

He started walking in the opposite direction of the hotel. He'd reach the Baikal Hotel within minutes on foot and could not risk Mia catching him making phone calls from a booth.

There was a bar a few blocks down—perfect.

While he walked, he thought about what a tender core Mia had. In her job nobody could touch her. Douglas had watched in amusement how she had handled Shurnik. She was kind but definitely strong willed and had put Shurnik, in a very gallant way, into his place when he had tried to tell her how to do her job. Hell, if Mia knew what a hardcore thug Shurnik really was. Of course, Douglas did not think of himself as a less dangerous person. But he was one of the good guys, right?

He smiled. Her hard shell sheltered a very soft heart. Once someone broke through the shell she was very vulnerable to pain. He knew she was mad with him right now, but there was no doubt he could win her back.

He casually walked around the block before he entered the bar. The snow had stopped and just a few pedestrians shared the sidewalk with him. He scanned the establishment. A young couple and an older man sat at the bar, and two streetwalkers lingered around the music box. They eyed Douglas, whispered, and giggled. Their skimpy attire gave their occupation away. Douglas did not pay them any attention.

The place seemed dingy. Cigarette smoke had yellowed the ceiling over time. The bar and furniture were made out of a dark wood, and years of wear and tear had left their marks. The floor was brown and beige checkered linoleum. There was a wooden swing door with a round, Plexiglas window in it behind the bar. It probably led to the kitchen. Two doors facing each other were at the end of the room. That must be the restrooms, he thought. The hallway leading to the bathrooms and beyond them was unlit, and Douglas could not see the end of it. Let's hope for a pay phone, he thought.

A heavy man in his sixties appeared through the swing door with an unidentifiable sandwich on a paper plate. He nodded at Douglas and served the old man sitting at the bar.

"What can I get you," the bartender asked Douglas.

"Baltika Lager on draft."

The bartender nodded and asked Douglas as he poured, "Where are you from?" Douglas was certain it was a staple question.

"Moscow," he answered and took a seat on one of the barstools.

"If you don't mind me asking, business or pleasure?" The barman eyed him curiously.

Douglas gave him a smile that would have made the Pope trust him even if he'd been the devil himself. "Business." And with a slight nod in the girls' direction he added, "Is there such a thing as pleasure around here?"

The bartender laughed and placed the beer in front of Douglas. He thanked the man and took a good swig. There was a long mirror behind the bar that showed Douglas the entire room, which wasn't very big. He also had a view of the outside through the windows.

He observed the place for a while, and when he felt secure, he got up and went to the bathroom. As he entered he heard the girls at the jukebox giggle some more. They probably wouldn't even charge him, but Douglas was apathetic toward hookers—they made good snitches, but never mind the sex.

To his surprise Douglas noticed a payphone, and as he walked back out of the washroom he lifted the receiver. Dammit, no dial tone.

He went back to take his seat at the bar. The young couple was gone, and the old man hovered over his sandwich. The bartender sat in the corner closest to Douglas, reading a paper. He lifted his head and asked, "Would you like another one?"

Douglas shook his head. "No thanks." He pointed a thumb over his shoulder and said, "Your phone is out of order." Patting down his pockets he added, "I must have left my cell phone at the office. Do you mind me using yours?" His eyes went to the cordless phone attached to the wall.

"Not at all." The bartender got up to give Douglas the phone.

He actually had the decency to disappear into the kitchen while Douglas dialed the number of his cell phone.

He considered the security of the phone line but didn't worry about it. The number would be re-directed twice before it actually reached the line. And thanks to the United States government, the line he was calling from wouldn't even be charged. The call would not show on any detailed bill—it frankly did not exist. And as long the call was made from a landline, it was impossible to trace.

"It's about fucking time," Ludvika answered, in a mood.

"How's the weather, Darling?" Douglas knew she was hiding somewhere outside getting snowed on.

"I finished the damn tests, and Shurnik offered his joint to hang out in until I could read the results. I think he thought to get lucky again," Ludvika reported.

"Can you blame the guy?" Douglas asked, trying to make her feel better, but that was impossible.

"I told him that unfortunately I had some other business to attend to, but I would call him with the results tonight. Then I left and parked the truck on the east side of the camp. I had to stay away several miles, because of the tracks in the snow."

Douglas pictured where she was. The bartender reappeared from the kitchen and signaled Douglas to take his time.

"Can you talk? Where are you?" Ludvika asked. Douglas switched back to his Russian. "I'm in a restaurant, sweetheart. I must have left my phone in the meeting. How are the kids?" Douglas watched the bartender out of the corner of this eye. The man went back to his paper, but could probably hear bits and pieces of Douglas conversation.

"Shurnik's still around. There's no change. Have you had a chance to search Lagunov's office yet?"

"No, sweetheart, I still have to continue the meeting, but I will call you tonight from the hotel." Douglas sang into his imaginary wife's ear.

Ludvika acknowledged and hung up. She knew every minute on the phone was vital.

"I love you too, sweetheart, kiss the kids." Douglas smiled and pressed the end call button.

Thanks to modern technology it would take about two seconds for the phone's memory to lose the number Douglas had called.

He thanked the bartender and stayed for a minute of small talk. He left a generous tip, and when he walked outside he noticed a flower shop across the street.

Chapter 43

Her cab stopped next to the truck.

Mia thanked the driver and paid him. She got out and walked around the car to the truck. It was locked, of course. She wanted to get the small carry-on piece she had brought today. It was lying on the backseat next to the suitcase Douglas had brought. Farland, damn you! Mia thought. She looked over her shoulder. There was no one in the parking lot. She would have to wait for him before she could retrieve her luggage.

Just as she turned away, it occurred to her that this was the same truck they had used on their excursion to Lake Baikal. And that thought led her to remember the hidden key. She stood for a moment and wondered if she should give it a try. It couldn't hurt, she figured. She might get lucky.

Trying not to get her wool coat dirty, she leaned down the side of the truck and searched the area where Douglas had hidden the key before. Yes! There is was. At least Douglas was a creature of habit.

She looked at Douglas' suitcase. She felt like tearing through it and leaving the contents strewn all over the parking lot. Now that would be childish, her common sense told her. But fun, the little devil on her shoulder encouraged. Common sense won out and she left Douglas' belongings alone. She locked the truck and left the key where she'd found it.

Boy, he could get her juices going. He had been so polite the last couple of days—and very sexy. But as charming he could be, especially when his southern drawl peeked through, he could be just as offensive with his damn cockiness.

As she walked across the parking lot, she noticed the snow had stopped. The gray clouds promised more, though. "Good afternoon," the receptionist at the hotel desk greeted her kindly. "Oh, Ms. Trentino, of course." She remembered Mia. "You will find your room just the way you left it. Well, cleaned, of course. Here let me give you a new key for it."

The receptionist swiped a new card key for Mia and handed it to her.

As she walked down the hallway to the elevator, she suddenly missed Douglas. It was just a few hours ago that they'd been together having lunch. He had teased her with innuendo about his appetite. Mia couldn't remember exactly what his words had been, but she remembered his gorgeous eyes on hers, getting her blood going.

Mia unlocked her room and threw her purse on her bed. She placed her luggage next to it and stopped short when her eyes caught something on the desk. There was a bottle of Newen Patagonia Merlot with a note attached. What in the world, she thought.

It was from her boss. "I hope you will find this before it turns into dust. Many thanks, Scott," it read. Kiss ass, Mia thought, but smiled. Scott knew what she had to deal with out here. And a sip of wine was just what she needed about now.

There was a corkscrew in the drawer of the small kitchenette. She couldn't find any wine glasses, but in her state of mind, a water glass worked just fine.

She did not expect any phone calls until later in the evening. She was sure that Shurnik would notify her about Dr. Yeltsin's findings. Mia had asked him to do so, no matter what time it ended up being. But it was still early. In the meantime, Mia was in the mood for a hot bath. Later she'd relax for a while and order room service, maybe even watch some TV.

Mia tried the Merlot, and it was nice. Not too spicy but with an earthy undertone, just the way she liked it. She'd let it breathe for a while. If it mellowed out a little it would be perfect.

She took off her coat and her suit jacket and hung them up. The purple blouse she had been wearing would have to go to the dry cleaner. She stepped out of her slacks and folded them just so. Releasing her hair out of its confinement, she rubbed her scalp.

In the bathroom she added a generous dash of lavender bath oil to the steaming water and inhaled the soothing scent. The moment she sank into the bubbling bliss, her stress about Douglas' behavior melted away and she decided not to think about it anymore.

Mia closed her eyes and indulged in her hot bath, listening to Bach's soothing *Sleepers, Awake* on her iPod. A half glass of wine sat on the tile floor next to the tub. Mia was letting her senses rest for a while.

Thump.

She was so focused on the music that the sudden sound startled her. She opened her eyes and wondered for an instant if she had fallen asleep. She removed the plug out of her right ear and listened, holding her breath.

Again, a faint thump then a knock. Someone was at the door.

You're kidding, she thought. Who could it be? But of course—Farland!

"Go away," she said quietly without moving. "If I have to, I forgive you, just leave me the hell alone"

Silence. Mia waited a full minute but didn't hear anything else. He must have given up. She was glad. Maybe a little disappointed, but definitely more glad.

She raised her hand again to remove the other ear plug and noticed that the skin on the inside of her hand was white and wrinkled. She'd been in this tub way too long. Reluctantly, she stood up and used the handheld showerhead to wash her hair and spray herself off.

The snow-white towels were a thick, Egyptian cotton and wonderfully soft. She took her glass of wine and stepped out of the bathroom. She was tired, but the bath had rejuvenated her senses.

Wrapped in the oversized towel, she dimmed the lights and turned on the TV. She sat on her bed and flicked through the channels. There was nothing that interested her, so she bent down and opened the cabinet door beneath the TV. To her surprise she found a whole entertainment system. It only took her a minute to figure out that it was compatible with her iPod.

She let a sip of the Merlot sit on her tongue. Getting better, she thought. She refilled her glass with another small shot and grabbed a towel to rub her damp hair dry.

Someone knocked on the door again.

She straightened up on the bed. "Who is it?" she asked in English.

There was a pause and someone said in Russian, "Room service for Ms. Trentino."

She hadn't ordered anything yet. She wondered if it was a mistake, and then Douglas came to mind.

What was his deal? she thought. Now she was getting curious. She padded barefoot to the door and stood on tiptoe to look through the peephole. The wide angle scope showed the bizarre image of a servant with a round face and an oversized nose.

"I have not ordered any food," Mia said through the closed door.

"Ms. Trentino, I have a message for you," the servant said politely. His voice sounded muffled.

"Can't someone call?" Mia asked. She wanted to get a look at Douglas' door across the hallway, but all she could see was the servant's huge face.

He hesitated and said, "Ms. Trentino, it is not a phone message." The bellboy started to sound a little desperate. Her own curiosity was killing her by now. She put the chain up and opened the door just as far as it would let her.

The servant was actually a nice-looking young man when his face was viewed in proportion. With his gloved hand he held a small silver platter in front of him. On top of a white cotton, lace-trimmed handkerchief was a perfect red rose. The bellboy did not say anything. He was obviously touched and a little embarrassed at the same time.

For an instant Mia just stared at the beautiful flower. A few drops of moisture clung to its petals like tears. She didn't know what to make of it.

Suddenly, Douglas appeared out of nowhere. He silently placed a folded bill on the silver platter and took the rose by its stem. The servant understood and instantly left.

Douglas held the crimson colored blossom in front of Mia and looked at her very intensely. Mia's gaze shifted from the rose to his eyes. She found remorse and a little sadness there. He did not say anything.

It must have been close to a full minute before Mia closed the door. She leaned her forehead against the doorframe and exhaled. Damn, he looked good tonight. Even earlier, when he had shown his ugly side, she had still felt attracted to him.

He had come to apologize—she had expected that. But the way he had done it tugged on her heart. She smiled. This was the most sincere way someone had ever asked her for forgiveness before: without words.

God, what was she going to do?

Mia was certain where this would lead to, if she let him in. Her common sense told her she shouldn't, but every inch of her body screamed at her to open the damn door again.

Douglas watched the door shut. He had never hoped for anything more in his life than to hear the chain unlock on the inside.

For a moment there was nothing, and then Mia opened it and looked at him. There was still silence. Then, she took a small step to the side, and Douglas took it as an invitation. Still holding the flower to his lips, he smelled its sweet scent. His eyes never left hers, and when Mia stepped back, he shut the door quietly and leaned against it.

How handsome he was. And he seemed even taller than before. Maybe it was because he was fully dressed in his suit, including his black overcoat, and she was wearing nothing but a towel. But before she could think about it more, Douglas reached out to her and cupped his hand around the back of her head. Very gently he pulled her toward him. Mia placed one hand on his chest to keep their bodies from touching.

"I'm still mad," she blurted out, helplessly fighting the effect Douglas had on her.

"I know," he said, his voice a murmur. "And you should be." He did not let go of her but softened his grip.

Mia fought with all her inner strength against his intoxicating boldness. His hand moved down her neck and under her chin. His touch was different than before. It was still gentle, but there was an arrogance attached to it.

He lifted her head up to him and asked, "Can you kiss while you're still angry?" It sounded like one of his jokes but it wasn't. He was not smiling, and his eyes revealed a desire new to Mia.

He didn't move. He was waiting for her to either stop it right there or to give him permission. Her hand still rested on his chest. But instead of pushing him away, she dug her fingers into his coat and closed her eyes.

There was no need for words. Before Mia could tip her head back, Douglas' lips were on hers. For an instant there was the same tenderness they had experienced before, but then Douglas gave his passion a bit more rein.

It only took Mia a second to realize how much Douglas had held back in the past. The intensity of his kiss stunned her at first, but quickly his hunger swept over her and she responded with the same eagerness. Before she realized it, she had her hands buried in his soft, dark hair. Then, they dropped onto his wide shoulders. She slipped his coat and suit jacket off and started to unbutton his shirt. Douglas helped her and let it glide to the floor.

The rose followed, and so did Mia's towel.

He separated himself from her just enough to glance over her body. For the first time since he had walked into her room, Mia saw him smile. And what a delicious and knowing smile it was. His usually intense blue eyes had darkened with passion, and the sweet pain of anticipation was written all over his face.

Douglas' strong hands softly caressed the sensitive skin of Mia's naked neck and back, not yet touching the velvety softness of her front. His touch triggered an unknown fire in Mia. It flared up inside her, burning away all her reservations. She lifted both hands to the back of his neck to cling against his warm body. He smelled so wonderfully masculine, like warm earth and rain.

As their kiss became more determined, her hands ran over Douglas bare chest and hard stomach. His muscles flexed under his skin wherever Mia touched him. She left hot trails of sensation as her fingers slowly teased their way through the black curls beneath his navel. A deep moan escaped Douglas' throat as she let her fingertips glide along the sensitive area at the rim of his trousers.

Exploring her completely, he cupped his hand around her breast—it fit perfectly in his hand. He let his thumb glide lightly over the rosy tip. An electric jolt shot through Mia's body, and she withdrew from his kiss, breathless.

Douglas watched Mia open her eyes, and the dark passion in them told him she was ready for him. He did not give her time to recover, but let his lips reclaimed hers once again. Effortlessly, he scooped her up off the floor. His probing mouth never left hers as he carried her the few steps to the bed. Carefully, he laid her on top of the sheets and stood upright.

The vigor he felt deep inside his core was a new experience. It was taking all his discipline to hold back a little while longer. He wanted to look at her, study her, caress her with his hungry eyes.

She was simply divine.

The dim light brushed a radiant glow over her skin that he had never seen before. For a moment he stood still, indulging in the beauty laid out before him. Then he undid his belt and let his pants drop carelessly to the floor, unable to take his eyes off her perfect body.

It was too dark in the room for Mia to see his face. But she could make out his wonderful, masculine shape. He was a beautiful man—strong, but incredibly sensitive. As he stepped closer to the bed, Mia's eyes found his.

She reached for him and whispered, "Come here." He took her hand and kissed the inside of her palm as he lowered himself onto the bed beside her.

As their mouths met again passionately, his lips joined his hands in exploration of every inch of her unbelievable body. He took his time and kept finding more ways to deepen her ache. She radiated sensuality and writhed beneath his roaming mouth. Mia's mind had shut off a while ago, and as her desire began to peak, she yearned to share her delicious agony.

She dragged her teasing nails over his hot skin, eventually finding her way to his groin.

Douglas inhaled sharply. "No," he rasped. It was his turn.

He repositioned her body with ease, and let his weight press her into the pillows. He pinned her wrists above her head with one hand while he continued agonizing her with the other. Just as a tremor ripped through Mia's body, he covered her mouth with his to suffocate her cry.

He propped himself up on one arm just enough to give her room to arch her body against his. His hips nudged her thighs apart, and when Mia began to beg him, he knew he could not wait any longer.

He watched her closely as he slowly entered her sweet depths. Her dark and luminous eyes told him not to hold back—but he did. For a while he let her drown in his eyes, until his own desire consumed him. He buried his face in her silky hair and began whispering her name over and over as he took her to a place she had never been before.

Chapter 44

DOUGLAS WAS THE FIRST to open his eyes.

Somehow Mia had ended up on top of him. Her head lay on his chest, and her soft hair was tickling his chin. He tried to look down but couldn't move his head far enough see her face.

Mia felt him moving and grumbled something he couldn't understand but she didn't stir. Had she fallen asleep?

Their hands were interlocked and lay on either side of their bodies. Douglas lifted one of hers to his mouth, wanting to kiss her awake. As he did, he noticed a faint bruise on the inside of Mia's delicate wrist. His stomach knotted up.

Dammit, Farland, he thought. You must have gotten a little carried away. He gently kissed the spot, hoping he had not been too rough with her.

"Are you counting my battle wounds?" Mia asked quietly, listening to his strong heartbeat.

"Are you okay, Love?" he asked carefully.

Reluctantly, she lifted her head. She wanted to lay like this forever. Douglas let go of her hands so she could prop herself up on his chest. Her cheeks were still flushed from her passion, and tiny sparkles danced in her dark eyes. Her beautiful face was framed by her tousled hair, and when she smiled mischievously, Douglas knew she was just fine.

"I'm not okay. I'm hungry," she said. It had not been very long since their late lunch, but the activity of the last few hours had worked off all her energy. "Should we order some food?"

He kissed her forehead and glanced at the alarm clock on the nightstand. It was almost seven o'clock. He still had time.

"You got it, Love. Let's get up." His deep voice was so wonderfully soothing to her. She felt a bit ragged and laid her head back on Douglas' chest to rest just a little while longer.

When she moved her hips slightly, Douglas body reacted instantaneously. It did not take much of her to get his blood going again.

Feeling something press against her thigh, Mia chuckled. She looked at him again and smiled teasingly. "Looks like someone's already up."

A new wave of lust rolled through Douglas as he saw the growing desire in Mia's face. "If you want food, you better move soon," he warned her in a raspy drawl.

"Yes, I better," she agreed as she rolled off of him. "For now, anyway."

Naked as sin, she strolled into the bathroom. Douglas looked after her, admiring the shape of her backside. She was surprisingly strong for her size. Her back and shoulders were defined and she had beautiful legs that had proven powerful when she'd wrapped them around his thighs earlier. Her hips were softly rounded, and he could almost fit both his hands around her waist.

He propped himself up against the headboard and scrubbed his face with both hands. Holy cow, what a woman. He'd been apprehensive about his involvement with Mia. He thought it might interfere with his focus on the mission. Surprisingly, it didn't. It felt natural to be with her. Yes, there had been times when it had been tricky to hold his disguise, but he had figured it out rather quickly.

"What's the serious look for?" Mia asked. Douglas had been in deep thought and hadn't noticed her step back into the room.

"You, Love," he said smiling at her. She had brushed her hair and fastened it in a loose pony tail on the back of her neck. Her freshly washed face still showed evidence of his satisfying her. She looked gorgeous.

"Well, what about me?" she asked curiously, closing the front of the hotel's bright white bathrobe.

Douglas grinned and said, "Do you know how long I've had this on my mind?"

She nodded. "I have an idea, but why don't you enlighten me?"

Douglas pretended to think and said, "About thirty seconds after you stepped out of the ladies' room when we first met."

Mia narrowed her eyes. What ladies' room? And then it came to her.

"Right. That was about the same time I was going to strangle you with that god-awful orange tie."

He laughed. He loved that tie.

"Would you order us something while I take a quick shower?" he asked her as he pushed back the sheets.

"Sure, what would you like?" Mia had to force herself to look up at his face and not stare at his muscled body. Just to look at him weakened her knees and she bit her lip.

Douglas walked up to Mia, his eyes on her mouth. He did not touch her but almost swept her of her feet with an intense kiss.

"I told you not to do that, Kid. Don't drive me crazy," he playfully warned.

He let her stand and disappeared into the bathroom. By the time Mia had recovered, he had closed the door and turned on the shower. She turned toward the bathroom door and raised her voice a little to get through to him. "You haven't answered my question."

"Which was?" He grinned while he washed his hair.

"Food! What do you want?" Her voice sounded a little impatient.

Douglas enjoyed her agitation. It would be good for her to get her emotions going again.

"You order for me, Love. I can't read the damn menu anyway."

Mia sighed. She felt like a slave to her own libido. This guy was unbelievable. She touched her cheeks with the back of her hand. I must be running a fever, she thought smiling. To focus on something other than Douglas' body, she took the room service menu off the table and studied it.

By the time Douglas stepped out of the bathroom, Mia had

organized his clothes and made room on the small table for dinner, which had arrived quickly.

Douglas was clean-shaven, and his dark hair was damp and uncombed. A few drops of water glistened on his broad shoulders and in the black curls beneath his navel.

He noticed that Mia had to swallow and grinned.

She tossed him his pants, and as she turned her back to him said, "You better put those on."

Douglas ignored his slacks and stepped into his boxers instead. Mia was leaning over the table removing the silver domes from their plates. He silently stepped behind her and wrapped his arms around her body. The plush fabric of her bathrobe felt nice, but he would have rather caressed skin.

He bent down to kiss her neck and grumbled, "Mmm, look at this—delicious."

Mia smiled. She was not sure if he meant her or the wonderful food on their plates.

Douglas let her go and sat. They shared the rest of Mia's wine and enjoyed a very nice dinner. After they had finished their meal, Mia's mood became a bit somber. Douglas watched her closely. He hoped she didn't have any regrets. Or was she thinking about his outburst from earlier today?

"What's on your mind?"

Mia stared at her empty plate, "Shurnik."

Douglas was relieved and played offended. He jabbed his thumb to his chest and asked, "You have this Adonis sitting in front of you, and you're thinking about him?"

Mia laughed and then rolled her eyes. His confidence was sometimes too much. "Okay, hotshot. I'm thinking about Shurnik calling us about the test results."

Mia got up to clean the plates off the table. She stacked them onto the tray the servant had left.

"Ah, we're back to work," he teased. Looking over to the alarm clock he said, "Good news. It should be another couple of hours until we'll find out. And I know exactly what to do to prevent boredom until then."

He reached for her arm and wanted to pull her toward him, but he missed the sleeve of her robe by an inch as she quickly stepped aside. He looked up at her, surprised.

Her eyes dared his as she mocked, "Oh, yeah? What'cha gonna do, hotshot?"

Douglas held himself very still and said, "I will have you for dessert." His voice deepened, and his longing eyes seemed to rip off her robe. But he just sat there, comfortably leaning against the back of his chair with his legs slightly parted and his arms confidently crossed in front of his chest.

Mia raised her eyebrows and took a step toward him to stand between his knees. "Really! Still feel like you need to prove your appetite to me?"

She laid both hands on his shoulders and stepped one leg over him to sit on his lap. The robe parted enough to reveal her smooth thighs but kept the rest of her body covered. He wanted to feel her sweet lips on his, but Mia would not let him. Playful, she looked into his eyes and bit her lip.

There was no way Douglas could draw it out like he had earlier. He knew now how amazing she felt. He leaned forward, grabbed her hips, and stood. It barely took any strength to take her with him.

She wrapped her legs around his waist as he moved to carry her back to the bed. Before he could lay her down she commanded, "Sit down." The playfulness in her voice had left, and her almost ruthless tone forced him to obey.

He sat on the edge of the bed with his back straight, and Mia bent her knees so she could stay on his lap. Douglas searched her eyes. He found the same deep passion he had witnessed before, but when he noticed rawness about it, he knew this time he would let her be the aggressor.

Ludvika picked up after the fourth vibrating signal.

"Where the hell were you?" Douglas asked. She was supposed to have his phone close by.

"Having a good time out here, so don't give me any shit." Ludvika sounded tired. She must be, Douglas thought. She'd been out there since early Thursday morning. It was Friday night now, and she had not had much sleep. Douglas had a few packs of self-heating food in his gear that he had left her, but besides the truck she was driving, she had no shelter.

"Anything to report?"

"Negative." Ludvika said briskly. She wanted to tell him that next time, he could go to hell if he needed her help. But then she remembered that she had volunteered. Shurnik's dead body would be worth it, she thought.

She was shivering, and Douglas could hear it in her voice. He was not sure how well she'd make it through the night.

"Do I need to come out?" Douglas asked her, worried.

"What for? To hold my hand?" she hissed back.

"Okay, sorry I asked. I'm on my way to search Lagunov's office. I will call you with my findings," he said.

"You have not done that yet?" she demanded, exasperated. "What the fuck have you been doing all damn day?" She knew that she was dangerously close to overstepping the boundaries of Farland's tolerance, but she didn't care.

"Having a good time, just like you, Bogdan," he said calmly.

With that, Douglas terminated the line. Damn, she had a temper. But Douglas knew better than to argue or show her any sympathy. She was a more effective warrior when she was on the edge. He had to ignore her fuming. It was better that way.

The phone booth he was using was just a block south of the Yukoil building. The streets were somewhat busy. It was just after 21:45, or 9:45 p.m., and the pedestrian traffic consisted mostly of couples walking to or from bars and restaurants.

It was easy for Douglas to blend in. He was on high alert but looked like a guy who was nonchalantly walking to pick up his date.

He had left Mia in her room just twenty minutes ago. They had made passionate love after dinner, and luckily Mia had fallen asleep in his arms. She had been completely wiped out. He had waited until her breathing was deep and regular before he had moved her arm off him. She had not stirred, and he quickly had gotten dressed and silently left her room.

He had retrieved his Five-seveN out of his room where he'd left it earlier. Now he could smile about his earlier mistake that he had caught just in time.

When Douglas had knocked on Mia's door with one long-stemmed rose in his hand, he was still wearing his gun strapped to his body. He had remembered it just in time and had unlocked his room to get rid of it. As he unbuttoned his shirt to remove the holster he'd had the idea to use the bellboy's help.

The bell of the Roman Catholic Church chimed ten times. Damn. He only had an hour or so until Shurnik called and woke up Mia with the test results. With any luck, Douglas would return and sneak back into her room before the call.

He hid in the shadows of a big maple tree in front of a busy restaurant and observed the entrance of the Yukoil building. Finally! He watched the last member of the cleaning crew close the heavy front door and the security guard lock the building. He spoke into a radio fastened to his shirt by his shoulder and left the premises.

Douglas was thinking about Mia waking up with him gone and the consequences. Well, it depends on how long she's awake for, he figured. As usual, he could not worry about problems that hadn't happened yet. If he did that, he'd quickly lose his mind over the what if's.

Chapter 45

The street was well lit, but the entrance of the Yukoil building lay in darkness. Douglas walked up the street on the other side of the road and crossed the street half a block away from the entrance. He stood on the corner and nodded, smiling, at an older couple passing him. A busy street was the perfect cover.

A quick look over his shoulder told him there was nobody behind him. He kept his eye on the older couple and followed them in a safe distance. Walking toward the entrance his senses went on overdrive. Now or never! A quick step to the right, and the darkness swallowed him.

He stood motionless, observing the street to both sides as far as he could see. Across the road he saw the restaurant and the tree he had stood under, watching, just a short while ago.

A brief check of his watch told him it was 22:06, six minutes after ten.

He scanned the Gothic entrance of the Yukoil building. Its architecture was outstanding, but Douglas had no time to admire the Russian art of masonry. His eyes were searching for any kind of surveillance devices and cameras. It was dark, and his eyes had not yet adjusted from the well-lit sidewalk. This morning, he had observed Yukoil's security system as thoroughly as the walk to and from the meeting room had allowed him to. Besides the usual motion detectors and locks, he had not seen anything he couldn't conquer. His bug detector would help him find the surveillance cameras once he was inside.

He took another minute but could not find anything out of the ordinary. The device he had used to pick the locks of the meth lab worked here as well.

In a short time he heard a faint click and he could easily turn the brass door knob and slipped through the heavy wooden door. The tiny green light on his device told him that both the motion detector and the alarm had been disengaged.

He loved modern technology.

Back in the States, Brian and Douglas had studied the blue prints of this building. Satellite surveillance had revealed the cleaning crew's work schedule, and entry with their involuntarily help had been discussed. Pressed for time, Douglas would not have had a chance to properly prepare. And they had calculated the risk of getting caught.

The photos had shown a possible way through the ventilation system, but if the building was empty there was no need. The team had made the decision that the front door would be the easiest way for Douglas to gain access.

Brian had told him, "I wish I could be there watching you walk through the front door like Al Capone in 1920s Chicago. Probably wearing a black coat instead of one of our high-tech bunny suits." Now that Douglas heard his partner's voice in his head, he smiled. He was indeed wearing his black overcoat, but he still wished Brian were there to cover his ass.

Douglas was surprised by the simplicity of Yukoil's security system. But then, this was a legitimate company with a vault in the basement for its computer files and whatever else needed to be locked away in case of a fire. A regular security system was good enough. The most valuable items above the basement were the oil paintings of the executives in the hallway.

The bug detector told him the location of a camera under the ceiling in the upper hall. He had missed it this morning, but it didn't matter now. Unless he triggered an alarm, the chances of someone watching tonight's tape were very small. And after Lagunov's arrest, the authorities—Interpol in this case—would confiscate the tape as evidence, and the Acronym would have Interpol destroy them.

He still stood against the wall in the foyer, listening to the darkness. There was nothing—it was time to move.

Lagunov's office would be a different story, Douglas was sure. He had to anticipate that Lagunov had his own surveillance system installed. The thought of one's image being on the Russian Mafia's most-wanted list could make one's stomach queasy, but Douglas was not worried about getting tracked and found. The Acronym was too good at what they did.

As Douglas approached Lagunov's office, the level of adrenaline in his blood increased, and as he crouched down to work on the lock he thought about what Brian had called him before—an insane pervert. Douglas enjoyed the fact that most thugs knew he was the one responsible for putting them away. The thought of his image being burned into a criminal's mind, fretting over him every single day for the rest of their miserable lives, entertained him. On top of that, Douglas liked the constant danger of someone spying through the thick walls of the Acronym. If he'd wanted security in his life, he could have stayed with the FBI.

The bug detector did not read anything behind Lagunov's office door. Douglas had expected that as he'd anticipated this being more a vault than a room. The camera detector was unable to reach beyond these walls.

He focused on the door.

Click—done. Douglas was impressed. He had not seen a lock like this one before. He didn't know if the Russians were leading in the field of vaults, but he guessed not. Otherwise he wouldn't have picked it so easily.

Of course, Douglas did not turn the light on. He could see well enough with the street lights faintly illuminating the room from outside. Before he placed even one foot into the room, Douglas checked his device again. Nothing.

Odd. He couldn't believe Lagunov did not have this place watched. Damn, what to do? He supposed he had no choice. He had to accept the fact that he might be videotaped—or worse, that someone was watching him live. There was always the possibility that Lagunov had the room scrambled so Douglas' equipment was useless.

That possibility ultimately made Mia a target. If someone found out right this minute that Douglas was here, they would assume Mia was a part of his op. Worst case scenario: They got to her before he could even leave the room.

His heart screamed, but he suppressed it. Sorry, sweet thing, he thought. The op was priority. He certainly could not pick up the phone to give her warning. The office was good sized. He scanned it with one sweeping look. He stepped into the center and stood very still, his breathing becoming shallow. Douglas had an extremely sensitive sixth sense. He closed his eyes and let the room talk to him. His partner, Brian, had watched Douglas find hidden objects before during training sessions. Voodoo bullshit, he called it.

A faint peep came from Douglas right wrist. He had set his Breitling to alarm him every fifteen minutes. It was 22:30, but Douglas did not move.

After a full minute, Douglas slowly turned on the spot, still with his eyes closed. He felt that sensation he was never able to describe and opened his eyes. Royal blue wallpaper above three feet of dark, wood paneling was all his eyes saw, but his senses told him something else.

Douglas walked to the wall and let his experienced hands glide over the paneling and the wall above it. No human eye could have spotted the thin seam. He felt it, and after a closer examination, he knew that there was a hidden door in the wall. Where could it lead to? He thought about it and decided it didn't matter right now. He was not looking for Lagunov's escape routes. Douglas was looking for evidence.

Even though his senses had not disappointed him, what they had helped him find was useless. He would come back to the hidden entrance if he could not find any other kind of safe.

He began his search systematically. Of all the places where people could hide things, many times they ended up choosing the same set of objects—behind pictures and mirrors, underneath desks and tables tops, or false bottoms in drawers and cabinets.

He found that Lagunov's thick, wooden office desk had a double layer. The top opened and there were three video screens behind glass. Douglas watched pedestrians and vehicles moving in and out of the scenes. One view was focused on the front door. Douglas had not seen the camera. It was probably hidden in the stones of the building.

While Douglas carefully searched the private bathroom his watch beeped again; 22:45. He stayed calm.

There were two framed paintings on the wall, neither one of them had a safe behind it.

Once again, Douglas took out his penlight and went through the drawers of Lagunov's desk. Nothing.

Douglas sat down in the overstuffed leather chair and closed his eyes. He pictured Lagunov and dug up in his mind everything he knew about him.

He had read his file. He looked like he was clean as virgin snow. Douglas did not know the details behind why the FBI had pointed their bureaucratic finger in Lagunov's direction, but they had recruited the Acronym, which meant they must have something on him they couldn't touch.

Douglas gave his senses one more chance. He opened his eyes and focused in on the first thing he saw. It was a photograph of a young family without their father. A very attractive woman sat on a big rock holding two small boys. Funny—Douglas was reminded of his own brother. He had not thought about him in months.

The photograph seemed to be big for the usual desk picture of one's family. Something made Douglas pick up the eight by ten and looked at the threesome closely. Cute buggers, Douglas thought of the two boys. Too bad you're gonna have to visit your dad in the dungeons in some northern Siberian jail.

Mom did not look like it would take long to find someone to console her. But then Douglas remembered that she was deathly ill.

Douglas turned the framed picture around and examined it closer. He noticed that it had been opened recently. The indentations the metal clips had left on the velvety back cover were in different spots that the clips themselves. He could clearly see one indentation beside each clip. He looked at the photograph again. It had the date handwritten on it in the lower left corner, almost hidden by the gold frame.

It was more than two years old. Why had it been opened?

There was absolutely no sound in the room. He retrieved his pocket knife and opened it. The snapping sound seemed unnaturally loud in Douglas' sensitive ears. Carefully, he inserted the tip of the blade underneath the clip and turned it sideways to open it. He could feel his blood rushing through his veins as his instincts screamed at him to open the photograph.

When Douglas finished turning the last of the four clips, the thick cardboard cover opened. A legal-sized piece of paper fell, light as a feather, to the ground. At first Douglas thought it was the photograph, but as he leaned down to pick it up, he saw computer print on it.

He placed the photograph on the desk and held the white page in front of him. First he scanned it quickly, then the words 238U and North Korea got his attention and he read the document more carefully. As he comprehended the words he was reading, an indescribable feeling overcame him—holy shit.

He read on. When he finished the last sentence, he just sat there, stunned. "Holy shit." This time the words escaped his mouth.

Again, Douglas looked at the page. The letters seemed to mock him, dancing in front of his eyes. He was not an easy to startle guy, but if this was anything close to the ongoing happenings, he had every right to panic.

Chapter 46

Mia startled and her eyes flew open—she was wide awake. Had there been a noise?

"Douglas?" she whispered.

She looked into the darkness, listening intensely. Maybe it was the phone, she thought, remembering Shurnik's promised call. No, the phone didn't ring again.

The digital numbers of the alarm clock illuminated the area to her right very dimly.

"Douglas?" Mia moved her right arm to her side in search for him and found empty sheets. She propped herself up on her elbows, to see if there was light shining beneath the bathroom door. There wasn't. The green numbers on the alarm clock showed that it was 11:03 p.m. Where was he?

She reached out to her bedside lamp and switched it on. Her eyes squinted shut momentarily, but she adjusted to the light rather quickly. Trying to remember the time frame of the evening, she figured that she must have fallen asleep around nine o'clock right after...

The memory of their love making came back to Mia, and it gave her a pleasant shiver. But only for a second. The warm fuzzy feeling left fast without Douglas there. Where could he be?

She swung her legs out of the bed and sat up. Looking around, she felt confused. Her eyes went to the chair where she had folded his clothes over so neatly. They were gone. He must have left to go to his room, but why? Why hadn't he stayed with her?

A suspicious feeling overcame her. Was he a guy who enjoyed the sex, but preferred to sleep alone? She just could not picture him being like that. No, there was no way.

But then, he had disappointed her before. Men, they were all the same, and Mia frankly did not know what to think or do.

She rubbed her eyes. Placing both hands on the edge of the bed, she straightened her back and dropped her head. An emptiness opened up inside her. Could he have really just left her like this?

Then she remembered that he'd used the computer before in the lobby. Mia lifted her head, and her spirits lifted, too. Yes— right after they had arrived, he had mentioned something about checking his personal e-mails. Maybe he just went downstairs. A small spark of hope ignited in her belly. Finally she got up, went into the bathroom, and studied her mirrored image. She looked refreshed from her sleep, but a small wrinkle of worry still lay between her eyes.

Suddenly she thought about checking on him. She knew it wasn't right. If he found out, he'd laugh at her. Or would he? Mia was not sure. It seemed like something a compulsive woman would do. But weren't all women a little bit compulsive?

Mia splashed water in her face and brushed her teeth. She kept eying herself in the mirror and finally made up her mind. She didn't dare knock on his door. The confrontation would be outright uncomfortable if it turned out he was the kind of man Mia so wished he wasn't. She'd have to deal with that later. For now a casual phone call to the front desk would not hurt. She hoped whoever was on duty downstairs would be discreet when checking the computer.

She walked back into the room and smiled, realizing she was unconsciously trying to walk quietly—sneaking. She knew she was doing wrong. Curiosity swept through her, pushing the worries aside. By know she was almost certain Douglas was sitting in front of the computer downstairs. She should let it go for a while and wait for him to return, but she couldn't help it.

When her eyes fell onto the phone, she remembered that Shurnik would be calling anytime now. The clock read 11:10.

She pulled out her cell phone to make sure it was turned on and fully charged. It wasn't. The battery indicator showed it was only three-quarters full, so she plugged it into the wall.

She sat back onto the bed and bounced right back up again. She started to pace. What would she ask? She felt a little silly and almost embarrassed by her behavior, but then she picked up the receiver.

For a second her right index finger hovered above the button with the word "front desk" in Cyrillic letters next to it. Then, she pushed it. Gnawing on her lower lip, and with a nervous flutter in her stomach, she waited for someone to pick up the phone.

"Secona," Brian answered briskly on the second ring. Douglas stood still. Leaning against the glass wall of the phone booth, he had his left forearm on top of the pay phone and was resting his forehead on top of it.

"Are you sitting down?" he asked Brian, who immediately heard something he didn't hear very often in his partner's voice—stress.

"You all right?" Brian asked, worried.

Douglas took a deep breath. No, he was not all right. Not really. But that was not important. He had to explain his findings, and he had to do it fast.

"Listen," he said. "You need to send backup right away. We're gonna have to stop the drug transport at once. We also—"

"Whoa, whoa, whoa," Brian interrupted. "What the hell is going on?" He needed Douglas to start from the beginning. This wasn't at all like Farland. He never rambled like this. "Start over, man! And calm down, for Christ's sake!"

Douglas lifted his head and straightened his shoulders. He scanned the area for anything suspicious. "I just got done in Lagunov's office, and I found more evidence than we had hoped for."

"Good. So what's his connection to the drugs?"

"Drugs?" Douglas sounded confused for just a second. "Forget the drugs. That's small stuff."

"What do you mean small stuff? As far as we know they are fixin' to head out to drown China with synthetic drugs, completely syndicating the market."

"Yes, I understand that," Douglas' eyes swept the premises again. "But that's just a test."

Brian was lost. What the hell was Farland talking about?

"Okay, here is the deal," Brian began to sound aggravated. "You either spit out what the fuck's going on, or this conversation is over until you come to your senses."

Douglas knew he now had his partner's full attention. He had to force Brian into more than just his normal state of mind in order for him to fully comprehend the severity of this case. In a few quick words Douglas repeated what he had read on the document in Lagunov's office just a short while ago. When he was finished, a deadly silence hovered between the two men.

Douglas could almost feel Brian's astonishment and disbelief. "Jesus Christ!" he finally said.

"Exactly."

"Baikal Hotel, front desk, this is Tanya speaking." Mia recognized the pretty voice of the older lady at the reception desk. She knew that Tanya did not speak English and said in Russian, "Tanya, this is Ms. Trentino in room 212, I was wondering if you would be so kind as to give my colleague a message."

Tanya knew right away who Mia was referring to. "I am sorry, Ms. Trentino. I have not seen Mr. Farland for a while."

Mia's heart sank. "Oh, so he is not using the computer anymore?" Mia tried hard to sound casual.

Tanya's eyes went across the foyer to the small, windowed room with the personal PC for guest access. It was empty.

"No, but when I started my shift this evening, I accidentally bumped into him as he was walking out the side door." Tanya paused, remembering how he had held the door for her and added, "Such a charming young man. He apologized profusely for running into me, even though it was my fault." Picturing Douglas treating the elderly woman with kindness, Mia smiled.

"Well, that was nice of him. Could you tell me what time that was?" Mia asked.

"Just before nine thirty. I believe he mentioned something about a quick walk," Tanya said.

Mia thought about what the receptionist had said and a weird feeling rose up in her. After a silent moment Mia said, "I didn't know you spoke English."

"Well, Ms. Trentino," the old lady lowered her voice as if she was embarrassed, "I certainly don't."

Then how could she have known what Douglas was saying? Was he picking up on the Russian language that fast?

"And you could understand Mr. Farland's Russian just fine?" Mia asked in disbelief.

"I most certainly did," Tanya said. "If I didn't know better, I would have thought he grew up in this country."

"And why is that?" Mia asked, afraid of Tanya's answer.

"He spoke without an accent."

It was 23:21.

Damn. Douglas had spent too much time talking to Brian. But after he'd told Brian about his discovery, they'd had to figure out what to do. Brian had agreed that backup would be on the way as soon as they could scramble a team.

He wanted to switch landlines, but there was no time to search for another phone booth. Douglas dialed his cell number and waited impatiently as the satellite redirected his call.

It rang and Ludvika picked up.

Before she could waste even one second of Douglas' precious time he said, "Bogdan, hang tight and listen. You need to sabotage the vehicles and prevent the transport at once." He paused. Ludvika must have recognized the urgency in his voice, she did not say anything.

"What's the status? Has Shurnik loaded his merchandise yet?" There was no response.

"Bogdan, you copy?" Silence. Shit. Was the battery low already? It couldn't be. Was she playing a stupid game? Douglas did not have time for any of it and ordered her firmly.

"Agent Bogdan, do you copy!?"

Yet another moment of silence gave Douglas a nauseated feeling. Suddenly he understood.

"Mr. Farland. I am glad you are telling me her real name." Shurnik's voice was very calm. "I have tried just about everything, but she wouldn't say."

Douglas felt like the earth had just swallowed him whole. His body tried to react sensibly to the commands of his overloaded brain. He was drowning in adrenaline.

"I dare you, Shurnik." Douglas could not say anymore, his mind was on the verge of being lost.

"Dare me? I am not certain that your position allows you to dare me." Shurnik sounded amused as he continued. "But I am willing to assist you in understanding this delicate situation."

Douglas forced himself to calm down. The initial shock slowly left and his instincts took over. "You are asking to negotiate." Douglas did not make the obvious sound like a question.

"Maybe. But why don't you and the lovely Ms. Trentino join us out here, and I am sure we all will find out." Shurnik sounded like he was inviting Douglas to a barbecue.

Tap, tap. Douglas looked up as he heard the noise of metal against glass. An older man had used the brass handle of his walking stick to knock against the door of the phone booth, looking at Douglas.

"The lovely Ms. Trentino has no say in this," Douglas said, not showing any hostility in his voice. He was playing Shurnik's game very well, but Shurnik knew better than to believe Douglas.

The man outside tapped the glass once again. Douglas smiled apologetically at him. He wanted to send him to hell, but could not afford any kind of attention.

"Ah, of course," Shurnik sang into Douglas' ear. And then his voice became very suggestive. "Mr. Farland, for your agent's sake here," he paused and looked at the unconscious Ludvika, who was tied to the chair she was propped up in, "I highly recommend you following my order. You can either bring Ms. Trentino with you, or we will arrange for her transportation. The choice is yours."

Shurnik's warning echoed in Douglas' head as he ran down the sidewalk. His black overcoat flapped around his legs, and the soles of his Armani dress shoes clacked noisily on the asphalt. Douglas didn't care if people were watching him now. He had slammed the receiver back on the phone, and pushed the older man aside as he swung open the phone booth door.

If he could just reach her in time!

Chapter 47

THE HOTEL PARKING LOT was well lit. Mia retrieved the key from under the left front fender.

This was a bit bold, but she didn't care. She unlocked the passenger door and threw her purse onto the backseat. As she walked around the truck, she checked her watch. It was almost eleven thirty. She could be there at two o'clock in the morning.

Am I overreacting? she asked herself as she sank into the driver's seat. Her hands were trembling. She needed to calm herself down. She leaned her head back and closed her eyes, trying to think more clearly. For the last twenty minutes she had agonized over one main question.

Why?

Why had Douglas hid from her the fact that he spoke fluent Russian? What could possibly be the reason?

Mia had replayed the last few days in her head over and over again. He had been a pleasure to work with, a perfect gentleman. Yes—perfect. That should have made her suspicious, because there was no such thing.

I trusted him, Mia thought. Trusted him and shared her experience with her work. She had given him huge insight on her job, and just a week ago she had sworn to herself she would not do exactly that.

And she had translated every goddamn word for him—what for?

Her thoughts intensified on Douglas' behavior. The only abnormality had been his aggressive outburst after the meeting this afternoon. And really, after she had gotten over the initial shock, it had not seemed as severe.

Yes, he had showed a side she didn't appreciate, but it certainly had not affected her so strongly that she'd refused to sleep with him. She had trusted his apology to be sincere. Of course, she had trusted him with her heart, too.

Trust, Mia thought angrily. What a joke!

Now that she sat in the truck, she could barely remember how she'd gotten there. It seemed like only a minute ago she had been sitting on the edge of the bed, holding the phone receiver in one hand and staring at the wall. She couldn't remember now if she actually said anything to the receptionist after she got the news. Her head had seemed to be in a thick cloud. She couldn't even remember the receptionist's name.

What was it? Tina? No, something Balkan. Tanya, right.

All Mia remembered now was the feeling of the walls closing in on her. Claustrophobic as hell, she'd damn near had a panic attack. Then it had gotten worse. Their unbelievable passion had flashed back into her mind. In that room, only a few hours ago, she had made love to a liar.

Disgusted and appalled, Mia had thrown on a pair of jeans and a sweater. She had not even taken the time to brush her hair or fold the business attire she had worn today. She had grabbed a few of her toiletries, her purse, and fled from her feelings of betrayal.

She opened her eyes. Are you overreacting, Mia? Again the question came to mind. She didn't now how else she was supposed to react.

She felt a bit calmer now. She could think more clearly. She wracked her brain trying to find a reason for Douglas' lie. She could only come up with one explanation. If he had kept her in the dark about his language skills, God only knew what else he was hiding from her. She was convinced by now that this had to be it: Farland wanted to take her position at Worldmove. He wanted to push her out of there.

At first it had really sounded far-fetched, but what else could it be? Mia thought about the many questions he had asked her. He had been so slick about it! He had literally sucked her knowledge out of her. Douglas calling Scott in Seattle was now another indicator.

Mia was kind, and yes, sometimes a bit naive—she was the first to admit that. Farland had used that kindness to his advantage. Mia could deal with someone who played the game unfair. That was just what the business world was like nowadays. But Farland had abused her trust and trampled on her dignity by sleeping with her. She had broken her own set of rules for him, and in return that bastard had shaken her self worth.

Defiantly, she stuck her chin out and lifted her head. Well, you messed with the wrong gal, Pal! Mia thought, hot-blooded. She had talked herself into it. There was only one way she could save her position.

Mia turned the key and started the truck. She found the light switch and put the transmission into reverse. She shot out of the parking spot, turned the wheel, and headed for the camp.

Douglas reached the north corner of the hotel within fifteen minutes. He slowed down and finally walked. He was breathing hard and soaked in sweat.

Hiding behind a four-foot brick wall adjoining the hotel's back side, he observed the premises thoroughly. Douglas had forced himself to use a different route back to the hotel. The shortest way would have been unsafe, regardless how badly he wanted to run up to Mia's room and get her the hell out of here.

They might have gotten to her already—the chances were high. It depended on how long ago Shurnik had caught Ludvika, and if the Russian had someone on standby here in Irkutsk ready to strike.

Bogdan! Douglas thought. He knew what she was going through right now. Especially after what she'd done to Shurnik.

Shurnik had found her.

Douglas was trying to imagine what Ludvika's mistake must have been. She had been at the camp to observe, Shurnik knew that as soon as he had caught her. But she could have been anybody. And then Douglas had called her "agent" on the phone. By doing so, Douglas had put Ludvika in an extremely dangerous position.

He should have called her by her code name. He should have known better. He had been trained to know better. Douglas had made a mistake.

Usually mistakes were of deadly consequences in his line of work.

Douglas had believed Shurnik. He'd said he couldn't get any information out of Ludvika. Which meant that he had already began to use forceful methods. Douglas tried to put himself into Shurnik's shoes, if that was possible. The fact that Ludvika had played Shurnik by seducing him would probably engage a higher level of hate and fury in him. His patience during the interrogation would be smaller, and the level of punishment for her silence would be greater.

Shurnik would not kill Bogdan. Not yet, anyway. She was bait to lure Douglas to the camp. Of course that's why Shurnik wanted Douglas to bring Mia along, too. So he could get rid of them all at once and go on with his plans.

Pretty simple plan—too simple. Douglas wondered if Shurnik had an additional agenda.

The hell with him, Douglas thought as he crouched lower behind the wall, getting ready to approach the hotel's back entrance. He wouldn't just roll over and give up trying to save his own skin.

Douglas was under a tremendous amount of pressure. He had to get to the camp as soon as possible, which meant at least two hours if he left right now. There was no way to reverse his mistake, but he had to do his very best to stop Shurnik before he destroyed a perfectly good agent.

But he had to take care of Mia first. He prayed she was in her room, untouched, sleeping safely beneath the covers. He'd wake her and get her to the airport and on the next plane to the States. He did not regret that she was still in Siberia. He had kept using her as part of his cover, and if Ludvika had not been caught, the cover would still be effective.

Cut the crap, Farland! Douglas told himself. Don't make another mistake by thinking about the past. He had to take care of the present situation. He had to get back into the right frame of mind and do what he was good at.

Douglas' heartbeat slowed and he calmed down. He closed his eyes and ran through the possible scenarios that might occur in the next minutes. He had his handgun on his side, but would only use it if absolutely necessary. A shot thug in a hotel would have the authorities here in no time.

He opened his eyes—he didn't have an extra minute to spare.

The truck fishtailed left.

Mia reacted by slightly steering into it. Don't overreact, she told herself. You're gonna put yourself in the ditch.

The dirt road had a few inches of fresh snow on it. No problem, just a bit slick. She knew how to drive through conditions like this. She had learned in Michigan—the winter in the Midwest was no picnic. Mia just had to be careful and slow down. The four-wheel drive would get her there. She just had to keep calm. The odometer showed that she had driven over forty kilometers. She had a quarter of the way behind her.

You still can turn around, her common sense told her. And then what—give up without a fight? her pride argued back. No, Mia had set her mind to it. She would drive to the camp and take care of business, and that was it.

Her cell phone peeped, letting her know it was desperately searching for a signal. She needed to turn it off or the battery would be drained soon.

As Mia turned it off, fright overcame her. There would be no service between here and the camp. If something happened...No, she wouldn't think about that.

Suddenly Shurnik came back to her thoughts. He had never contacted her tonight. He had been behind his scheduled call when she'd left the hotel. Regardless of the test results, Mia had asked him to call her immediately with any news from Dr. Yeltsin.

Mia was sure that Farland was behind that. He probably had told Shurnik to call him instead. Maybe Farland's reservations about

Shurnik were just part of his game. Behind her back he'd been doing business with the Russian.

Mia was getting more upset. "You damn manipulative chauvinist!"

She was gone.

Douglas stood in Mia's room. Had they gotten there before him? The thought almost made his blood boil over.

Douglas scanned the room. The digital alarm clock showed 11:41 p.m. There was no sign of any struggle. He took his time visualizing what it had looked like before he had left. His eyes fell on the small table next to kitchenette. The dirty dishes with the silver covers still sat there, just the way Mia had arranged them. Her brown leather purse had been underneath the table. It was gone now.

Would they have let her take her purse? Definitely not.

Douglas turned and walked into the bathroom. He found the hair clip she had been wearing this morning and her brush, but the violet-colored makeup case he had noticed next to the sink was not there anymore. Neither was her toothbrush.

He was certain she hadn't been abducted from this room. She had left in a hurry, but voluntarily.

A relieved feeling overcame him. She was safe—or was she? Leaning onto the sink, Douglas looked at himself in the mirror.

"Where the hell are you, Mia?" He asked out loud, watching himself speak the words. Sweat-damp strands of short, dark hair were glued to his forehead. His eyes seemed a bit sunken in, but were still bright and alert and his focus fell on the open collar of his dress shirt. He needed to change. His black camo suit was still at the camp with the rest of his gear. Man! He sure hoped Bogdan hadn't been caught hovering above his equipment.

Douglas had a pair of black jeans and a thin black turtleneck sweater in his room. It wasn't the classic attire for a stake out, but it would do. Luckily he had another pair of combat boots in is room as well, and with the addition of his Five-seveN, he could almost call himself prepared.

Still standing in Mia's bathroom, he looked himself in the eyes. Where could she be?

Back at the door, he looked through the peephole. As far as he could see, which wasn't very far, the hallway was deserted. Very slowly he opened the door and scanned both sides. He retrieved his card key from the back pocket of his slacks and walked across the hallway.

He opened the door and slipped inside.

Leaving the lights out, he quickly changed his clothes. Douglas drew his weapon and checked his clip. He knew he didn't need to, but did it anyway. Suddenly he turned his head toward the door. Had he just hear someone approaching out in the hallway?

He thought about an escape plan, not wanting to use the confined area of the hallway. Standing behind the open curtain, he looked out the window. For a while he observed the parking lot below him.

There was no movement. He had to get out of here quickly. It was just a matter of time before he encountered resistance. The window was hinged on the left side. It would open to one side by turning the handle and pulling it inward. He swept the outside of the building with one look. As he climbed on to the narrow windowsill, he found himself two stories above the asphalt parking lot. A jump would be out of the question. He'd end up with a broken ankle.

Douglas carefully leaned to his left and saw a mid-sized pine tree. Its highest branches barely reached beneath the window. He'd lucked out. An old bus was parked right next to the tree. If he could jump far enough into the tree to get a hold of a couple of branches, it would slow down his fall and he could bounce off the bus roof.

Douglas evaluated his chances. Could he make it without injury? Possibly. Should he turn around and use the hallway? Definitely not.

What would his next steps be? Get to a phone, report to Brian, and then look for Mia? He couldn't. He had to go after Shurnik. Even if they got Mia, they would not kill her. If he could get to Shurnik fast enough, he'd fake negotiations to let Mia go. With any luck Bogdan would be still alive by then as well.

In his mind, Douglas' plan looked doable. He took a breath and focused on the bus roof twenty feet below him. And just as he jumped his eyes went over to the end of the parking lot where he had parked the truck today.

It was gone.

Chapter 48

Lagunov sipped his blue-labeled Johnny Walker. How much he enjoyed Scottish Whiskey. The long-legged flight attendant asked him if he wanted a refill before takeoff and he thankfully agreed.

He eyes followed her, glued on her mid-thigh-length skirt. Legs like hers got him easily excited. His wife had legs like those. Long, slender, and smooth. And when she wrapped them around him after the boys had gone to bed...Well, his wife was ill, and it had been a while.

Of course Lagunov would never cheat on her, but it certainly was not cheating letting his eyes lick the insides of the flight attendant's thighs.

The captain informed the passengers of a slight delay in takeoff due to the weather. They would have to deice the engines once again to guarantee a smooth ride. He added that now would be a good time to shut off all electronic devices.

Lagunov leaned against the backrest and unbuckled the seat belt of his oversized seat. He retrieved his cell phone out of the pocket of his Italian-made suit and turned it off. He had spoken with Shurnik just an hour ago. Everything was going according to plan. The Americans would stay the night in Irkutsk, and Shurnik would take off due southeast to the Mongolian border. Shurnik had arranged for a convoy of three trucks to follow parts of the Trans-Siberian and

Trans-Mongolian railways. The 2200 kilometer drive would take him close to thirty-six hours.

Lagunov's golden Rolex told him it was 11:35 p.m. His flight was scheduled to arrive in Vladivostok at 5:15 am Saturday morning. A meeting with Sergei Selkin was planned for that afternoon at the Hotel Equator, where Lagunov would stay.

He regretted being unable to bring his wife along. The sunsets over the Vladivostok's harbor were the prettiest he had ever seen, and his wife loved sunsets.

Well, maybe when she got better he would take her there for a romantic get away. For now, he had to focus strictly on business.

The ice cold water hit Ludvika hard.

Gasping for air, she instantly regained consciousness. She slowly lifted her head, and sharp pain pierced her face again.

"Time to wake up, sweetheart." Shurnik stood in front of her with a plastic bucket in one hand. "Let's continue our little chat, shall we?"

Ludvika let out another anguished cry as he grabbed her hair. The pain of him brutally pulling her head back added to the agonizing ache deep inside the right side of her face. Her eye socket was fractured and her right eye was almost swollen shut. She was disoriented and could not move. She was on the verge of losing consciousness again, and her one good eye was rolling back into her head.

"Fuck you." She could barely speak with her swollen, bloodied lips. They were the only words she had told Shurnik in the last hours.

Hours of pure agony. It seemed like the punishing eternity of hell.

She wanted to sleep. Not die, just sleep. He had not yet broken her will to live, but he might be able to do so during the night. But he would never break her will to keep silent—never.

Her foggy mind tried to convince her battered body to block out the excruciating pain. She was still able to comprehend, and her brain was on overdrive, but she was so tired. She had never been so tired in her life.

Ludvika was lucky. She had already lost consciousness again when the thick bottom of the plastic bucket crashed against her right temple, crushing her cheekbone. The momentum sent the chair she was tied to toppling over sideways, and Ludvika's head slammed onto the concrete floor.

You are going to kill her, Shurnik thought as he watched the blood gushing out of Ludvika's nose. He turned the bucket over and sat on it. He would give it a minute for her to come back around. He knew she would. She was tough—incredibly tough, especially for a woman.

Shurnik had handled men in the past who had been trained to withstand the effects of torture. It was all about mind control, and he had watched men breakdown long before they had experienced what she was going through.

He crouched down to look at her more closely. Where the hell did she come from? Her Russian had a slight accent, but he could not quite place it. Eastern Europe, probably. By her looks she could not be from south of the Caucasus. Maybe she originated from somewhere in the Balkan region.

Agent Bogdan. If that was her real name, she could be easily traced. But Shurnik didn't have the time. He should be on his way to Ulaanbaatar very soon. He checked his watch—01:06. He had scheduled his departure for three o'clock in the morning and the crew was ready. He'd had to put them on standby because of the necessary delay in departure. Shurnik had to wait for the Americans to return and take care of them.

It was still under control. No need to involve Lagunov. By the time Shurnik had brought her here, he had been unreachable, anyway. Shurnik knew Lagunov's itinerary, and his flight should have left over an hour ago.

Discovering her had been a pure coincidence. And she had reacted very quickly when he had surprised her in her hideout. She hadn't been able to pull the trigger, but when Shurnik had kicked the weapon out of her hand she'd already had it pointed to his chest.

At first Shurnik hadn't been sure who he was fighting. Her face was disguised with a black mask, and her blond hair had been covered as well. He had been able to rip the mask off during their encounter, and a moment of disbelieve had given her an advantage and Shurnik a cracked rib.

She had put up a hell of a fight.

Shurnik had thought he could play with her; but very soon he had figured out that she had been trained extremely well. But she hadn't just fought like a black belt. Her style proved her skills reached far beyond that. She had the speed and agility of a trained guerrilla combatant and fought very smart.

By the time Shurnik had realized he would need all his expertise to beat her, she had already done him some damage. The only reason he had been able to overpower her was due to pure muscle strength. She had lost because she was a woman, not because she was less of a warrior.

Douglas accelerated.

After realizing the truck was gone, he'd started trying doors in the parking lot, not wanting to waste the precious time it would take to pick a lock. He'd had a moment of pleasure when he'd tried the handle of the brand new GAZ 3120 and it opened. The Russian mixture of an American Jeep and Hummer was perfect for the terrain.

The pleasure was fleeting, however. Deep inside Douglas' unsettled core, he knew what the missing truck meant and where Mia was headed. He had no idea exactly how far she was ahead of him or why she had decided she must leave in the middle of the night. He planned on calling the hotel front desk to ask if they had seen her, but priorities first.

The GAZ was loaded with extras. It had a navigation system, which would be an advantage for Douglas when he approached the camp, but the disadvantage was that the GPS was probably traceable. Hopefully the vehicle would not be reported stolen until the morning.

His eyes scanned the inside of the GAZ while he made his way toward the city limits of Irkutsk. The car phone was operational, but wasn't even close to being a secure line.

Douglas weighed that risk against the time he would save by talking and driving at once. It didn't take long to decide. He dialed a landline at the Acronym instead of Brian's cell number.

"The Baltimore Avenue Bed and Breakfast, how may I help you?" the Acronym's planted receptionist greeted in her lovely voice.

"04 for 02." He hated having to go through the security ordeal He didn't have the time to waste. "How many people in your party?" she asked, meaning Douglas' code.

"040102." The line got connected to Brian's office.

"Where the hell are you calling from?" Brian was upset. The Acronym's lines were strictly reserved for code red situations only.

"From a very cool Russian Jeep, hauling ass. Now shut up and listen." He gave Brian the rundown of the last hour, starting with his conversation with Shurnik right after he'd gotten off the phone with Brian.

"You screwed up, Doug!" Brian said baldly.

"No shit, smart guy, but I should be there within ninety minutes. I think she'll be all right."

"If she lives, I'll tell her you said that." On the other end of the line, Brian was squinting his eyes as his stomach turned. He could only imagine the position Ludvika was in. "So what's your plan?"

"I'll tell you in a minute. First you need to know that we might have an additional problem." He paused as he passed a police patrol car. He was going just a bit over the speed limit, and hoped he wouldn't have to add "high speed chase" to his growing list of troubles.

When he saw the cop wasn't going to follow, he continued. "Mia Trentino is heading toward the camp, somewhere between twenty minutes and an hour ahead of me."

"Aw geez, what happened? I thought she'd be outta there by now." Brian held his head in his hands. What was his partner risking her for?

"My cover was still good until Shurnik found Bogdan," Douglas explained.

Brian understood and reluctantly nodded. "Are you going to be able to catch up with her?"

"I sure hope so," Douglas said, meaning it.

"Okay, maybe when you get all your girl trouble sorted out you can go back to catching the bad guys. By the way, this just came through—Lagunov is reported to be on his way to Vladivostok. He used false papers, but Interpol still traced him."

"They're not gonna arrest him, are they?"

"No, there are no charges as of yet. But you need to get your ass out there as soon as possible. Backup is not far behind you." Brian's voice was getting fuzzy. The satellite signal was getting weaker. He only had a few seconds left before he'd lose Brian if he didn't stop the Jeep.

"Brian, I'm gonna lose you. I will contact you from the camp, if I get the chance."

"Roger that." Brian was gone.

Douglas eyed the rearview mirror again to make sure neither the patrol car or anyone else was following him.

He turned sharply onto the snow-covered dirt road that would lead him to the camp. He floored the gas pedal, and the powerful diesel engine obeyed. There were fresh tire tracks in the snow.

Mia, Douglas thought.

He hadn't had the chance to call the hotel's front desk before the line went dead. Now he would not be able to find out if or at what time anyone had talked to her or even seen her leave.

I'm behind you, sweet thing. I won't let anything happen to you, he thought, knowing he couldn't really make that promise.

He rubbed his hand over his face and a sudden burn on his left cheek made him jerk. Again, he glanced into the mirror, lifting his head to see what had caused the sting. He noticed a bloody scratch right on top of his cheekbone. He must have gotten it when he'd slid through the pine tree on his way to the roof of the bus. He hadn't even noticed.

Drawing blood, he thought. He was sure Bogdan had drawn more blood than him by now.

His knuckles turned white as he clamped his hands around the steering wheel.

"Girl trouble," Brian had said. If Douglas didn't hurry, both women would end up in a little more than just "trouble."

Chapter 49

"They're coming." Oleg stood in the door, looking at Shurnik.

He tried to ignore Ludvika, but as his eyes brushed past her, he couldn't help but wince. He knew she was the enemy, but she was still a woman, and a beautiful one. Well, she used to be, anyway.

His hazy focus went back to Shurnik, who asked with emphasis, "Have you had any today?" Shurnik referred to the meth Oleg has been smoking lately.

"No, Boss," he lied. He had smoked, but just a little to keep the urge under control. He felt calm and very confident. Nothing in this world could harm him. He was ready for the task.

"You keep your eye on her. I will take care of the Americans. She's out now, but she might regain her consciousness soon. She'll try to plead with you. No matter what she might tell you, do not get close to her. Is that understood?" Shurnik pressed.

"Of course, Boss." Oleg answered keenly.

Shurnik looked from Oleg back to Ludvika. He had propped her back up, including the chair. Her shoulders and head were slumped forward. Blood still trickled heavily out of her nose, but not as bad anymore. In this position, even if she didn't come back around, she would be able to breath and not suffocate on her own blood.

He had hoped she would have woken back up by now. He had not been able to get a damn word out of her. Now he had to leave her and worry about the Americans—especially the man. Shurnik anticipated heavy resistance from him.

He gave Ludvika one last look before he left. What was he going to do with her? For some reason it didn't feel as easy to get rid of her as the other two. Killing her seemed wrong and unnecessary—a sensation totally new to him. He had some time to think about it, he reminded himself. With that issue deflected, he turned around and went through the heavy metal door, through the cold meth lab, and up the stairs.

Mia saw the dim lights of the camp. A deep feeling of relief overcame her as she drove down the hill. It had taken her a little while longer than she had thought. Snow was a treacherous thing to maneuver in, but she had managed well. Now it was almost two thirty, and the night was pitch-black without a moon in the cloudy sky.

You made it, she thought and yearned for sleep. She'd sneak into her yurt, set her alarm for five, and curl up in bed.

Thinking about how she should handle the situation, she hoped, more than ever before, that the test results would be negative. That way she would be able to finish up her task today and leave by this afternoon. It would be hard with just a few hours of sleep, but she was going to sleep for a week once she got back home. If Scott ever approached her with another assignment in Russia, he could shove it.

Thinking about Montana and all the good things that came with it had kept her going in the last three hours. But what if the tests showed contamination? Well, she'd deal with that, too. Think positive, she told herself.

She drove around and parked behind the mess hall. Three heavy trucks, two of them with machinery strapped to their flatbed trailers, were parked in a row. She wondered what that was about, and then remembered Shurnik saying something about accompanying equipment to Vladivostok on Sunday.

Despite her fatigue, her curiosity won out, and she walked over to see what was tied to the flatbed. She noticed a motor on each trailer, covered in clear tarp, and figured they must be replacement parts.

Shurnik watched her, hidden in the shadows. He was very surprised to see her come alone—or was she? Was it Farland's plan to make it look like she had and then count on the effect of a surprise attack?

He decided to stay where he was and continue to watch her.

She took a bag out of the backseat and walked to her yurt. She did not observe her surroundings or try to conceal her presence in any way. If she was an agent, she was either very brave or crazy, Shurnik thought. She was walking unprotected toward her barracks, not something a trained combatant would do in a situation like this.

She kept her head forward, looking straight ahead of her. Shurnik ran his eyes over her body. Her jeans were tucked into her lace-up boots. She'd never be able to reach an ankle holster quickly. She carried her jacket over her arm, and he could see both of her hands. The sweater she was wearing was too tight to conceal any kind of weapon.

His instincts told him that this woman was what she had come here as—Ms. Trentino from Worldmove, Inc. There was no doubt in his mind. But what the hell was she doing here in the middle of the night? Had Farland sent her knowing she would be a target? Would she have agreed to whatever reason he might have come up with to send her driving out here at this time?

Shurnik was utterly confused and dying to find out.

He stepped just far enough out of the dark that she could see him. "Ms. Trentino."

Mia let out a faint scream as she dropped her bag. Her brown eyes were huge, like a deer staring into headlights of oncoming traffic. "Oh, God," she exhaled.

Shurnik smiled. She was undoubtedly by herself. "I'm sorry I startled you, Ms. Trentino. Isn't it a bit late to be driving through the Siberian taiga? Especially in this weather?" He wanted to ask her about Farland, but let her speak first.

With her heartbeat thumping beyond anything she could manage while she was running, she looked at him. "Mr. Shurnik, good evening." Unbelievable—she was still polite. "I hadn't heard from you. Do you have the results?"

It took Shurnik a moment to figure out what she was talking about.

He smiled again. "Yes, we do. It took longer than expected. The good Doctor just called me."

Mia's tiredness vanished. "Oh, good."

Shurnik's gray eyes penetrated her as he took a step toward her. "You will be excited to know that the tests were negative." He paused and added. "Mr. Farland and you will be able to return to the U.S. very soon. Did he not accompany you on your drive?"

Mia looked at Shurnik. She had noticed the icy color of Shurnik's eyes before, but now she was mesmerized. What had he just said? Negative tests? Mia forced herself away from those glacier-colored eyes. Negative tests? She thought again, and then it sank in.

A huge wave of relief washed through her, pushing away the last traces of the effect the long drive had left on her. She smiled at Shurnik and felt like hugging him, but of course didn't. "That's wonderful news! Yukoil must be thrilled," she said happily.

"Yes, they certainly will be."

Mia then realized Shurnik's earlier question. He had asked about Farland. No, he was definitely not with her. But if he wasn't here, where was he?

Mia was not sure how to ask Shurnik, so she just blurted out, "I thought he was back here in camp. He hasn't arrived this evening?"

Shurnik narrowed his eyes. Was she playing him? "Did you and Mr. Farland not leave together in one vehicle?"

A flush of heat rolled through her body. Of course, she realized. How could she have been so stupid? She had the truck. He couldn't have driven out here to work things out with Shurnik.

Then where was he?

"No," she said finally. "Mr. Farland has not come with me." She did not want to explain. She wouldn't know how. And to Shurnik, it should not matter. The job was done. She'd gather her belongings, type her final report in the morning, and then she was out of here, with or without an explanation from Farland.

That decided, she turned and began walking toward her yurt. Shurnik hadn't offered to carry her bag for her. He had simply wished her a good night and let her walk on—probably so she wouldn't be freaked out by him following her to her sleeping quarters in the middle of the night with no one else around. What a courteous person.

Mia had just enough time to finish the thought before the impact on the back of her neck robbed her of consciousness. She was out before she hit the snow-covered ground.

Oleg stared at Ludvika's breasts. Her arms were tied behind her back, and the top button of her black camo jacket was ripped off. The blood did not bother Oleg much. It just stained the dark clothing darker.

She was still out like a light, and he dared to move a little closer. Shurnik had tied her ankles to the two front legs of the chair; her thighs were parted and her knees bent. Her long, blond hair was a mess and had some blood in it, but Oleg thought that it looked like a waterfall of silken gold and wanted to touch it.

The jacket was tight over her breasts and his excitement grew. He knew what Shurnik had told him, but couldn't help it. His hands glided from Ludvika's hair down her uninjured cheek toward her neck. Her skin was so soft. He bent his knees to get closer to those big breasts he yearned to touch. He watched her breathing and didn't notice any change. She was unconscious and in no position to give him any grief about his fondling her.

His eyes went to her mutilated face. She had been so beautiful when he had seen her last. With eager hands he feverishly opened another button and his focus went back to her chest.

Suddenly she let out a cry and her body launched forward with unbelievable speed. He didn't have time to comprehend what had happened before he found himself on his back, unable to take another breath, with Ludvika on top of him. Her hands were steel clamps around his throat, both thumbs pushing his larynx toward his spine. One knee crushed the bottom third of his sternum, thrusting life out of his solar plexus.

It took him a while to die, and he did so with a look of surprise on his mealy face.

Ludvika rolled on her side, her hands already trying to find a way to untie the knots on her ankles. Her face throbbed much worse now. Earlier she had been able to deflect the pain by concentrating on very carefully wiggling her way out of the first shackle behind her back.

Shurnik had cut her during their fight in the woods, and that was her luck. The deep wound in her lower right arm had saturated her shackles with blood, making them just slick enough for her to free one hand.

It had taken her all her willpower and strength to keep rotating her wrist to free herself. The tight shackle had restricted her circulation after a while, and the pain of the deep cut had been unbearable. But it had been her only chance, and she had known it.

A few times she had almost given up. But then she remembered her partner who'd been killed by Shurnik, and the promise of revenge urged her to go on. The deep, cold emotion of hate had been stronger than the pain.

Chapter 50

THE GPS WORKED WELL.

Douglas was still over five miles out when he noticed that he was in reach of a satellite. The small points on the screen indicated that he was close to receiving a signal.

And there is was. Douglas stopped at once. He studied the screen, locating the area where the camp must be. He pushed the button and the field zoomed in. It took a minute to reestablish the full range on the display, but he could make out that there was drivable terrain on the west side of the camp.

Perfect. He could sneak in close enough to quickly get to his gear on foot.

He had thought about the dangers. If Shurnik knew about Douglas' hideout, he'd expect him there first. But Douglas had to take certain risks, and that was one of them.

Mia's tire tracks were illuminated by the jeep's headlights. He would turn off the road now. It had begun to snow again, and Douglas hoped it would continue so his own tracks would vanish soon.

The pale, orange lights of the jeep's dashboard made it hard to see as Douglas continued with just the lower driving lights on. He found a little wheel underneath the light switch and turned the dashboard lights off. The only lights left now were the grayish-blue screen of the GPS and the tiny orange dots of the digital clock. It was 02:54.

The terrain was difficult to drive through, and Douglas had to force himself to be careful. Ludvika and Mia were counting on him not making another mistake.

The minutes seemed to have raced away by the time he finally decided he was close enough to continue on foot. He killed the lights and the jeep's engine. He turned off the interior lights and opened the door.

He stepped out, and it was completely dark. The GPS was removable, and he unplugged it out of the cigarette lighter. He did not know how good the batteries were, or if it worked on charge. It didn't matter. With any luck he'd find his way to the camp quickly through the thick woods.

She was still in terrible pain. Ludvika had torn off parts of her shirt and wrapped them around the injured part of her face and the deep cut in her arm. Blood was quickly saturating the cloths, but at least she wouldn't leave a blood trail.

She crouched low behind the canvas. She was just in time to see Shurnik knock Mia unconscious. In a distant part of her mind not consumed by thoughts of survival, she was surprised and wondered what the other woman was doing back at camp. Regardless, though, without weapons and in her shape, she would be lucky to take care of herself, much less Ms. Trentino.

When Shurnik disappeared with Mia toward the tents, she carefully made her way in the opposite direction. As far as she could see out of her one good eye, nobody else was around. The loss of blood was making her light-headed, and she was not sure how long she could last.

She noticed several different boot prints in the snow and hurried in wide steps, zigzagging through parts of the camp, trying to conceal the direction she was going. The closer she got to the edge of the camp, the fewer footprints she saw. He'll find me, she thought, but she did not have the strength to go all the way around the camp. If she could make it in time to Farland's hideout, she could arm herself with his M40.

Suddenly, Ludvika slipped on an icy patch of snow and fell forward onto her injured right arm. The sharp pain shot through her nerves into her whole body. Agonized, she lay on the ground moaning loudly.

Shut up, she told herself. She wanted to lay there on the snow and go to sleep so the pain would go away. But she couldn't. She had to push on just a little longer till she reached the hideout.

Somehow, she did. The distance was not very far, but to her battered body it had felt like miles. The night had swallowed her, and without any lights, nobody would be able to see her tracks or her as she huddled in the brush underneath the big trees.

Now that she was sitting still, feeling safer with Farland's sniper rifle on her lap, she started to shiver. Shock was creeping over her body like a silent snake stalking its prey.

Stay awake, she told herself. The rifle in her lap wouldn't do her any good if she passed out.

She scooped up a handful of snow and carefully pressed it against her swollen eye. The cold numbed the pain ever so slightly, and she dared to let the snow touch her fractured cheek. The raw nerves protested with an electric shock of pain that almost knocked her unconscious.

Okay, just the eye.

The shock progressed, and her body shook violently. Desperately she tried to keep herself awake by thinking rational thoughts. She figured out quickly why Shurnik had focused on battering her face. He must certainly know there are especially pain-sensitive areas in the body. She had no doubt in her mind he had felt them himself in pressing confessions. But more than that, he had concentrated on her face because that's what she had used to weaken him. When she'd seduced him, he had told her he'd never seen anyone as beautiful as her. He had to make sure that she would never be able to do that again and so destroyed her features.

Ludvika didn't care about her looks. She didn't care about scars or worse. Not now, anyway. Right now all she cared about was staying awake and defending her life.

Douglas could hear Ludvika's muffled moans and chattering teeth, but he could not see her. He must be close, he thought. He was somewhere behind her, pressed against the trunk of a big tree, inching himself closer. He didn't know if Shurnik or someone else was with her, keeping her alive and using her as bait.

He strained to see in the dark, but all he could make out was the outline of the tree he suspected Ludvika was sitting against. Holding his breath, he listened hard. He could not tell if there was anyone else. He had to take his chance.

With his weapon in his both hands, he lay on the ground. Suddenly he could make out that Ludvika's head had slipped sideways from against the tree. He could barely see her blond hair hanging down to the ground. He watched as her upper body started to slide sideways as well. She didn't fall all the way to the ground, but just sat there, lifeless like a string puppet without its master.

Douglas could not hear her breathing. The sudden certainty that she was dead welled up in his mind.

No, it can't be. Don't let her die, he frantically thought, but still didn't move. He waited to see if someone tried to wake her back up. Without making noise, she wasn't good bait. But there was nobody. Nobody tried to squeeze more pain out of her to lure Douglas closer. She was alone.

Still on his stomach, he crept closer. When he reached the tree Ludvika sat under, he saw the tip of his rifle sticking to the left. He crouched behind her and placed his hand over her mouth. With a sudden, muffled scream she woke up. "Shh," Douglas kept his hand where it was. He barely whispered, "It's Farland. Are you alone?" A faint nod of hers told him he could let his hand go.

Relieved, he let himself down next to her. He could just barely see her face, but what he saw was enough to make his heart wrench. The one open eye reflected deep fear, and the other side of her face was double the size of what it should be.

"Bastard," Douglas whispered hatefully. He knew it was just a matter of time before she went into shock. If she didn't get help quickly, she could die.

"Bogdan, where else are you hurt?" Douglas asked, cupping his hand very carefully around the good side of her face. Her skin was cool and damp.

When she felt his tender touch, Ludvika realized she was safe. A tear rolled down her cheek and wetted Douglas hand. She could not speak. The pain was too great in her jaw. She lifted her right hand off the rifle in her lap and Douglas took it instantly.

He could feel the wetness of the primitive bandage around her lower arm. The consistency of it told him that it was blood—lots of it. He opened the wrap but couldn't see the injury. He had to look at it. If a main blood vessel was severed she could bleed out within a very short time.

He dared to turn on his penlight and held it between his teeth to inspect the severity of the wound. The cut was deep and about four inches long. The location made it clear that it was a defense wound. It still bled considerably, but he could probably stop it with a tight pressure bandage.

He ripped a new piece of cloth off her shirt and pushed it onto her arm, applying a moderate amount of pressure. She winced but did not make a sound.

How brave she was. "I'm sorry, Bogdan," Douglas whispered, meaning more than just the pain he'd inflicted on her arm.

He needed to stay with her for a while. Maybe he could get the bleeding under control and prevent her from going into shock. He carefully helped her lay down and held her arm elevated from her heart. Douglas had many questions for her, but he knew she couldn't speak. He wanted her to feel safe and placed the palm of his hand tenderly on her forehead.

A tone escaped her throat, and he was not sure what she meant. He shushed her. "You'll be fine. Brian sent backup. They should be here very soon," He hoped he wasn't lying. They might get here too late.

She whispered something he couldn't understand, so he lowered his ear down to her split and swollen lips.

"He took her." Douglas could barely make out her words. He took her? Was she talking about Shurnik? Douglas did not dare to ask but had to. "Did Shurnik take Mia?" Ludvika nodded faintly and Douglas' worst nightmare became true.

"Did you see where he took her?" Douglas tried to picture the possibilities in his head.

It took Ludvika all her strength to say, "...hit her hard...carried her...to tent..."

With that Ludvika passed out.

Douglas tried very hard to comprehend what Ludvika had just told him. Did he understand her right? Shurnik had hit Mia? Hit her hard—is that what she just said? And he had carried her to a tent? Jesus, what for? Douglas did not allow his brain to imagine what Shurnik might be doing to Mia. But as soon as the thoughts had finished forming, that was all he could think about.

The sudden uproar of several diesel engines in the distance made him look toward the camp. He carefully placed Ludvika's hand on her stomach and rose. Taking a few steps toward the noise he could see more clearly through the trees. Three trucks were lit from above by the main light of the camp's center. Men were mounting the trucks. He could not make out who they were, but Douglas knew one of them must be Shurnik.

They were leaving, transporting the drugs due southeast to China. Testing the safety of the route for their next, far more dangerous load.

Douglas took his M40 rifle from Ludvika's lap and looked through the high-powered scope. Shurnik was easy to make out. His size and those confident, long strides as he walked gave him away. He was carrying something, but Douglas could not see what it was. The Russian had his back to him.

When Shurnik turned to approach the back of the second truck in line, Douglas suddenly understood. He had his right index finger on the extremely sensitive trigger. If only he could just pull it. Her brown hair dangled over one arm, and her legs hung lifelessly from her knees down over the other.

Douglas had never felt as helpless as when he was forced to watch Shurnik take Mia away.

Chapter 51

HE NEEDED TO MAKE the call.

Douglas went back to Ludvika. He found his cell phone in her pocket. He checked her pulse and breathing and decided she was okay for now. Her status could change fast, but he had to trust in her strength.

After the second ring the line got picked up. "The Baltimore Avenue Bed and...." Douglas interrupted her. There was no time for security measures.

"040102. I have a code red. Repeat, code red."

The receptionist at the Acronym did not say anything and patched Douglas through to Brian's landline.

"Go," Brian said.

"I've got Bogdan. Alive. But she needs medics ASAP. The Russians moved out." Douglas paused. He did not mention Mia.

Brian answered. "I'll call medics, you pursue. You've got reliable wheels?"

"Positive," Douglas said quickly and added, "You need Big Eye to cover for me."

"Roger that." It would take Brian one call to have the satellite's watchful eyes on Shurnik's path. Maybe he could even pull a string or two at the Air Force, but that would take time. Brian knew they would be all over Shurnik and his load if he was transporting the real goods, but this was just a drug bust for now. It would be hard to talk the military into assistance.

"How bad is she?" Brian asked.

Douglas turned his head down to Ludvika. "She's bad. Out now, but she'll be okay if they get here in time. So get your ass on the phone. Tell them they'll find her in the travel trailer on the southeast corner of the camp, just west of the helipad."

Douglas terminated the line before Brian could ask about Mia. She didn't matter to Brian or to the Acronym. Brian would only warn Douglas about the sensitivity of the op. "Just tail, no rescue," that's what Brian would have told Douglas, and he did not want to hear his friend say those words. Brian knew about Douglas' past with the FBI's hostage rescue team. It was in Douglas' blood to go after her. But this was the Acronym, not the FBI. The rules were different. The mission was absolute priority, not the safety of a citizen. Brian would only have pressed the issue, and Douglas wanted to avoid the conflict if he could.

He carefully scooped Ludvika off the cold ground. Her clothes were wet from lying in the snow.

It was just a short distance to the trailer, and Douglas was not concerned about being seen. Shurnik's convoy had left the camp, and he was concealed in the darkness. Douglas wouldn't be surprised if he could move around freely now. He was not worried about the surveillance cameras in the trailer, either. This was, after all, just the field of a Siberian oil company. The remainder of Shurnik's crew probably did not know about the drugs and the little side job he was doing.

Douglas laid Ludvika on the bed without turning on the lights. He carefully positioned her arms by her side. The bleeding seemed to have slowed down considerably. She moaned and was half conscious.

"Hey," he said gently, touching the uninjured cheek. "Help is on the way. You just rest for now. They will be here to get you very soon."

Ludvika understood through the haze of pain. Douglas could make out that she barely nodded, and her half-open eye looked at the door. A very small gesticulation, but Douglas knew what she meant.

She was telling him to go get after the bastards.

Douglas touched her forehead once more—he would not tell her goodbye—and silently left.

"You are now allowed to use your electronic devices," The long-legged flight attendant informed the passengers with a purr.

Lagunov sighed. He had just woken up from a whiskey-infused catnap. He felt good, not tired at all. The excitement of the following days would give him just the right amount of adrenaline to be alert.

He got out his cell phone to turn it on. Momentarily he retrieved a short text message. "Aunt Lucy died." It read. He raised his eyebrows in astonishment. What? Who's Aunt? He didn't have... Of course. The code words that had been explained to him. It had been a few weeks, and Lagunov stared at the phone's screen, trying to remember what that meant.

Suddenly, it came back to him. Aunt Lucy was the coup. Death meant trouble. He looked out of the window as the plane taxied to the terminal. It was still dark outside. An unsettled feeling swept through him.

Shit, he thought, wondering what could have happened.

The planning of this operation had been going on for almost a year. The Mafia had tested Yukoil efficiency through smaller coups, mostly money laundry. Yukoil had proven itself to be a competent partner for the Mafia's future ventures. It had not always been easy for Lagunov to keep his involvement concealed from the rest of the board members, but his smart business sense and his trusting karma had kept him from being exposed.

Through members of the ex-soviet military, the Mafia had known about the underground premises close by Yukoil's oil field. It had been Shurnik who had come up with the drug laboratory idea.

Lagunov rubbed his jaw. His mind replayed the conversation with Sergei Selkin just a few weeks ago when he had visited St. Petersburg.

"U-238," Lagunov could still hear Selkin's voice in his head, "will be our ticket to a very prosperous future."

Lagunov had looked confused, not knowing what Selkin was talking about. Was U-238 a new designer drug? That question and other facts had not been explained in the document sent to him.

But then Selkin had said, "For a long time now, unit one of the nuclear power plant in Beloyarsk has been shut down. However, we have very good connections with important workers in the plant."

Lagunov remembered now, his stomach knotting up at the words "nuclear power plant."

He had asked, "What kind of connections?"

"Very, very good connections, Mr. Lagunov." He had paused and then continued. "Unit one has been dead for over twenty-five years, and the plant's management has changed positions in those years. Not everyone is in perfect understanding about some of the treasures Beloyarsk has to offer."

"Treasures? I wished you would be more explanatory, Mr. Selkin." Lagunov hated it when people didn't spit out what they had to say. Selkin had played a guessing game with him and Lagunov had wondered why.

"Yes, treasures. And we have found a very lucrative way of turning these treasures into hard currency, Mr. Lagunov. We have to wait and see if Shurnik's way of transporting the methamphetamine is a safe route. If it is, we will use the same route to transport our treasure from Yukoil's oil field to Vladivostok."

"Why to Vladivostok? Aren't the drugs being transported to Jilin, China?"

"Yes, Mr. Lagunov. However; the delivery of the U-238 will continue to Vladivostok," Selkin had explained.

Lagunov had had enough. "Mr. Selkin, would you mind sharing your secret about what U-238 stands for?"

Selkin had been enjoying himself and smiled. "Certainly. U-238 stands for uranium-238, which will be bred into plutonium with a little help of the nuclear enrichment unit at a breeding reactor in China."

Lagunov had looked baffled at Selkin who had further explained, "And as you might know, Mr. Lagunov, plutonium can be used as a fuel source in a nuclear reactor—or for thermonuclear weapons."

Lagunov's face had burned as if someone had slapped him hard. He had barely dared to ask the question, "Nuclear weapons for Russia?" Selkin had laughed at Lagunov's naiveté.

"No, of course not. The enriched U-238 will be sold to our neighbor just a few hundred kilometers south of Vladivostok—to the great country of North Korea."

The captain turned off the fasten seat belt sign, and the faint dinging noise brought Lagunov back to the present time. Once again he looked at the message on his cell phone, and then deleted it. He let the phone slide into the inner pocket of his suit jacket and stood. He was sure that someone would contact him again very soon.

He stepped out into the aisle to collect his carry-on suitcase. As his eyes went over the back of the flight attendant's legs for the last time, his wife came to mind. The brain tumor deep inside her head could not be operated on. It was growing rapidly, and without removal she would die. They had told him that he needed to get her to the United States for radiation treatment. She had been there now for several weeks undergoing very expensive therapy in a private cancer research and treatment clinic.

Ironic. He was using stolen nuclear power to enrich himself so he could afford the nuclear radiation his wife so desperately needed to be healed.

Chapter 52

Mia smelled the lavender.

It was deliciously sweet. She turned around and saw Douglas running toward her. He was so handsome! She wanted to run to him, but suddenly could not place one foot in front of the other. She was paralyzed. There was a wide, bottomless gap in front of her. She screamed at Douglas to warn him, but he could not hear her soundless words. In horror Mia watched Douglas step into the gap, and it swallowed him right in front of her eyes.

Mia tried to reach out to him, but could not move her arms, either.

Gasping for air, her eyes flew open. She tried to inhale, but her mouth was taped. A small amount of her own spit ran down her airway and triggered her reflex to cough, but she couldn't. She panicked. Oh my God, I can't breathe, the insides of her screamed. She tipped over to her side, scrambling to get out of whatever it was confining her movement, but it would not budge.

It was dark in front of her eyes, and Mia hoped she was just floating between nightmares, but the throbbing pain in the back of her neck told her this was real.

Why can't I breathe? Mia tried desperately to inhale through her mouth, but the duct tape did not let through the smallest amount of air. Her brain automatically switched the source of air intake and her nostrils flared open.

Thank God.

"Easy, easy," a male voice said in Russian. A cloth sack was lifted from her head. She squinted. The room was dark with a light source above her. He was behind her, so she could not see him. A strong hand pushed her throbbing head onto the filthy ground. The voice said, "Promise to behave, and I will take the tape off."

Mia tried to scream, but only a muffled noise penetrated the tape. The strong hand went over her nose, robbing her of precious air. Her scream died and panic set back in. Her confined hands balled into fists behind her back as she tried to jerk her head away from the strong hand, but she couldn't.

"Behave if you want to breathe," the voice commanded.

Suddenly Mia lay still, understanding that she could not fight this. The hand moved, and Mia inhaled deeply, supplying her starving lungs with much needed air. She squeezed her stinging eyes shut, trying to suppress the urge to gag.

"That's better," the voice said. The hand moved to the side of her taped mouth, and before Mia could finish her next thought a sudden, painful heat blossomed over her lips and cheeks as the man ripped off the tape.

"Don't make a sound," he warned her immediately. Mia gagged and coughed. And just as she thought he would tape her mouth again, he helped her to sit up. She could breathe easier in this position and the man held her by the shoulders until she regained her balance.

"Too bad the boss told us not to touch you. I've been eying you all week," the man said. Mia had not heard the voice before. But the lustful meaning of his words made her shiver in disgust.

She tried to understand where she was. All she saw was the dirty inside of what seemed to be the loading space of one of Yukoil's big trucks. Green canvas was draped over freight. She could not see what it was. They were driving on a bumpy road, and she smelled the exhaust from the diesel engine.

The obvious dawned to her. "I've been kidnapped," she whispered, and the cold truth ran like ice water through her veins.

"Smart girl," he said. She wanted to see his face, but could not turn her head enough. Mia heard him say, "She's awake." A tinny voice crackled back, "Any trouble?" "No, not really."

He had talked to someone on the radio. Mia thought she'd made out Shurnik's voice on the other end, but she was not sure.

"Where are you taking me?"

"You'll see. Don't talk," the man commanded.

"I want to know where you are taking me." Mia's voice rose, but she stayed calm, and now she sounded commanding herself.

She was startled by a loud ripping sound. His arms went heavily around her upper body from behind, holding a roll of black tape in front of her face. He ripped off a piece.

"What's it gonna be, sugar? Tape or no tape?"

Mia understood. She stayed quiet. The rumble of the rough road shook her, and it was difficult to sit upright and keep balance without the use of her tied hands.

What in the world had happened? The last thing she remembered was arriving at the camp and Shurnik talking to her.

Oh, God, Douglas! Panic swept through her. Strangely, she was suddenly concerned about him. She was the one who had been kidnapped. If he hadn't lied to her, she wouldn't have driven to the camp in the middle of the night, and she wouldn't have...

Her thoughts went crazy.

The truck seemed to slow down and finally stop. The diesel engine rumbled as it idled low. Mia heard the door of a vehicle open, and the truck shook as the door was slammed shut. She heard the footsteps approaching her direction. Her heart was hammering in her tight chest.

The canvas flew open to one side, and Mia recognized Shurnik as he climbed into the back of the truck. He ducked as he stepped over the tied-down equipment and sat on a canvas-wrapped bundle in front of her. He had something in his hand—a white plastic pouch of some sort.

Oh, no. He's gonna drug me, Mia thought, horrified. Her body started trembling.

Shurnik's face was close to hers. Mia did not dare to say anything. She just looked at Shurnik with big, frightened eyes.

"Do you promise to be good?" Mia did not react to Shurnik's question. Pure horror had paralyzed her. "You can make this relatively easy for yourself. You will not be hurt. I know that it is your main concern. You will not be harmed or killed." He looked at her with those cold, gray eyes. He added, "That is, if you are going to be good and not cause any problems."

Mia saw something else in his eyes. She wanted to believe it was honesty. But how could a man like him have any honesty in his body?

Slowly Mia nodded her head. Her petrified eyes went from Shurnik's down to his hand. He was still holding the white pouch.

He asked, "How is your head? I know it must hurt."

It took all of Mia's courage to speak. She whispered, "Where are you taking me? What do you want from me?"

"One thing at a time," Shurnik said and squeezed the plastic pouch hard with both hands. Mia heard a pop and then a swooshing sound. Shurnik moved the ends up and down, mixing its contents. As he raised the pouch toward Mia's head he said, "Here, that should relieve—" He did not get to finish his sentence.

Mia tried to scramble backward to get away from him, but her back was already against an object. She lost her balance and fell over, slamming her head into a metal crate. She cried out in pain.

When Shurnik reached for her, Mia swung her tied feet forward from underneath herself and kicked him in the shin. He cursed and quickly moved his legs.

The same strong hands from earlier propped her back up, rougher than before. Mia was unable to move with those heavy hands on her shoulders. Shurnik glared at her and raised one hand, ready to strike her. Mia shut her eyes, expecting a blow in the face. It never came.

"You are not helping your situation. You will stay with us for several days. It is up to you what kind of privileges you will be granted. It is all up to you."

The back of Mia's head had hurt before, but now the side she'd slammed into the metal crate was in a lot worse shape. For now, she had to give up. She just had to believe they wouldn't hurt her, or worse.

"Okay, I understand." She kept looking at Shurnik, who said,

"This is an ice pouch I was going to hold to your neck. It will relieve the swelling and the pain. I know you don't want to, Ms. Trentino, but you just have to trust me."

With that, Shurnik raised the pouch again to place it on Mia's neck. He was not exactly gentle, but he could have handled her a lot worse.

Mia lowered her head and closed her eyes. The icy-cold pouch felt good and she exhaled.

Shurnik watched her relax just a bit. "Very good, Ms. Trentino. Now I will explain the situation to you. You will be held for several days. I can't promise you a very comfortable stay, but as I said earlier, you will not be harmed. And if you comply, we will not harm your friend either."

Mia's blood froze. She instantly raised her head. A deep thump of pain in the back of her skull punished her immediately. She ignored it. "What? You have him, too? Where is he, is he all right?"

Shurnik smiled to himself but kept a straight face. He was sure his bluff would work. "Yes, he is okay. He is in the other truck, obeying our orders. So you better make sure you obey ours as well. That way nothing will happen to either of you."

Shurnik got up. She looked after him as he lifted the canvas to climb back out of the truck. It was getting lighter outside, a new day was born. The day when Mia should have gone home.

A heavy knot began to build in her throat, but she would not allow herself to cry.

Chapter 53

SHURNIK CLIMBED BACK INTO the driver's seat. He smiled. Ms. Trentino certainly was feisty. He liked that about her. He respected her, and that's why he had told his men not to touch her. Shurnik had seen his men looking greedily after her and had threatened them with severe punishment if they tried to rape or even just touch her.

He rubbed his lower leg. He could feel the swelling beneath his pants. She had stood up for herself even though he knew how frightened she must have been. But her demeanor had changed quickly when Shurnik had mentioned the American's name. He had known it would keep her in check.

She had still been out when they'd crossed into Mongolia just a little while ago. Border patrol had not searched the trucks, but Shurnik knew the border into China would be much tighter. Now that she was awake, she would have to be hidden when they crossed into China. Shurnik was certain she would cooperate if she believed Farland would be harmed if she didn't.

She had driven back from Irkutsk by herself in the middle of the night. Shurnik didn't care about her reasons, but it had been a gift to him that she had come. The second he had found Bogdan, he knew the operation was in great danger. He didn't know how much they knew.

And then he had gotten Farland on the line, another advantage for him.

Yukoil is going to be exposed, he thought. Or was it?

Shurnik had kidnapped Mia for insurance. He would try to use her to negotiate with whatever agency Bogdan and Farland worked for. Shurnik was almost certain they wouldn't, which would place him in a very delicate situation with the Mafia. The plan to use Yukoil as a cover for future expeditions would deteriorate, and he was aware of the consequences for failure.

The American company Ms. Trentino worked for might pay a nice amount of ransom. It would hopefully get his neck out of the Mafia's tight string.

Just before the convoy had left the camp, he had notified Lagunov. He had sent him a text message he should have received by now. Shurnik checked the time. Yes, it was after eight o'clock in Vladivostok. Lagunov had arrived.

The fact that he had not notified Selkin in St. Petersburg might compromise the trust the Mafia had in him, but reporting directly to them was out of the question. He had a problem, and he would take care of it.

It was the same situation as when he had discovered Bogdan missing. He had not notified St. Petersburg. Finding Oleg dead had not really surprised him. Oleg had needed to be taken care of, anyway. He was worthless.

He had calculated the severity of damage Bogdan's escape could do to the coup and had decided to move out immediately instead of searching the premises. The arrival of the American had to be anticipated, and a confrontation needed to be prevented.

Douglas stopped in the city of Ulan-Ude.

He was still in Russia. Big Eye had reported that Shurnik's convoy headed toward the Mongolian border, so far without an incident.

As long Big Eye provided a visual on the convoy, Douglas didn't need to. He would take a much faster route than Shurnik. The Russian had to stay low with his cargo and would probably use easier access through the borders on unpaved roads in terrain that would slow him down. Douglas had to prevent the convoy from entering China. And he still had time. He would have passed them by the time he reached Mongolia's capitol, the city of Ulaanbaatar.

He needed to ditch the GAZ. It would have been reported stolen by now, and he could not afford any time delay from a police investigation. Parking it at the train station of the Trans-Siberian railway had seemed like a good idea. Douglas looked for a pay phone and found one just inside the green and beige, three-story, cinder block building.

He called Brian's cell phone direct. The big clock inside the terminal showed 06:05. The sun had not yet risen, but a glow faintly lit up the eastern sky.

"Secona," Brian picked up the line. He sounded tired. It was 5:05 p.m. in Maryland.

"Am I disturbing your afternoon snooze?" Douglas asked, knowing his partner had had just as much sleep in the last twenty-four hours as Douglas himself.

"Where are you?" Brian asked.

"Ulan-Ude, ditching the Jeep. I'm fixin' to get me new wheels. How's my backup?" Douglas hoped they would join him soon.

"You are scheduled to rendezvous in Ulaanbaatar," Brian said. He knew it was unacceptable, but there was nothing he could do.

"You're joking, right?" Douglas asked, knowing his partner wasn't. "Doesn't Interpol have someone here?"

Brian took a deep breath. "Yes, they do. But after what happened to Bogdan, Interpol is a bit leery about sending in another agent."

Douglas eyed a small group of tourists standing close to him—three young men with huge backpacks. They spoke in German and said something about breakfast and beer.

He turned his back to them and spoke lower.

"I guess I can understand their position. How is she?" Douglas hoped Brian would have a report on Ludvika's status by now.

"Already in surgery," Brian was happy to report. "Get this, when I notified the Irkutsk's police chief about her situation, he scrambled a chopper. I have no idea where that puts us, but he said that he commanded the Lake Baikal rescue medics to get her, instead of just the Ambulance. She must have left a lasting impression on the good old cop."

Douglas smiled. He was glad to hear that. "Good, so she'll be all right after all."

"Yes. It's too early to say what the outcome will be, but she's gonna live."

"Any encounter with the medics at the camp?" Douglas asked.

"Nope. As far as I understood it they were in and out. Took 'em not even five minutes between landing and liftoff to get her out of there. The pilot had reported a visual of just one heavyset, older lady."

Helena, Douglas thought and smiled again. He was very relieved that Ludvika was going to be okay.

Douglas debated with himself for a second. He should tell Brian about Mia's abduction. There should not be any secrets between them—they were partners. And just as Douglas finished his thought Brian asked him, "Why don't you tell me what else is going on, Doug?"

God, Brian was spooky that way.

"What do you mean?" "Come on, you know as well as I do that something's bothering you," Brian guessed correctly. And than he added, "It's that Trentino girl, ain't it?"

Douglas took a breath. Brian needed to know. "Yes, it is. Shurnik took her when he left the camp."

Brian nodded. He had been afraid of something like this happening. "You know what that means, don't you, Doug?" Brian said calmly.

Douglas did not want to hear it. "Don't worry, the op will stay priority."

"I have no doubt in you, Doug. But I could run it by Quantico. What do you think?"

Douglas had thought about it, too. Now that Mia was involved, the FBI would have jurisdiction over the case. The Acronym could not care about the abduction, but the FBI certainly would.

"It's your call, Doug. Is she worth the risk?" Brian had sensed Douglas' position toward her a few days back. He was asking Douglas if it was worth taking the risk of the FBI's bureaucracy potentially being a disturbance to the mission's success.

The Acronym had bent the rules as usual, but not yet too far to prevent the FBI from being able to get involved.

"Yes," Douglas said with emphasis. "She *is* worth the risk, but hold off for now. I think I'm gonna be able to take care of it. For some reason I believe Shurnik will use her as bait. I really don't think she is in that big of a danger."

"Spoken like a true lover," Brian said dryly. "We can always call the feds later on and let them roll in the big guns. I'll wait on that one—it's your decision. You know, if this damn cast wasn't keeping me tied to this fuckin' office, I'd be out there with you right this minute."

Douglas knew how true Brian's sentiment was. He nodded into the phone and said, "I know my friend, don't you worry. There are plenty of bad guys out there we'll sink our teeth into together."

With that, Douglas hung up the phone.

He pictured Brian back in Maryland, sitting anxiously in his office. His right leg was in a cast clear up to his thigh. Douglas had heard something about a young colt bucking Brian off out on the Colorado ranch.

Douglas stood for a minute and scanned the people around him. The train station was busy on this weekend morning. His eyes found the backpacking tourists as they sat down at a bar. Douglas had to grin. Germans—each one of the three had a beer in front of them.

After a quick bite to eat, Douglas found a bathroom and refreshed himself as well as possible. He bought a newspaper at a kiosk and took a seat in the waiting area close by the entrance.

His eyes fell on a Russian-made Jeep someone had just parked outside the glass doors of the train station. Not as good as the GAZ, but it would do. The male driver and his female passenger retrieved two bags out of the Jeep's rear compartment. After they closed the doors, the driver locked them and said something to his lady friend.

They laughed to each other, holding hands as they approached the entrance.

Weekend tourists, Douglas thought. They would not miss the Jeep until they'd return, and by the size of the bags, it could be two or three days.

Douglas kept watching them as they bought tickets and pointed to the board above them, where the arrival and departure times were displayed. The driver kissed his lady friend tenderly on the cheek and took her by the arm. He whispered in her ear and again they laughed and disappeared in the crowd.

Douglas waited a good fifteen minutes and stepped outside. He casually walked to the Jeep. It didn't take twenty seconds to pick the lock.

The jeep was too old to have a security alarm on board, but it was in good enough shape to get Douglas where he needed to go. He opened the driver door and placed his black duffel bag next to him on the passenger seat. He had retrieved everything out of his hideout before he had left the camp.

Knowing Ludvika was safe, Douglas could concentrate fully on the next step in his mission. He believed what he had told Brian, that Shurnik would probably not harm Mia in a serious way. But every minute she had to spend with this scum was a minute Douglas could hardly bear.

Chapter 54

Sergei Selkin slammed the receiver down.

Who in the hell did Shurnik think he was? Selkin just got off the phone with Lagunov. He was in Vladivostok with a message from Shurnik saying that the coup was endangered. Shurnik had notified Lagunov, but not Selkin himself in St. Petersburg.

Selkin was furious. He'd meet up with Shurnik and personally watch over the operation from now on. He knew Shurnik's route—the convoy should be on its way to Ulaanbaatar right now. Selkin checked his watch. The flight would take him longer than Shurnik's drive to the capital city of Mongolia.

Selkin cursed. It was very dangerous for him to leave the safety of St. Petersburg. But Shurnik hadn't left him any choice. He dialed a number in Ulaanbaatar.

"Yes." Selkin's man answered the line.

"Hold the load, I'm coming in."

"Understood. Problems?"

"Of course," Selkin answered angrily and hung back up. He had groups of men along the route on standby for situations like this.

The truck stopped suddenly and the hard rumble shook Mia awake. At first she couldn't remember where she was, but when she smelled the diesel and felt her hands still tied together, the gruesome reality came back to her quickly. Her throat was dry as she swallowed hard.

What time was it, she wondered. She didn't know how long she had slept. She was lying on her side, and someone had covered her with a gray wool blanket. It was cold in the back of the truck, and she shivered despite the cover.

Her head still hurt, but not as bad as yesterday. Light shone through the little holes in the canvas where ropes went through to hold it in place. It must be late in the morning. She wondered if she had indeed slept through most of the night.

Drowsy, she tried to sit up. Her hands and feet were still bound, and her wrists ached badly where the ties held them together. She noticed the bruises from her fighting the ropes. But at least they had bound them in front of her, so her shoulders had stopped hurting. She squinted her eyes a few times and lifted both hands to her face to swipe some hair away. Her hands were filthy.

The truck idled a little longer and then they turned off the engine. Where am I? she wondered.

There was a different man from yesterday sitting opposite of her, watching her now. She felt the vibration as the truck door opened, and she could hear Shurnik without understanding his words. He spoke to at least two other men. Mia could make out the different voices.

She held her breath, straining to understand what they were saying. She let her tongue glide over her dry and chapped lips. God, she was thirsty.

They started to argue. Something must be wrong, she thought. Within the chattering sounds of the men's conversation, she suddenly heard her name. Was that a good sign? Her heart jumped, and heat flushed through her body like a burning stream.

The men's voices died, and Mia could barely hear the sound of footsteps in the dirt. Suddenly the canvas swung open, and bright sunlight streamed into the back of the truck and over Mia. She was immediately blinded. The sunlight shot through her eyes like a laser and triggered the dull pain in the back of her neck to flare up again. Her eyes shut, and she turned her head to the side and sat still. The feeling was extremely nauseating and she silently begged for it to go away.

By the time her grainy eyes had gotten used to the light, the canvas was pulled back down again. What was that? Who was there?

Nobody said a word to her and she could hear them climbing back into the cabin of the trucks. Mia wanted to shout at them, but knew it wouldn't do any good. She had tried it yesterday.

Her demeanor had changed throughout the day. First she had been frightened, very frightened. Then she had complied with what Shurnik had told her. She had sat quietly for hours, just staring at the back of the rumbling truck, trying very hard not to go nuts. Finally she had become restless and started talking aimlessly, but the watchman had just ignored her.

He had ignored her when she had asked for a bathroom break. He had ignored her when she had repeatedly asked about Douglas' whereabouts. He had ignored her when she had demanded to know where they would take her. And after several warnings, he had taped her mouth again.

They had not reacted to anything she said yesterday, so why would they today?

Last night they had let her out after it had gotten dark and had given her some water. No food, though. She probably would have just spat it back into their faces anyway. Someone had taken her by the arm to the side of the road and given her a minute by herself. She had looked for signs of Douglas, but had not seen or heard anything.

For hours Mia had tried to figure out why this was happening to her. Had Worldmove done something awful? Was her boss involved in some shady business? Was Douglas behind all this? Her brain was on overdrive, and before she could lose her mind, she had been exhausted and fallen in a deep and dreamless sleep.

Once she had woken up, freezing and feeling incredible vulnerable and lonely. Her thoughts had gone back to Douglas. She wanted to believe that he was safe somewhere and not involved in this terrible, terrible thing. She had swayed between worry and hostility thinking about him. Mia had just not been able to figure anything out.

The truck was in motion again now, and she almost lost her balance. She repositioned herself against her backrest and could do nothing more but wait. It did not take very long. Mia had her head onto her arms when the light suddenly disappeared. The sound of the engines got louder and she heard an echo. She lifted her head and stared at the canvas. The diesel engine stopped again. We are in a building, Mia thought. But where? Was this the end of the drive?

Her own mind was slowly driving her crazy, already agonizing over the same unanswered questions from yesterday and there were more every minute! Mia heard men dismounting the vehicles. The voices were louder now and echoed, impossible for Mia to understand. It was darker inside. She could still see, but it was much darker than when they had been driving.

She looked at the huge man sitting across from her, but he just stared in front of him like she was not even there.

Mia tried to get up.

"Sit," the watchman suddenly said in a sharp tone. "Sit down, they will get you." He looked at her.

"Get me and then what? Where are we?"

The man shook his head. He said, "You need to give it up. The boss will be here, soon."

Who's the boss? Shurnik? Mia thought.

The canvas was once again removed. Mia could see two faces.

"Get her out," it was Shurnik's voice.

The watchman got up momentarily and took Mia by her elbow. She could not stand his touch and jerked her arm away from him. She glared at him. "Don't you touch me."

The watchman just laughed and grabbed Mia by the arm again and pulled her up. He was rough with her, and the top of his shoulder punched Mia in the stomach as he threw her over his left side. The sudden move knocked the air out of her lungs. She could not even make a sound. The man was very strong. He climbed out of the back of the truck with Mia over his shoulder as though she were a sack of rice.

She could hardly see and as she regained her air, she started to kick. "Let me go, you bastard," she yelled at him.

A strong hand grabbed her hair and jerked her head back. Cold eyes she had not seen before looked into hers and someone warned her in a very calm voice. "Ms. Trentino, I thought we had an understanding."

She gave it up and didn't move.

The watchman carried Mia across a long hall. The footsteps echoed off the concrete floor. There was no artificial light, and someone shut the big gates so it became even darker inside.

"I'm going to set you down," the watchman said. "You move a wrong muscle and you'll be sorry." As he shifted Mia's weight off his shoulder, he placed his hand onto the back of her upper thigh. He squeezed it with a groping paw as he set her down.

They stood on one end of a huge building. It felt like an empty warehouse to Mia. She looked past the men toward the gate they must have come in through. All three trucks she had seen at the camp were parked in here, including the trailers. Otherwise the building was empty.

Was Douglas still in one of them? She wanted to shout out his name, but a hard grip around her upper arm caught her attention. She looked into the same cold eyes from earlier. They sent a shiver down her spine.

"Ms. Trentino, my name is Sergei Selkin, and I am so very pleased that you have joined our little family." Mia did not know the man. He was only her height, with a moderate frame, sandy blond hair, and not very old. But his cold eyes were set close together and looked intelligent and very scary.

Mia stood still, her feet still bound. Her heart hammered in her chest. The blond man lifted one arm and held his hand right underneath Mia's chin. She noticed a metallic object in it just as she heard a blade snap open. The sound froze Mia's blood, and she inhaled sharply, just to hold her breath as he held the knife right at her throat.

"Mr. Shurnik has told me that you two have had a little talk. Are you going to keep your word and not cause us any trouble?" His Russian sounded like he was from far west. Moscow or St. Petersburg. Mia instantaneously hated him with more ferocity than she had ever hated anything or anybody in her life.

The constant fear she'd been experiencing for the last twenty-four hours was suddenly gone, pushed aside by the blinding rage of hate. She withstood his probing cold eyes and glared back at him. He gave his knife to the big man, watching Mia with his face just inches from hers, trying to intimidate her.

The same man who had groped Mia earlier bent down to cut the ropes around her ankles. She wasn't even thinking. Just as she felt the pressure lessen and the ropes slide to the ground, she raised her right leg and kicked as hard as she could at the big man. The tip of her boot caught him in the stomach and sent him flying onto his back. Her own momentum almost knocked her off her feet.

Instantly the other men laughed. The huge watchman got back to his feet quickly and shot forward to attack Mia. Selkin held his arm up without taking his eyes off of Mia. The watchman stopped in his tracks.

"Oh, I see," he said, amused. "We have us a tough one. Well, let me tell you something about little ladies like you, trying to be tough. Usually they don't last very long. So you might as well give it up now, while you still can." He paused and added, "You're not only jeopardizing your own well being, but that of your American friend as well."

Mia remembered Shurnik telling her the same thing, and something deep inside told her they were both lying. But she did not react.

The moment she had kicked the watchman, she'd thought she was going to die. It was a stupid thing to do, but her body had automatically tried to defend itself without the permission of Mia's usually very reasonable brain.

Someone pushed down hard on Mia's shoulders from behind, and her legs buckled. She sat hard onto a chair. Selkin bent his knees to be eye level with her. Mia's feet were still untied, and she could have tried to kick after Selkin as well, but he knew she wasn't that stupid. He placed his hands on Mia's legs, the touch appalled her, but she still didn't move. Selkin's cold and intimidating demeanor was beginning to show its affect on her.

"Just as Mr. Shurnik has told you, you behave and you will get out of this unharmed," he assured her.

Mia didn't believe him. She had seen all of the men's faces. She could easily identify each and every one of them. Cold sweat ran down her neck as she realized, sooner or later, they were going to kill her.

Chapter 55

DOUGLAS HAD ARRIVED IN Ulaanbaatar earlier than he had hoped for. The border into Mongolia had not given him any grief. His disguise as the usual tourist had worked out perfectly.

He was sitting in the stolen Jeep, thinking that it should be time to change vehicles again, when his cell phone rang.

Only Brian had this number. "What's up, brother?"

"How ya doin'? Where're you at?"

"On Marx Avenue looking at a Lama Temple."

"No shit! You are already in Ulaanbaatar? Did you drive straight through?" Brian asked with amazement.

"Yep. I'm extremely sleep-deprived and very cranky. So give me some good news," Douglas said, grinning. He had just taken a catnap in the temple's overcrowded parking lot. Sure, he was tired, but still alert and anxious to succeed.

"Well, I have good and bad news. What's it gonna be?" Brian asked. The bad news was actually really bad news.

"Good news first. Is it my backup?" Douglas sounded hopeful.

Brian was glad he could give him this much. "Sure is. I got Bao lined up to rendezvous with you at twenty-one hundred hours, your time."

Douglas checked his watch. Nine o'clock tonight would only be three and a half hours from now.

"That's great, Brian. How in the hell did you find Bao this quick?" Douglas asked, picturing the little ass-kicking Asian fellow.

"Long story, Doug. And for Christ's sake, don't call him Chinese again—he'll rip you a new one. You know he's Cambodian."

"Right, I forgot. They all look the same to me."

Brian laughed and said, "I know, but you won't look the same when Bao has twisted your ass into a freakin' pretzel, man!"

Douglas laughed, too. The situation needed a little humor—otherwise a guy could loose perspective really easy.

"Ready for your bad news?" Brian sounded like his serious self again.

"Ah, shit. Okay, hit me."

"Big Eye lost the convoy about two hours ago."

"Damn. Where were they?" Douglas had been worried about losing signal. It was to be expected the way they were headed. But the satellite should pick up on them soon.

"Was it the desert that screwed up the satellite?"

"No, they're already in Ulaanbaatar as well, Doug."

"Holy shit, how did they make it so fast?" Douglas sat up straight in his stolen Jeep. The very last feelings of exhaustion blew out of his body. He needed to go after them if they left Ulaanbaatar to head toward the border to China. He told Brian so.

"Yes, I know, Doug. But they haven't left the city yet. The satellite lost them as they disappeared into something that looked like an old hangar."

Douglas' forehead wrinkled in thought as he considered what Brian had said. "What do you mean? They parked the trucks?"

"Exactly. The satellite images show an old runway about ten miles southeast of the city. It hasn't been used in years, and there are several old buildings still intact on it. They were headed toward that hangar and on the next image they were gone."

Douglas knew what that meant.

"I can't wait for Bao."

"Doug, don't be stupid, you're gonna have to. What are you gonna do, just waltz in there and get her?" Brian knew he should have waited longer before he told Douglas.

Douglas was getting anxious. "Why didn't you call me earlier?"

"Because you needed to rest."

"As if you knew I was sleeping," Douglas snorted.

Brian understood why his partner was upset. "Listen, man. You need to wait because we need to get closer to Lagunov, first. He's under surveillance. He has checked into the Equator Hotel in Vladivostok, but nobody else has shown up yet. Selkin has apparently left St. Petersburg, but that is not yet confirmed. So you need to sit tight." Brian paused and then continued with emphasis.

"They cannot know you are on their heels yet. We know they will be expecting us, but if you move in now, you'll scare them off. We need to wait until they contact Lagunov. You understand that, Douglas, don't you." It wasn't a question.

Douglas sat still. Of course he understood. He had to keep the op priority and not get carried away trying to free Mia.

"Yes, I do—" He wanted to say more, but Brian interrupted him fiercely.

"Listen, Doug. We anticipate Selkin rounding up Lagunov very soon. The minute he does, you'll know and you can go after her. Goddammit, Douglas. Don't you think I know how hard this must be? Just hang in there and do not compromise!"

"I won't," Douglas said and punched his phone off. There was nothing more to say.

Mia was so thirsty.

She'd been sitting on the dirty concrete floor of this building for hours. Her back was resting against the wall and her tied feet were stretched out in front of her. They had kept her hands bound, and they were numb from the wrist down. Her throat was so dry that it hurt. She yearned for water, but pride held her back from asking. She would not beg the bastards for anything.

The cold from the cement floor had crept into her body and a consistent tremor had taken over. Mia was tired, hungry, and still full of fear. But her anger outweighed all the other emotions and feelings. She wondered why that was.

She was glad to be angry. She certainly did not want to feel like a victim and beg them for her life. They would just laugh at her weakness, and she would not allow that.

First she had kicked Shurnik, then she had hurt the big man. She had shown them her courage, but that same courage had also taken away all privileges, as Shurnik had called them before. No food, no water, no bathroom until she acted like a good girl. At the word "good girl," Selkin had looked at his men, and they had laughed at her.

Mia shuddered at the memory.

Selkin seemed to be the leader, now. Shurnik had been the boss since Mia had first stepped foot into the camp an eternity ago. She didn't know Selkin. She had no idea where to place him or what his role was. Neither did she know what this whole thing was all about.

She didn't care. All she wanted to do was to wake up from this horrible nightmare and leave this awful country.

Her thoughts went back to all the things she was missing from home and another knot built up in her throat. She swallowed hard and winced in pain. She felt like crying but wouldn't allow herself to. Her eyes went far across the building, and she watched the men hovering around Selkin.

He sat on the back of a truck, talking to his men. He was mesmerizing. He had seemed so inconspicuous at first. With his young age—he couldn't be far into his thirties—and relatively small frame, compared to the other men, he looked like a college kid. But there was something about him, his eyes, his speech, and his confidence that made his men, including Shurnik, hang on his words.

She could not hear what they were saying. Her eyes left them. She could not bear looking at them for another second. These men were everything evil stood for.

Another swell of freezing cold and sadness shuddered through her, and the shivers intensified. She looked down to her bound ankles and tried to move her numb hands. Finally she could not stare at all the ugliness anymore. Mia closed her eyes and took a deep breath. She tried to ignore her physical condition and focus on the good things in her life. Things she probably wouldn't see again. Sorrow sat like a hot, glowing rock in her chest, crushing her heart; but she forced herself to visualize. She had to if she didn't want to lose her mind.

Blue popped up in front of her, and as she pictured him in his woolly cuteness as a puppy, she drifted off into an exhausted sleep.

Douglas watched the sun go down. It felt like Mother Nature was playing a trick on him and taking an extra long time to allow darkness to prevail.

The minutes ticked away like hours, and Douglas thought about his backup.

Bao Shuang, a thirty-something-year-old individual whose father had fought the Americans as a Vietcong.

The Acronym did not have much on Bao, but he was highly trusted and very capable. He did not belong to any specific agency and was proud to call himself a "freelancer." He was only five-foot-two but as fast as a bullet, and he had whooped Douglas' and Brian's asses at the same time during a training session in Colorado.

Douglas smiled. Thinking back on it, he had felt like a big clumsy bulldozer with that agile whirlwind dancing just out of reach around him.

Douglas watched the religious wandering toward the temple for their evening prayer. Buddhism was widely spread in these parts of the land, and Douglas admired people who believed. He had witnessed too much human distortion in the world to be able to believe in something greater. He would have liked to, though. I need to retire, he thought dryly, getting sentimental as he watched the red-clad worshipers step up the stairs to the Lama temple.

Douglas leaned his seat back. With his eyes closed, he ran through the next hours. As soon as the sun had set he would trade his transportation in. He had already picked out what he'd steal next—the four-wheel drive sat two rows behind him, slightly to the left. He would have to wait for Bao before he made the switch, or so his common sense told him.

He would wait for his Asian partner and work on a plan to inch closer to Shurnik's crew for surveillance until Brian had a green light from Vladivostok. Then he and Bao could move in, free Mia, and hopefully take Shurnik into their custody without having to kill him. Douglas wanted to keep his promise to Ludvika to let her get a chance with Shurnik sometime in the future.

It all looked good in his head. The only problem was, he had no idea how long it would take until he could move in on Shurnik.

The op was priority, Mia wasn't, he had to tell himself again and again.

Suddenly Douglas' eyes flew open. Who was he kidding? He turned his head and observed the mass of people gathering in the parking lot in front of the temple. Tonight was some special religious festival planned here in downtown Ulaanbaatar.

Douglas collected his gear from the backseat, and by the time he had visualized a plan, the early darkness of the evening had swallowed him already.

Chapter 56

THE RUNWAY WAS SHORT.

Weeds had pushed through cracked cement and stood knee high. The never-ending wind was blowing dead brush like tumbleweeds from east to west. The sun had disappeared a while back and given way to yet another cold, high desert night. The temperature had dropped considerably as soon as the bright moon had set.

Dressed in all black and armed to his teeth, Douglas crouched behind one corner of what seemed to be the smallest of the three buildings. No doubt this was an old hangar. Just as Brian had said, it had not been used in a very long time. There were no outside lights, and thick, dusty sand covered the concrete patches in front of the buildings.

Douglas could see the tire tracks. They led to the other building across the field from his current location. There was no movement outside, right now. Douglas had been taking his time observing. He could not afford the slightest mistake. He silently retreated and made his way around the back side to the other end of the big building. He was certain to find Shurnik and his crew hiding in there.

The hangar had no windows and only two big sliding gates in the front, which were tightly closed now. The only way for Douglas to enter the building was from above. He had noticed a dome-like cupola on top of the roof. He suspected an air shaft of some sort underneath it.

Douglas had watched the three men rotating as they prowled the premises, on the lookout for anything or anybody. They carried Uzis and stayed out of the way of anything that could detect their presence.

Douglas checked his watch. He had forty-five minutes until Bao's scheduled arrival. Looking up to the roof of the hangar, he was sure he could make it in time to take Brian's call.

The hangar was made of thick metal, which would reduce the sound of Douglas' movements to a minimum.

Douglas stayed close to the other building, avoiding the sandy dust as much as possible. The back end of the main hangar had an old water tower close to it. Douglas evaluated the distance from the fifty-foot-high water tower to the rooftop of the hangar. Too far to jump. He'd never make it. Plus his impact onto the metal roof would be heard throughout the entire building. He would have to claw his way up the metal building on the outside. Douglas studied the ridges between the sheet metal—he had no other choice.

Running back to his gear bag, he retrieved his necessary equipment, already carrying his Five-seveN and his rifle. His gloved hands retrieved a black, nylon mask from his bag, and he slipped it over his head. Neatly wound up black rope and karabiner followed. He changed his combat boots for thin, rubber-soled shoes, similar to the ones athletes use for rock climbing.

It took Douglas over half an hour to climb up the outside of the hangar. He cut his hands twice through the gloves on the sharp edges of the sheet metal, but ignored it. The tips of his thin-soled shoes found just enough support on the narrow metal ridges to give himself enough push upward.

He was drenched in sweat despite the biting wind-chill, which intensified once Douglas reached the forty feet high roof top. The slanted roof was not very steep, and Douglas slid carefully onto his stomach. Pushing himself toward the dome, he could hear faint voices. Just another ten feet and he would be able to peek through the air shaft.

A sudden metal-on-metal sliding noise froze his blood in his veins. One of the karabiners attached to his harness had slid off and glided slowly toward the edge of the roof. Douglas held his breath. The sound was way too loud not to be heard inside the hangar. In dismay he looked after the karabiner. It kept sliding toward the edge, gravity increasing its speed and therefore the noise.

Douglas was certain the men inside heard it and were on their way out to check the premises. If the damn karabiner fell off the roof, the men would find it, and Douglas would be trapped on top. The next thing he imagined were the men's Uzis ripping big holes through the metal roof and then through him.

His heart jumped up his throat just as the karabiner should have disappeared over the edge. An old rusted screw, used to attach one sheet of metal to the next, was raised above the metal only an eighth of an inch. It was just enough to catch the karabiner on its snap, preventing it from falling.

Douglas stared. It was dimly illuminated by the moon, but he could barely see it. When he was sure it would hold, he exhaled. That was close. Be more careful, Farland, he told himself.

He pressed himself against the roof, wondering if the men were outside looking for the cause of the noise. He didn't move for a full minute, concentrating on anything and making sure it was still safe for him to continue.

He pulled himself forward and finally reached the dome. He had been correct. There was an air shaft underneath the cupola, approximately thirty-five inches in diameter. He could fit through it without his gear strapped to his back, but for now he only observed.

The inside of the hangar was dimly lit. Just the driving lights of two trucks were turned on and shone upon a group of men. Douglas could see Shurnik forty-five feet below him, but Shurnik was just a bystander. The men surrounded somebody else, and that person seemed to be the only one speaking. Douglas could not see who it was.

Sweeping the hangar with his eyes, Douglas noticed the trucks he had seen in the camp. They were indeed parked here for whatever reason. Douglas thought of Mia. Was she in one of the trucks? Helplessly bound and scared to death? Or had they gotten rid of her already, dumped her body in the muddy waters of the Chikoy river? Douglas forced that paralyzing thought far into the dark depths of his consciousness.

From his current position he was only able to see half of the hangar. Very carefully he slid sideways to reposition himself on the opposite side of the dome. Now he lost the men and the trucks out of his field of vision and he scanned the faintly lit darkness of the far side of the building.

Suddenly he saw her.

Mia sat with her back against the wall on the cold, cement floor. Her legs were out in front of her. The tips of her boots were slightly tipped outward, and her head was slumped to the side, which told Douglas she was not conscious. He could not see her face—it was covered by her dark hair.

Douglas stared at her. At least she seemed okay. Well, as okay as a person in her position could be. He did not want to think about what they might have done to her. He couldn't. If he allowed himself to get enraged about it, he would lose his cool and make mistakes.

He knew now that he had to wait for Bao. He would not be able to get her out by himself. Just as he was moving backward to retreat, he heard the men's footsteps below him. They were still out of his vision, but they were clearly walking toward Mia. Douglas lay still, waiting for them to appear. First he saw a smaller guy approaching Mia, followed by two others. One was carrying something Douglas could not make out.

The smaller man stood in front of Mia and used his foot to wake her up. Douglas clenched his jaw as he saw Mia startling awake when the man tapped his boot on her leg. She looked up to him, and now Douglas could see her face clearly. It was pale, and she said something he could not hear.

The small guy stepped back and someone else grabbed her by the arm and pulled her up. She shook her head; they must have asked her something. The big guy bent his knees and cut the ropes around her ankles Douglas had not been able to see earlier. They took her by her arms and walked her toward the other side of the hangar. I hope they're not moving out, Douglas thought.

Suddenly the smaller guy lifted his head and pointed toward the door. In an instant Douglas recognized his face. Selkin. Douglas was sure, and just as he was asking himself what the hell the Mafia boss was doing there, his cell phone vibrated in his cargo pocket. Douglas was not really in any position to answer phone calls, but he carefully moved to retrieve the cell and pushed the button.

"Brian," he whispered. "You won't fuckin' believe it!"

Brian heard his partner whisper and instantly had a bad feeling.

"Where the hell are you?" Brian asked. Douglas ignored the question and said, "Sergei Selkin is not meeting Lagunov in Vladivostok. They must have had a change of heart."

Brian lost his speech for a second. Did he understand Douglas correctly? They had planned on taking Lagunov into custody as soon as his involvement with the Mafia was confirmed through a meeting with Selkin.

"How do you know, Douglas? Have you heard from our men in Vladivostok?" Brian asked, wondering how that would have worked.

"No need to," Douglas whispered.

"Then how do you know that Selkin ain't there?" Brian was confused.

"'Cause I'm looking at the bastard right now."

Brian listened as Douglas gave him a quick explanation of his position. He then told Douglas that Bao was on the other line, ready to get instructed on where to meet him. Douglas arranged to meet Bao at a landmark not very far from the hangar in forty-five minutes. When Douglas ended the call, he had lost his visual of Mia and the men. They had walked across the hangar toward the trucks. He had to hurry. There was no time to observe any further.

Crawling toward the far end of the roof, Douglas allowed his thoughts for a moment to go back to Mia. Her face had been pale and very frightened. He could see it from that far above looking into an unlit room. Goddamned sons of bitches! His adrenaline rose beyond the red line of his inner scale. He was so ready to face them. He'd meet Bao and be back in no time. A plan had already taken shape in his head.

Douglas snapped the rope to his harness. Easy now; he warned himself, scanning the area beneath him. It was clear. He silently stepped to the edge, and the only sound was the faint whir of his equipment as he repelled himself off the roof.

Chapter 57

Bao saw the landmark Secona had described. He wondered if Farland was already there. Killing the headlights, he steered the car by the deserted gas station to observe. He drove slow, trying to keep the sand from whirling up from underneath the tires.

A half mile down the dirt road, he turned around to approach the gas station yet again. He had not seen anybody or any other vehicle since he had taken the turnoff. There was a wide ditch behind the now-empty five thousand gallon fuel tank, perfect to conceal the car for now. He let the vehicle roll down the shallow embankment and quietly opened the door. Bao let himself glide next to his car and just sat there.

His instincts had to adjust to the surroundings, but he could already sense the American. Bao crossed his legs and centered his inner core. He closed his eyes and relaxed his face. Farland tried to sneak up on him from behind. Just as he felt Douglas' presence on the other side of his car he said, "No need, Farland. I could smell you from across the desert." Bao spoke with a heavy Asian accent, missing the *r* in every word. He pronounced Douglas' name "Faalaan."

Damn that little guy was good.

Douglas sat next to Bao onto the sandy ground. "How ya doing, China man?" he teased. They had not seen each other in quite some time. Douglas was glad Bao was here, he was just the man he needed.

Bao still had his eyes closed as he said, "Tell me about the op. Secona did not give me any details."

"I'm sure he didn't. Did he mention anything about a hostage rescue?" Douglas got straight to the point and was pretty sure of Bao's response.

He opened his almond-shaped Asian eyes and stared at Douglas, not saying anything.

"I guess that's a 'no,'" Douglas guessed correctly.

Officially there was no hostage. Even at the Acronym the only person who knew so far was Brian. He had only briefed Bao about Douglas needing backup to tail the convoy into China.

Boa finally spoke. "I take it we're not going to China?" Douglas studied the small Asian man huddled with his back against the car, next to him.

"Well, we still might, I really am not sure yet. But let me tell you what I have in mind for now."

Douglas shared his plan, and Bao did not interrupt.

"You Americans watch too many movies," Bao simply said. Douglas grinned. If the situation wasn't so serious, he would have laughed. Boa sounded just like Ludvika right now.

"Did you bring any Gorex?" he asked hopeful.

Bao smiled at Douglas for the first time. "Would I be Chinese if I didn't travel with a good dosage of Gorex in my trunk?"

Douglas liked this guy. "Chinese? You're telling me, Bao!"

Mia sat back down with her back against the wall. They had let her go outside for a little while and given her something to drink. Still nothing to eat, though, and she felt weak and light-headed. The cold night was getting to her, too. The chill from the cement floor was sinking into her bones. Finally she could not handle it anymore. She asked the watchman for a blanket. He laughed and told her he had a different idea about how to warm her up. Mia got quiet quickly, not wanting to give the man any more wrong ideas.

It was painful to sit up. Her lower back was killing her, and she lay down onto her side on the dirty, cold, concrete floor and closed her eyes once again. They had not demanded anything from her, had not asked her any questions at all. Not knowing what they wanted was by far worse then not being able to give them what they'd asked for.

Mia hugged her knees with her bound arms, trying to get the shivers of her body under control.

Climbing the building was so much simpler with two men and the help of their descenders.

Douglas had left the rope from earlier attached and hidden behind the sheet metal. Standing on the ground next to the hangar, Bao lifted his head, looking up the side of the building, and found the rope. He attached it to his harness and asked Douglas, whispering, "How did you get up there before?" Douglas pointed to the three inch deep ridges between the sheets he had used for his foot work and the narrow overhang he had locked his fingers in.

Bao nodded and whispered, "I'm impressed. Not bad for an older, non-athletic, white guy."

Douglas grinned. He had no doubt that Bao could climb this building in just about half the time he had needed. He said suggestively, "You just watch that they don't cut your Chinese balls off, once you're inside."

Just before Douglas and Bao had left their hideout, Douglas had called Brian and inquired about any movement from the hangar. The satellite had not shown any trucks or men around the premises.

On top of the roof, Douglas went ahead of Bao, and they dog-crawled to the dome. Douglas looked through the air vent first. He signaled Bao to stay where he was. He bent his neck just a little bit more and could see Mia. She was curled up in the fetal position, lying on the floor. Douglas could feel the heat of rage swelling up in him again, but he had to stay calm. A big man was sitting next to her on some sort of a bundle. He was facing the middle of the hangar, toward the area where Bao would repel down to. Bao would have no chance of an unnoticed descent like this. The timing and the right effect of the next step was crucial.

Douglas lifted his hand and pointed two fingers to his eyes and then to Bao, telling him he needed to trade spaces with Douglas to view the situation. Bao crawled to the dome and took a minute to evaluate his next move. He clicked another rope to his harness and retrieved the small remote control out of his pack.

Douglas rolled carefully onto his back. He could feel drops of sweat running down his temples. He retrieved his weapon and attached the silencer to his Five-seveN. He wished he had his rifle, but he could only carry so much gear. The handgun could be attached to his thigh, but the rifle had to be carried on his back, and he had needed space for additional climbing gear.

Bao looked at Douglas. Sitting on his heels, he was ready to move. Douglas gave him a nod, and Bao pushed the red button on his device. The loud boom of the explosion filled the air momentarily, and within a second Selkin's men came crawling out of the trucks and ran toward the gates in loud commotion.

Mia thought she would have a heart attack. The man next to her jumped up from his bundle and headed toward the gate. Selkin pointed to the watchman and hollered, "Stay there and watch her."

Everything went really fast. Just as Mia saw the watchman walk toward the gate, something came flying down from the ceiling. Mia thought she was dreaming as a black something hovered right above the watchman, but only for an instant. By the time Mia realized that it was a man, the watchman was already lying on the ground.

A small man dressed in black leaned over the one on the ground, and Mia could not see what he was doing. To Mia everything seemed like a dream. When the small man sprinted toward her, her first reaction was flight. But her feet were tied and she was too paralyzed with fear to move.

The man said something, but Mia could not understand him. A loud humming noise in her ears blocked out any words. He moved so quickly, and he wore a mask. Mia tried to find his eyes, but everything was happening too fast. He bent down and cut her ropes, first the ones on her ankles, then on her hands. Then he turned around and grabbed Mia by the arm. Mia stood still, unable to move, with her back pressed against the wall. Bao knew what needed to be done. He took just enough time to remove his mask and looked at her.

"Mia," he took her hands and squeezed them, "I'm here to help you. Let me get you out of here. But we have to go now!"

Suddenly Mia's foggy brain understood. Her tired legs moved, and Bao took her to the spot where the watchman was dead on the floor.

Mia stared at him, standing still. Bao tugged her arm again. "Let's go!" Very quickly he fastened a harness around Mia's waist and upper thighs and looked up.

Before Mia could realize what was happening, she was already fifteen feet above the ground. She instinctively held on to the black rope in front of her eyes and suddenly a muffled voice said quietly, "Give me your hand." What? Mia thought. Where was he? "Give me your hand." A little louder.

It was only ninety seconds after the explosion when the fireworks went off in the distance. Douglas didn't know what else Bao had planted, but his concentration never left Mia. He stood above the airshaft with her weight on his harness. He grabbed her by both arms and lifted her through the narrow air shaft.

This moment was crucial. He had to let her go to get Bao out. But he was afraid she might panic, especially if she recognized him. Hostages could react in an extreme way to their rescuers. If it was hostile, sometimes they would even fight them. The possibility of Mia suffering from a milder form of the Stockholm syndrome this soon was highly unlikely, but Douglas had to expect anything. He said in a commanding but quiet voice.

"I need you to sit down." He didn't wait for her reply, but pushed on her shoulders to emphasize his order. To his surprise, Mia complied. She didn't sit, but crouched down with her knees bent.

Within twenty seconds Bao was retrieved and through the dome. They grabbed their gear and ran toward the far side of the building. Douglas checked his watch—two minutes and fifteen seconds. Longer than what he had planned, but with any luck Selkin's men were still in awe of the happenings outside.

Bao went down first. As Douglas was letting him down, he could feel Mia's eyes on him. Was she figuring it out? He did not look at her. She might recognize his eyes. The rest of his face was concealed by the black mask.

Douglas retrieved the rope and attached it to Mia. She froze as she realized the height of the building.

"No," she said.

"Yes." Douglas grabbed her arm and squeezed it hard. "There is no choice. Go now."

Mia shook her head and started to scramble backward, away from the gaping depth of darkness.

"No," she almost screamed.

Damn. This was what Douglas had been afraid of. He added pressure to her arm. He was sure he was hurting her bad.

"Mia, you have to go. Otherwise you will die." It was hard to explain new danger and death to people who already thought they would be killed.

He watched Mia look down. Bao stood helpless on the bottom of the building, looking up at them. This was taking way too long. They should have waited and snatched her while the transport was on the move. But Douglas had had a good point when he had voted against that.

Suddenly Mia realized that this was her only way out. She sat on the edge, and the strong man behind her held on to her rope as she let go of the roof.

She landed softly on her feet, and Bao was instantly unsnapping her harness. Mia watched as the strong man slid off the roof and went down very fast, his rope being his only lifeline.

"Run." The small man grabbed her by the arm, but let her go once she was up to speed. Mia's survival instincts kicked in and gave her wings. She followed the small man as he sprinted closely in front of her. Once he looked over his shoulder to tell her to run ahead. They both picked up tempo until they reached the outskirts of the airport.

Douglas stayed behind. He retrieved the gear and made sure their tracks were covered as well as possible. Bao's fireworks had distracted the men long enough for him and Mia to get away. For now, anyway. Once they realized Mia was gone, they would move out like a swarm of angry wasps. Douglas would further distract them. He'd eventually meet up with Bao later. But for now he had to stay put and observe Selkin's behavior.

"Go go go," the small man said, pushing Mia into his car. He scanned the area. So far he could not see anyone. Bao jumped into the driver seat and told Mia to buckle up. The drive might get quite rowdy. The little car fishtailed as he floored it, and Mia let out a shriek as Bao shot down the dirt road with the headlights still off.

Chapter 58

SERGEI SELKIN WENT BACK inside and instantly saw the man lying on the ground. He drew his weapon and took cover behind one of the trucks. "Man down," he shouted to the rest of them still standing outside. His head poked out from behind the truck, and his eyes searched along the far wall of the hangar. It was semi dark, but he should have been able to see the woman's silhouette against the wall.

He didn't.

Selkin cursed and signaled to one of his men to make his way to the back and check the situation.

"Clear," the man shouted after a while. He was crouched down, trying to find a pulse on the dead watchman's neck. He looked up as Selkin approached and shook his head.

Selkin studied the dead man. He was lying on his side and had scratch marks on his face and neck. His pants were pulled down to his knees. His side arm was still in his holster but his knife was gone. A stab wound just below his heart and very little blood indicated a fast death.

What had happened here? Selkin wondered. He circled the dead man slowly, running through the possibilities. It looked obvious to him. The man had tried to rape the woman while the rest of the men were outside. And the woman had fought him back—killing him?

Selkin narrowed his eyes in disbelief. The man in front of him surely had not been the brightest one in his crew, but he was big and as strong as an ox. And that tiny woman overpowered him? With her hands bound?

Selkin looked for the ropes and found them lying beside where she had sat. He rubbed his jaw. Something wasn't right. He thought back. Yes, the woman had shown bite and aggressiveness earlier today, but he had also seen the depths of fear in her eyes. Fear a warrior would not have. Or had she played them and waited out the perfect situation for her escape?

Selkin was stunned. He looked around. What else could have happened? Did the fireworks have anything to do with it?

He looked back at his men. Everyone had returned inside and the gates were closed. She could have sneaked around to the left side of the trucks and disappeared into the darkness while they all were frantically trying to figure out what was going on outside.

That little bitch, he thought. He checked his watch. Five minutes must have passed by now. She could not be far, but if she had experience, five minutes would be all she needed. For now he decided to let her go. He would get his chance to track her down. This continent was not big enough for her to hide forever, and neither was America. No matter what rat hole she disappeared into, he'd find her. Nobody outplayed Sergei Selkin.

Bao slowed down to the speed limit once he had reached the turnoff. The road leading to Ulaanbaatar was busy, so he peeled the top of his black bunny suit off.

Mia watched silently as he checked his appearance in the rearview mirror and smoothed down the wrinkled collar of his Hawaiian shirt. He was very small, in height and in frame. Mia had never seen anybody move so quickly before.

He felt her eyes and turned his head. He winked at her and said, "You run like a man, Mia. I'm very impressed."

Mia had calmed down a little, and her mind was trying to process what had happened in the last fifteen minutes. She wanted to ask a million questions, but seemed to be unable to speak.

"My name is Bao Shuang. I work for the American government." Bao pulled a face. That really didn't sound right. "I'm FBI," he lied instead.

Mia was still speechless. The FBI? She turned her head and looked out the window, only to turn her head right back to look at him again.

"Bao Shwang?" Mia asked, still baffled.

He narrowed his eyes. "No, Bao Shuang. And don't think I'm Chinese, because I'm not."

Twenty minutes later they pulled into a motel parking lot on the east side of Ulaanbaatar. The tourist traffic was less here, but it was still busy enough to blend it. Bao retrieved room keys from the glove department and looked at Mia. She had not said anything in the last fifteen minutes, which was odd. She should have showered him with questions by now. Instead she looked very pale and fragile to him. Bao hoped she'd be okay, at least until Farland showed up.

"You are going to be fine. You are safe now." There was no reaction from her. "Would you like me to contact a female officer for your comfort?" He had no idea how he would manage that, but the question made sense to him. No answer. "Do you need medical attention?" He certainly hoped not.

Still, she just stared right in front of her, completely absent. Damn, Farland. Get your ass here now, Bao thought. He had no experience with hostage victims and was not sure what to do. His senses told him that she was in a state of shock.

He decided that, for her own safety, she needed to get locked up again. He pulled the car around to the back parking lot where the rooms were located. Bao parked and turned off the engine. After he stepped out and scanned the area, he went around the car and opened her door.

"Please follow me. The other agents will be here shortly. I promise you, you are safe now," he said again. Those must have been the magic words. She finally looked up to him and took a deep breath. She stepped out of the car and followed him inside the motel.

It was noting special, just a regular motel, but with very little traffic. Bao did not see anyone and was glad that Farland had arranged for this room in advance.

They stepped inside and Bao locked the door. He immediately went to the window and checked the outsides. Not a soul out there.

"How can you promise?" Mia asked suddenly. He turned around to her. She sat on the edge of the bed with a straight back and stared at the dead TV screen.

It had just fully dawned on Mia that she was not with those evil men anymore. This man here seemed trustworthy. But she had trusted before and where had it gotten her?

The phone rang and Mia startled. Bao picked it up after the first ring and didn't say a word into the receiver.

He heard Douglas' voice. "Bao, I called a few times. You had me worried."

"Sorry, we just got here."

"How is she?"

"Not too good. Are you on your way?" Bao wanted Douglas here now.

"Yes." Douglas hung up.

Bao turned his head to Mia and said, "That was our other agent, he'll be here very soon."

Mia looked at Bao. He sat across the room from her on a chair, giving her as much distance as possible in the small room. The small man radiated warmth and calmness. For some reason she felt comfortable around him. She had wanted to go to the bathroom for a while and wondered if she should ask.

Douglas raced back to the city. He took a different route than Bao. Two blocks away from the train station he parked the Jeep and walked through the dark alleys. He found a spot to quickly change his clothes. He shouldered his gear bag and stepped out into the road and flagged down a cab. Within minutes he arrived a block away from the motel and took his time approaching it. He had to be absolutely sure nobody had tailed him.

Bao stood at the door, awaiting Douglas. He opened it before Douglas could even knock. Douglas was nervous. He had no idea how Mia would react. From the time he had spent with her, he anticipated a certain amount of hostility, and he couldn't blame her. She'd gone through hell and back in the last two days. He still didn't know why she had left the Baikal hotel and driven out to the camp by herself, but it must have had something to do with him. Therefore, the horror she'd just gone through had been, at least in part, his fault. She probably hated him, but he hoped he could convince her to stay with him and Bao for now.

Douglas stepped into the room, ready to do whatever was necessary to stop Mia if she started to draw attention to them. Bao pointed his thumb toward the bathroom door. He whispered, "She's been in there for a while now. I have left her alone." Douglas nodded.

Mia sat on the edge of the small tub. She looked around. The bathroom was old, but she didn't care. She got up and washed her hands and then her face. She did not look at herself in the mirror until she had washed her face several times and dried it off.

Her skin was pink from the hot water, and she had dark circles under her eyes. Her hair was messy and dirty. She almost did not recognize her own features. Her cheekbones stood out and her lips were cracked. There was a bloody scratch on her left cheek—she didn't even remember how that had happened.

She pushed the sleeves of her arms up to wash her hands yet again. She scrubbed and scrubbed and could not feel clean. The soap burned where the ropes had rubbed the skin of her wrists. She had never yearned for a shower so bad in her life, but wanted to wait for something. She did not know what. She drank the water out of the faucet until her stomach rebelled and she gagged some of it back up.

A faint knock on the door and the Asian accent asked, "Are you okay, Miss? Can we get you anything at this time?"

Mia realized that she had been in the bathroom for a long time. They were probably worried about her. She needed to pull herself together. They were agents—she could trust them. She straightened her back upright and instantly felt dizzy. "Yes, I'm okay. I'll be out in just a minute." Mia tried to be thankful, but her words just sounded weak. She unlocked the door and opened it. The Asian man stood by the main door and smiled at her openly and friendly. Out of the corner of her eye Mia saw someone else. As she turned her head in that direction, she took another step forward into the room.

She looked the other man straight in the face and froze. It took her mind several seconds to realize that it was Douglas who was standing there. She wanted to take a step forward but could not move. Blackness spread in front of her eyes and her legs buckled. Before she could hit the floor, Douglas had already reached her.

Chapter 59

Douglas carefully placed Mia on the bed. She had passed out. Maybe that's a good thing, he thought. He knelt beside her and tenderly touched her forehead. You're safe now, sweet thing, he thought.

Bao looked at Douglas. There was no need for an explanation. He could feel the strong bond between Farland and the woman, but he could also feel something negative, like a bad aura. Bao closed his eyes and focused on the negative energy. It felt like disappointment.

He looked at Douglas and said, "I will get us some food. You try to figure this out." Douglas knew Bao didn't mean the continuance of the op, but his own situation with Mia.

Bao stood and walked over. He said, "Let me take your cell, so I can call you here from outside when I return."

Douglas gave it to him. "What are you going to tell Brian when he calls?" Douglas asked. Bao answered honestly. "The truth."

Bao left and Douglas rested his forehead on top of his and Mia's hands. He couldn't remember the last time he had prayed—maybe as a child? But now he silently thanked God for letting him find her unharmed.

There was movement. Mia stirred and Douglas was sure that if she was dreaming, it wasn't pleasant. He sat close to her side and woke her gently by kissing the sensitive inside of her hand.

"Hey, Love. Wake up," he said quietly.

Mia's eyes opened. For the first time in several days she didn't startle as she woke up. Instantaneously she felt peacefulness spread over her. With dark eyes she looked at Douglas, who still held her hand. The memory of the last week echoed through her mind. She needed a while to understand where she was and what had happened. Finally, she pulled her hand away from him.

"Liar," she simply said, and Douglas' heart hit rock bottom.

She sat up with her back against the headrest. She was not scared of him, but unconsciously grabbed a pillow to hold on to, as if she could use it to keep distance.

"Can I explain?" Douglas asked calmly.

Mia looked the other way. Clearly he had saved her life, but who had endangered it in the first place? Wasn't it all his fault?

Mia's eyes showed dark clouds as she looked back at him. "Explain? Which part are you gonna explain? Like why you speak Russian?" She blurted out the first thing that popped into her head. Why should I believe you anyway, her insides screamed.

So that was it, Douglas thought. He had to know, "How did you find out?"

Mia shook her head. "What does it matter? All that matters to me is that you've lied. I trusted you," she said loudly, paused, and added more quietly, "With everything." She wanted to sound a lot angrier than she did. She felt so weak and helpless. One of those hated knots crept up in her throat and she swallowed it away hard.

Douglas saw the tears coming, but they never spilled. She was too proud to cry. He knew exactly what she was saying. In that second he swore to himself he'd never lie to her again. He'd explain everything if she wanted to know. Of course he wouldn't give it to her voluntarily, but he would answer every damn question she had truthfully. Douglas knew he could not force her to trust him again. He'd have to give her time and hope for the best.

"How is your arm?" He asked her matter-of-factly. Mia had no clue what he meant. He pointed at her. "Your arm. I squeezed the hell out of it. Does it still hurt?"

Mia remembered. Oh, God, that had been Douglas. She knew it! She had not recognized him at first in her state of mind, but later it had dawned on her.

Not knowing where to start, she asked, "Who are you?"

"I asked you first. How's the arm?" Douglas switched from his worried mode into a cooler demeanor within a second.

Angry, Mia pushed the sleeve of her sweater up and held the black and blue bruise under his nose. He could see the colored imprint of his fingers perfectly around her upper arm. Damn, he thought. That had to hurt.

"There, are you happy?" Mia snapped at him. If she wasn't so tired she'd scratch his eyes out.

Douglas got up and sat in one of the chairs. She wouldn't tolerate his closeness right now.

"Who the hell are you?" Mia asked again. "And don't tell me you're some damn geologist from Seattle."

Douglas took a deep breath. How much should he tell her for now? The phone rang. Douglas was glad about the interruption. It was Bao, with food.

Mia's narrowed eyes looked quizzically at Douglas, but she did not ask.

"It's the pizza man," Douglas said as he rose and went to the door.

Mia's jaw dropped as Douglas drew his handgun and held it nozzle up as he looked through the peephole. Bao stood in front of the door and grinned like an idiot into the peephole. All Douglas could see was a wide row of snow-white teeth.

Douglas opened the door and Bao stepped it. His eyes fell on Douglas' hand holding his Five-seveN and Bao said dryly, "Oh, I'm glad to see you guys are working things out."

The two men completely ignored Mia, and within seconds they hovered over the huge pizza Bao had brought from down the street. Douglas had peeled off his black leather jacket, and Mia stared at the brown holster and its gun underneath his arm.

Bao followed her eyes. "Doug, you're scaring her. Put that thing away." He was joking, as he sat there with his own handgun snug by his side.

Mia swayed between angst and hysteria. She didn't know what to think or believe anymore. Finally her stomach overruled her worried mind. She slid to the edge of the bed and took the piece of pizza Douglas was holding out to her. She took a bite, and even though the spicy pizza sauce burned her cracked lips on touch, she thought that it was the best damn pizza she had ever had in her life.

After they ate, Douglas suggested Mia relax in the shower for a while. He'd explain things after she was finished. He asked her to at least trust him this much, and she nodded and disappeared into the bathroom.

"Have you told her?" Bao asked Douglas, sipping water out of a plastic cup.

"No, it'll take time."

Bao leaned toward his partner and put a hand on his arm. With wise, Asian eyes he looked at him and said, "I know you have a hard time with what I say sometimes. But believe me when I tell you that there is a lot of positive energy around her. She's got a very strong spirit."

He was right. Douglas did have a hard time with Bao's spiritual nonsense, but only because he didn't understand. Hell, sometimes he got scared by his own inner strength.

Bao volunteered to make the rounds and take first watch. They compared their wrist watches and set the time for Bao to trade with Douglas in three hours. Mia needed to rest. And as long as Brian didn't call to let them know that the Russians were on the move, there was no need to leave.

Douglas switched the TV on but muted the volume. He listened for Mia in the shower and stretched out on top of the covers. He followed the scenes on the TV screen, but wasn't really watching. He needed to think about the next few days. It all depended on when the Russians got back on the move and where they headed. Mia's escape might turn the whole scenario upside down, and Douglas needed input from Brian's side.

Douglas was deep in thought when Mia poked her head around the edge of the door. Her eyes went over his body. He was lying on the bed, still wearing his black jeans and had one heavy boot crossed over the other. He hadn't taken off his tucked-in shirt or even removed that awful gun. The sleeves of the shirt were pushed up to his elbows and he sprawled with usual confidence with his hands behind his head.

"What do you think you're doing?" Mia asked him briskly.

Instead of getting into an argument about whether he belonged on the bed or not, he simply grabbed the covers and held them up in an inviting gesture. He suppressed a smile and kept his stony gaze onto the TV. "Lay down and shut up," he said. He knew that offense was the best defense, especially with her.

Mia was too tired to argue. She had put her filthy jeans back on, but was just wearing the gray t-shirt she had been wearing underneath her sweater.

She sat on the edge of the bed as far away from Douglas as possible. Not knowing if she should or shouldn't, she decided she'd be more comfortable without her dirty jeans on. She sighed, slipped them off, and quickly slid under the covers with her back to him. She wanted answers, but just as she'd figured out what to ask him first, her mind put an end to it by falling into a deep and dreamless sleep.

Douglas still stared at the voiceless TV screen. When he heard Mia's relaxed and steady breathing, he looked over to her. All he could see was some of her shower-damp hair and the outline of her underneath the covers. He was so thankful she had not been harmed.

He carefully slipped closer to her—how peaceful she looked. Ah, what the hell, he thought and sat up. He took his holster off, secured his weapon, and placed it close to him on the nightstand. Then he stretched out close to her and wrapped one arm around her. She didn't move as he held her tight. "I'm gonna get you out of this, Love," he whispered and was asleep momentarily.

Chapter 60

SELKIN GAVE THE SIGNAL.

His men started the trucks and one opened the gates. They had collected the dead watchman's body. The Gobi desert was full of corpses, one more wouldn't matter.

Selkin had just gotten off the phone with St. Petersburg. After explaining the situation to them, they had decided to go forward with the expedition. Shurnik would separate once they reached China. He had to answer some sensitive questions in St. Petersburg. Kidnapping the American woman had been a very dangerous move and was completely senseless. Shurnik had only tried to benefit himself. The operation had gotten out of hand and he had wanted her as insurance. Now, that his mistake had been uncovered, Shurnik would have to pay for it.

Selkin's priority had changed. For now he needed to deliver these drugs to China. He could not worry about the transport of the U-238. He was certain, however, that once they'd restructured, the U-238 mission was still possible. Lagunov had been notified. He sat on hold in Vladivostok. Selkin would meet with him after the drugs had been delivered.

The sun just came above the horizon, and as the last truck exited the hangar, Selkin swept with his eyes over the empty building one last time. It was dark inside and he could not even see the wall on the other side.

Just as he turned, he noticed a sudden light illuminate the middle of the room. A beam of early morning sunlight had caught the top of the dome high above Selkin's head. He followed the sunbeam with his eyes, and they stopped at the air shaft fifteen meters above him. He had not noticed it yesterday. It had been too dark. He took his time observing and rubbed his jaw in thought. Was it possible? He stepped right beneath the air shaft and studied it as closely as the distance would allow him. He asked himself again the same question—was it possible?

His eyes did not let go of the covered hole in the ceiling. He took his phone out of his pocket and pushed the speed dial number for St. Petersburg.

Douglas' cell rang. Finally, he thought. He pushed the button and answered, "Good news?"

"You're telling me, Doug." Brian did not sound happy.

"Well, are our Russian friends on the move?" Douglas asked.

"They are, but it doesn't matter anymore."

Douglas looked at the dragon statue outside the motel. He had just taken over the second watch and was making an early morning round.

"What are you saying, Secona?"

"That it's over. For now, anyway. Good job on the rescue, by the way," Brian said calmly.

"Dammit, Brian, what are you talking about?" He was going to tell Brian about Mia's rescue, but had that little Chinese guy jumped the gun on him?

Brian took a deep breath. This was not going to be easily explained.

"Listen, Doug. The CIA tabbed and unscrambled a cell phone call an hour ago. We believe it was Selkin. We're not sure, but it doesn't matter. The context of the call matters, though. He had used the words 'American woman' and 'escape.' That's all it took. We are still in command, but I have the FBI breathing down my neck now that they know about the abduction."

Douglas held his head in his hand. How could it have been a mistake to free Mia?

Brian went on. "With your findings in Lagunov's office and the other evidence we have, we'll get Lagunov on at least the lesser charges involving the distribution of the drugs, Doug. The uranium will be discovered. Interpol is already on the way."

Douglas had to take a seat. He was utterly stunned.

"What about Selkin?"

Brian continued. "Bao will meet up with a group in China and take them down for the meth. With any luck, Selkin will still be with them. If not, we'll have to let him go. Don't worry, buddy, we'll get his ass next time." Brian tried to sound encouraging. He knew how much of a disappointment this must be for Douglas. And then he added sadly, "You're off the case, my friend. You're gonna have to bring her in."

Douglas was not easily sickened, but the probable answer of his next question would twist his stomach.

"She is a free citizen. Do I dare ask what they want her for?"

Brian hated this, but he knew it was necessary. "She's gonna have to testify against Lagunov."

"What? Are you out of your fucking mind?" Douglas had to work hard to keep his voice down. "I might as well shoot her right here."

"Relax, Douglas. The FBI has a new safe house—" Brian got rudely interrupted.

"Safe house my ass, Secona! There is no such thing. Protective custody doesn't always work. Especially when you have the Red Mafiya glued to your ass. Goddammit, Brian, we're talking about the very bottom of the scum here."

Douglas got suddenly silent. He held his hand to his chin and let his brain do its work. After a full minute he said very calmly. "Brian, I will bring her in, but only to my terms."

Brian tried to talk him out of it quickly. "Doug, you can't possibly—"

"Listen, Secona. If they want her in, that's gonna be the *only* way!" He hung up, not being able to keep the discussion up any longer.

Douglas sat on the stone bench behind the motel. If he was seen by someone now, he'd be an easy target. His forearms sank onto his thighs and his hands went through his dark hair. He studied the tips of his boots. How could this have happened? Circumstances and mistakes, he thought. That's all it was. Mistakes happened in every mission. Some smaller, some crucial. He had made a few minor ones. Combined, they had been potent enough to blow this whole goddamn thing out of the water.

He looked back. Would he have done something different given the chance? Nope. He had worked to the best of his abilities. Maybe I do need to retire, he thought and smiled. Go back to the Mississippi swamp where he had come from. Buy a houseboat, take Mia, and live happily ever after.

Douglas pulled a face. In his line of work, there was no retirement. If he sat still long enough to kick his feet up, some pissed off thug from the past would find him and blow his ass—including the houseboat and Mia—to the moon.

Douglas rose and stretched. Fine. The past was the past. If they had to let Selkin slip through the net, there would be another mission just in his honor. For now, Douglas had to focus on the present. He had one mission in mind. And he'd be goddamned if he screwed this one up, too.

Chapter 61

Douglas stood in front of the motel room door. He heard a faint laugh. It was Bao. Douglas knew what this meant. Mia was in a state of shock now that she'd realized her safety. Her mind was running in high gear. Sometimes victims like her would be lethargic for days, and sometimes they'd have a reaction like she was having.

She was laughing and charming Bao with her innocent sweetness. Whatever the story she was telling him, she was able to take the worry away from someone who had seen worse than death. That's what Mia did. She lightened one's life just with her presence—even when she'd been in a horribly victimizing position twelve hours ago. And Douglas was not going to let anything jeopardize her precious existence anymore.

He inserted the key and opened the door. Bao was wiping tears off of his face, he had been laughing so hard. Mia sat fully dressed in a lotus position on the bed and looked a lot better than just a few hours ago. Earlier she was still angry with him, but as the wave of hysteria seeped out of her body, she was glad to see him.

Bao pointed at Mia. "Can we take her everywhere we go? She really takes the edge off."

Bao's question was meant in a funny way, but its cynical truth cast a shadow over Douglas' face. "Yes, we can," he said, and as Bao's laughter suddenly died Douglas added, "and we will."

Afraid he would intimidate Mia, Douglas sank onto the bed and faced her. She looked at him with open curiosity. It was heart-breaking. But before Douglas could bring the news to Mia, he looked at Bao.

"I spoke to Brian. I'm off the op. You are going to join a team to finish up in China. I have been instructed to bring this precious cargo home."

Boa held his breath. Did he just understand correctly? He did not know all the details of the mission, but if he took Douglas' hint... Bao did not dare finish the thought.

He asked flat out, "Are you taking her to Colorado?" Douglas nodded silently and Bao understood. He rose from his chair and said. "I'll be back in an hour. We should move out, then."

"Agreed."

Mia was starting to get uncomfortable. What was going on? Someone needed to explain some basics to her. She had slept soundly through the night and when she woke up, Douglas was gone and Bao had been sitting there watching over her. He had not explained anything. He had been very reassuring, though. How things would be explained to her, how she'd be just fine, how she was safe, now, and would go home soon. After a while Mia had relaxed and they had continued talking until it had escalated into Mia's sudden attack of hysteria.

Mia looked after Bao as he left the room. He took that soothing, comfortable feeling with him. Her eyes went from the closed door to Douglas. How sad he looked. Was it just another of his games to regain her sympathy?

Douglas got up and sat across from her in a chair. He could not be close to her and tell her that her life was going to change dramatically very soon. He took his time. There was a lot more to explain than what he could put into an hour. He started with the most important things, and when Mia raised questions, he held up a hand to stop her.

"I promise you, I will answer all your questions truthfully to the fullest extent, but for now please just listen." He added, "Trust me."

Mia shook her head. "I need to know one thing right now. Who are you and who are you working for?" She asked him with probing eyes. She would not tolerate an evasive answer.

Douglas took a deep breath. He owed her this. "Okay, my name is real. I am an agent. My employer planted me at Worldmove to—"

Mia interrupted. "An FBI agent?"

Christ, she was going to make him begin at the wrong end. He thought she would be more curious about other peculiar things, like if Scott Hensley was involved, but her sharp mind went right to the point.

Douglas shook his head. "No, not FBI. I used to work for the feds. Now it's on a private basis."

Mia frowned. "What are you saying? After all the lies you have told me, you still want me to trust you, right? So you better start spitting out some facts!"

Douglas tried to read her. She was calm on the outside, but her voice told him that she better got some information soon, or she'd walk out the door.

"Mia, are you willing to completely leave your life the way you have known it behind you and start over?" Douglas knew that this question would not make much sense to Mia at this point, but he had to ask her anyway. He continued, "It is very important that you understand. I know it sounds crazy, but if you want to know the whole truth behind all this, you won't be able to return to your life as you have known it."

His bright eyes penetrated Mia's to underline the seriousness of what he just said. Mia thought about his words. It sounded like a bad movie to her, but this was no movie. This was the hard reality of a very wrong situation.

"Why?" she simply asked.

"Why, what? Why change your life?"

Mia nodded.

Douglas studied her pretty face. She looked very alert and calm, despite the circumstances. She could take it, he thought. So he explained, "The agency I'm working for is called the Acronym. They work on a private basis with other agencies, sometimes even the military. The public doesn't know about the Acronym. They cannot know. That's why your life will have to change, at least for now. They will keep you until they trust you enough to let you return to what you've been doing."

Mia's eyes went wide. "Keep me? Keep me where?" But Douglas wouldn't let her interrupt.

"Listen, Mia. You have to believe me when I tell you that I know what is best for you. If I don't tell you about the agency I'm working for, they will place you in an FBI safe house. And it isn't safe. I know! The place I have in mind is a lot safer than what any federal institution could offer you. And they would only protect you until the trial, anyway."

Aw shit, he should have waited with that. But what the hell. She wanted the truth. He just hoped she could handle it all at once.

She asked the obvious question. "What trial?"

"You will be a star witness to lock up Lagunov. You want to get the people who did this to you, don't you?"

"Lagunov? But he wasn't there. It was Shurnik. You're mistaken. Lagunov is the CEO of Yukoil," Mia rattled, confused. Douglas had to slow down. If she wasn't so damn curious and would just let him explain the way he wanted to, she'd be better off.

"Lagunov is a dirt bag. That's all you need to know for now. I will explain it to you another time. And there will be plenty of time for that, but just not now. Now we have to go."

"So where're we going?" Mia asked, wanting nothing more than to go home.

"Colorado," Douglas said. He couldn't wait to get her there.

"What's in Colorado?"

"Safety," he said and took her hand. He had slid the chair across the room to be close to her again. He leaned forward and sat eye level with her, looking at her very seriously.

"Mia, we have to get you out of here and get you to Colorado where they can't find you." Douglas knew that he was scaring her now. And as much as he hated it, she needed to be scared. She needed to understand that he was here to bring her home. She needed to trust him and not be difficult on the way there.

"We need to go to Colorado? But Bao said we're going home. Montana is home for me, Douglas, not Colorado." She was so naive.

Douglas loved that about her. It made her so damn innocent and vulnerable.

He had to crush that innocence with the hard and brutal reality. "You will get home, Mia. But for now we'll get you to a very safe place in Colorado. You'll love it, I promise. And I know that they can't get to you there."

"Who won't get to me there?" She was frightened. Douglas' intensity had started a flow of adrenaline in her system she had not known before.

"The Russian Mafia, Mia. That's who is hiding behind Yukoil."

Mia looked incredulously at Douglas, and just as he thought her facial expression might change for the better she said, "You are crazy!"

She jumped of the bed and grabbed her coat. Douglas was ahead of her, blocking the door within a second.

"Get out of my way," Mia demanded. "Get the hell out of my way, Farland—or whatever your name is!"

Her dark eyes glared at him but she stood at a safe distance. Douglas did not move. He crossed his arms in front of his chest and said, "I'm afraid I can't do that."

Mia felt panic swelling up inside, and Douglas could see it coming. He wanted to take her by the arms and shake her until she understood. But instead he tried to explain.

"Mia, listen to me." She did look at him, waiting for what he had to say, but her body trembled. She felt confined yet again. Douglas hoped she wouldn't go berserk. If she screamed, he'd have to tackle her and shut her up. That really wouldn't help him to regain her trust.

"I know it sounds crazy, but everything I have told you in the last hour is the truth. You've gotta believe me."

Mia realized that Douglas would not let her get even close to the door. She was trapped. She thought about screaming, but decided to talk herself out of there. She straightened her back and defensively crossed her arms in front of her.

"I'd like to know one good reason why I should believe you. You have been lying to me from the first moment you opened your mouth. Who says that you are not as crazy as Shurnik? For all I know you could be working together and this is just an easier way to get me where they wanted to take me in the first place." She was getting angrier by the second. "I am just a person who is trying to make people's live better. I want to go home and forget about this awful place."

Her arms sank to her side and her hands balled into fists. Douglas watched her and knew what would be next.

She was furious now and her voice rose. "I have been lied to, these mindless people kidnapped and almost killed me, I've been scared to death, and I don't know who to turn to. And I certainly don't believe a word you say, because you are the worst of all of them!" Angry tears rolled down her face. "So get the hell out of my way, 'cause I'm going home!"

Her enraged mind stopped working sensibly and she shot forward. He was a big man, and armed with a gun, but that didn't matter to Mia. All she wanted was to step foot through that door and get away from this god-awful place.

Douglas caught her with both arms. What was she thinking? That she could just walk right through him? He certainly would not fight her. He just confined her by wrapping his strong arms around her and trying to talk sense into her. She boxed him in the sides, but her strength left her as the tears started to flow in a heavy stream of hopelessness. Douglas just held her. She gave up as the uncontrollable sobs trembled through her body.

"Shh, Love," he whispered into her hair. He raised one hand and cupped it softly around her head as she cried into his chest. "It's okay. I know how bad you want to get home, and I will get you there."

By the time Bao returned from his surveillance rounds, Mia had calmed down. Douglas had held her for a while until she had peeled herself out of his soothing embrace. She wanted nothing more than to believe him—believe that he would get her home—but could she?

She had stopped crying and hated herself for the self pity she had allowed. Now she felt only sadness covering her like a heavy blanket. Bao saw the anguish in her eyes when he walked through the door. He looked at Douglas, who silently nodded. Bao stepped in front of Mia. Her eyes did not leave the ground. He retrieved something out of the inside pocket of his coat, and Mia lifted her head to see what it was.

Bao held a small piece of paper under Mia's nose. It was an old, faded photograph of a young, smiling Asian girl.

"She was fourteen in this picture. It was the last one taken of her before she got kidnapped and shipped to Shanghai. They drugged her and forced her into prostitution." His voice stayed steady but it sounded very sad. "By the time we found our daughter, it was too late. The drugs had done their damage and she died of an overdose shortly after." Mia looked into the almond eyes. They reflected a broken heart, but showed determination as well.

"That's why I am doing this, Mia. She is the reason I'm on this job, and will be until the day I die. I don't know how much Douglas has explained to you about the Red Mafiya in the last hour. I can not imagine what you must be feeling right now, but one thing is for certain. We are here to protect you."

Bao had found a reliable car for Douglas and Mia. He would split and follow Shurnik's trail into China. The Acronym would not need long to have the FBI issue papers through the U.S. Embassy in Ulaanbaatar for Douglas and Mia.

This was it—they would be out of there within twelve hours.

The car was parked just outside the back entrance. Bao had made certain nobody suspicious was roaming around the premises. All three stepped out of the hotel. Mia walked between the two men. She felt better now that Bao had talked to her. She had decided she would give Douglas a chance to do right. Bao had explained in more detail what Colorado was all about and how slim the chances of survival were if she chose to just leave and go home to Montana.

Douglas opened the driver side door and threw his gear into the backseat. He scanned the area, his senses on high alert. There were a few other cars parked, but not a person in sight. He looked at Mia and signaled her with a short nod. He walked around the car and opened the passenger door for Mia. She stepped out of the motel's shadow into the open and bent down to climb into the car.

The sniper had his crosshair aimed right at the tall man's forehead, but just as he was about to pull the trigger the man moved.

"Either one," Selkin had ordered. Either the woman or the man.

Best case scenario would have meant both of them, but the sniper knew that that would not happen.

He focused on the woman. She moved a lot slower and therefore was an easier target.

Mia never heard the shot. Something very hot suddenly pierced her back, and by the time the impact of the bullet threw her upper body into the car seat, she was out.

Douglas draped himself quickly over her. Instinctively, his hands covered her head and out of the corner of his eye, he saw Bao running in the direction the shot had came from.

Douglas slid onto the asphalt and shoved her legs into the car. Just before he slammed the door shut, he saw the blood. It had already penetrated her coat. He drew his weapon and hunkered behind the vehicle. He sat still and listened. No other shots followed.

Bao was hiding in some bushes behind the hotel and scanning the area where he thought the projectile had come from. On top of the grassy hill across the back parking lot was a small apartment building. From what he could see, there were eight balconies facing this way. No movement, though. He knew that by the time he'd make his way up there, the sniper would be long gone.

Bao decided that Douglas would need his help. If the bullet hadn't killed her, Mia had to get to an emergency room as soon as possible. He stayed within the brush, in case the sniper was aiming for more, but Bao made his way back toward the parking lot. He got there just in time to see Douglas' taillights disappear around the corner.

Chapter 62

PRETTY, WHITE LACE CURTAINS swayed faintly in the light breeze. The magnificent mountains far behind them were snow covered on top and a fresh, Hauser green with small dots of yellow and red the rest of the way down. Softly rounded cotton-ball clouds puffed through the light blue sky with incredible ease. Just outside the window was a tall maple tree, and its bright golden leaves shuffled soundlessly in the wind, distributing the sweet aroma of autumn and happiness.

She felt weightless, almost non-existent. The soft, white sheet felt light to the touch on her skin. There was no pain, just the soothing feeling of a very long sleep. I must be dead, Mia thought. It was a calming feeling, not frightening at all. Then she tried to move her hands. She wanted to touch her face to see if she was real.

"Hi, Love," a very soothing, dark voice spoke softly to her from the other side. Mia recognized the voice at once and turned her head a little. It was Douglas. She wasn't dead after all, she realized. He was sitting next to her, holding her hand in both of his.

"How are you feeling?" he asked her, looking at her with such tenderness her heart clenched.

Mia moistened her lips. Her throat felt dry as she tried to speak. "Fine," she could only whisper.

Douglas was holding a cup. "Are you thirsty, Love?"

Mia tried to push herself up, and as she put weight onto her right arm a sharp pain went through her body. She gave up quickly and rested her head back into the pillow.

"Here, don't move." Douglas was fast to help her when he saw her pain-stricken face. He slid his hand behind Mia's neck to lift her carefully up, just enough for her to have a refreshing drink of mild, hand-warm chamomile tea. She was still on an IV drip. Her body had everything it needed, including hydration, but the thirst still must be unbearable.

Mia took a few satisfying swallows and closed her eyes. A sudden fatigue overcame her, and she did not feel as light anymore as she did when she first woke up.

"Sleep, Love," Douglas said tenderly. "Go back to sleep." He placed the cup back onto the nightstand and leaned over her again to brush another soft kiss onto her forehead.

The nurse came back into the room to change Mia's dressing. He nodded at her and quietly went outside. Brian sat on the front porch watching his new colt being worked in the round pen. He had his cast propped up onto an ottoman and looked at Douglas as he joined him. Douglas took a seat in one of the cushioned, natural colored wicker chairs.

"Have you ever seen anything like it?" Brian asked, looking at his colt. The two-year-old was giving the man who was working him a hell of a time.

"Spunky," Douglas commented. They watched the scene for a while.

"I should have called him 4B's," Brian said.

"And what would that stand for?"

"Bold, beautiful, and bucking like a sunovabitch," Brian answered, smiling.

"I have a better idea. What about 'femur-creamer,'" Douglas suggested and knocked his knuckles against Brian's cast.

Brian laughed. He loved his horse's spirit, even though it had cost him a broken leg and a bunch of office time back east in Maryland.

"You wanna try a round?" Brian asked Douglas and smiled. He knew Douglas was a good rider, but did not want to know anything about breaking a young horse. Especially not one as strongly willed as this one.

"No thanks," Douglas said honestly. "I'd rather put my energy somewhere else right now."

"So, how is she?" Brian inquired. He refilled his ice tea and offered the glass carafe to Douglas.

"She woke up again for a minute. It's frustrating. The doctors predicted she'd sleep a lot. They say her body would be on some sort of a standby mode while it heals. But it's hard to just watch her lay there." Douglas sounded tired.

"Maybe we should have given her more time in the hospital. It's only been four days since surgery," Brian observed.

"No way. She's taken care of just as well here. And she's safe." Douglas would not even allow an argument.

The doctors in Ulaanbaatar had been able to stabilize her with the damage the Russian 7N1 bullet had inflicted on her back and stomach. She had been incredibly lucky. The little steel knocker within the projectile should have propelled forward on impact, and the nose of the bullet would have been destabilized and mushroomed out. Mia's whole interior midsection, including some of her vital organs, should have been destroyed by the lethality of this sniper load, but for some reason it had not ripped her apart. The bullet had not done even a fraction of the damage it usually would have. The doctors had argued about the distance it had had to travel, but Douglas had not cared. She'd lived. That's all that had mattered.

The U.S. embassy had reacted quickly and held a press conference about a gunned down and killed American in the streets of Ulaanbaatar. It had given Douglas time to get her stable and out of the country before Selkin could receive any seeped through information.

Mia had been flown from Mongolia directly to the U.S. Army Hospital in Fort Carson, Colorado. They had done more surgery there. Her severed kidney had finally given up, and they'd had removed it. She would live just fine with one, they had explained, but the recovery would take time.

The warm sponge felt soothing on her face. Mia opened her eyes again and saw the friendly round face of the nurse smiling at her. She felt better every time she opened her eyes. Sometimes she thought she had died. I wonder why that is, she thought. Maybe because she almost had. She wished she could think of the nurse's name. She had told her before—Mia remembered being talked to more clearly now.

Gosh, how long have I been lying here? And where am I? Her eyes went back to the window. It was so beautiful outside. The window was open a little, but Mia did not feel cold.

It must be a wonderful autumn day, but where? She did not remember Mongolia being so colorful. Isn't that where she had been? Yes. More memories started to become clear in her mind. She remembered cold hospital rooms and people in white. She remembered Douglas sitting next to her. She remembered a little Chinese man—Bao. And she remembered Shurnik. Suddenly the feeling of being shackled came back and she shuddered.

Mia raised a hand to look at her wrist. She could not see any bruises from the ropes. They had healed up days ago.

"Are you all right, Miss?" The friendly face asked her and looked concerned.

"Yes," Mia spoke weakly. "A memory...where am I?"

"You are in Colorado. How are you feeling?" The nurse was obviously very glad to see her awake and talking.

Mia thought for a moment. She actually felt pretty good. Still tired, but the pain in her back was not as sharp anymore.

The nurse watched Mia closely. Her cheeks showed a bit more color, and her eyes were not glassy anymore. After a quick check of Mia's blood pressure and pulse the nurse said, "There is someone who would be very pleased to see you like this. I'll be right back."

The nurse disappeared and Mia carefully propped herself up higher against her pillow. She was thirsty and saw the cup next to her on the nightstand.

Chamomile tea. Douglas had given her a sip of it before. She just couldn't remember if that was earlier today or yesterday or the day before that.

"Mr. Farland!" The nurse called out. She stood on the big wraparound porch of the mansion–sized, two story log home. She listened for a reply, but could not hear him. Her eyes went from the front yard, neatly landscaped with fall flowers, out to the lush, green pastures.

Just as she was about to shout out Douglas' name again, he appeared from inside the barn.

"Everything's okay?" He asked her, worried, as he walked toward the house.

"Yes, yes," the nurse was excited and clenched her hands in front of her round body. "Please come quickly," she beamed at him. Douglas felt excitement rise up, like a young boy just before opening Christmas presents.

He took the four steps leading up into the great room with one big leap. Douglas knew what the nurse was so happy about. He had instructed her to tell him the second Mia woke up again. Breathless, he stepped into Mia's room. And there she sat, with her back propped up against a white pillow holding the tea cup in both hands.

"Hey, look who's up!" He blurted out, beaming at her. His heart jumped for joy and he hurried to her side. To Douglas she had never looked more beautiful.

Mia had been thinking about him. The memories had almost returned completely, and she leafed through the mental notes and the feelings inside. There were so many questions that had to be answered, but one thing was for sure—no matter if she liked or disliked those answers, she for certain loved this man.

Chapter 63

A FEW DAYS LATER one of the doctors from Fort Carson made a house call to see in person how well Mia's health was progressing. He had driven north through Denver to the mountains of Estes Park, where he had been awaited by two men in a dark van with no windows. Even though the good doctor was a member of the military, the classified information of the ranch's location was not to be compromised by anybody.

Douglas greeted him on the front steps. He shook Douglas' hand and said, "Quite the operation you've got here, and a beautiful spot on top of that." Douglas smiled, expressing secrecy, and invited the doctor to sit on the porch for a while.

Mia was napping in the huge hammock—it was her favorite spot. Curled up like a cat in the late summer's sunshine, she was covered with one of the many colorful quilts one could find throughout the house.

The doctor looked at her face silently, not yet waking her up. He wanted to talk to Douglas first before he examined her.

"She looks a lot better. Seems like she put a little weight back on. Is she eating okay?"

"Yes, she's got a good appetite, and I have to hold her back with her activity. She wants to get better sooner than her body is allowing her. She's frustrated," Douglas explained.

"That's common. Keep talking to her and slow her down. Her remaining kidney can handle the job just fine on its own, but needs time to adjust. How is her mental state?"

Douglas was afraid of this question. He took a deep breath and looked at Mia sleeping on the far side of the porch. Her behavior was not easily explained. "Let me put it this way, Doctor. I am not a man of medicine or any other kind of science. I can only explain to you what I observe, and I have been watching her very closely for a long time, now."

Douglas paused and the doctor looked at him very intensely. "She is going backward, isn't she," the doctor stated.

Douglas looked at him, surprised. "Exactly! Her body seems to gain more strength everyday, but mentally she seems to get weaker. I have tried everything in my power to lighten her mood, but sometimes she seems to disappear deep inside herself for long periods at a time. Her demeanor has been changing quite drastically." Douglas didn't know how else to explain it.

The doctor nodded. "She is depressed. That's to be expected. She is suffering from PTSD."

Douglas had heard that term before. "Post traumatic stress disorder."

The doctor nodded again. He explained calmly, "I'm not sure what exactly went on, sir. You know more than me. All I know is that this young woman had been in a foreign country for some time and ended up being shot and almost losing her life. She's here now, which is obviously not her home. She must have flashbacks of the incident."

The doctor paused, studying Douglas, and continued. "As I said, I don't know the details, but I would not be surprised if the trauma she experienced is not responsible for her emotional detachment. Think about it, Mr. Farland, and put yourself in her position."

The doctor got up and added, "You don't want her to slip into a clinical depression, and those are hard to get to. In the military we have to deal with them all the time. I'm sure you have heard of the term 'combat stress reaction' before, or even had to deal with it yourself." Douglas nodded thoughtfully and the doctor finished up his lecture by saying, "Then you know that you need to do whatever is possible to prevent it. I can give her a mild anti-depressant for now, but it is not a long-term solution."

The doctor walked over to gently wake her up. He would examine and improve her physical health, but could not do much to help her mental state of mind.

Douglas smiled at her as she peeled herself out of the hammock with the doctor's help. As they walked inside, Douglas stayed behind, sorting through his thoughts.

She had been in Colorado for almost three weeks now, and her wounds had healed up nicely. He had taken her on short walks to help her regain her strength. She had moved from the downstairs bedroom into one of the five upstairs. Douglas had stayed in the one adjoining to hers, but had insisted on spending the nights next to her bedside, sleeping in a comfortable chair with his gun on his lap.

He had been around her every second of the day, patiently answering all her questions about his past, the Acronym, and what the future would hold for her.

He had told her many times, "You worry too much, Love. Why don't you heal up first, and then we'll figure out what we need to do."

She had listened but had grown impatient the last several days. She wanted to explain to her family what was going on, but Douglas had not let her make more than just one quick phone call to Michigan.

"The danger isn't over, Love. Please understand that we have to wait a while longer," he had told her time and time again.

Mia had turned out to like Brian. He and Douglas were very close, and they had included Mia in some of their conversations about the current situation so she'd know that she could not be in any safer place in the world right now.

Mia enjoyed the beautiful surroundings of the ranch. There were acres and acres of lush pastures, and she liked sitting on the front porch and laughed as they watched the horses graze and play. The heart of the Rocky Mountains stood majestically right in front of them, and she had seemed interested when Douglas had explained the formations and their names.

They had spent the evenings sitting in the hammock and enjoying the colorful sunsets together. The porch faced due west, and the snow covered peaks reflected the sunlight in soft oranges and pinks. Mia had leaned into Douglas and let him keep her warm by wrapping his arms around her. That had been the only time she had instigated physical contact.

Douglas had managed to get a lavender bush from some nursery and had planted it close to the front steps. Even though it would not blossom again until next year, its narrow leaves distributed the faint scent Mia loved so much. He had cared for her with all his love and ability and talked to her for hours. But she still seemed to slip further and further away.

What could he do to save her fragile spirit? He could not let her go home to Montana yet, and she knew that. She had agreed to let Douglas handle her life for a while, but it must be very hard without her friends and family like this.

Douglas watched Brian as he came out of the barn, still on crutches, being followed by one of his older horses. Suddenly Douglas shot up and stared at the horse. Brian noticed Douglas and called out to him. "What's the matter, Doug? You look like you've just seen a six point."

Douglas smiled widely as his idea took shape in his head. "No," he said. "Better than that. Much better!"

He turned on his heels and walked inside. The door to the downstairs bedroom was not quite closed. They used the room for examining Mia since she had moved upstairs. Douglas lowered his head and softly knocked on the door frame.

"Doctor, before you leave, I have another question,"

"You can come in, Douglas," Mia said from inside. He hesitated at first, not knowing if he should. But then, she had offered. Maybe she wanted him in there with the doctor and the nurse.

Mia sat with her back to him on a stool. Her yellow shirt was down around her waist and Douglas noticed the thin straps over her naked shoulders. The doctor was peeling off the bandage on her wound. Douglas stepped closer and pressed his lips together. He had not yet seen the severity of the entry wound. Fresh pink scar tissue surrounded the indentation where the bullet had entered. Suddenly he realized it was the very same spot where the 9 mm had penetrated his own back. It had been years and he did not think about it very often.

The doctor was happy. "It looks really good. I don't think we're going to have to redress this."

"Oh, good. What about this one?" Mia turned around and lifted her shirt away from her mid section. The exit wound was bigger, but had healed a lot faster.

The doctor nodded in approval. "Yes, ma'am. Must be the tender care you are receiving around here." He looked at Douglas and winked.

Mia looked in the antique oval mirror standing across from her, eying her mutilated body. She said sadly, "I guess I won't be wearing a bikini any time soon."

Douglas saw the sadness in her eyes. She was beautiful to him, scarred or not.

"If it is any consolation to you, I've got scars just like that," His attention went to the doctor. Their eyes met, and Douglas slightly motioned toward the door. I'll meet you outside, they seemed to say.

The doctor closed the door so Mia would have privacy getting dressed. Douglas stood out on the porch. "I might have an idea for therapy," he said as the doctor walked up.

"Good," the doctor said, "She needs it. What do you have in mind?" Douglas motioned toward the horse, which stood sleeping and untied next to the barn.

"Can I get her on one of these?" The doctor thought for a moment and said, "I don't see why not. Of course she is in no shape for a race, but a quiet ride would not harm her injuries."

Douglas smiled. That's what he wanted to hear. He turned to the doctor, shook his hand, and said, "We very much appreciate the trouble you went through to come out here, sir."

The doctor nodded and looked toward the rugged peaks of the Rockies. "You know, Mr. Farland, they don't let me out much, so believe me when I say that the trip was worth it just to see the mountains."

Chapter 64

THE FOLLOWING MORNING WAS one of those breathtakingly beautiful autumn days in the heart of the Rocky Mountains. The eastern sky was still illuminated in soft pastels of pink and orange, but promised to turn an unbelievable blue, and the early-morning mist glittered over the green pastures like a blanket made of a million diamonds.

Douglas was in the barn. He had fed the horses early, and was now arranging the tack he would need for today. He had watched Mia sleep for a while this morning, thinking about what this day might bring. He hoped she would give him a chance. Only time would tell if she was ready to move on.

He heard the faint screeching noise of the screen door opening. He walked outside the barn, leading the dark bay horse to the hitching post to tie him up.

Mia was standing on the porch, lifting her nose into the calm fall air. She had her eyes closed and inhaled deeply. How wonderful it smelled. The lavender's scent always greeted her when she walked through the door. Douglas had been so amazingly considerate she thought, and smiled.

The orange-red blossoms of the huge mums looked like drops of copper in the sunlight. Along the stone walkway someone had planted blue asters and red chrysanthemums side by side. They marched all the way down to the barn, and so did Mia's eyes, until she saw Douglas. He looked so tall and very handsome in his black cowboy hat, dark red shirt, and blue jeans.

He gave her a huge smile. "Good morning, Love. How are you feeling?" Mia stretched her back carefully. She had slept through the night without her back being bandaged. It felt much better today.

"Really good, how about you?"

"I woke up and got to watch you sleep. How do you think I feel?" Douglas answered truthfully. Mia smiled. He showered her with kindness and sensibility every chance he got. She was amazed. It must be his true side. Nobody could keep this up for so long if it wasn't genuine.

"Why don't you come down here and say hi to these guys," he suggested. And just as if he had planned it, another horse walked nonchalantly out of the barn. He was not wearing any halter or headstall and parked himself next to the dark bay, like he knew he belonged there.

"Very good," Mia approved. "How long did it take you to train him to do that?"

Douglas laughed. "He is just being a gentleman, as usual." He walked toward her. "Come here, Love, and meet them," he invited.

Mia had not been around horses much, and these seemed awfully big to her. Especially when they weren't tied to something solid connected to the ground, like the brown one—he was just running free. "It's okay. They look good from up here."

Mia was afraid of them, and Douglas could see it. He took a breath, hoping this was a good idea. He walked up to Mia and did something he hadn't done in so long—he didn't wait for Mia to initiate a contact. He planted himself in front of her and embraced her in a tender hug. At first he could feel her hesitation, but as he carefully wrapped his arms around her warm body, she relaxed a little and leaned her head against his chest.

It's been too long, Douglas thought. He held her for a while and kissed the top of her head. He avoided the injured area on her back, but gently caressed her upper back, and he could feel her let go of her tension some more.

"Mornin', Love," He drawled again. "I hope you will have an amazing day." She looked up, and he moved his head back to see her eyes.

"What's going on?" Mia was curious, a good sign. He smiled, promising, but did not answer.

He kept one arm around her shoulder and gently steered her toward to barn. He finally spoke again. "I haven't asked you in a while, but I will ask you now to please trust me." Douglas' voice was low and calm. It had its usual relaxing effect on her.

She let him lead her right next to the untied sorrel horse, which seemed to be sleeping. His eyes were half closed. Mia looked at him and thought he was pretty. His color reminded Mia of a copper penny, and he had a diamond-shaped white mark on his forehead.

Mia lifted her hand—she felt she did not need to be afraid of him. She laid her hand right on top of the white diamond and asked, "What's his name?"

"Buster," Douglas simply answered.

Buster opened his eyes as Mia touched his head, and he nickered gently when she repeated his name.

"He has such gentle eyes." Mia was fascinated that a big creature like him would just stand there, obviously enjoying her touch.

Douglas watched her getting closer to the horse. The sorrel began to investigate the pockets of her jeans for anything edible. He gently moved his lips on top of Mia's hands, and she instinctively turned the palms up to let him lick any leftover traces.

"He smells the apple I ate earlier, doesn't he?" Mia asked.

"He sure does," Douglas smiled. So far, so good.

Mia let her hands wander through the horse's soft coat. She loved the feeling of the warm, silky hair against her hands. Stepping to the side of Buster, she combed her fingers through his mane and petted his neck.

He was just the right size for her, Douglas thought. Mia rubbed her fingers on top of the horses back and must have found just the right spot. Suddenly his neck grew longer and the tips of his lips looked like they were reaching for a treat just in front of his nose. Buster squinted his eyes and laid his head sideways.

"What is he doing?" she asked, laughing.

"He's enjoying your company."

Brian sat on the porch, watching the scene down at the barn. Douglas had told him about his plans for today. There was nothing Brian hoped for more than for this to be a life-changing day for Mia. By the time they had finished breakfast, Douglas had talked her into it. She was excited, but a little scared, too.

"Look what happened to you, last time," she had said, pointing at Brian's cast. He had laughed and said, "You can't really compare a wild, two-year-old colt with old Buster. They're not even the same type of animal."

Douglas had kept telling her that it would be okay if she didn't trust him, but it would not be fair not to trust old Buster.

"You're just trying to make me feel bad," she had said.

"Yes, is it working?" Douglas had smiled.

Next thing she knew, she was sitting very comfortably on Buster's back. Douglas stood next to her with the reins in his hands.

He had estimated the stirrup length beforehand and they fit perfectly. Douglas pointed to the saddle horn. "I know you won't need it, but hold on to it for a while until you find your balance. And remember, the more relaxed you sit, the easier it is."

Douglas walked around Buster's front and touched her leg on the other side to make sure her boot was securely in the stirrup. His eyes went over her body, lingering on her hips for a second. He smiled up to her and said, "I just knew it."

Mia could feel his eyes. "Knew what?" Douglas jumped into his saddle and gently pushed his leg into his horse to move next to Mia's so that his knee touched hers. He looked deep into Mia's eyes and said, "I just knew how good you'd look in those jeans on horseback."

With that he rode on, ponying Buster on one rein. Mia thought about it for a minute, and by the time she realized when she had heard him use these words before, she found herself headed toward the mountains.

Douglas watched her. Her face was relaxed and her hands lay easy on her thighs. She just let Buster carry her without any sign of fear. He swung the one rein over Buster's head and laid it across the horse's neck. He showed Mia how to gently neck-rein her horse if she wanted to steer.

"You should have your reins in one hand, but I doubt that you'll need them. Old Buster here will stick to this lady's side like a magnet."

"They like each other, don't they?" Mia looked down to Douglas' horse.

"Yes they do. They're always together." Douglas stretched his arm out to her, and Mia put her hand in his. He raised her hand to his lips and told her, "You look absolutely beautiful."

Brian had watched them ride away. Mia was a natural. She sat straight and her hips and legs were relaxed. She looked like she was born to be in a saddle. He nodded his head and walked inside. Douglas had arranged for a little surprise when they returned from the mountains. Brian had to make a pone call to check on its status. When this worked out as planned, they had more serious business to take care off.

They rode for a while. Mia was speechless at the magnificence of the mountains and how close they were. They saw a group of deer, and once Douglas pointed out an eagle way above them, gliding majestically in the bright blue sky.

Douglas had picked an easy route, and Mia looked back a few times to see in which direction they were headed away from the ranch.

"This valley dead ends behind the ranch, doesn't it? There is only one way in and out," Mia observed. "Yes, the ranch sits in this valley completely surrounded by the mountains. There is only one way to get to with a vehicle, otherwise you'd have to come in by chopper."

"I've seen the helipad down by the stream. Is that how I got here?"

"No, they transported you via ambulance from Fort Carson. It's close—not even a hundred sixty miles from here."

Mia wanted to ask more, but she told herself to relax. The ride was too soothing. She just wanted to enjoy it in silence. Every few steps the horses took, white butterflies fluttered into the air around them. The grass was still green and knee high. It was just a perfect day. She closed her eyes and lifted her head. The autumn sun felt warm on her skin, and the air was filled with life.

Mia could feel the tension seeping from her body. The injury was just a dull feeling, not really a pain anymore. It was a consistent reminder of something terrible, but the memory faded away a bit more every day.

Suddenly her horse stopped and she opened her eyes, squinting into the sun. Douglas had already dismounted and had stepped next to her, looking up.

He raised his arms up to her and said, "Come here, Love. I'd like to show you something."

They had reached the very bottom of what seemed to be the beginning of the steady climb toward the foot of the mountains. Mia swung her right leg over the saddle, trusting Douglas to help her dismount. At first she was a little unsteady on her feet, but that quickly passed. She still had one rein in her hand and Douglas said, "Just let him go. He'll stay right here." She had noticed that Douglas had done the same with his horse and she had instantaneously begun to graze.

Douglas wrapped one arm around her shoulders and took her up a small embankment to a formation of big rocks. She looked around. The ranch had disappeared and she looked straight up but could not see the top of the mountains—they were that close to them.

On one of the boulders in front of them, Mia noticed what looked like something a third grader must have drawn onto the rock with colored chalk. But then she understood.

"It's an old Indian grave site," Douglas began to explain. "A very spiritual place. The Kiowa tribe buried one of their leading shamans here."

Mia was captivated by the rock drawings and asked, "A shaman? Isn't that something like a medicine man?"

"Yes, indeed. The Indians would come here to gather strength to fight illness."

He looked at her, and she realized why he had brought her here. He wanted to help her heal. She knew that her physical health was progressing fast, but she was also aware of her hurting soul. Mia didn't know what to say. It was touching to see that a man like Douglas would trust in an old belief like the Natives had done.

She stepped forward and pressed the palm of her left hand on the rock and closed her eyes. She did not have to bend down. The boulder was as high as she was and several feet in circumference. Mia listened deep inside her own self. Yes, she did want to get better, and yes, she did believe that this would help. She focused on the energy the rock radiated, and after a while she thought she could feel it spread deep inside of her body. Amazing, she thought. It was like a warm flow of vitality made its way to her inner core.

She did not know how long she had been standing there, but when she opened her eyes and turned around, Douglas was gone. He had walked back down to the horses and was lying in the grass with his hands behind his head, chewing on a piece of hay. His hat was pulled over his eyes as if he was sleeping.

"How long would you keep doing this for?" Mia asked him as she walked toward him.

Douglas kept his eyes closed and lazily crossed one boot over the other. "Doing what, Love?"

Mia stretched out next to him on the grass. "How long would you continue to care for me like this?"

Surprised, Douglas pushed his hat back, opened his eyes, and looked down to her. She had cuddled up to him, and his arm came around her to hold her tight.

Tenderly he said, "However long it takes."

Chapter 65

DOUGLAS AND MIA HAD taken their time and returned hours later. He had held her in his arms and she had let him, and now she felt better than before she had almost lost her life. She was able to talk about it, too. On their way back, Mia had begun to open up to Douglas and told him about all the sadness almost consuming her in the last weeks. With every word she spoke she felt more and more rejuvenated and freed of the terrible tension which had seemed to be suffocating her.

Brian watched them reappear and hobbled down to the barn to help Douglas with the horses. Mia stood beside them and beamed at Brian. He had never seen her like this and understood why his friend had fallen for her.

"How was it?" Brian asked. He undid the cinch and lifted the stirrup up to hang it onto the saddle horn.

"It was amazing. But I'm sure you knew that it would be," Mia answered. Brian looked at her knowingly and saw the sparkle in those brown eyes. He nodded and smiled at Douglas.

"Well, I had an idea about what kind of influence old Buster here can have on a lady"

"I like the conspiracy, thank you." She squeezed Brian's arm and went to Buster's head. "And thank you for letting me do this." Just as if he had understood, the horse gently nudged her side with his nose.

Both men looked at Mia as she laughed out loud. It made her stomach wound ache, but she didn't care. She hadn't laughed like that for a long time.

Brian smiled at Mia. "He says you're welcome. By the way, there is something waiting for you in the great room."

Mia looked surprised. "What is it?" Brian shrugged and remained silent.

The men worked quietly on their horses and Mia hurried inside. She felt fatigued from the ride, but her mind had not been this alert in weeks. She climbed the stairs to the entrance and opened the door. Just as the two men exchanged silent looks they heard her scream, "Oh my God, Blue!"

Mia embraced her dog. He was patiently waiting for her. She went down to her knees and buried her face in his thick coat. Tears were streaming down her cheeks in seconds, and she took her time to thoroughly greet him. Blue was wagging his tail and licking the salty tears from her face. Mia looked up and saw some of her personal belongings neatly packed and stacked on the great room's huge log table.

Brian had stopped in his tracks and said to his partner, "You do know how to work out your girl trouble, don't you?"

Brian had barbecued a feast to feed an army and they ate heartily. Mia had helped Brian clean up the kitchen and afterward found Douglas in the hammock. The sun had already gone down and it was chillier than the previous nights. Winter was coming. Douglas could smell the snow.

Mia stood in front of him, her facial expression soft. "Here, Love, sit down." Douglas shifted to make room for her, but she shook her head. She just stood there looking at him.

In the dim light of the kerosene lamp her dark eyes reflected the passion he had thought was lost for good. She had his attention without saying a word—their eyes did all the talking. Mia reached her hand out to him and he stood. The spine-tingling memory of touching her warm body waked in him. He knew what she wanted, but he wasn't sure if it wasn't too soon. He took her in his arms. "Are you sure?" he drawled quietly

"Yes," she whispered. "I am sure."

He took her upstairs. As soon as they stepped into her room, he embraced her and held her close. Before his lips met hers, he took his time studying her beautiful face. That enticing flush was back on her cheeks, and her eyes definitely would have branded her a liar if she'd tried to say "stop."

The following days were filled with serious talks. Douglas took his time to thoroughly explain what the Acronym was negotiating. Mia's mental comeback had continued. Now she was running on all cylinders again.

They spent the days preparing her to make that vital decision. And the nights together were simply amazing.

Douglas said, "You have told me that all you wanted to do is better people's lives. And I have watched you work with such passion. You have the very best chance to do that from right here." He stopped and smiled at her and then continued. "But first we'd have to relocate *you*."

He made certain she saw the sacrifices she'd be making if she stayed for good to work for the Acronym. But he also loved her and had told her so. Douglas returned to Colorado between assignments and that fact simplified the final step of her decision.

"I still have to work in the field, and you know how dangerous it is," Douglas warned her several times. He pressed the issue, making sure she could handle it. He did not want her to regret her decision later on.

"Yes, I know, and I will be a warrior's woman," Mia replied just as often. Douglas had always nodded, but this time he didn't.

He looked at her very intensely from across the great room's wooden table, and Mia had to swallow hard. "I don't want you to be a warrior's woman." He paused as if it was too painful to go on.

He has changed his mind. The thought shot through Mia's head like high voltage. And just as she thought her blood would freeze in her veins, Douglas continued. "I want you to be a warrior's wife."

Mia just stared at him. Suddenly, she felt light-headed. What did he just say? She narrowed her eyes, trying to fathom the statement. Douglas smiled and let go of her hand. He leaned back to reach into the pocket of his jeans and revealed a tiny gold band with one inlaid, polished stone.

As he slipped it on Mia's left ring finger he said, "I hope you don't mind that it's not a diamond. It's a chip of the boulder from the Shaman's grave." He looked at her and started getting nervous. She was still staring at her hand, not saying a word. He rattled on, "I thought this stone was more appropriate, thinking of—"

"Shut up," Mia interrupted. She did not need an explanation. Her eyes found his and she reached across the table. She grabbed him by the shirt and pulled herself to him. Her long and very tender kiss was all the answer he needed.

Mia let him go and breathlessly sank back onto the bench. There was moisture lingering in Douglas' eyes.

"So, big men do cry." She smiled and a wonderful feeling of peace and serenity spread through her body.

The call came only three short days later. It was Ludvika. She had returned from her own recovery and notified Douglas and Brian from St. Petersburg. She was on Selkin's heels. Bao had managed to assist Interpol with the arrest of Shurnik and his men just after crossing the border into China, but the Mafia boss Selkin had disappeared shortly after the assault on Mia.

Ludvika had made it her personal vendetta to go after Selkin. Her focus had shifted from Shurnik to him. Shurnik had just been a tool she had realized, and since he had been arrested he was unreachable. Lagunov was in custody as well and awaited his trial early next year in the United States over Mia's abduction. Interpol was still very interested on bringing Selkin down and Ludvika stayed on the case. Her agency was relying on the Acronym's assistance once again.

Mia's first assignment came sooner than she'd thought. The Acronym was bringing in an older couple from Italy in a few days to stay there until the FBI had coordinated protective custody for them. They had witnessed some sort of a bust in Sicily involving an American fugitive. Mia wasn't sure what had gone on, but she would take care of them, doing what she did best—helping them to move from the safe haven of the Acronym's ranch. They were going to stay in the U.S. to testify.

Douglas had asked Mia where she wanted to get married. She had chosen Michigan—she wanted to have her family close by. Mia had been able to talk Douglas into contacting his estranged brother, Wayne, in Texas, telling him over and over that family was more important than anything else.

"You are turning me into someone soft and mushy," he had playfully complained. She had laughed and nudged him in his rock-hard stomach, "It wouldn't hurt you any to soften up just a little."

The first snow had fallen the previous night. The valley looked like something out of a fairytale. The pristine mountains had a fresh glaze on them, and every fine ridge of the granite peaks was easy to see. The snow-covered pastures reflected the sunlight with such intensity, it was blinding. Mia and Douglas had watched the horses run and play in the fresh powder for a while. Now they stood on the big front porch having to say their good-byes. The helicopter was waiting for him.

But the world around them did not exist at that moment. Douglas looked deep into Mia's eyes. "Don't you worry, Love. I'll be back in a flash," he said in his wonderful, low voice. Mia held him tighter. She was afraid to let him go, to let him go out there into the danger, and she knew that this was what it was going to be like every time. The awful feeling of an uncertain future was heavy in her stomach. She forced herself to smile, wanting Douglas to know that she'd be all right. She rested her head against his chest and listened to that strong heart like she had done the night before.

He had told her that every time his heart took a beat, it called her name. Mia closed her eyes and took a long, deep breath; she inhaled his scent and kept it in her lungs until they burned.

Finally she exhaled quietly and calm. It was time for her to let him go. She lifted her head and his wonderful blue eyes smiled through sadness. She swallowed away a tear and he softly kissed her again. His voice was a whisper. "You know how much I love you. No matter what happens, I promise I'm right here with you." He lifted her left hand to his lips and brushed a kiss onto her ring.

Then he let her go. He needed to do what he was born to do. But he would do it faster to return to this amazing woman who would very soon be his bride.

She did not follow him down to the helipad. She could not bear to watch him walk away. He quickly climbed in and fastened the harness. The chopper took off, and as it passed her by he gave her his incredible smile. She smiled back and blew him a kiss just before the chopper turned the front porch into a snowy storm of glistering ice crystals.

Mia watched the chopper shrink into the blue sky, and as it finally disappeared over the mountain she could already feel loneliness creeping up inside. She allowed just one big tear to roll down her cheek and immediately fought the overpowering urge to cry. She decided she needed to be strong. Not just for her self but for her warrior as well. It was time for her to focus in on her new job and her new life which lay ahead.

Suddenly Blue jumped up the stairs and sat next to her, leaning slightly against her leg. She reached down and gently patted her dog's head. She thought about Douglas' last words to her before he took off, and more to herself than to Blue, Mia said, "Don't you worry. He'll keep his promise. He always does."

Epilogue

Finally, now, the Tumbler falls:
one end and one beginning;
Here, another Trail calls—
the Weaver's card is spinning;
Hold on as surely as you can:
the Path is steep and churning;
hold Truth securely in your hand—
Tomorrow is returning.

A shaman's poem